Pleasing Mr. Parker

Elle Nicoll

Rose Hope Publishing

Copyright

Content Warnings—This book is intended for adult readers only and contains profanities, detailed sexual acts and issues concerning mental health and addictions.

*To everyone who loves a grumpy alphahole...
And of course, to Rosie, for bringing happiness and inspiration... and a load of bird poop to our little spot in
the world.*

Contents

Chapter One

Maria

"THAT'S IT, BABY. TAKE my cock. Take all of it."

The picture of a plane shakes on its hook. Each vibration from the wall sends another ripple through its frame.

Do not fall.

I swear if I'm left clearing up shards of broken glass, then the man-whore next door really will have something to shout about.

There's muffled female moans, and the sound of skin being struck.

Slap!

"You love my cock, don't you?" Whimpered sounds reverberate through our interconnecting wall as he groans again. "Tell me how good my cock is, baby girl. Tell me!"

Before his companion has time to answer, the sound of what I assume is his palm connecting with her ass rings out through the wall again, followed by a low growl. I may as well have a bedside seat to the show.

"So, so big!" a female voice pants.

"That's right, baby. I'm filling you with my giant cock."

Seriously? This guy? Surely, he can keep it down. He must have figured out he can be heard, groaning at a volume to rival that of a jet engine. Then again, maybe that's his kink, knowing other people can hear him talk about his cock over and over.

I raise my fist over the wall, ready to bang against the plaster. Not that it would do any good. By the sound of the woman's increased panting and accompanying words of encouragement, the only banging they will hear is their own. With any luck, they'll be finished soon.

I abandon my open suitcase and stalk out of the bed-room—letting the door slam shut behind me—and head into the open-plan kitchen and lounge, trying to get as far away as possible from my very own private porn audio show. Two doors and one hallway reduce their liaison to an almost acceptable level. He didn't even give me a chance to unpack my speaker before he began his vigorous evening activities. I mean, who even has sex like that at nine o'clock on a Sunday?

Not me, that's for sure.

I grab the TV remote and bring up the first music channel I find, turning the volume right up. My shoulders relax as P!nk starts to play, and I wander over to the window with a smile on my face as I lean against the frame. The twinkling lights of Manhattan spread as far as I can see. This is my home for the next six months. An all-expenses paid apartment in the private residences of The Songbird, New York's most prestigious hotel, while I manage their newly renovated spa. After that? Who knows? I guess, it depends on how these next six months go.

My cell beeps on the coffee table and warmth blooms in my chest as I read the message.

Nan: I hope you are settling in? Good luck for your first day tomorrow, my love.

I snap a picture of the view from my window and text it back. It's two in the morning over in the UK, where she lives.

Me: Almost, just some more unpacking to do. What are you doing up so late?

Nan: Had my head stuck in my book. Stayed up late to finish it! Give me a text tomorrow, love, let me know how it goes.

I chuckle softly as I text goodnight. That's Nan all over, always reading her romance books. Our family was worried when she lost my grandad that she would be lost. But she has gotten herself out and joined a book group, whom she speaks with every day. I swear it's kept her going. Although, the one downside is that now she's looking at every new man I meet as the potential new hero of my story. She won't have it when I tell her real life doesn't happen like that. And I should know.

My shoulders tense, but I brush the memories away before they can claw to the surface and ruin my night. Now is not the time to dwell on the past. And right now, I'm looking forward to my new future as a spa manager at The Songbird. I wrap my arms around myself and gaze out of the window dreamily. Griffin Parker, the owner, headhunted me personally for the position months ago.

He said he had heard about my spa back in Hope Cove, just outside LA. His mother and father visited for their wedding anniversary and raved about it. He wants to bring the same success to The Songbird that I created there.

I built the spa in Hope Cove from scratch. So many extra hours and late nights out with friends missed. But I would do it all again in a heartbeat. I wasn't just creating an award-winning spa there; I was re-inventing myself. And now I'm about to do it all again. Except this time, I know beyond doubt I can do it.

It's a dream I would never pass up.

It took months of video meetings and contracts to finalize the plans with The Songbird's HR team. I don't want to just be a manager. I want to make the decisions, run it in a way I know will make it dazzle. Make it somewhere all of New York wants to be. The floor plan of the spa alone is triple the size of the one in Hope Cove, plus all the clientele that visit. It's easily five times busier. I'll barely have time to think. I agreed to take the position on the condition that they gave me the freedom to run it how I choose.

A cab swerves across every lane of traffic to pick up a fare. New York is a different world. Everything is fast-paced compared to home. Not that Hope Cove was my home. But it is the closest thing to feel like one in a long time. My fingertips tingle as excitement bubbles in my chest. I am here. I am actually here. I can even see Central Park peeking around the corner of the building.

It's perfect.

The sound of female giggling floats in from outside, and despite myself, I walk over and peer through the spyhole. A woman in a tight black dress has her back to me as she flicks her long, blonde hair over her shoulder and giggles again. Her male companion is obscured from view, standing inside the apartment. The only glimpse I get of him is his hand, and the gold class ring on his pinkie finger as he reaches out and cups the blonde's ass. She murmurs something that sounds like encouragement, and he chuckles darkly, squeezing it.

Finally. Now I might get some peace to unpack and run through my plans for tomorrow. It's my first day, and also my first meeting with the spa product suppliers. I can't wait to meet them and get started. I've already got some new ideas for the products I want to introduce. I've researched everything I can about the hotel and current treatments the spa offers. The hotel is the most coveted place to stay in Manhattan. Award winning restaurants, unrivaled views over Central Park, luxury rooms that are constantly named as having the most comfortable beds in the world.

There's a year-long waiting list for a night in its top penthouse suite. The British royal family has even stayed there. The price for one night is a closely guarded secret. But judging by what I've been encouraged to set treatment prices at in the spa, I would say it's one of those where, if you have to ask, then you can't afford it.

I'm about to turn away when a second woman emerges from next door. She is all long blonde hair and tight dress, too. She and the first woman look so alike they could be twins.

I almost roll my eyes but stop myself. So what if they are all having great, hot, and dirty sex on a Sunday evening? Just because it's been months since I had any. Scratch that. I have *never* had sex like what just went on next door. I don't even mean the threesome. Just the passionate, earth shattering, toe-curling, shout out loud fucking that these three have just had.

I'm envious.

I can't even pretend that I'm merely annoyed that I had to be a non-consenting witness to their antics. I'm envious that someone is getting great sex around here. And despite being excited, I'm also nervous about tomorrow. I need what those two women just had—a good fucking that clears my mind and stops me from being able to think straight, even if only for an hour.

I go back into the living room and sink down onto the large sofa. This apartment is beautiful, all soft white furnishings and deep cream carpets. It's the perfect sanctuary, apart from my noisy neighbor.

I press my fingertips to my temples and rub in small circles.

This isn't like me. I'm calm, level-headed and someone who knows what I'm doing at work. I can run a successful spa with my eyes shut; been doing it long enough; building up my own business, making it a success. *Proving people wrong.* But I've never worked for Griffin Parker. He's the most prominent hotelier in New York. Rumor has it he either likes you or he doesn't. At only thirty-three years old, he's already on Forbes' rich list. I doubt he got to where he is without being ruthless. I don't think anyone would want to be on the wrong side of Mr. Parker.

I remember our first meeting months ago. How his handshake was firm, and that his eyes lingered on mine a little longer than was professionally acceptable as he told me how pleased he was to meet me in person. The way his short, dark hair is a direct contrast to his crystal blue eyes—eyes that burned into me throughout our meeting.

He was polite, sure. And his passion for The Songbird shone through when he spoke—in his voice, his eyes, his entire demeanor. It was something I really admired, and one reason I knew I had to take the position. But as far as liking me? I am still on the fence. I think what I've achieved impressed him. Yet there was something he was holding back. Something in his eyes I couldn't place.

That isn't necessarily a bad thing, though. When I am at work, that's it. I'm focused. Nothing can distract me. No one will ruin this for me. I'm stronger than that. I've proven it. Time and time again. It's harder for women to succeed in business, and I'm not about to jeopardize this chance for anything or anyone.

If there's one thing I have learned, it's that you never mix business with pleasure.

Not unless you want to get burned.

And my scars have only just healed.

Chapter Two

Maria

THE SONGBIRD SOARS INTO the sky, a majestic creature, just like her name. I haven't gone inside the main entrance yet. I'm still taking it all in. I went out of the private residence's door this morning and took a walk in Central Park to clear my head. And because it was dark when the cab dropped me off from the airport last night, this is the first time I'm seeing the hotel's main frontage in all its glory.

Pulling my shoulders back, I take in a deep, cleansing breath. It's magnificent. All regal, stone architraves with gold accents around the windows. It looks old and luxurious in its French Renaissance style. *Elegant and timeless.* That's how I described my vision for the spa in my first meeting with Mr. Parker. Working here is going to be magical—I can sense it.

"Impressive, huh?"

I turn. Bright eyes watch me in amusement.

"Hi!" I grin at Harley, Griffin's personal assistant. I've spent more hours than I can count talking to her on video calls and setting up my move to New York.

"Is that all I get?" She laughs, her light, breathy voice matching her appearance perfectly. Her light blonde hair and hourglass figure make her a modern-day Marilyn. But all those video calls that veered off work talk and on to more fun topics mean I'm not fooled. Harley may look sweet, but she's feisty and impulsive and very driven. I know we're going to be good friends. And thank God because I know absolutely no-one in New York.

"Come here!" She pulls me into a hug, beaming brightly. "I can't believe I'm actually seeing you again in person—finally!" Her eyes rake over my face and down my long, dark hair, which I've straightened and left down. "Oh, my God! You're even more beautiful than I remember."

I chuckle at how naturally she tosses out compliments. It's something that struck me about her when she accompanied Mr. Parker to LA for that first meeting. She spent ages talking to all the staff at the hotel there, laughing and joking with them. Spreading positivity like a ball of luminous sunshine. I don't think she realizes quite how beautiful that makes her.

"Thanks." I laugh as she bounces on her toes and her eyes light up.

God, I remember being in my twenties and having that much energy.

"How's the apartment? Did you sleep okay your first night?"

"I did, thank you. Well, after my neighbor's guests left, anyway." I shake my head, recalling the loud session that served as my 'welcome to the building' party.

10

"I didn't realize he had guests staying." Harley wrinkles her nose before shrugging her shoulders. Before I can ask who—or explain that they weren't the out-of-town family type of guests—she links her arm through mine and pulls me across the plush sidewalk carpet and up the steps toward The Songbird's main door. "Come on, let's go in!"

I say good morning to the doorman as he tips his hat and gives me a warm smile.

"Good morning, Ms. Taylor."

"How did—?"

"Oh, it's Earl's job to know everyone around here. Isn't it, Earl?" Harley stands on her toes and gives him a kiss on his gray whiskered cheek. The action draws a twinkle to his eyes, and he shakes his head at her.

"You'll be getting me into trouble, Harley." He chuckles.

"I don't know the meaning of the word." She winks at him. "How's pigeon-gate going?"

I look between them in puzzlement.

"Earl's been having problems with some locals and the sidewalk welcome carpet." Harley tips her head to the deep pink carpet we're standing on.

"Pigeons," Earl mutters. "Every morning, I shoo them away. But sometimes they've already left us a gift. I have to make sure the evidence is gone before Mr. Parker arrives."

"Yeah. That would not go down well." Harley snorts. "He's a control freak, as you'll no doubt find out, Maria. If it's not perfect, then he demands to know why."

"He's not so bad," Earl adds, looking at me and smiling kindly. "If you're good to him, he'll be good to you. I've worked here for forty years, in various positions around the hotel. First for senior Mr. Parker, and now for Mr. Parker. They're a wonderful family who hold trust and loyalty highly."

"Thank you, that's good to hear." I smile back.

"Forty years, Earl?" Harley shrieks. "You don't look a day over thirty-five."

His eyes crinkle at the corners. "You've made an old man's day, Harley, even if you do need glasses."

"Never! Mrs. Earl is a lucky lady." She grins at him and pulls me in through the main door.

Earl holds it open for us and chuckles as we head inside.

My jaw almost hits the floor, and I compose myself before I look like a star-struck idiot.

Holy... Wow!

"I know, right?" Harley laughs. "And you thought outside was impressive."

She leads us across the giant cream marble lobby, and underneath a crystal chandelier the size of a small country. The online video tours of the hotel I watched online in preparation did not do it justice.

"It looks so much... bigger in person," I say as I swallow down a tiny bubble of anxiety dancing in the pit of my stomach.

I'm not usually nervous. And Mr. Parker wouldn't have chosen me personally if he didn't believe I was capable. What the hell has gotten into me? I can do this job standing on my head. I know I can. It's just, talking about contracts, and looking at photographs and videos is not the same as standing here in person. Not even close. The Songbird is simply breath-taking. It would be enough to make anyone nervous.

I press my lips together and take another subtle look around. The nerves in my stomach turn into flutters of excitement as it sinks in. This is me now. This is my challenge for the next six months. To hell with being nervous. From this moment on, I intend to enjoy every second.

Harley smiles at me. "Come on. Let's go find Mr. Parker and say good morning. Then I'm giving you the grand tour before all the boring 'welcome to the company' paperwork begins."

I laugh as Harley feigns a yawn, and we walk across the lobby toward a bank of elevators. Even the thought of filling out a pile of forms cannot deter the warmth that is spreading in my chest. All the creams, golds, and deep pinks—this place is hotel class at its finest. I can't describe it, but something here feels right—like I'm exactly where I'm supposed to be. I know working here will push me into achieving something spectacular.

Harley scans her employee ID card to the elevator control as we step inside. "We need to get you one of these. We'll take you to security later and get your picture taken." She reaches out a glossy pink nail and presses a button for one of the high floors.

"Mr. Parker's office is near the top?"

"Yes, almost. The big penthouses take up most of the higher levels. But we have a section of offices in the east wing. We've got a great view of the park from there. Mr. Parker's office has the best view, naturally." She laughs and checks her watch. "This time of the morning, he'll be in his office making calls."

"Right." I nod, even though I don't have the first idea what the routine for someone like him is. Harley told me she has been Mr. Parker's assistant for the last five years. His routine is second nature to her. She probably knows it better than him.

The elevator doors slide open slowly and I walk along-side Harley into an open reception area. A young man in a suit with short blond hair gives us a dazzling smile from his seat behind a giant curved marble desk. Behind him is an office full of people working at desks.

"Maria, meet Will."

I raise a hand in a wave and give him a bright smile.

"Will is your go-to guy for anything around here. You need something fixed in the spa? Call Will. You need an emergency outfit because you spilled coffee all down yours? Will. Emergency condom for a hot date? Will." Harley ticks off things on her fingers as she talks. "Of course, these are just examples. No-one has ever come to you for condoms, right, Will?"

I look between the two of them with a raised brow, and Will laughs as Harley gives him an exaggerated wink. Then he turns his attention to me.

"It's so nice to meet you, Maria. I've heard all about your visions for the spa. They sound incredible. I'm sure you'll love working here at The Songbird. We're a friendly bunch. Like Harley said, if you need anything, you just ask. My official role here is head of hotel administration. But as Harley's wonderful introduction said, whatever you need, just ask. If I can't help, I can find someone who will."

"Thank you."

I'm going to love it here, if Harley, Will, and Earl are anything to go by.

"Right. Let's go see Mr. Parker." Harley spins away from the desk.

"He's in his office making calls," Will says.

"Glad to see he's on schedule," Harley calls over her shoulder as we walk down a wide corridor. "Seriously, Maria, you could set your watch according to Mr. Parker. He likes to do things a certain way. I'm sure you know what that's like, having already run your own business."

I nod as we walk past a long glass-fronted office with closed blinds and stop in front of the door. I know what that's like. I'm exactly the same. That's part of the passion for running your own business. You want things to be perfect.

The sound of a deep, throaty voice talking inside filters out. I expect Harley to say we will come back later. He's obviously on a call, but she lifts her hand and knocks on the glass door.

"Come in," the voice calls.

Harley opens the door and stands back so I can enter first. The second I cross the threshold; cool blue eyes lure me in. Mr. Parker is standing by the window; Manhattan's magnificent skyline behind him.

He assesses me coolly, subtly taking in my fitted red dress. It hugs all the right places, but in a powerful way. A way which, when teamed with my shiny, heeled pumps, says, 'this woman knows what she's doing.' At least that's what I thought it said. Now I feel like it was the wrong choice entirely. I dart my eyes to either side of him quickly before coming back to hold his gaze and giving him a polite smile.

Maybe he hates the color. Judging by his office—all black, chrome, and glass—he doesn't strike me as a lover of bright things. Even his designer suit is charcoal, and his tie deep gray. Then again, it makes the crystal blue of his eyes stand out. Maybe that's his plan. Distract his enemy with his hypnotic gaze. It takes me back to our first meeting. This is obviously how he is. Brilliant at what he does—The Songbird is like stepping into a magical world of luxury, where you can imagine your dreams coming true. But he is also cool and calculated. It makes sense. This is business, after all, not the PTA bake sale. I'm not here to make friends. I'm here for one thing, and one thing only—to create something special.

Taking in a deep breath and clearing my throat, I square my shoulders back as he says goodbye to whoever is on the other end of the line and drops the phone onto his desk. I'm being stupid and forgetting what's important. Frankly, I don't give a shit whether he likes my dress or not. I'm here to do a job, not to please him with my wardrobe choices.

"Ms. Taylor." He gives me a formal nod as he rounds his desk and holds his hand out. The scent of something fresh and invigorating follows him, like the air in a tropical garden after rain.

I reach out and take his hand, staring into his eyes. He finally smiles at me, but it seems to take a great effort to do so. I'd even go as far to say he looks pissed.

"My apologies if we disturbed you," I offer with my best business-like smile as his large, warm hand envelops mine. It's another thing I noticed about him when we first met. His hands are huge. Strong and masculine, with long fingers and clean, neat nails. I always admire a man's hands. They can tell you a lot about someone. My ex, for example, always had dirty nails. I hated that he didn't care enough to wash them properly. It's not like he even worked outside or in a job where they got dirty every day. He had no reason for it, except downright laziness.

Mr. Parker keeps my hand firmly in his as I hold his gaze. "And please, call me Maria."

Something seems to shift in him, like he's remembered where he is, and that Harley is standing next to me. He slides effortlessly into business mode, giving me a warm smile, which, when added to his dark hair and jawline that could cut glass, makes him look like a Greek god dressed in Prada.

"Maria. It's a pleasure to see you in person again. I can't tell you how excited we are to have you here, joining us at The Songbird." He places his other hand over mine, completely trapping it between his. "Please, call me Griffin. I hope your first night was comfortable?"

I hold back the smirk that's threatening to take over my face as the gold class ring on his pinkie finger glints at me. The same one I saw last night, squeezing the blonde's ass in the hallway.

Oh, Mr. Parker. I've got you figured out.

Harley told me he has a penthouse in the building. I just didn't expect to be given the one next door while I'm working here.

"It was brilliant, thank you. Although the sound proofing between apartments could do with updating." I raise my eyes to his.

He's studying me intently, his brow furrowed. "Really?"

"Yes." I stare back into his eyes. I bet he's great at poker. His face gives nothing away. He's got balls; I'll give him that. I've as good as told him I heard him fucking two women all evening, and he's totally unfazed. Then again, why wouldn't he be? He doesn't have to explain himself to me.

"Well, I'm sorry if it affected your ability to relax. I'll get someone to see to it straight away." He takes both of his hands back, and the cold air hits my skin.

"That's very considerate of you, thank you." I smile as he runs a hand down over his tie, his eyes never leaving mine.

"Has Harley given you a tour yet? I'm sorry I can't do it myself, but I have a meeting this morning, which couldn't be rescheduled." He clears his throat and looks at Harley.

"That's next on our list. We came to see you first."

"Excellent." He turns and walks back around his desk. "Harley can help you with HR and security, getting everything organized, and I will see you this afternoon."

"This afternoon?"

"At the meeting with the spa product suppliers," Harley adds, as I frown.

"Yes, I'm aware of the meeting. I just didn't see your name on the attendees' schedule that I was sent over." I direct my statement to Mr. Parker.

"You wouldn't have, Maria. I'm not on it." He looks down at a pile of papers on his desk and starts flicking through them.

My stomach tightens.

You're not on it because there's no reason you need to be there.

It's exactly the sort of meeting I would run back in LA. And exactly what I thought we'd agreed I would do by myself when I took the role up here. I don't need him breathing down my neck, checking I know how to do my job properly. If he doesn't think I'm capable, why did he hire me?

"I thought I could make the introductions, seeing as you haven't met before." His eyes leave the paperwork on his desk, and he looks up at me, arching a brow.

Why, you arrogant...

I smile politely, not buying a word. "Of course. That's kind of you. But I'm more than happy to attend alone. I'm sure you have a busy schedule."

Harley's eyes dart between the two of us.

"You're welcome. But I insist, Maria." He smiles at me, his brow arching higher over his intense gaze.

I wasn't thanking him. Cocky, self-assured—

"Right, we'll leave you to it." Harley cuts in, steering me out of the room and closing the door behind us before I can object any further. She waits until we're at the end of the hallway before she turns to me. "Oh, my god."

"I know," I tut, shaking my head. The bloody nerve of him. I can see working with him is going to be harder than I thought. Mr. Parker is obviously not a man who is used to giving up control.

"I've never seen him like that before." Harley's eyes widen. "You know what that was, don't you?"

A controlling ass in a suit?

"Mr. Parker not trusting me," I huff out.

She wrinkles her nose in confusion. "No, Maria. That was sexual tension at its absolute finest." She grabs my arm, and I look at her like she's deranged. She ignores me and grins, her eyes gleaming. "No one ever affects Mr. Parker. You being here is going to be so much fun!"

The rest of the morning whizzes by. Harley is the perfect host, giving me a tour of the hotel, and telling me gossip about things guests and members of staff have gotten up to. Especially at some of their famous charity galas, which a close family friend of Mr. Parker's runs. Maybe that's what it takes to earn his trust—years of playing in sandboxes together as kids. I only have six months to show him what I can do. But it's enough. He will eat one of his silk ties when I show him what I'm capable of.

After seeing the spa and meeting the team there, we head to lunch. The hotel has multiple restaurants, but Harley insists we go to her favorite deli around the corner, saying we need to escape 'the nest' before we go 'cuckoo'.

"You okay? You're kind of glowing." Harley looks at me as we join the line in the deli.

"Is it that obvious?"

She raises her brows and then breaks into a giggle. "It's pretty spectacular, isn't it?"

"That's one word for it." I can't help my wide ear-to-ear grin that's been there ever since we went into the spa. It's like no place on earth. One foot in through its large, ornate doors, and you are stepping into heaven, or the Garden of Eden. You're surrounded by lush, green plants, the sound of running water, and incredible giant columns made of Jerusalem limestone flown in from Israel. I saw pictures of it before moving to New York, but they did not do it justice.

"A guy in London who owns a global property re-development business designed it. Him and Mr. Parker are good friends," Harley says as she scans the menu board behind the counter.

"Yes, I read about Mr. Grayson. How long have they known each other?"

"Um, just over three years. They met while I've been at The Songbird."

I rub my lips together as I take in this new piece of information.

"What happened to the lady who was the spa manager before me?" I ask as we reach the front of the line.

Before Harley can answer, the server takes both our orders. Harley takes her card out, ready to pay.

"Oh no, you don't." I place my hand over hers and pass the server a twenty. I ask for a receipt and Harley's gaze lands on my wallet as I neatly fold it and place it next to the rest of the receipts, which are squeezed so tightly inside that it's almost prevented from zipping closed.

I slot the wallet into my purse, and we take our food and drinks and walk over to a free table.

"Thanks for lunch." She smiles as we take a seat. She lifts the lid off her latte and inhales deeply. "Ah, come to Mama, baby." She catches me smiling and looks pointedly at my cup. "Trust me, Maria. You'll want to kiss me. No place makes them better. Not even The Songbird."

I laugh and take a sip of mine. "You know? I think I must agree." I swallow the sweet, creamy liquid as Harley clinks her cup gently against mine.

"Yes! Latte sisters." She laughs.

I smile at her as we unwrap our sandwiches and eat.

"Okay. The last spa manager," she says after finishing a mouthful. "Where do I even start?"

I wait as she purses her lips in thought.

"She was okay. Gwen, I mean. The spa was doing well. But then there was all this stuff with the formulations for the signature products going missing. It was suspicious. There were only a handful of people who had access to them. Gwen being one of them. It all got weird. Then she and Mr. Parker broke up, and she left. No one really knows what happened."

I stop, my sandwich poised halfway to my lips. "Hang on. They broke up?"

"Yeah. They were dating for a while. Two months, I think."

I put the sandwich down and lean back in my seat. Mr. Parker dated someone at The Songbird? I would expect him to want to keep his work and personal life separate, like I do. But then, he isn't me. He's a billionaire. That kind of wealth and power buys you the luxury to do whatever the hell you want.

"He never looked at her the way he does at you, though," Harley says, observing me.

"What? God, no, I'm not thinking that."

"Really?" She raises an eyebrow.

"No! No, no, no." I protest as Harley's lips curl into a small smile.

She goes back to eating her sandwich, her eyes on me. I cannot believe she thinks I'm asking about them dating because I'm interested in him *like that.*

"I'm just surprised he dates people he works with, that's all," I say as I take a sip of my drink.

"There was only Gwen. And he hasn't dated anyone else at work since. He learned that lesson the hard way," she says. "Well, I thought he had. Until I saw the way he looked at you when we came to LA, and again today."

"You're wrong."

My skin prickles as I picture his cool blue eyes assessing me. If anything, I would say Mr. Parker doesn't even like me. Not personally, anyway. He must have chosen me because he knew I could do a great job. But outside of a professional capacity, I cannot see us having anything in common.

"Maybe. But I doubt it. I can read men very well. It's a skill I'm well rewarded for."

I narrow my eyes at Harley in interest. "Sounds intriguing. I'm guessing there's more to that comment?"

She laughs. "Come for drinks one night with me, and I'll tell you all about it. Right now, we need to think about heading back. You've got the supplier meeting this afternoon, and we still need to go to security to pick your pass up. It should be ready now."

"Oh, yes," I groan.

The meeting, which Mr. Parker is hijacking.

I can't wait.

Chapter Three

Griffin

"WHERE'S MS. TAYLOR?" I ask Harley as she walks toward my open office door, obviously on her way back from lunch, judging by the takeout coffee she places down on my desk as she enters. She insists on bringing me one back every day, even though I told her The Songbird coffee suits me fine. What I haven't told her is I'm in talks with the owner of the deli to open a branch in The Songbird's east wing lobby, by the hotel boutiques. She isn't just a diligent PA; she also knows her shit when it comes to coffee.

"Maria? You know she said you could call her Maria, remember?"

"Yes, I recall," I huff out, shoving my hands into my pant pockets. "Maria. Where is she? Had enough of us already?"

Harley shakes her head at me. "Not likely. That woman is driven. She asked me to show her to the conference room early. She said she had some paperwork to go over."

"I see." I glance at the wall clock. There's still twenty minutes before the meeting starts.

Harley follows my gaze. "I can hold your calls from now, if you like?"

I realize I'm grinding my teeth. Maria is merely a few doors down in the conference room, preparing for the meeting. Exactly what I'd hope she would do in readiness for her new role here. So, why the thought of her sitting down there in that red dress of hers bothers me; I've no clue.

"That won't be necessary, thank you. Hold them from the time we previously agreed," I tell Harley, turning to look out the window at Central Park as she leaves.

This is what I wanted. I headhunted Maria for the newly available role of Spa Manager after my parents couldn't stop gushing over how incredible the spa she ran near LA is. Her achievements and awards meant I was ninety-nine percent convinced I was offering her the role before I met her face to face. That's where the one percent came in. The one percent that has long, dark hair and sensual hazel eyes. The giant fucking one percent that had me beating one out in the shower this morning.

I'm not an idiot.

I won't make the same fucking mistake twice.

I finish up with some calls in my office and drain the last of the takeout coffee before getting up and putting my suit jacket back on. The conference room looks empty as I walk past the window. It's only when I enter through the open door that I see her. She has her back to me, laying out bound folders at each of the four places which have been set up—one each for me, her, and the two reps from the supply company who will be attending.

"I thought Harley already put the agendas out in here?"

Maria glances at me over her shoulder, not in the least surprised at my interruption. It's like she already knew I was here.

"She did."

"What are these, then?" I walk to the table and stop in front of a folder, scanning the fancy font underneath The Songbird's emblem on the front cover.

"They're the agendas, same as before. I just added a few items I'd like to discuss, that's all," Maria says as she leans over her notepad on the table and jots something down.

I take a slow breath in, fighting to maintain composure. "You made some changes?"

"I emailed them to you," she continues, "but maybe you didn't see them yet."

"No. I was at a meeting all morning, and then on calls just now." I scan the folders again, the hairs on the back of my neck pricking up.

"Oh." She looks up. "I'm sorry. I hope that isn't a problem?"

I stare back into her eyes in silence. It should impress me that it's only day one, and she's already showing initiative, just as I expected her to. Yet, part of me wants to tell her that yes, there is a problem. A big fucking problem.

I don't like things not to be run past me first.

"Of course not." I smile in the way I've been told makes me look charming, but Maria has already turned away.

"Okay, great." She picks up one of the bound files and comes to stand next to me. "Plus, I found some discrepancies in the reports I want to raise with the suppliers." She flicks to a page in the file and points to some figures. "See?"

She turns her face to the side and looks up at me. Her hazel eyes are fanned by long, dark lashes as she waits for my reaction. Heat fires across my neck, underneath my collar, as the scent of her perfume reaches me. It's sexy and elegant, and smells like a workplace sexual harassment claim waiting to happen.

I peel my eyes from hers and look at the page.

"Where, exactly?" I frown at the invoice. At a quick glance, the totals all add up.

"Here." Maria points to the price our supplier is charging for a body scrub. "One of the key ingredients is coconut sugar. Yet, they're charging us almost the same as the lotion with the pure rose oil in." She looks up at me again, her eyes bright before continuing. "It made little sense, so I did some digging." She turns to her bag, which she has placed on the chair, and pulls out some more documents. When she turns back to me, she's even closer, and the bare skin of her arm brushes against my jacket sleeve.

"Look. This is what the grower in The Bahamas is charging our supplier for coconut sugar. Over double what I expected to see from last year's prices with the same grower."

She presents the accounts document to me and leans in, reading it at the same time as I do. The curve of her breast brushes my bicep and I clear my throat, taking a small step to one side, breaking contact.

"How did you get this?" I skim my eyes over the fig-ures. She's correct. The grower is charging our product supplier two point three times as much as they charged last year.

"I couldn't fall asleep last night. So, I went online and did some research. I have some contacts in The Bahamas from my spa in Hope Cove. And I'm familiar with this grower. I met him once, years ago."

I raise a brow, closing the folder and placing it back on the table.

"This is certainly interesting. Maybe I should cancel the team who are booked to add some insulation to the apartment next to yours. It seems the noise may aid you in your work."

Her eyes widen, and her lips part at my suggestion, as though I've spoken out of turn. She takes a moment before responding.

"As *thoughtful* as that suggestion is. I would rather my neighbor"—she looks at me pointedly—"maintain his privacy, along with my peace, if you don't mind."

She turns and busies herself with some more papers in her bag. If I weren't so drawn to looking at her whenever I'm near her, then I wouldn't notice the subtle tensing in her shoulders.

But for some unfathomable reason, I am. And so, it seems my mind is intent on noticing every single thing about her.

Like the tense muscle in her cheek as she frowns.

Something has bothered her.

"Was there something else?" My question comes out like an accusation despite not intending it to.

"No. Just coconuts. Round, firm fruit," she mutters under her breath, her cheek tensing again.

Great. I've hired someone who is bat-shit crazy.

There's a knock at the door.

"Mr. Parker, Maria? Todd and Serena are here," Harley announces brightly from the doorway.

I drag my gaze away from Maria, who hasn't looked at me since my comment about the insulation.

"Thank you. Show them in, please."

After the initial pleasantries and introductions, the four of us take our seats at the large conference table. Maria and I on one side, Todd and Serena on the other. The Songbird spa has been using them for several years now to supply the products. I've never had a problem with either of them before today, but the way Todd's eyes keep dropping to Maria's chest when he thinks she won't notice doesn't escape my attention, and I find myself scowling at him over across the table, my jaw clenched tight.

"I see what you mean, Maria," he says. *Chest glance.* "I can't believe we never picked it up." *Chest glance.* "You've got a good eye." *Chest glance.*

If you're not careful, Todd, you're about to lose both of yours.

He looks up at me with uncertainty as he studies the discrepancies Maria has found. Serena takes notes next to him, marking up the accounts with a red pen until it looks like a scene from a horror film.

"I'll cancel the contract with the grower. We'll get someone else." Todd rubs his hand over his chin.

Maria shifts in her seat next to me. "No. If you don't mind, I would like to talk to the grower first. I met him once a few years ago. I never bought from him as he couldn't source what I needed. But he put me in touch with someone who could. He didn't strike me as a dishonest man. I'd like to see what he has to say before we rule him out."

Todd turns and smiles at her, his eyes glowing. "That's very understanding of you, Maria. Let me give you my business and personal cell numbers, and we can set something up." *Chest glance.*

I swear his pretty-boy blond curls are taunting me to smack him square in the jaw.

I stretch my fingers out on top of my legs beneath the table as I suck in a sharp breath.

"Thank you. That would be great." She smiles back. "Mr. Parker, is that okay with you?" She turns to me, and I swear there's a challenge in her eyes. It's almost like she wants me to disagree with her.

I purse my lips and nod. "Of course. You're the manager. If you want to get to the bottom of it with the grower, then please be my guest." My hands tighten into fists, dragging over the material of my suit pants.

"Why don't I call you tomorrow, Maria? And we can discuss it some more." Todd looks like Christmas came early as he stands and shakes Maria's hand. "I think it's going to be wonderful working together. I can see you're going to be an asset to The Songbird." *Chest glance.*

"Todd." I swear my blood has almost reached boiling point as I take his hand. The corners of his eyes twitch as I squeeze tighter than usual, picturing crushing his hand to dust inside my own. I smile before I release him.

"Good to see you again, Serena," I add as I shake her hand too.

"Well, they seem nice," Maria says after they leave.

"Mmm," I grunt.

"Have you worked with their company for long?"

Too long, I'm thinking.

"A few years," I answer, not wanting to waste another second's thought on Todd and his 'I'll give you my personal cell shit'.

"His hair is amazing," Maria says, more to herself as she gathers her things together to leave. "I wonder what product he uses."

I bristle, then straighten my shoulders immediately.

"Why don't you ask him? When the two of you speak on his personal cell," I bark, smoothing my hand down over my tie. "Now, if you'll excuse me." I turn and leave the room before she has time to answer and stride down the hall toward my office.

I glimpse at my profile reflected in a mirror that I pass—short, dark hair.

I snap my eyes away, swallowing down the bubbling anger burning inside my gut.

Fucking pretty boy with his blond curls.

"Hey, what's up with you? You've got a face like a whipped ass."

"Jerk," I mutter as I slap Reed on the shoulder and walk past him into the apartment.

He chuckles as he closes the door and follows me.

"What exactly were you up to last night, anyway?" I ask, casting my eyes around the apartment, expecting to see his guitar, or another source of the noise Maria referred to.

"Why? Who's been talking?" Reed looks at me warily, his eyes darkening.

I shake my head. "Nothing like that, don't worry."

He runs a hand back through his deep brown hair. "Thank fuck. Now is not the time for the press to go chewing on bones."

I smirk as he heads to the fridge and passes me a beer. "There never is a time with you. That's what you get for wanting to run for Mayor—everyone watching your every move."

"Bloody media and their fucking circuses," he curses as he takes a swig from his bottle. "Still, it's nice to take a little break from California for a few days. Relax, make new friends, you know?" He shrugs a shoulder as the corners of his lips curl.

"How many new friends are we talking about?" I sink back into his couch, kicking off my shoes and putting my feet up on the coffee table. I use my free hand to loosen my tie. I like to relax after work. And after today, I feel like I've earned it.

"Two new friends. Underwear models." Reed grins, dropping onto the couch next to me.

"Really?" I raise my brows. "What were their names?"

Reed shrugs. "Baby... and... Babe."

"Figures." I snort, knocking back a mouthful of cool beer.

Reed is one of those guys who always has different female company. None of whom he cares to ask the names of. It seems to suit him. He comes across as happy as a pig in shit when we get the chance to catch up. It's not as often as we used to. Not since he moved to LA to run for Mayor. But in politics, anything can change. I know for a fact he has his sights set on the New York Mayor's office. And after my meeting there this morning to discuss some planning I'm applying for downtown, I'd say he's in with a shot. The entire staff there seemed on tenterhooks. Hushed conversations, worried glances. There is definitely a shake-up on the horizon.

"You know you have a neighbor as of last night?"

Reed stops drinking his beer.

"Seriously? On that side?" He tips his bottle toward the wall that connects to Maria's apartment.

"Yeah. The new spa manager."

He tips his head back and blows out a breath. "Shit. We may have given her a show last night. It got loud."

"When doesn't it with you?" I smirk, remembering many nights in our shared college dorm. We had a code. If a tie was on the door, then one of us had company.

If the tie's hanging, inside we're banging.

Crass, I know. But we were testosterone-fueled young men with freedom and seemingly unlimited energy... and we knew exactly how to put it to use.

"What can I say? I'm on a mini break, blowing off steam, catching up with my buddy." Reed looks at me, amusement dancing in his eyes.

"Yeah, well. Expect some guys around tomorrow to improve the insulation. It should help muffle the noise next time you choose to entertain."

Reed chuckles. "Look, I'm sorry. I didn't know. I thought I had the floor to myself."

That was the original plan. Although he's on a break, he has work-related meetings going on in New York. The two advisors traveling with him are staying on the floor below. And the floor above—where Maria should be—had a leak in the master bathroom the day before she arrived. Harley set up the apartment next to Reed's at the last minute.

"Yeah, well, you know now." I rub a hand over my eyes as I lean my head back against the couch and let out a sigh, my shoulders loosening as tension slowly drops from them.

"Tough day?" Reed asks.

"Nothing major. Just issues with a supplier. Maria thinks a grower in The Bahamas is overcharging them for an ingredient for one of the spa products, and they're passing the increase onto us."

"Maria?" Reed's ears prick up. I swear he's like a fucking blood hound at the sound of any new female name he hasn't heard me mention before.

"Yes. The new spa manager." I take my hand away from my eyes and catch the glint in his.

"She hot?"

"I work with her. And I will be for at least the next six months of her initial contract."

"You didn't answer my question." Reed takes one look at my unimpressed expression and chuckles. "That's a yes, then. What are we talking? Hot, but you can ignore it? Or hot, all you can think about is what she looks like naked every time you see her?"

I say nothing. I've learned with Reed, that's usually the wisest choice in situations like this. He forgets nothing. He's like some ridiculous Mensa genius, with an IQ of 156. It doesn't stop him from saying or doing stupid shit sometimes, though.

His chuckle morphs into a full-blown laugh as he slaps his hand against his leg.

"Yeah, yeah. Ha-the-fuck-ha!" I grumble, waiting for his laugh to die down before continuing. "I work with her. She's going to be great for The Songbird. That's it."

My thoughts turn to how she found all the discrepancies for today's meeting. I was right about hunting her out. She will be an asset to the hotel.

"She's had an impressive first day. Made an impression on Todd from the supply company." I scowl, remembering the prick's roaming eyes.

"That guy? Does he still look like he should be on the Johnson's no tears shampoo commercial?" Reed grins.

Despite being halfway through imagining wringing the curly-haired fucker's neck—and smiling to myself at the mental image—I turn my attention to Reed and nod.

"Sure does. Although, he's not so baby-faced now. Harley even said she thinks he's handsome."

"Harley did, did she?" The grin drops off Reed's face.

I've noticed recently that whenever her name comes up, he does this—looks like a sulking kid with his brows drawn low and his lips curled down with a hint of a pout. He swears I'm seeing things and point-blank refuses to engage any further. As far as I'm aware, they've only met in passing when he's visited me at the office.

Whatever it is about her that riles him, it's obviously something he doesn't want to share.

"Just as well you don't dip your pen in the company ink then, eh, Griff? Looks like Tiny Tears Todd might give you a run for your money." He blows out a breath, and his expression turns back to one of amusement as he turns the conversation back to Maria.

"Did that once. Got the stain to prove it," I mutter.

I still don't know whether my ex, Gwen, was responsible for the signature product formulations going missing or not. But that wasn't what ended it. Our relationship was on the rocks long before, doomed from the start. She was good at her job, but nowhere near as dedicated and insightful as I needed her to be.

Not like Maria.

I rub my eyes again, stifling a yawn.

"Age getting the better of you?" Reed asks.

"Fuck off. I'm barely three months older than you." I sit forward and drain the rest of my beer. "I have an early start, though. And I want to get a run in first. You still up for breakfast after?"

"Sure am," Reed answers as I get up and head toward the door to let myself out.

"All right then." I lift a hand and give him a wave, then step out into the hallway, closing the door behind me.

"Good evening."

I take a second to process the voice as I turn.

Maria is at her apartment door, key poised, about to unlock it. She's changed out of her red dress, *thank fuck.* That was the kind of dress that made me need a cold shower after seeing her in it. Now she's wearing workout gear, like she's just been for a run. Her face is flushed, beads of sweat running down her smooth, exposed skin toward her breasts. I tear my eyes away as a stirring in my groin fires up.

The red dress suddenly seems the safer option.

I give her a friendly smile, despite the muscles in my shoulders going rigid beneath my suit jacket.

"Maria. I hope you're enjoying your evening?"

"I am, thank you. I thought I'd try out the residence's gym."

I fight to keep my eyes on her face, and not let them drop over the curves of her body in the skin-tight outfit.

Skintight and hugging every ample feminine curve.

"Wonderful. It's there for you to use as you please. If you need anything else, you only need to ask."

She gives me a polite smile, her eyes darting to Reed's closed door behind me. "Going out tonight?"

"I…"

She thinks this is my apartment. Technically, it is. They all are. I own the entire building.

I roll my lips as she waits for my answer. "Just visiting a friend."

"Oh, I see." She flicks her long, dark ponytail over her shoulder, eyeing me a second longer, before dropping her gaze to the keys in her hand.

I fight to keep the amusement from my face. She heard Reed doing God knows what last night and thinks it was me.

"Well, don't let me keep you. Good night," she says quickly, opening her door and disappearing inside before I can correct her.

"Good night to you, too," I say to the closed door.

I head back to my apartment with one thing stuck firmly in my mind—the flash of annoyance in her eyes when she thought it was me who she's been hearing through the wall these last few nights.

The same fiery annoyance that caused her eyes to darken as she looked at me, setting a whole host of images coursing through my imagination.

All of which keep wickedly thrusting and spilling into every inch of my mind, firing me into a stupor.

Images that keep me company that night in bed.

And are still there when I shower the next morning.

Chapter Four

Maria

My first week at The Songbird passes by in a blur. *I love it.* The spa therapists are an amazing team who all help one another and strive for excellent client satisfaction. The day-to-day appointments and bookings run like a well-oiled machine, leaving me time to design a new treatment menu, and come up with some new special packages. The other hotel staff I've met so far are all warm and welcoming. And living in Manhattan and waking up to the view of Central Park is like being on a movie set every day.

I love it.

Every. Single. Thing. About. It.

"Maria?"

Except one.

"Good morning, Mr. Parker." I lift my head from my position behind the spa reception desk and lock eyes with him. It's early and the staff members aren't here yet. I wanted to come in and get a head start on preparing for the new weekly team meetings I've implemented.

"Griffin," he says curtly.

I give him a tight smile. It feels strange calling him Griffin. Too familiar, like we should be friends. And we are definitely *not* friends. He doesn't even seem happy about me calling him by his first name, but this is the second time he has corrected me, so I really should use it.

"Griffin," I repeat.

"You're meeting Todd from the suppliers today," he states, his jaw ticking as his blue eyes assess me with their usual coldness.

Jerk.

I straighten my spine. I didn't inform him about the lunch with Todd I have scheduled today. I shouldn't have to, and he knows it. He's obviously checked my schedule. Once Todd and I have agreed on the next step about what to do over the grower in The Bahamas and the discrepancies, then I will give Griffin a full report. Exactly the process things should follow with me being Spa Manager.

"I am." I smile again, despite him not deserving it.

I've hardly seen him this week, which has been a blessing. Because each time I do, his score on the jerk scale rises. I don't know what it is about me that makes him so downright grumpy. He looks like he's swallowed something sour whenever he addresses me, which is a shame, as he is a handsome man. Like ridiculously tall, dark, and handsome, *handsome.* He looks so much better when he's smiling. And I know he can do it, because I see it every time he talks to my spa team, or Harley, or Earl. When he talks to any other person.

Anyone that isn't me.

If I didn't love this place so much, then I could tell him to shove his job up his overpriced designer suit-clad ass. But I'm not a quitter. And I'm not about to start because of Griffin Parker.

"Where?" he growls, making the word sound like an accusation. Of what, though, I'm not sure.

I want to roll my eyes at his complete lack of manners. How the hell I thought he was charming at our first meeting in Hope Cove is a mystery now. Maybe it was all an elaborate act to get me to accept his offer.

I stare back at him as he presses his lips together.

You've got perfect white teeth that dazzle people when you smile. Use them!

"Greenhams," I answer finally, not wanting to give him anything more.

He nods once, thrusting his hands deep into his pockets. "Excellent. Well, I look forward to a full update."

"Of course." My shoulders relax as I turn my attention back to my notes on the desk.

"This afternoon," he adds. "Two o'clock. In my office."

I snap my gaze up and back onto him, my fingers tingling at their tips with the overwhelming urge to strike out and poke him in his crystal eyes.

But he's not worth the trouble of ruining a perfectly beautiful manicure.

"Absolutely!" I smile brightly with fake enthusiasm.

"Are you... are you being disturbed less?" His voice softens, and for a moment, I consider he may actually care about my answer.

But despite the soundproofing being a giant improvement, I'm still aware of the fact he's had visitors to his apartment every night this week. Now it's muffled bangs and the occasional high-pitched scream if he's doing something she really likes. They never stay overnight, luckily. At least I can guarantee that by midnight the latest Cinderella will have departed the ball—or departed *his balls*. And from who I've seen leaving, they all look the same.

He must have a thing for blondes.

I hold the fake smile on my face as my cheeks ache. "Yes, thank you."

"Good." He smiles the first genuine smile at me he has in days. "I'm pleased to hear it." He turns to leave, but then hovers at the door. "Maria?"

Just hurry up and go. Please.

"Yes?"

"Make sure you put lunch on your company account, won't you? I don't want you to spend your own money. Not if it's a *working lunch*." His eyes hold mine long enough for a tiny flicker of heat to spark in my stomach at his words.

"I will. Thank you."

I hold the puzzled look off my face until he strides out of the door, taking his fresh rain-cleansed air scent with him.

Why did he emphasize the words *working lunch*? Like I would ever use the company card for anything non-business related. Is that what he was suggesting? That must be what this weird feeling in my stomach is—anger at his insinuation. Only, I think he meant it sincerely. And if he did, then that spark is something else entirely. Because him being concerned that I may use my own money when I shouldn't have to means something to me.

It means everything.

"Maria, it's so great to see you in person again." Todd stands from his seat in Greenhams restaurant as I approach and places his hand on the small of my back. I barely have time to take in the relaxed coastal-themed décor before he leans in and kisses me on the cheek.

"Oh, yes, you too." I smile politely as he pulls my chair out for me.

Maybe a week of phone calls and emails about business matters has now moved us to the 'kiss greeting' stage in his mind, rather than the handshake I would have offered. Either way, we are here to talk about work, so should get on with it.

"I thought we could begin with—"

"You look beautiful." He grins at me as his eyes skim over my olive-green silk blouse.

Or maybe not get straight on with it.

I sigh internally, reaching down into my bag to retrieve some costing reports. I really don't want to seem rude, but I have a ton of work to be getting on with when I get back, so I would rather cut the pleasantries. However, he is representing the supply company who has worked with The Songbird for several years. So I should at least be able to engage in some light non-business talk to maintain a good working relationship. Besides, he's just being friendly. My run-in with Griffin this morning has just set me on edge, that's all.

"Thank you," I reply, injecting more warmth into my tone.

"How are you settling into life in the city?"

I place the reports on the table. His eager face has guilt gnawing in my stomach as a result of my rudeness.

I soften my shoulders, lifting my eyes to his.

"Good, thank you, Todd. Great, actually. It's been a whirlwind first week, so I haven't explored much yet. But I'm going to rectify that this weekend."

"That's great." He smiles. "I know some places you shouldn't miss if you need a tour guide?"

"Oh." I smile politely. "That's really kind of you, but Harley has already made plans for us. She has a whole itinerary set up."

"Ah, Mr. Parker's PA?"

"Yes."

Todd nods in understanding. "Well, I hope you have a great time." He grins as a server approaches and takes our orders. "Shall we get started, then?" He gestures to the reports on the table.

We spend the rest of lunch with our heads bowed together over the reports, discussing ingredient costs and new products that will work well with the signature fragrance blend I've made. It's an essential oil blend that I want to add to the products at formulation stage, so that each product used in The Songbird holds the signature fragrance, which will be entirely exclusive. I did the same thing at my spa in Hope Cove. But where that scent was beachy and light, this one will be sultry and darker to fit the urban setting. It's something Mr. Parker was extremely insistent upon me developing when I accepted the job. Now I understand why. If their previous signature formulations went missing, like Harley told me about, then he will want new ones, which his competitors can't replicate.

"I really like these ideas, Maria. It's definitely something we can do." Todd looks up and smiles at me as the server heads over with the bill. He hands her his card and pays without a second's thought, before turning back to me.

"Thank you, I appreciate it." I smile as Todd pulls my chair back for me, and I stand.

He puts his navy suit blazer back on, his broad chest filling out his crisp white shirt.

"It was so good to see you. I'll call you next week and we can set up that meeting with the grower. I think in-person will work best, don't you?" he asks.

"Yes, I think you're right."

I'm too busy mentally considering the logistics of booking my first work trip to the Bahamas to notice Todd leaning close.

He brushes his lips against my cheek.

"It was a pleasure, Maria," he says softly into my ear before kissing my cheek.

I clear my throat, taking a step back and subtly placing more distance between us.

"Yes, it was lovely. Thank you for lunch."

Todd smiles at me. "Maybe we can do it again? Outside of work?" He raises an eyebrow in question.

He's handsome, there's no denying that. His blond hair, and easy, big bright smile make him the polar opposite of someone else—Griffin. God, why am I even thinking of him? He's rude and abrasive. Frankly, if I'd known what I was letting myself in for coming to work with him, I might have given it more thought.

I open my mouth to respond to Todd, but my words die in my throat.

It's like thinking about him has conjured him up, as if by magic.

I stare back at the pair of cool blue eyes assessing me from a table across the restaurant.

The hairs on the back of my neck rise and my body tenses at the unwelcome intrusion. His lunch date seems unaware that his focus is not on her and is instead burning a hole right through me as he glowers over at me.

Really? Of all the places to go for lunch. I know for sure I told him I was coming here. It's just another example of his controlling micro-management. I'm surprised he refrained himself from coming over to join us, so he could make sure not to miss a word.

This is not what I agreed to when I took this role.

It's time he and I had words.

Stupid, annoying, control-freak Griffin Parker.

What the hell is his problem?

Chapter Five

Griffin

Two o'clock on the dot, there's a determined knock at my office door.

"Griffin, I'd better let you get back to work. Thank you for lunch."

Emily stands from the large leather sofa and picks up her purse.

"Don't mention it. Give the family my regards, won't you?"

Emily's eyes drop to the clasp on her bag as she fiddles with it. "Of course. Dad's always asking after you."

"I'll have to grab a drink with him. Join him and my dad at the club next time they're in the city."

A small frown passes Emily's lips. It's no secret that she's always had a tense relationship with her father, Owen, my dad's best friend. Too many drinks once at one of many family get-togethers, and he announced to the room how he had never been blessed with a son. I think life as an only child was lonely for her. She lived for all the holidays our families used to take together so she could hang out with me and my two brothers.

"Take care, Em. I'll see you soon."

"You can count on it. I've got some ideas for the fundraiser I want to run past you."

"Of course," I answer her as I open the door, but my eyes are drawn to Maria, who is standing behind it, heat radiating off her as she fixes her gaze on me.

"Ah, Maria. Thank you for coming. This is Emily. Emily, this is Maria, The Songbird's new spa manager." I step back as I make the introductions.

Emily looks at me in surprise, her brows shooting up her forehead, before recovering quickly to smile at Maria.

"Of course. Maria, it is so nice to meet you. Griffin was telling me you had started. And you've come all the way from LA. How have you found your first week?"

Maria's gaze moves from me to Emily, and her face takes on a beautiful, open smile.

"Oh, it's been interesting." Her eyes flick to me again, then back to Emily. "It's a stunning spa. I have some great ideas for it."

"I would love to hear them"—Emily glances at her watch, her forehead wrinkling—"but I have to go."

"Please don't let me hold you up. It was lovely meeting you," Maria says.

Emily smiles at her. "I'm so sorry to rush off. How about I come in next week? I'd love to spend more than one minute talking."

"That sounds great."

Emily nods at Maria and then turns to me, placing one hand gently against my chest as she reaches up and kisses me on the cheek.

"I'll call you."

My eyes meet Maria's over Emily's shoulder as she hugs me. Maria only breaks eye contact when Emily turns back to her.

"Bye, Maria."

"Nice to meet you," Maria says, watching Emily leave and close the door behind her, before whipping her eyes back to me, a trace of annoyance flashing in them.

"Maria, have a seat."

I walk over to the large black leather sofas to one side of my office and undo the top button of my jacket with one hand, waiting for Maria to sit first before I sit opposite her.

"How was your lunch with Todd? You two looked rather comfortable together."

Her shoulders pull upward as I say his name, her eyes pinching at the corners ever so slightly.

"Really, Griffin?" Her top lip curls as she shakes her head in what I can only describe as disgust.

I hold my hands up, studying her. How that little muscle tenses in her cheek.

"Merely an observation," I say, dropping my gaze from her cheek, to her lips, then back to her eyes.

I could tell from across the restaurant just how close that fucker was getting. The thought irks me, and I run a hand down over my tie.

"If you are implying that I cannot be professional and keep my personal life separate from business, then you're very much mistaken." She narrows her eyes at me.

"Of anyone in this hotel, you can trust me the most not to blur the lines."

I stare back at her, and she refuses to drop her eyes away from mine—a silent challenge. She hasn't denied there's something going on between her and Todd. But I decide to leave that topic of conversation—for now.

"It sounds like you're talking from experience?"

I lean back on the sofa, one arm slung casually over the cushions, and rest one foot over my other knee as I study her. I know everything there is to know about how she works and her achievements in LA. But the real Maria, who she is outside of work, what made her into the person she is—I'm clueless.

She drops her gaze, ignoring my question.

"Lunch was productive." She sweeps her long, dark hair over her shoulder, and I sit mesmerized as my eyes follow it.

Does she even know what that does to any sane man?

Images of curling it around my fist flash through my mind.

"Of course, you could have joined us and heard it all for yourself. You were there, after all." She appears irritated, her lips pursing as she stares back at me.

My lips curl slightly at the corners.

She *is* irritated.

"Greenhams does great fish. In the city, that isn't always the easiest thing to find. When you mentioned it before, it reminded me I haven't been there in a while," I say calmly.

"Convenient," Maria clips, her eyes assessing my casual position as she sits up straight, her hands clasped in her lap. The corners of her red glossy lips turn down before she takes a breath. "If you don't trust me to take meetings alone and run the spa myself, then why did you approach me when I was in LA?"

And there it is. The reason I can't get her out of my mind.

Another trace of amusement passes over my lips, and I hide it before she sees. I sit forward, resting my elbows on my knees. This is one thing that impressed me about Maria when I first met her. She's direct. To the point. You don't wonder where you are with her. And in business, that can save a lot of time and a great deal of wasted energy. It's a sign of confidence and strength that I greatly admire.

"Maria. I don't trust anyone completely. I've learned that lesson the hard way." She parts her lips to speak, but I smile softly at her and continue. "I came to find you because I knew you were the best person to bring in for the role. You are what The Songbird needs. You have passion, drive, and determination. You bring something unique that no one else can. It was only a matter of time before someone else made you theirs. And I wasn't about to let that happen."

Her expression softens an iota, but her eyes remain fixed on mine.

"You're right. I am passionate about what I do. And I am determined to make The Songbird even more successful than it already is. But in order for me to do that,

I need to have the ability to make decisions, and know that you support me."

She fixes me with a look that tells me she's waiting for my compliance.

So I take my time answering, enjoying the way her red lips press tighter together with each stretching second.

I run my finger back and forth over my lips before finally nodding.

"I understand. I want the same things you do." My eyes drop to her lips and back up again. "My interests are purely with the hotel and its continued success. Nothing is more important to me."

"Good." She seems to accept my answer as she reaches into her bag and takes out her cell phone. "So, you wanted an update on today's meeting? Well, Todd and I—"

I scoff. *Todd and I.* Sounds fucking cozy.

Maria looks up from her phone and arches a brow at me before continuing.

"Todd and I were discussing the grower in The Bahamas. We've decided a face-to-face meeting is best. I'm going to suggest to him we book a flight for next Friday." She types into her phone. "I'm putting it in my schedule now. So you'll know where I am if you decide to check it."

She looks up at me again, and I fight the compelling urge to snap a comeback at her, but instead I take a breath before I answer.

"Why would I do that? You've just told me where you'll be. I don't forget things easily, Maria."

She swallows and purses her lips, then slides her phone back into her bag.

"So, you'll be flying out early and coming back that evening?"

"Actually, it may include a one-night stay. The flight times don't work out," she replies.

"I see." My shoulders tense as I run my hand down over my tie again. "Will Serena be accompanying you?"

"I don't believe so. We can handle it."

"I've no doubt you can, Maria."

My brow furrows as I stand and invite her to do the same. I bet Tiny Tears Todd thinks all his fucking Christmases have come at once. Staying overnight in The Bahamas with Maria? He can ogle her till his balls feel like they're going to explode.

"Once we've spoken to the grower, we can make plans going forward. I know we can source coconut sugar cheaper elsewhere. But I know this grower, and his quality is high. And you've used him for a long time, haven't you? Loyalty perhaps counts for something." She tilts her head to the side, her eyes narrowed as though she's testing me.

"Hmm." I realize I've been standing with my jaw clenched instead of showing her out. "Yes, loyalty, of course."

"It's becoming rarer, wouldn't you say?"

She's still looking at me, her eyes glinting. It's like I'm on the fucking witness stand being cross-examined.

"Not for me." I stare back at her, challenging her to say whatever it is she's obviously thinking.

Instead, her eyes drop over my dark gray suit for the tiniest fragment of a second, before she speaks.

"Always a pleasure, Griffin. I'll see myself out."

She walks to the door and my gaze wanders down her long legs, and her high black stilettos with red soles as she leaves, clicking the door shut behind her.

I walk around my desk and reach my forearm up, resting it against the cool, hard glass of the window. Central Park spreads off into the distance. A young boy chases a group of pigeons just inside the entrance.

What the fuck was I thinking? I went to Maria, just as she's said. *I* headhunted *her*.

I headhunted a woman with a sharp mind, who isn't afraid to use it and call me out. A woman with long dark hair that I picture wrapping around my fist as I remind her which one of us is really in control. A fist, which has had to make do with wrapping around my hardened dick day and night, trying to banish this ridiculous interest she has piqued inside me.

I don't mix dating and work. Or sex and work. It's a recipe for disaster.

No... just no.

I headhunted *her*.

What the fuck have I done?

Chapter Six

Maria

"HERE IT IS!" HARLEY'S eyes light up as she pulls me through the entrance of a trendy looking bar with low lighting and a long, sleek, black marble bar. "It's *the* best place for cocktails after work on a Friday, believe me. Mid-town has its fair share of bars... and I know most of them."

She giggles as she pulls me across the polished concrete floor and over to a small booth. The bartender is mixing a cocktail in a shaker as we pass the bar and my mouth waters at the scent of lime mixed with salt. I hope to God Harley suggests making the most of the long cocktail menu she said this bar has. After today's lunch with Todd and his lingering lips, and then the awkward meeting with Griffin this afternoon, I need a drink.

A strong one.

"You made it!" Harley grins and throws her arms around a pretty woman with short, honey-toned hair.

"Maria." She turns to me, her face glowing. "This is Suze. Suze, this is Maria who I told you about."

Harley slings her bag down and then throws herself into the velvet padded seat, pulling me with her.

"Hi, nice to meet you." I smile at Suze as I sit down next to Harley.

"You too." She gives me a friendly smile. "Harley said you've just finished your first week at The Songbird. You're working closely with Mr. Parker. How's that going?" Suze takes one look at my frown before laughing. "Rather you than me. From what Harley tells me, he isn't the easiest man."

I laugh back, relaxing into the seat. "I can already tell you and I are going to get on," I say as Harley giggles from her place in between us.

"Hey, he's not all that bad. I've lasted five years, haven't I?" Harley grins as she hands us both a cocktail menu from the table.

"Ugh, thank God. I did not want to be the only one drinking tonight." I exhale heavily as my eyes roam over the menu.

"Um, Maria. You're with me and Suze, here. There isn't a cocktail on this menu we haven't tried, at least four times."

Harley bumps shoulders with me and I smile, so pleased that I came out tonight and didn't head back to my apartment alone with just a bottle of wine and Griffin's late night activities next door to keep me entertained.

"You should go with the 'Boss Lady' cocktail," Harley says. "After your first week running things in the spa like a queen!" She bounces in her seat excitedly.

"Clashing heads with Griffin, you mean?" I roll my eyes. "I swear he's scrutinizing every move I make."

Harley looks at me sympathetically. "He does that to everyone in the beginning. Don't worry. It won't last. He's a pretty great guy under the alpha boss-hole exterior. Just keep doing what you're doing in the spa. You are going to blow his mind, I know it." She stands and squeezes past me. "First round is on me, ladies."

She heads off to the bar as I turn to Suze.

"So, how long have you and Harley been friends?"

I don't want to spend the evening talking about work, and I'm also aware it must be boring for someone outside of The Songbird to listen to. Tonight is about letting go and making new friends. And judging by my first impressions of Suze and her unfiltered opinion of Griffin Parker, I would say we've got lots in common already.

Suze leans forward onto the table, resting her chin in her hands.

"Oh, just since Harley tried to sleep with my husband. Two years ago, now."

My eyes widen and my mouth drops open as I do a double take and stare at her.

"I'm sorry, what?"

I knew things were going to be different in New York from LA. But befriending your husband's mistress? Surely not.

Suze dips her head, laughing, before meeting my gaze again.

"It's true. He was totally up for it as well. Jerk," she mutters, shaking her head.

"You talking about Curt?" Harley asks as she comes back to the table with three cocktails balanced between her hands.

"Ooh, you star. Thank you." Suze grins as she helps Harley and passes one to me.

"Cheers! To your first week in your new job. And to new friends," Harley says in a singsong voice as she clinks glasses with me and Suze.

I take a sip of the sweet, fiery liquid. It's grapefruit with a hint of ginger, and completely delicious.

"Hang on." I hold up a hand and take a bigger gulp, placing my glass down on the table with a loud sigh as I look at Suze. "I'm sorry, I think I needed that for this conversation."

I switch my gaze between her and Harley, and they both snort with laughter.

"I don't even know why I'm laughing," Suze says, wiping at her eyes. "It's not even funny."

"Someone please explain, because after the week I've had, I'm starting to think I moved to the twilight zone, not Manhattan."

Harley takes a sip of her drink.

"Okay... I have a second job as a honey trapper. But hardly anyone knows, especially not Griffin. You *cannot* tell him."

I blink, staring at her.

She giggles. "Fine. I know you won't tell him. You two barely communicate with words as it is. You just do your sexual tension thing whenever you're in the same room instead."

What?

There's no way there is anything remotely resembling sexual tension on my part when I'm near him. And I'm confident in saying the same for him. But before I can correct Harley, she continues.

"I needed the extra money. And I've learned a lot about men from doing it." She rolls her eyes. "But I also made a fab friend." She grins at Suze.

"I don't get it. Did you hire her?" I direct my question to Suze as I look from one to the other.

Suze drops her voice. "I did indeed. I suspected Curt had been having *extra company,* shall we say, after I had to go to the doctor for something that turned out to be a sexually transmitted infection."

"No! That's awful."

I reach across the table without thinking and grab her hand. I know all too well what it's like to have your trust completely betrayed by someone who is supposed to love you.

"It was." She squeezes my hand back. "But it meant that I could finally get the balls to do something about it. I've known Curt for years. And his reputation means a lot to him. By getting the evidence that he would easily choose to be unfaithful, I could make him a lot more cooperative about our divorce and the plans for the kids."

"Suze has Emmerson who's five, and Mason, who's eight. They're the most adorable kids," Harley adds.

"I found a company who came highly recommended by another mom at school and called them. They sent

Harley to Curt's favorite bar after work, and that was that." Suze knocks back the rest of her cocktail and winks at Harley.

"And you what? Strike up a conversation with them and see if they suggest taking it further?" I look at Harley, images of sleazy guys slipping off their wedding rings swirling in my mind.

"Basically." She shrugs. "I flatter their egos a bit, flirt, bat my eyelashes. I can tell straight away which ones are going to be the easiest. They don't even try to hide the fact they're checking me out when I sit next to them at the bar."

"Curt was one of the easiest," Suze says in disgust.

Harley smiles at her sadly. "You're better off without that jerk."

"But how did you two meet? Do you have a debrief after with the wives?"

"No, no, no." Harley shakes her head. "This one"—she jerks her thumb toward Suze— "decides to come and see for herself. Nearly blew my cover."

"I had to see it with my own eyes, you know. I didn't want to believe it," Suze says. "Ten years of marriage—gone. Just like that. He didn't even take off his wedding ring and try to hide the fact he had a wife at home. Just brazenly sat there and asked Harley if he could take her to a hotel."

"Asshole," I mutter, my mouth dropping open.

If there's one thing I can't stand, it's liars.

"I found a seat out of view and watched. I would've gotten a report back through the agency, but I knew seeing it with my own eyes would give me the strength I needed to act on it. Once Harley turned him down and he left the bar, I went over and told her who I was. We ended up having a great night... and one too many cocktails." Suze smiles at Harley. "The entire night he was texting and calling me, asking me when I'd be home. I told him I was out with a girlfriend. The next morning after breakfast, I asked him to leave."

"And she's never looked back since." Harley grins, wrapping an arm around Suze, who hugs her back.

"Exactly. Sisters before misters, as you say."

The two of them laugh, and a warmth spreads throughout my chest. Even in our darkest times, there is something good just waiting to happen.

A new friend for Suze after she was betrayed.

My old spa taking off in Hope Cove for me, shortly after the betrayal that nearly brought me to my knees.

No one's negativity is greater than us, more powerful than we are. No one can hurt us beyond repair. Watching Harley and Suze laugh together, their friendship and love for each other radiating from them in waves proves it.

Nothing can keep us down.

Nothing can keep me down.

Not even the thought of having to work with Griffin Parker again on Monday morning.

Todd: Everything is all booked for Friday. Would you like to share a cab to JFK?

I click out of the text without replying and glance at my watch. If I'm quick, I'll have enough time to grab a coffee from the deli Harley took me to. God knows I need it after being kept up late by Griffin's 'entertainment' again. How the hell he can look so fresh at work all the time when he is up half the night is a mystery. It must be all the orgasms, working like a miracle anti-fatigue treatment.

I step out of my apartment door into the hallway.

As if the universe isn't punishing me enough with its overdose of Griffin, it decides to go one step further and thrust him in front of me when I'm tired and un-caffeinated.

"Good morning." He gives me a curt nod as he steps out of his door and into the corridor.

"Is it?"

My eyes narrow as they drop over him. Black suit today, with a pale blue shirt that makes his eyes even more vibrant as he looks at me.

Why does he have to be so insanely good-looking? Prick.

He opens his mouth, but I hold up a hand before he can speak, annoyance at another interrupted night fueling me.

"You know. It's up to you what you do in your own time. I just wish I didn't have to hear it through the wall." My voice rises. "It's like living next door to a zoo of horny baboons! Some of us like our sleep. Maybe you could visit your friends at their place once in a while? Or practice the art of mime? You know, put someone else first, be *considerate*?"

The corners of his mouth twitch as one perfect, dark brow rises over the crystal blue of his eye.

"Maria, I am considerate. I let others come first. *Every* time."

Heat flares across my chest, my blood boiling at his blatant cocky reply. I'm sure Harley said he has a close childhood friend who runs charity galas at the hotel. It's got to be Emily. And from the way she looked at him in his office after I saw them at lunch together, and the way she hugged and kissed him goodbye, I'm sure there's more to that story than just friends. It's bad enough that he's got different women in his apartment every night. But it's a whole new level of being a jerk if he's dating Emily while doing it.

"I wonder what Emily thinks about you entertaining so many guests in the evenings," I mutter, turning my back on him to pull my door closed.

"Say that again!"

The scent of air after rain surrounds me, and I spin back around as he grinds to a halt inches from me. He towers over me, the molten heat from his eyes sending electricity all the way from my head to the tips of my toes. I press my back against the door and my lips part as I stare at him. Even in three-inch heels, I have to crane my neck to meet his eyes.

The back of my neck grows increasingly hot, and my mouth goes dry. I dart my tongue out to wet my lips and his eyes darken as they follow its path.

"Say. That. Again." He glares at me, his eyes penetrating deep into mine, his jaw tense. His chest expands as he draws in a breath and then lets it out in the small space that still exists between us. Mint mixes with the scent of him, and without thinking, I lean closer and inhale.

"I..."

"Hey, Griffin! You forgot your coffee," a voice behind us calls.

I tear my eyes away from Griffin's and peer around him. A tall guy who looks about Griffin's age is standing in the open doorway of the apartment next door. He sees me and flashes a bright white smile as his eyes light up.

"You must be Maria?"

I look back at Griffin, who's still glaring at me. He hasn't moved, and I'm aware of how close we are—me backed up against the door, his chest practically pressed up against my breasts.

Toe to toe.

Breath to breath.

The other guy seems kind of familiar as I give him a polite smile. "Yes, I am. Hello."

"Griffin said I've been a little loud." He runs his hand around the back of his neck as he bites his lip with a smile. "Sorry about that. You'll be pleased to know I'm heading home soon."

"Heading home?" I wrinkle my brow in confusion, aware that Griffin's eyes haven't moved from my face. He's still standing over me, his breath fanning over my cheek as his chest rises and falls with each deep inhale.

"Yeah, back to LA. Just been in town a couple of weeks catching up with this ugly fucker." He tips his head toward Griffin's back and laughs.

My eyes widen as the penny drops.

"You're Reed Walker? Running for Mayor of LA? I saw your campaign ads before I moved."

"The one and only." He straightens his shoulders as he grins at me. "Why don't you drop by after work later and we can talk about all things LA?"

"Piss off, Reed," Griffin says without turning.

Reed laughs and throws a hand up in the air, waving goodbye to me. The hallway light catches the class ring on his finger.

The same one Griffin has.

"Good luck working with this grumpy son of a bitch, Maria. You must have the patience of a saint."

"I said *goodbye*, Reed." Griffin slams one palm against the wall above my head, his eyes staying glued to me.

"Actually, you said, piss off."

Griffin snaps his head around and glares at Reed, who chuckles as he heads back into the apartment.

"Nice to meet you," he calls to me before the door closes.

The hallway falls silent.

I allow my eyes to trace up and along Griffin's freshly shaven jawline before he turns back and pins me in place with an icy gaze.

"Reed is the one staying next door?" I swallow.

He smiles, but there's no warmth to it. "Yes. It's Reed."

"Oh... I thought..." I stand rooted to the spot, waiting for him to say something else.

"I'm well aware of what you thought," Griffin's deep voice rumbles, and the vibration hits me straight in my core.

His dark brows pinch closer together as he studies my face with an unapologetic entitlement, like he has every damn right to look inside my soul should he wish.

To claim it as his.

I don't know what it is about him. I would usually hate someone with such arrogance looking at me like they could own me if they should so choose. But it sends a shiver of unexpected pleasure down my spine as I stare back into his piercing crystal gaze.

"Maria. Let me be clear on something," he growls, his eyes boring into mine. "If I were dating a woman, there would be no room in my thoughts for anyone else."

He leans forward, the fabric of his blazer grazing the front of my dress. Tingles spread from my fingertips all the way up my arms and across my chest as he brings his lips to my ear. Warm breath dances against my skin. I'm surrounded my him—his scent, his heat, his energy. I drag in a breath as his voice turns low and gravelly.

"If I were dating someone, Maria, she would be everything to me. All. *Mine*."

My heart races in my chest as he draws back, looking at me with his clear blue eyes one last time.

Then he turns and strides off, leaving me washed in a wave of intoxicating air after a storm.

Chapter Seven

Griffin

I STRIDE DOWN THE hallway and punch open the staircase door, not wanting to wait *with her* for the elevator. What does she think she's playing at? Suggesting I would be in a relationship with Emily and then do whatever God-forsaken kinky shit she's heard Reed getting up to next door? She must think so little of me from her short time here, if that's the kind of man she's decided I am.

I fly down the stairs, across the lobby and out into the street. There's a direct route into the hotel from the private residence's wing, but I need the air to calm down. I put my hands onto my hips and suck in a deep breath through my nose as I force my feet to slow down and walk around the building to the main hotel entrance on the other side.

"Good morning, Mr. Parker."

I pause on the sidewalk as I nod back a greeting.

"Morning, Earl. How are you today?"

I've known Earl since I was a boy, when my dad ran the hotel. He still insists on calling me Mr. Parker, even though it sounds wrong coming from him. He used to pick me up when I skinned my knees from running around the hotel too fast, and make me and my brothers hot chocolate in the restaurant kitchen when we were waiting for Dad to finish late night meetings.

He smiles as he runs a hand over his stubble.

"Oh, grand, grand. Can't complain. I meet the most interesting people doing this job, as you well know. I remember the day your dad brought you boys here when they were filming that movie. We had Tom Cruise abseiling down the east wing wall. Drew quite a crowd. He does all his own stunts, you know?"

Earl's kind, weathered face beams in delight, and my earlier frustration ebbs away.

"I remember. That was a great day." I smile as I recall how excited we were to be coming to watch the filming.

"Rumor has it we may have some more action unveiling on this very carpet?"

I chuckle at his raised brows and glowing cheeks.

"Well, the rumors may just be true."

"I knew it!" He clicks his fingers as his eyes twinkle. "Make sure you put in a good word for me, won't you? If they need any extras."

"I'll remember to tell the producers." I pat him on the back.

Exciting news travels fast. I'm due to announce to the staff this morning that the LA FBI TV show, *Steel Force*, is coming to film some scenes at the hotel soon. The main actor, Jay Anderson, is well known, and has an army of devoted fans. All the spare rooms at the hotel booked up the second there was a sniff of the show coming here. No one at the hotel except me knows the exact dates they're coming to film. Yet, people have still booked up in case they get a chance to see Jay. Little do they know he's having his own floor with a private elevator and back entrance—anything to maintain our high-profile guests' privacy when they stay with us.

A flash of white draws my attention to the side, as something wet lands on my shoulder, splashing the side of my face.

"Argh, what the..." I swipe my hand over my cheek and study the shoulder of my blazer. "Fucking pigeons!" I curse, lifting my gaze up to where a speckled white and gray one eyes me beadily from its new perch on a windowsill.

"We're getting on top of it, Mr. Parker," Earl says.

"With an exterminator, I hope." I grit my teeth as the bird brain coos at me from a safe distance. "Rat with wings," I mutter.

It tilts its head side to side, then turns and lifts its tail, dropping another shit from its feathered ass onto the carpet as I jump to the side.

"You know, it's supposed to be lucky?" a voice says.

I turn and am pulled into Maria's hazel gaze. She gives me a small smile, seeming unfazed by our interaction outside her apartment a mere ten minutes ago.

"Not for the bird when I remove its head and use it as a ping-pong ball," I reply as she passes me and heads inside the hotel, her long dark hair tumbling down her back in loose waves.

"She's right, you know." Earl comes to stand next to me. "Maybe you're about to get some good news."

I look at him and shake my head. "Don't you start, too."

His chuckle echoes behind me as I stomp off into the hotel, complete with pigeon shit on my face.

And it's not even eight am.

"We've got something. It's not much, but we're working on it."

I purse my lips as I stand at the window, my hand gripping the phone until my knuckles turn white.

"Good. Do whatever it takes. And do it fast. I need to know."

"Yes, Mr. Parker."

I hang up and throw the phone down on my desk. It clatters against the glass as I drag my hands back through my hair. It's been months and nothing. *Nothing.*

What the fuck am I paying them for?

There's a knock at the door.

"Come in!"

Fuck's sake.

I clench and unclench one fist as I try to push the phone conversation to the back of my mind—for now. The last thing the hotel needs is for me to lose my head.

"Mr. Parker?"

"It's Griffin!"

Maria pauses at the door, her head jerking back as though my words hit her like a slap to the face, before she pulls her shoulders back and walks into my office, closing the door behind her.

Regret swirls in my stomach. "I'm sorry, I—"

"Bad start to the day?" She looks at me. "I understand. Here." She holds out a cloth and a small bottle.

"What's that?" My eyes drop over her delicate hands.

"According to Will, it's the one thing that can save your suit."

Her hands stay outstretched as I stare at them. It's the first time I've noticed her wear pink nail polish. Usually it's red, or a cream color that blends in with her skin. I've always wondered why women wear that. It makes their hands look like an '80s mannequin. The pink suits her. It's softer. *She* seems softer today. I look up at her face. The frown she often wears in my presence is missing.

She tuts and rolls her eyes when I don't move, brushing past me and walking around my desk to my chair.

"What are you doing?"

I watch as she tips the bottle and decants some contents onto the cloth and then blots the shoulder of my blazer, which I slung on the back of my chair after brushing off as much bird crap as I could.

"I'm apologizing." She narrows her eyes as she concentrates on the stain, which is growing fainter with each blot.

"Apologizing?"

She flicks her eyes to mine, then back to my blazer as a trace of pink moves over her cheeks. "For saying you were like a zoo of horny baboons."

"Right." I cross my arms over my chest. "Anything else?"

She finishes cleaning my blazer and straightens up. Her gaze drops to my forearms where I have rolled my shirt sleeves up, and her lips purse as she snaps her eyes up to meet mine.

"I don't know what you mean."

Heat spreads through my veins in response to the fluttering pulse in her neck. Such delicate skin covering something so full of fire and passion.

"You're not sorry for implying I'm a liar and a cheat?"

One side of her mouth lifts into the trace of a smile, her eyes trained on mine.

"That's worse than being called a baboon?"

"To me, it is."

She nods as the other side of her mouth joins the first, crafting a beautiful smile onto her face.

"Then, yes. I'm sorry about that, too. In fact, I'm most sorry for that."

"Reed, on the other hand." I blow out a breath. "Feel free to call him a baboon as much as you like."

Her eyes sparkle, and she tips her head back to laugh. The sound makes my chest light.

It sounds fucking awesome.

"I'll remember I have your blessing for that next time I see him. Or *hear* him." Her laugh dies down as the two of us stand and look at each other.

I allow my attention to indulgently rake over her hair, which is tumbling down around her shoulders.

"You look—"

The intercom on my desk buzzes, cutting me off.

"Yes?" I hit the button, connecting Harley on speakerphone.

"Is Maria still in there with you?"

I raise my eyes and hold Maria's gaze as I answer. "Yes, she is. Do you need her?"

"I've got Todd Wright on the line. He wants to know if she got his message about sharing a cab to JFK. He's booking it now."

I grind my teeth together as Maria raises her brows and nods agreeably.

Silence.

"Mr. Parker?"

Maria stares at me, her pupils dilating as that fluttering pulse in her neck tries to steal my attention again.

"Tell him yes, Griff—"

Tension seeps through my jaw, radiating down my neck and to my finger, which is poised over the intercom button.

"No, Harley. You can decline his offer. She has her own car booked."

"Okay, I'll tell him."

Maria frowns at me as I cancel the intercom with a hard jolt.

"I could have shared a cab with him. It would make sense."

My hands go to my hips. "No."

"You said I had my own car booked. I don't."

"You do now."

"Says you?" Her brows shoot up her forehead as she shakes her head at me.

"Yes. Says me." I stare back at her, refusing to be the first to look away.

The corners of her eyes pinch as she huffs and looks to the ceiling. "You know, last time I checked, I was a grown woman."

I can't help my gaze dropping to the exposed skin and hint of pink lace camisole visible by the top button of her shirt.

I bet her breasts are fucking incredible. Full and fuckable, with tight nipples that would roll over the contours of my tongue as I suck on them.

"Last time I checked; you were too," I answer, bringing my eyes up to meet hers.

Her bottom lip drops open, pink tinging her cheeks, but she recovers quickly, pulling her mouth into a straight line.

"You don't need to answer for me."

The heat of her anger fills the space between us. Reaching out, toying with me. Asking me to dance with the devil.

"Todd doesn't want to take no for an answer."

"It's just a cab to the airport!" Her voice rises as she glares at me.

I thrust my hands into my pockets so she can't see them clenching into fists. She is all fired up, passion burning in her eyes with enough heat to power hell.

"It's never *just* anything," I hiss.

"He's a business contact, Griffin. Don't insult me by implying there is anything more to this trip than understanding the pricing discrepancies. The ones that *I* discovered." She taps her chest with a pink nail.

"And you did an incredible job finding them." I walk around my desk so I'm standing next to her. "I know what men want, Maria. They can't be friends with a beautiful, single woman. He'll want more from you."

"What if he does? I can handle it. *Alone.*" She takes a step closer to me, her voice dropping as she narrows her eyes at me. "You know, I'm thinking of putting a donations box in the spa lobby."

I narrow mine back at her. God, she's pushing it. Why can't she just do as she's goddamn told without all the dramatics?

"What for? Please, enlighten me," I clip out each word.

She leans closer, close enough that I could see down that pink lace camisole if I were to lower my gaze.

I press my lips into a firm line as the heady floral scent of her perfume invades my senses.

I swallow, meeting her gaze as she pants in front of me, her perfect tits shaking with the effort of holding back her full anger.

"For the 'Pigeon Appreciation Awards' I'm running," she snaps.

Then she spins on her heels and stalks off, leaving my office door wide open.

"You do that!" I shout after her.

I stare at the open doorway, surprised there isn't a trail of smoke behind her.

Pigeon Appreciation Awards?

Fucking hell.

I shake my head with an unimpressed grunt.

Well, she's not getting a cab with Todd, at least.

I pick up my jacket, inspecting the now-perfect material on the shoulder, all trace of bird shit gone.

Lucky, my ass. This day just keeps getting better and better.

Chapter Eight

Maria

"THEN I TOLD HIM I was starting a collection for pigeon awards."

"You did not!" Harley slams a hand over her mouth and falls back onto my bed in a fit of giggles.

"Did too." I smirk as I pull a shirt from underneath her before it gets wrinkled.

"I wish I could've seen his face."

"He looked like he'd just swallowed a fart."

"Maria!" Harley shrieks and kicks her legs in the air as she laughs. "I've never heard you use such profanities before."

I fold the shirt and place it in my suitcase. "He brings it out of me. I find him so..." I screw up my face and let out a tiny scream.

"Demanding?"

"Yes!"

"Irritating?"

"Yes!"

"Sexy?"

"Ye—No! God, Harley!" I turn to her. She's rolled to lie on her front and is looking at me with a grin on her face.

"It's okay, you can admit it. I notice these things."

I stare at her. "At what point in our conversation did you get the insane idea that I think he's sexy?" I grab a skirt and throw it into my case.

"Oh, I didn't get it from anything you *said.* It's what you didn't say. That, and the way your cheeks flush when you say his name."

"They do not."

I run my fingertips over my cheeks. They are hot, but that's because I'm running around my apartment trying to pack for this trip to The Bahamas. Packing always makes me stressed.

Too many memories.

"And those." Harley tilts her head to my chest.

I pull my cardigan around me, covering the peaks of my nipples, which are trying to fight their way out of my thin tank top.

"It's cold in here," I mutter.

"They only did it when you started talking about him." She arches a brow at me and then smiles. "Fine. Live in denial. Just remember, I want front row seats at your wedding."

I drop the swimsuit I'm about to pack, muttering as I bend to scoop it up.

Harley grins at me.

"I'm kidding! Sort of, a little bit, okay, not at all." She sighs. "He's a billionaire, Maria. You've seen how he runs the hotel. You would have an amazing wedding. I'm not missing it."

She hops off the bed and heads over to my wardrobe, rummaging around and then coming back armed with the tiniest bikini I own. It's a red one that ties up. Completely inappropriate for a work trip. I didn't even know I still had it. It's from a girls' holiday I took years ago. I doubt it even still fits.

Harley stuffs it into my case and winks at me.

"Ooh, talking about the hotel. Don't forget Emily's fundraising gala is the week after you get back."

"How could I forget?" I roll my eyes. It's all the team at the spa have spoken about since I started working there. Apparently, the galas that Emily hosts in The Songbird, with Griffin's approval, are legendary.

"I've already sorted it with Will. He's going to fix us up with outfits from the hotel boutiques."

"Should I ask whether that's allowed?" I smirk at Harley.

She places her finger to her lips.

"Ssh, we do it every time. We scratch their backs, they scratch ours. It's all good."

"If you say so." I laugh as I close the lid of my suitcase and zip it up.

Todd: I'm so sorry, Maria. I'll be on the phone as much as you need me for the meeting. Let me make it up to you with dinner when you get back.

I shake my head as I read the other new messages I received while on the flight. Todd called before I left my apartment to say he was no longer coming—some family emergency he needed to help with. I'm not angry. These things happen. Instead, I made the most of the early morning champagne on offer in the car Griffin sent. As much as him acting like a controlling ass rubs me up the wrong way, the car was a welcome sight following my five o'clock alarm.

I lean my head against the cool leather of the car sent to collect me from San Andros airport—also courtesy of Griffin. The sun in the azure blue sky shines brightly through the window, its heat warming my skin through the glass. There are much worse places I've been in the name of business. I'm heading to a meeting with the grower this afternoon, and because my flight back isn't until tomorrow morning, I'll get the evening to enjoy to myself.

The car pulls up to the hotel and I gasp internally, excitement bubbling in my chest as the driver comes to open the door for me.

Hotel Atlantica is beautiful.

A large, colonial style building makes up the main reception, with smaller, low-level wings of guest rooms winding off into lush tropical gardens. I almost wish Griffin were here so I could see his reaction. It's completely different to the old-style grandeur of The Songbird, but beautiful all the same.

"Ms. Taylor?"

"Yes... oh, I'm sorry," I apologize to the driver, who has already unloaded my case.

"Please, don't apologize. This is where I bid you farewell, and a safe stay." He nods at me with a friendly smile.

"Thank you so much."

He gets in the car and drives off. I take hold of my suitcase and walk into the open foyer, across the shiny marble floor, its pink and cream hues like the inside of a beautiful shell.

It really is stunning.

"Madam, allow me, please." A staff member in a smart, deep green suit arrives and takes my suitcase from me. I thank him as he places it on a brass trolley next to a deep tan leather holdall. "Please, check in, and I will take this to your room for you."

"Okay. Thank you." I head over to the large reception desk, where a young woman is smiling at me.

"Welcome to Atlantica. I'm Lori. Are you checking in?"

"Yes. Thank you so much."

I smile back as I rest my hands on the cool marble desk. A tropical breeze flows through the open-plan lobby and my shoulders relax. New York feels a million miles away.

"I have a booking under Taylor," I say to Lori.

"Ah, yes." Her smile grows. "I'll take you to your room."

She hasn't even typed anything into her computer. I'm impressed if she can remember where each newly arriving guest for the day is staying without needing to consult a booking system. I wonder if we can adopt a similar welcome at The Songbird. It would enhance the guest experience and feeling of being a valued customer.

I follow her along an outdoor marble path that snakes through beautiful, fragrant yellow and white frangipani bushes. My eyes flutter closed with their scent—pure, bright, and ethereal. It pulls me back to one of the first ever aromatherapy blends I made for myself when I was a teenager.

"Here you are," Lori says, stopping in front of a door and inserting a key card to open it.

"I think there must have been a mistake." I look from side to side at the row of individual thatched huts we've stopped in front of. The trolley of luggage has arrived, and the young man takes the tan leather holdall off first and walks to the hut next door.

"No mistake." Lori smiles, bringing my attention back to her.

I glance up at her and then side to side again. I owe Harley a night of cocktails after this. She's booked me a private hut... this is incredible.

Lori motions with her hand for me to enter first. She gives me a tour of the room, and I run my hand over the voile drapes of the giant four-poster bed as she explains about the 24-hour room service and concierge service.

"The pool is shared with the eight villas in this row."

"I'm sorry?" I stare at her with wide eyes. "Pool?"

She walks over to the back wall and presses a button on the wall. The large white curtain slides back effortlessly to reveal a small private deck with lounger, and the clearest water stretching from side to side, like a meandering river running between all eight huts. Beyond it, pale sand, and the shimmering turquoise of the ocean.

"It's beautiful. Thank you."

My stomach flutters. I'm so thankful I packed a bathing suit. A swim in there tonight, under the stars will be incredible. That's one thing I'm missing since leaving California—the water. And the way the air by the coast is so clear... so calming.

As soon as Lori leaves and my case is delivered, I step out of my heels and pad barefoot out onto the deck, dropping to sit on the ground with my feet dipping into the warm water. I tilt my face up to the morning sun and take a deep breath, tranquility seeping into my pores with each lick of the sun's ray on my skin.

"This is like a dream." I sigh, leaning back on my hands and closing my eyes.

"Breath-taking, isn't it?"

What the...?

My hand flies to my chest where my heart has just leaped into my throat, and I gasp, snapping my eyes open.

I lean forward around the dividing bamboo screen, peering to the deck of the next-door hut. I don't have to look to confirm it, though.

I would know that voice anywhere.

"Quickly turning into a nightmare!" I huff as I stare into crystal-blue eyes. They're even bluer here, inviting like cool pools of water on a sweltering day. Maybe it's a trick of the light, and it's the ocean reflecting off them or something.

"How was your flight?" Griffin asks from his position on the next-door deck before he looks away, making the mesmerizing blue pools disappear from my sight.

I can't answer him. I stare out at the ocean and force myself to take deep breaths, trying to pull my body temperature down to an acceptable level now that my blood has been set boiling.

How does he do it?

Manage to be the most irritating, pig-headed, self-assured, egotistical bastard I've ever met? All without a hair out of place. It comes so naturally to him. It *is* him.

I was even starting to think he wasn't that bad. The way he lightened up when he made the joke about me calling Reed a baboon in his office. Sending the luxury car to take me to the airport this morning. Insisting I don't pay for company lunches myself. I was beginning to see a likeable, charming side of Griffin Parker, which everyone else seems to benefit from, except for me.

But it was merely a fleeting figment of an idealistic imagination.

I study him from the corner of my eye. He's standing, looking out toward the ocean, hands resting on his hips. He's still in a full, light gray suit. He must be baking. It's still early, but the humidity is unmistakable in the surrounding air.

"What are you doing here?" I stop paddling my feet in the pool and stand up, walking to the edge of my deck closest to his.

"I heard Todd couldn't make it." His eyes stay trained on the ocean, his dark hair shining in the sunlight.

"Family emergency," I reply.

"That's unfortunate." His lips stay pressed into a firm line.

"You didn't answer my question. What are *you* doing here?" I fight to keep my voice even as my body tenses. I'll be damned if I give the smug asshole the satisfaction of knowing he's affecting me.

This is another power play. One further example of what a control freak he is.

At first, I wondered if it was me. If I gave him any reason to doubt my ability to do the job. Gave him cause for concern, somehow. But now I know it's just Griffin. *Griffin control-freak Parker.* Because heaven forbid anyone can do something as well as him.

He turns to me, his eyes landing straight on mine. Butterflies set loose in my stomach, swirling and dancing with sudden vigor. God, it must be the plane food, or the champagne from this morning disagreeing with me.

"I have some personal business to attend to here. It made sense to move my trip to today so I can accompany you to the meeting—make sure you don't miss Todd." He juts his chin forward as he says 'Todd,' his eyes darkening as he watches me, as if waiting for a reaction.

I swallow down the butterflies which are now attempting to shoot up into my throat.

"Well, you're certainly not him. But we'll manage."

A muscle in his jaw ticks as he looks at me, pinning me to the spot with his blue gaze.

"Why don't you order some breakfast, Maria? I have calls to make. We leave in two hours." He turns, effectively dismissing me.

"Fine," I snap at his back.

He goes inside his room, then I head inside mine.

I stomp over to the bed, flopping down and grabbing a cushion.

Then I scream into it.

Chapter Nine

Griffin

Two hours later, Maria yanks the door to her room open, and I'm met with a fiery gaze.

"Ready to go?"

"Absolutely." She gives me a tight smile, which might as well be a 'fuck you', for all the warmth it lacks.

I stall at the door as my eyes rake over her.

"You look... very nice." I admire her blouse and suit shorts, which she's wearing with heels that make her legs look like a long list of reasons as to why I should have stayed in New York.

"Thank you." The corners of her eyes twitch, and she purses her lips, taking in my tie-free, open-neck shirt and rolled-up sleeves. "I should say the same. I'm not used to seeing you out of your full suit."

"Not many people do."

I rub my hand across my jaw, taking in her serious expression. I don't know how we have gotten off to such an awkward start in our working relationship. I swear she dislikes me more each time she sees me. It's like I offend her by existing.

"The suit fits in New York. But here... turning up to a business meeting on a plantation, in full suit and tie, when it's almost one hundred degrees? I'd look like a pompous jerk. Don't you think?"

Maria smirks and raises an eyebrow. "You said it."

My lips twitch as her face softens, and she takes another look over me, her eyes lingering on my forearms.

"Shall we?"

"Hmm?" She rolls her lips, her head tilted to one side as her attention stays glued to my arms.

"Get going?" I ask, canting my wrist and pretending to look at my watch.

Her eyes follow and then snap away.

"Yes! Of course." She steps out of her door and pulls it shut. "Let's go."

We collect the car I've organized from the hotel valet and drive most of the journey in silence. The local radio station plays island tunes, and Maria sits in the passenger seat, gazing out of the window. Each time I cast my eyes her way, she's wearing a serene expression—a small smile on her lips as she stares off over the water.

"You seem relaxed?"

She looks at me for a brief second before she turns back to the window and sighs.

"I am. It's the coast... the water. I used to be able to see it from my house in California."

"Nothing can match being by the water. New York's concrete jungle isn't quite the same. I get it." I smile as I keep my eyes on the road.

"Do you?"

I glance at her apprehensive expression. "I do. Believe me, Maria. I do."

She's still studying me as I turn off the main road and into the small driveway. I've been to this grower's house once before, when I set up the initial contract with Todd's company. It's been a few years, but the place looks the same. A few goats are running about freely in the driveway, and coconut palms stretch as far as the eye can see behind the modest house.

"There's Ken."

Maria waves at a man approaching the car and climbs out. Ken has already got her hand between both of his and is shaking enthusiastically by the time I walk around to them.

"It's wonderful to see you, Maria. You look even more beautiful than you were all those years ago when we met." Maria laughs in response, and he grins. "Trust me. You get to my age; you never forget a beautiful soul."

He looks over, as if just noticing me.

"Mr. Parker." He grabs my hand and gives it the same attention as Maria's, his cloudy eyes crinkling at the corners as he smiles at me. "Maria called to say Todd wasn't coming. I didn't expect you to accompany her instead. This is a truly wonderful surprise," he says with complete sincerity. "Come, come. I will show you the palms you asked about in our emails, and then we can have some tea."

We follow him up the path and around the back of the house. He walks with a limp, which he didn't have when I first met him. Maria looks at it and then raises her eyes to meet mine. I shake my head at her. She may feel bad that we are here to ask uncomfortable questions and potentially sever our contract. But this is business. Not a place for personal feelings.

"Here." Ken turns with his arms out wide, a proud grin plastered over his face. "The beautiful coconut palms." He laughs and leans over to kiss a trunk, patting it beneath his hand. "Come closer. Look, look." He takes Maria's fingers and places them against the tree. "You feel that? Pure island magic."

"They're magnificent. Aren't they, Griffin?" She turns to me, her cheeks glowing.

I stare at rows upon rows of coconut palms. I expected to see the remnants of a fire, or the aftermath of a pest infestation. Some explanation why Ken has been ripping us off to the tune of two point three times the price for his coconut sugar. But this?

They're fucking thriving.

I see red as I glare at him.

"Is this a joke? We come all the way out here and discover your plantation is perfectly healthy?" I jab a finger at the offending trees.

"I... I... don't know what you mean?" Ken looks at Maria and then back at me.

"I wasn't born yesterday. You're taking me for an idiot. My hotel is paying Todd's company through the nose for something you're practically drowning in here. Tell me, is he in on it, too? Are you cutting him in?" I wipe some sweat off my brow and ignore Maria's widened eyes as she stares at me. "Is that what this is? Screw The Songbird and the guy who owns it? God..."

I shake my head, raging internally at myself. How could I have been so stupid to have missed this? It's so obvious now. Maria spotted the price discrepancy on day one, for fuck's sake. How did Todd not pick it up? Or Gwen when she was spa manager? How did *I* not pick it up?

"No, Mr. Parker. I'm sorry. It's not like that. I'm an honest man. I've a family." Ken's eyes bulge in his head as I wave a hand at him.

I've heard enough.

"Forget our contract. We'll find another grower." I spin on my heels back in the direction of the car.

"No! Please. Mr. Parker, I'm a good man. I promise you," Ken sputters.

I mutter under my breath. I'm not in the mood for his excuses or sob story. No one crosses me and gets away with it. He can kiss any future deals with The Songbird away.

I will not be anyone's fool.

"Just a minute, Ken," Maria says in a calm voice.

She catches up with me and grabs my arm.

"What are you doing?"

Irritation swirls in my gut and pricks at my skin like a thousand tiny needles as I spit, "We're leaving. Get in the car."

"No!" She glares at me, her fingers still curled around my forearm.

Why can't she ever do as she's told?

My voice comes out deep and throaty as I fix my eyes on hers, staring deeply into them as I suck a breath in through my nose.

"Get in the car, Maria. I'm not asking."

"I. Will. Not."

Liquid fire bubbles in my chest as she holds my gaze, her eyes burning into mine.

"Get. In. The. Car."

She yanks her hand away from my arm and screws her nose up, lowering her voice. "You want to leave? Then go. I came here to find out why we're being overcharged. And I'm not leaving until I understand the real reason."

I tip my chin over her shoulder toward Ken, who is standing watching us from the trees, wringing his hands in front of his stomach.

"There's your reason. Someone who saw a chance to rip me off and took it," I hiss through gritted teeth.

"Are you even going to ask him?" Maria raises her brows. "Or are you going to be the judge, jury and executioner all in one?"

"What can he possibly say to explain the fact he has a complete load of fucking trees with coconuts on, yet he's charging us as though they're harder to find than the holy fucking grail? Damn it."

Rage tears through me without mercy, and I kick a stone off the path with force. Maria looks at me like I'm a toddler having a tantrum.

"Well, I'm going to ask Ken about it." She turns to walk back. "Are you going to at least let him have his say?" she says over her shoulder to me.

I don't reply.

She rolls her eyes and clicks her tongue in a tut. "Suit yourself."

Oh, for God's sake.

"Fine! I'll listen to whatever bullshit he's no doubt rehearsed," I mutter as I fall into step beside her, and we walk back over to Ken. "And then we leave."

Ken darts his eyes between the two of us as we reach him.

"Mr. Parker, Maria. I'm so sorry. I've not meant to deceive you. I only do what is best for them." He extends a hand toward the treetops.

"For who?" Maria asks gently.

I side eye her. This is the woman who built an award-winning spa in California single-handedly, from nothing. Now I'm asking myself how she managed if this is the approach she has. It's not kindergarten. She may as well be patting Ken on the back and saying 'there-there' and offering to put a band-aid on his boo-boo.

Fuck me, maybe hiring her was a mistake.

Ken's face breaks into a grin and his eyes shine as he points up. I follow his and Maria's gaze, shielding my eyes from the sun.

"The birds," he whispers.

A flash of black and yellow rustles the leaves at the top of the tree and a bird appears, whistling a tune.

"They're special." Ken beams. "So very special."

I snort. This is fucking great. Not only is he ripping me off, he's also stark-raving mad. Probably thinks the feathered little shits talk to him.

"He's cheerful," Maria says, watching the bird. "But Ken, the reason we came all this way was to talk about the prices you're charging. The coconut sugar has more than doubled... Why?"

My adrenaline from earlier subsides as my interest in Maria's approach grows. Within a matter of minutes, she has made Ken's expression morph from looking like his worst nightmare is coming true, to pure delight.

"It's the birds," Ken says again as another yellow and black one flies over to join the first. "They are Bahama Oriole."

"They're what?" I cut in as I stare up at the pair of them.

"They are very special. Critically endangered. I can't disturb them." Ken smiles up fondly at them like a proud father.

"What about the other trees? You've so many?" Maria asks.

"Ah! But there are more of them." Ken turns and points from tree to tree. "I see some here, and over the far side of the plantation. They're breeding! There are only a few places I can get the coconuts for your sugar from without disturbing them."

"That's why you put up the price?" Maria asks.

Ken nods in confirmation.

I shake my head and blow out a long breath as Maria looks at me.

I would have preferred Ken to be a raving lunatic over this.

Fucking birds.

"You have to be kidding me. It's like the pigeons in New York. This is just..." I drag my hands through my hair and let out a deep, frustrated groan before jabbing a hand at the treetop, my jaw tightening. "Just move them. They can find somewhere else to go."

"Mr. Parker." Ken's mouth drops open. "I can't disturb them. They are endangered! It's a miracle that they chose my home." He looks back at the tree in awe.

Jesus Christ.

Maria catches my eye and I swear she finds this funny, judging from the way her eyes are glittering, and she's twisting her lips together, as if holding back a smile.

"You think it' s acceptable to charge over double because you can't disturb a bunch of birds?" I tip my head back to the sky with a humorless laugh, my hands going to my hips.

"I'm sorry. I must protect them. The Bahamas, we need them." Ken looks at me like one of those charity adverts—with big, pleading eyes—the ones I switch channels to avoid.

"And you expect me and my company to pay the price?" I stare at him.

His face falls as he meets my eye. "You don't understand. My wife... she loves them. I want to keep her happy. When you meet a good woman, you would do anything for her heart to remain sweet for you."

I roll my eyes. "I think we're done here. Maria?"

I look at her, but she's not paying any attention. Instead, she's wandered over to a basket on the floor and is holding up a yellowy-orange thing that resembles an oversized ugly lemon.

"Ah, my cacao pods." Ken walks over to her. "I had a great year with it. It grows big and strong."

"Really?" Maria furrows her brow as she peers in the basket at the pile of similar pods. She turns to look at me. "I need more cocoa butter for some formula ideas I have."

I walk over and stand next to her, frowning at the unfortunate looking fruit.

"You need these?"

Her eyes are buzzing with energy as she nods at me, and I can just tell she's imagining her new creations in her head right this second. She has this brightness about her, this glow that she had the first time I met her in California. The passion flowed from her then. And captivated me.

Just as it is doing now.

God help me.

I was an idiot for thinking we could work together, and it would go away if I simply ignored it.

"Maybe we can work something out?" She smiles at me, sending blood pounding in my ears.

I breathe in. Once. Twice. Holding her gaze as she stares into my eyes, her dark eyelashes framing each blink against the tropical sun.

"Ken?" I turn to him. "Let's have that tea you mentioned and talk."

"This is incredible. I can't believe you got such a good price!" Maria flashes me a bright smile as she holds up the cacao pod.

I pause as we approach the door to her hut.

"It's the least he could offer us, after we've been paying all that extra for months," I mutter, biting back a smile as she smirks at me.

"Oh, come on. It was the way you negotiated with him. You won him over in the end."

"In the end?" I raise a brow, and she laughs.

"After the steam stopped coming out of your ears." Her laugh dies down and she looks up at me, her brow furrowing as she takes in a slow breath. "Harley told me about the signature spa formulations going missing. I understand why you felt angry. It makes sense that you hate the idea of someone abusing your trust."

She gives me a gentle smile, her pink lips plump and inviting.

"Someone stole them and leaked them to a competitor, Maria."

Her eyes widen as her fingers reach up to her parted lips. "You think it was on purpose?"

"I don't think. I know."

My jaw stiffens as I recall the day I found out someone had done it. Larry Vincent couldn't help calling from his office at The Manton to gloat about being offered them in exchange for a fee. He took delight in telling me how one of my staff was likely responsible, and that I ought to tighten up my ship. Our hotels have been rivals since our grandfathers ran them. Both men moved in similar social circles, where they met my grandmother. She was smitten with my grandfather from the get-go. Larry's grandfather took a while to accept that fact.

"Griffin. That's awful. I'm so sorry." Maria reaches out and lays her hand on my arm.

"It was one of my staff," I say through gritted teeth. "That's what cuts deepest. It was someone I placed my trust in."

I shake my head as I look into her eyes. To this day, I still don't know who is responsible if it wasn't Gwen. I swear whoever it is will regret it for every second of their worthless lives when I find out.

She holds my gaze, her hand still on my arm. "I get it."

Something about her voice makes my eyes narrow so I can study her. Faint lines crease the corners of her eyes, pain flashing through them momentarily.

"Sounds like a story there?"

She drops her eyes to the pod in her hands and re-moves her hand from my arm, stroking the pod as a sad smile settles on her face. Apart from her spa in LA, I barely know a thing about her—about her history before that, where she came from, what drove her into starting her own business.

Now the realization is hitting me.

It's *all* I want to know about.

She tucks a long dark strand of hair behind her ear. "Yes." She winces, exposing a vulnerability to her I've never noticed before. She's always in control, always professional, always...

"Maria?"

She lifts her gaze to meet mine and I'm caught in her stunning hazel eyes.

"Have dinner with me?" I say before thinking, knowing I'm probably her last choice for a dinner companion. "I've stayed here before, and the food is outstanding—"

"Yes," she breathes, looking at me, two lines forming suddenly between hers as though she regrets her answer already.

"Okay." I nod, clearing my throat.

"I'll meet you at the pool bar in an hour." She hands me the cacao pod and disappears inside her room.

I look down at the knobbly yellow fruit in my hand.

"See you in an hour," I murmur.

Chapter Ten

Maria

I'M HAVING DINNER WITH Griffin.

Fuck, fuck, fuck!

Why did I agree to it? Not just agree, but say 'yes' in a breathy, ridiculous voice that probably made me sound all flirty, or like some air-headed damsel in distress.

As I apply my makeup after a shower, I go through all the reasons I should have declined Griffin's offer in my head.

One, he's an irritating, control-freak who crashed my trip spectacularly because he doesn't trust me. But then, I know why he has issues with trust, and I can't say I blame him. I haven't been at The Songbird long yet. He obviously trusts people once he has known them awhile. Like Emily, for example. He trusts her to host her charity galas at the hotel and deal with it all herself. I don't think he gets involved with the planning at all, from what Harley says. So that's explainable, which just leaves irritating.

He's definitely still that.

Okay, reason two. He's my boss, and... wait, this isn't a vacation This is a business trip, so this is a business dinner. Surely *not* having dinner with him would be seen as rude. So that's not a reason, either.

Reason three... I comb my fingers through my hair. Reason three... trois... tres... the third installment... shoot, I have nothing.

I sigh at my reflection in the mirror. My eyes are bright—excited. Why the hell do I look excited about having dinner with the alpha boss-hole in the hut next door? No. It must be the new deal we agreed with Ken today. That's it. That is definitely it! I smile as I recall the way Griffin calmed down and smoothly slotted into Mr. Parker, charming businessman role as he chatted with Ken and met his wife, and we had tea on their porch. It's the same Mr. Parker I've seen glimpses of around the hotel when he's speaking to... well, anyone who isn't me.

I head over to the wardrobe in the bedroom, where I hung up some of my clothes. I've not brought a lot with me, as it's only one night. Luckily, I packed a dress in case Todd and I went to the hotel restaurant tonight. I pull it off the hanger and step into it.

Todd sent a text earlier to say everything was sorted with his family, after I asked if all was okay. He brought up taking me to dinner again when I get back, but I don't want him to think it's a date, so I suggested he come to Emily's charity gala with me as my business guest next week instead. That way it's a work function, and he won't get the wrong idea.

"This will do," I mutter as I zip the red dress up.

I twist my hair up at the back of my head and clip it into place, pulling some strands down around my face. It's far too hot right now to wear it down. I slip on a pair of high nude wedge sandals, grab my purse, and head out.

The walk to the pool bar allows me to clear my head. I always told myself I would put all my energy into work after I split up with my ex. And that's what I'm doing now. I think I'm doing a pretty great job, too, if I'm honest. The spa has received incredible feedback, and Vogue magazine wants to do a feature on us in their next issue. Everything is moving in the right direction. Just how I dreamed.

I round the corner to the pool bar. I feel him before I see him. The tiny hairs on the back of my neck stand up and my spine straightens as I dart my eyes around. A deep, intoxicating, blue stare pulls me through the small tables filled with couples having pre-dinner drinks. I weave between them as the fairy lights in the surrounding gardens twinkle off the surface of the infinity pool. My eyes never leave his as I walk over to the bar where he's sitting on a stool, looking like a runway model—light blue casual linen shirt, cream slacks, and a smile on his lips that makes my mouth dry.

He stands as I reach him and pulls out the stool next to his for me. I slide onto it as he sits down next to me, pulling his closer so our knees touch. His gaze drops over my tight, red dress subtly before he looks away, raising his chin to the bartender.

"What would you like to drink, Maria?"

I swallow down the flutters in my chest from the way he says my name. Maybe it's the first time, or maybe I've never noticed it before, but the way he says it makes it sound special. Like the most beautiful name in the world.

"Something strong."

He looks at me, the corner of his mouth twitching.

"Two of your strongest cocktails, please," he says to the bartender.

He leans his elbow on the bar, pointer finger tracing back and forth over his lips as he studies me.

"What?" I ask.

"Nothing." He shakes his head with a smile. "You just surprise me. Few people do that."

"By asking for a strong drink?" I smile back at him, relaxing into his proximity as I cross my legs and my knee brushes his thigh.

"By being you."

I pull my head back in confusion as the bartender places two cocktails down in front of us. They're bright yellow with a swirl of something dark and inky on the top.

"It's a compliment, Maria." He hands me my glass and then lifts his own to clink against it. "To new business deals."

I wait until the glass is to his lips.

"And to drinking cocktails the same colors as the birds who made it possible."

He inhales some of the liquid and then coughs, placing his glass down on the bar.

"What?" He frowns at the glass as though just realizing. "For fuck's sake," he mutters, running a hand around the back of his neck. Then he laughs and raises his eyes to mine. I laugh too, desperately trying to ignore the flush of heat that's infused itself between my thighs as I stare back into his eyes. They're open, honest. He looks back at me, and it's as though I'm seeing his soul.

This is the *real* Griffin Parker I've been aching to see.

The way he laughs so easily here—a deep, smooth sound that warms my insides, his eyes crinkling at the corners—is magical. He's like a different person to the serious control freak I'm used to.

Could it all be a front and I've had him wrong all along?

"How's your collection going?" he asks, breaking into my thoughts.

He raises a brow at me over the rim of his glass as he has another drink, this time without almost choking.

"Collection?"

"For the pigeons." He smirks.

I press my lips together to stifle my smile. "Very well, thank you for asking. I'm even thinking Emily may like to consider the cause for one of her future galas."

"Really?" Griffin leans closer to me.

"Mmm-hmm."

I concentrate on drinking my cocktail, so I don't have to meet his eyes. The fresh scent of his aftershave—or maybe it's just his skin—reaches me, and I shuffle in my seat, as the earlier intimate heat infusion intensifies in my core.

He smiles and shakes his head. "Today was impressive. We got a good deal with Ken."

"You did, you mean? You negotiated the price."

"It was both of us. You saw an opportunity and turned the situation around. We work well together."

Together.

I tilt my head and smile at him.

"Two compliments from you in five minutes. What did I do to deserve this?" I take another sip of my drink.

"You were you," Griffin states, as though that explains everything. He furrows his brow and then looks back at me, his eyes dazzling in their intensity. "Do you think I don't notice how talented you are? That I don't appreciate you?"

It's my turn to almost choke on my drink.

I place my glass down and lick my lips, Griffin's eyes following my every move.

I take a deep breath. "You turned up at the meeting with Todd and Serena on my first day. You turn up here for the meeting with Ken. You *don't* think I can do my job."

"That's not it." His gaze darkens as he looks at me, effectively drawing my eyes to his again until I can no longer look away, no matter how hard I try. "I know you're perfectly capable. I wouldn't have hired you if I didn't have complete faith in your abilities."

I remember the words he said in his office after I went to lunch with Todd.

Someone else would have made you theirs... I wasn't going to let that happen.

"Then, why?" I whisper.

"I told you. I don't trust people easily. Even when logic tells me I can." He lowers his head and shakes it, breaking the spell I'm under from his eyes, and allowing me to breathe again. "It's something I struggle with."

"The formulations that were stolen." I nod in understanding as I recall our earlier conversation about them. No wonder he's so hesitant to trust new people. When you've had someone betray you when you thought you could rely on them, it scars. It leaves a dirty black mark which doesn't wash away. I know all about those marks. I'm still wearing one.

He raises his eyes to meet mine again and the betrayal and hurt is tangible in them, like I could reach out and dust it with the gentle sweep of a fingertip.

I wish I could. Then I could brush them away, set them free on the breeze, never to affect him again.

Erase all black marks for good.

"Only a handful of people had access to them. People I *trusted.*"

"Gwen?" I ask, testing out something I've heard the spa team whispering about.

He nods. "She was one of them."

Griffin straightens and downs his drink. He obviously knows about the rumors around the hotel that his ex, Gwen, took them. It seems convenient that she left to work for a rival hotel shortly after they went missing. The theories range from her being approached with a considerable sum of cash to take them, to her being part of a larger operation, and planted in the first place, to grow close to Griffin, and use it to her advantage later to do something that would affect The Songbird. And if he was in a romantic relationship with her, the deceit would be all that more hurtful.

"Looks like our table's ready." Griffin looks over my shoulder.

I turn toward the beach. There's a scattering of tables for two set up on the sand, a path of hurricane lanterns with candles lighting the path to them.

"Wow, they look..."

"Inviting?" He catches my eye.

The word romantic freezes on my lips.

"Come on. I could eat a whole damn flock of birds."

I laugh as we stand and Griffin places his hand on the small of my back, guiding me out of the bar and over to the sand.

We spend the next hour drinking cocktails and eating the most incredible dinner of island fruits, followed by freshly caught lobster. I try to ignore the fact we are surrounded by honeymooners and romantic vacationers, dreamily gazing at one another across the white linen tabletops. I guess this is what you get when you stay in the best hotel on the island.

"Okay. I must agree. The food is outstanding, like you said." I smile at Griffin as I place my napkin down on the table, unable to eat any more.

"I *told* you." His lips curl into a smug smile as I roll my eyes at his lack of modesty.

I lean back in my chair and exhale, allowing the sounds of the waves gently brushing the shore to completely relax me. It's a beautiful evening. And having dinner with Griffin has been nowhere near as unpleasant as I would have expected prior to this trip. He's actually wonderful company out of work, more loose, more talkative. He's been telling me about how his grandfather bought The Songbird, and it has become a family business, moving down generations. They've opened other hotels now. One in San Francisco, and one in Boston, both run by his younger brothers. I bet family gatherings are interesting, judging from the stories Griffin regales me with about his brothers, an easy chuckle flowing from him with each one.

"Now you know about my family history. Tell me about yours." He leans back in his chair, mirroring my posture.

"Not much to tell." I look out over the ocean, and then back at him when his eyes don't leave my face. "Fine." I sigh, picking up my drink and taking a huge gulp. I place it back down on the table and my heads swirls, signifying just how many cocktails I've had tonight. They are delicious, though.

"I spent a lot of time with my grandmother and grand-father growing up. Mom worked a lot, and my dad..." I pause. "... Dad wasn't around much."

Griffin's listening and watching me closely, which just makes me want to say it as fast as possible so we can move back onto other topics of conversation. I hate talking about the past. What good does it do?

I turn my head so I'm not looking into his eyes.

"My dad was an addict. Poker, mainly. He would lose his wages before even making it home on pay day. Gone. Just like that." I grimace at the memory. Even as a child, I understood it wasn't normal. None of my friend's parents fought like mine did.

"Mom took on extra hours to help cover the bills. She never told my grandparents what was going on. They moved to the UK when I was a teenager to live near my uncle, who needed their help when his wife got sick." I glance at Griffin. He's still watching me closely. "Once they were gone, Dad didn't bother even trying to hide it. The whole town knew. Neighbors would drop off casseroles, offer to fetch groceries for Mom from the store, give me their kids' old school textbooks. We were *that* family. The one that everyone pitied."

Griffin clears his throat. "That sounds shit."

I give him a small smile, grateful that there's no trace of pity in his eyes. He's just watching me, his expression serious as he nods for me to continue.

"As soon as I could get a job, I did. I worked as much as I could, giving all my wages to Mom. It was at a fragrance and skincare counter in a big store. That's where my love of it began."

Griffin waits patiently as I gather myself. I haven't spoken about this in so long. I don't even know why I'm telling him.

"The day I came home and found Dad in my bedroom, all my drawers riffled through, clearing out my purse, was the day I left home. He swore he would get help, enroll in a program and everything. But it was too little, too late. He and Mom broke up. They live separately now, even though Dad's finally on a better path."

"And the spa in Hope Cove?" Griffin sits forward in his chair, leaning his elbows on the table, caught on to my every word.

"That came later. I saved up and paid to do a college course on formulations and then business management. Then I got a job as an apprentice in the best spa I could find and worked my way up to senior therapist. I heard about a small beauty room available for someone to start up by themselves in a little hotel outside of LA. I applied, got the job, and after a few years, as the hotel grew, so did the spa. It became what you saw when you visited."

Griffin's eyes glitter like two sapphires. "I knew you had built that spa up from scratch. But I didn't know just how hard you worked to get to that point. It's very impressive, Maria. You should be proud."

I look down into my glass, which is now empty.

"It almost didn't happen." I raise my eyes to Griffin's as I scrunch my nose. Somehow, what I'm about to say is worse than what my dad did. Worse, because I should have known better. Should have seen the signs. Like that saying, fool me once, shame on you. Fool me twice, shame on me.

"Why not?" He furrows his brow, and I swallow the lump in my throat, tasting the shame that's settled there with it.

Sour and clogging.

"Damien, my ex, started coming home late, saying he was busy at work with a project. I suspected he was cheating. Then I opened a letter from a debt collection agency. He'd forged my signature on a loan agreement and wasn't keeping up with the payments. My dad's weakness was poker. Damien's was a stripper called Mercedes in the next town over." I snort out a humorless laugh, expecting Griffin to do the same.

He doesn't.

Instead, my hand is cocooned in warmth, surrounded by strong fingers as he pulls it to his own and wraps it up.

I stare at it, shame heating my cheeks.

"He was a fucking fool, Maria. If he couldn't see the incredible woman who was right in front of him, then he didn't deserve you." He looks at me with an intensity that makes the breath catch in my throat. "I would kill any man who did that to..."

He lets my hand go, as a cross between a growl and a hiss escapes his lips. He turns, looking over to the ocean, and the muscle in his jaw ticks, his nostrils flaring as he draws in a breath.

I remember his words in the hallway outside my apartment that morning.

If I was in a relationship, she would be everything to me. All. Mine.

Looking at his face now, the deep furrowed brow, stormy eyes, I can tell—if you are the woman in Griffin Parker's life, you will never be treated like anything less than a goddess.

I'm still staring at him with my lips parted when he turns back to me and his blue eyes land on mine. They lose some of their anger, his brows relaxing.

"Enough about my depressing past. Tell me something interesting," I say, leaning over the table toward him, my eyes dropping to his hand, which was holding mine moments ago.

"Like what?"

"Like, whether you really had private business here to attend to, or whether it was all your control-freak nature taking over when you heard I was on my own."

His face fully relaxes as he chuckles. "Control freak?" He nods. "It's fair, I suppose. But I really was here on business. If you'd like to check my calendar..." He raises a brow at me and I smirk "... then you'll see I was originally due here in two weeks' time. I just brought it forward."

"Because Todd couldn't make it?"

"Precisely."

"You don't seem bothered that you had to change your schedule." I run my fingers up and down the stem of my glass.

Griffin smirks. "Because I'm not. It's the best damn luck I've had since that pigeon shit on me."

Chapter Eleven

Griffin

"BECAUSE I'M NOT. IT'S the best damn luck I've had since that pigeon shit on me," I say.

Maria's hazel eyes widen.

She looks down at the table, a faint blush blooming on her cheeks as she tucks a loose strand of hair behind her ear. She's tied it up tonight. It exposes her neck, and the way her pulse fluttered just below her ear when I took her hand earlier.

I force down the surge of anger, which is threatening to build again. What she told me about her father and then her ex... she's been abused by men. Taken advantage of by those who should be willing to trade their last breath for her happiness.

Assholes.

"We should go." Maria looks at the surrounding tables, which have slowly emptied.

We are one of only two couples remaining on the beach.

"Sure." I stand and move around the table to pull her chair out. She sways a little as she stands and then giggles.

"Those cocktails were strong."

"I gave you what you asked for," I say, catching her eyes drop to my lips for a second.

"You're right. You did." She smiles and lets out a contented-sounding sigh. "Now all I'm asking for is the moonlit swim I promised myself in that pool." She smiles dreamily as she looks up at the starry sky, then back at me, her mouth dropping into a little 'O' shape. "I said that out loud, didn't I?"

"You did."

I smile back at her. Her cheeks are rosy, and her eyes glassy, the cocktails' effects in full swing. Is it even safe to swim alone when you're a little drunk? What if she feels ill suddenly in the water?

I should sit on my deck so I can make sure she's safe.

My eyes drop over her red dress, hugging the curves of her hips. Then again, sitting there with an erection tenting my pants while she swims will make me look less like a concerned boss and more like a pervy creeper.

We walk back toward the huts through the fairy-lit walkways. Maria links her arm through mine, steadying herself, and I slow to match her pace.

"Griffin." She stops short, pulling us to a halt, and closes her eyes, inhaling deeply through her nose. Then she exhales, her shoulders sinking as she opens her eyes. "Do you smell them?"

She reaches over to a flower in the bush next to the path and strokes its petals.

"Frangipani. I like to think they smell like soap from heaven." She smiles at me, and an unfamiliar warmth floods my chest.

I pluck one of the delicate yellow and white flowers from the bush and place it in her hair, wondering what the hell my hands are doing. She isn't the only one whose senses have been taken over by strong island cocktails. My brothers would rip the piss out of me if they saw me now, acting like I'm the lead role in a romantic movie.

"Come on." I turn and walk again.

"Are you getting the same flight back as me tomorrow?" Maria asks as we reach her door.

"No. You're getting the same one back as me."

Two lines appear between her eyebrows. She's stunningly beautiful. But there's something about the way she looks so sweet when she's confused. Looking at me for clarification. Looking at *me*, and me only.

It has my dick fighting for attention.

"I arranged another flight. We check out at nine am."

"Oh?" The two lines disappear, then come straight back again. "I didn't think there was another morning flight."

"There is now."

"Oh? Okay." She reaches into her bag to retrieve her room key.

The smooth round peaks of her breasts are exposed by her low neckline, and I swallow the thickness in my throat.

"Are you still going swimming?"

"Yes. Are you joining me?"

She snaps her eyes up, closing her mouth quickly, as though regretting her words the second they come out.

I ignore my hammering pulse in my ears. "Of course."

Five minutes later, I'm in the private pool that runs along the back of the huts, my back resting against the side. The water is warm, and so is the air. The only sound is the ocean behind me. These huts are perfect. Set far enough away from the main hotel building that they are quiet and undisturbed. No one is on the beach this late, either.

It's just me here.

A door opening draws my eyes up and I fight to prevent my jaw from dropping as Maria steps out onto her deck next door.

"What's the water like?" She walks to the edge and sits down, her long legs trailing into the pool as she submerges one foot, then the other.

There are thin red strings around her neck, holding her bikini top up. And even thinner ones on her hips, keeping her tiny bikini bottoms from falling away.

I clear my throat. "Why don't you come in and see for yourself?"

She looks at me and then lowers herself into the pool. My brain turns everything into slow motion, my attention glued to where the water slowly rises over her lower stomach, into the dip of her belly button. Then over her ribs and up to her breasts, covering the full weight of them as she parts her lips and lets out a small sigh, which speaks directly to my throbbing dick.

She swims over and stops in front of me. The depth of the water means it stops directly below her nipples, the hardened outline of which are visible through the thin fabric of her bikini top.

Who makes swimsuits like this? That's right, probably a man.

Fuck, give me strength.

"Are you okay?" Maria tilts her head to one side as she looks at me.

I'm clenching my jaw and staring at her. What must I look like? A man who's barely holding it together?

"Yes. Fine. Perfect. *Dandy.*"

She narrows her eyes at me and then laughs. "What was in those drinks? Griffin Parker saying the word *dandy*?" Her eyes are bright. "Whatever it was, I need some to take back to New York."

I press my lips together as she moves closer.

"Why? What does it do to you when I say it? *Dandy,*" I murmur, causing a whole new fit of laughter, which makes her tits shake against the surface of the water. "*Dandy...*" I growl again, reaching out and grabbing her by the waist and pulling her to me.

Fuck, what am I doing?

She comes easily, then snakes her arms up around my neck, her eyes holding mine as her laugh dies down.

I widen my feet, pulling her between my thighs, right up against my body. My breath mingles with hers and my cock presses into her hip. But I don't care. All I care about is her—her beautiful golden eyes, pinching a little

127

in the corners as they search my own. There is hesitation in them; it practically screams from them.

I shouldn't have touched her, pulled her to me. I've crossed a line. Gone too far.

"Maria—"

She crashes her lips against mine, stealing my words before they can form as she kisses me with frenzied heat and passion, panting against my mouth. She slides her fingers into my hair and grabs fistfuls of it.

Any hesitation I imagined vanishes with her kiss, along with all my self-restraint.

"Fuck!" I groan into her mouth, before spinning us in the water so her back is against the side.

I press my entire body into hers as I run my hand from her waist up over her ribs and to the curve of her breast. She moans as my fingertips graze her nipple, and arches into my hand.

I've got her.

She wants this.

And that knowledge makes my dick throb, power coursing through my veins and beating out a relentless pulse through my hardened length.

"Fuck," I groan again in response to her gasp when my cock brushes over her.

I grab her throat with my other hand and slide my tongue inside her mouth. Tasting her, drawing out of her what I want. What I *need* from her. Her fingers loosen in my hair, and she relaxes her neck against my hand, tilting her head back so I can deepen our kiss.

Trusting me.

"Why did you pack such a sexy little swimsuit?" I growl, my lips sliding from hers, along her jawline and toward her ear. "Were you planning on *fucking* Todd while you were here?"

"What?" Her breasts rise and fall, squashed against my chest as her breath shudders in her chest.

"You heard me," I say into her ear before I run the tip of my nose down the side of her neck and pause at her shoulder.

"Of course not!"

"You haven't thought about him fucking you?"

I open my mouth and lick slowly with the flat of my tongue up the side of her neck and back to her ear. The idea that she packed this tiny scrap of material to wear in front of him has adrenaline crashing through my chest like a tsunami.

"No," she replies.

But her voice is tiny, barely a whisper.

"Don't lie to me, Maria." I flex my hand against her throat and twist her chin so her eyes meet mine.

"I'm not!" She glares at me. "Not everyone lies to you, Griffin."

My jaw tenses as I stare at her, blood racing in my ears as my cock grows painfully hard in my trunks.

"Who then?"

Her forehead wrinkles as she opens her mouth to speak.

"Who do you think about?" I cut her off, my eyes dropping to her jaw as I rub my thumb over it. Back and forth. Back and forth. "When you come? Whose face do you see? Who do you think of?"

"I..." Her eyes dart between mine.

"Too long." I tut. "You took *too fucking* long to answer." I rub my thumb higher, so it presses against her plump bottom lip. "I'll make it easy for you to answer next time."

Her eyes widen as I let go of her throat and grab both of her hips, lifting her out of the water and onto the side of the pool in one swift move.

Arousal surges through me as I place my palm on her chest and push her backward so she is leaning on her forearms.

"Griffin, the other huts." She glances side to side.

I chuckle darkly as with one flick of my wrist, I undo one tied side of her bikini bottoms, followed by the other.

"What about them?"

"The other guests?"

"Sweetheart, you can scream as loud as you like when you come on my face. I booked them all. There's no one here but you and me."

I smirk at her as her brows shoot up her forehead.

"Now stop fucking interrupting and spread them."

She looks back at me.

"Spread. Them," I grit out, lifting her feet from the water and placing them on the ground as I pull her bottoms out from underneath her and hurl them across the pool onto her deck.

She parts her legs slowly, watching my face.

"Wider."

Her feet inch along the edge of the pool away from each other, so her pussy is spread open, pink, and inviting, and shining with wetness.

"Fuck."

I grab one of her hip bones with one hand and then drop my head to the side to admire her. My other hand goes inside my trunks to my cock, which I squeeze, then leisurely stroke a few times to take the edge off the ball-crushing ache that's going on down there.

One glance at her flushed face and parted lips as she gazes at me in anticipation tells me I won't have to wait long for that glorious moment of tasting her release on my tongue.

It will be mine. *All. Mine.*

"Watch," I growl, dropping in the water so my head is at perfect pussy eating height.

She moves forward a little, and my cock weeps in response to the glorious bolt of pleasure taking over her face as I spit on her.

Then I lower my mouth and claim her.

"God!"

She drops her head back and moans as I spread her lips with my fingers and delve deeper, licking and tasting her. Every soft fold of skin, every drop of sweet wetness like the most incredible high against my tongue.

"Look. At. Me."

She forces her eyes back to me and watches as I take my time with her, savoring every shiver her body makes against my tongue, devouring every wave of wetness she sends to me.

And fuck, does she send them. Her cunt is dripping with the need to be filled and fucked.

But I want this first.

I *need* this first.

Her taste... it's... it's perfect.

She tastes fucking perfect. Just how I feared she might.

My sucking and licking increases with my growing desire to claim her next orgasm as mine. It's all I can do to stop myself from freeing my cock and climbing up and pounding into her tight, wet heat. I want her first to be on my face with her eyes glued to mine. I want to watch and see the moment she realizes that a part of her will always be mine from now on.

No matter what she does, in this moment, Maria and her pleasure belong to me.

I place my mouth over her swollen clit and suck. Her eyes widen and she shudders, panting as she climbs toward her release.

I stop without warning and draw back.

"Tell me."

"Tell you what?" She writhes against the ground, lifting her hips toward me, desperately chasing after what she almost had.

What she almost succumbed to on my tongue.

I stare into her eyes and place my hand flat over her pussy, pushing it down to the ground. She squirms against my hand, trying to create friction for her needy cunt.

"Tell me whose face you'll see when you come from now on."

"Griffin," she moans, reaching for me.

"Tell. Me."

"Yours... yours... please..." Her face is screwed up. She rolls her hips, trying again to grind against my palm.

I tear my hand away. She's so pretty and swollen. Leaning down, I take a slow, deep breath and inhale the scent of her arousal.

"That's right, Sweetheart," I murmur. "*Mine*."

She whimpers and then I sink two fingers roughly inside her, surprising her and making her cry out. Her body wraps around them snugly and squeezes.

"This tight little cunt is going to remember me, Maria," I growl.

I work her into a frenzy, adding a third finger and pumping in and out of her, my skin coming out slick from her juices as the sound of it crackles in the air between us.

"Griffin..." Her hands are curled into fists by her sides, her knuckles pale. Her eyes fixed on me.

"Mine," I growl against her clitoris as I lap at it with my tongue. "All. Mine."

She gasps and bucks up into me, spreading her taste further around my face.

"Say it."

She grinds shamelessly against me, her lower back arching off the ground.

"Say it," I repeat, pushing her down so our eye contact isn't broken.

She looks me right in the eye, licking her lips. "Yours."

I smirk and suck the little ball of nerves between my lips. She struggles to stop her eyes from rolling back in her head. She writhes against my face, her body shaking and shuddering, fighting to get away from the over sensitivity as I graze her clit with my teeth.

No, you don't, Sweetheart.

I suck again, swirling my tongue over her and twisting my fingers inside her, my chest expanding with delight as I soak up the perfect moment where she tenses and then spasms, coming hard on my face.

"Fuck yes! Give it to me," I groan into her, my tongue gathering up every drop of her, not wanting to miss one. "Don't hold anything back. Give it to me!"

She wriggles and pants and moans and gasps.

And I bathe in every single movement and sound she makes.

I fucking *bathe* in it.

I slide my fingers out of her and grab both of her hips, dragging her closer and sinking my face into her, breathing deeply, calmness washing over me in waves.

My ears fill with the sound of my own deep groans as I rub her all over me, relishing the tiny aftershocks as I drink her up until she's quiet and quivering beneath me, her fists loosened, her breath slowing.

That pleasure. Her pleasure.

It's mine now.

One night underneath a starry sky in The Bahamas.

One orgasm that exploded with the strength of a hurtling comet against my tongue.

It will always be mine.

All. Mine.

She lies limp and spent, fallen back against the ground as she stares at the night sky, lost in her own moment of bliss, sweat glistening between her perfect breasts as they rise and fall with each steadying breath she takes.

There's no fucking way she'll ever forget my face.

Chapter Twelve

Maria

I GAZE AT THE stars as I breathe. In and out. In and out. Every sound is strange and muffled in my ears as I come back from wherever I've just been. *Heaven*, I think. Of course, it's not heaven. I'm not that drunk despite the cocktails. But Griffin's mouth... if heaven was a place on earth, it would be there. Underneath his soft lips, behind his perfect, white teeth; on the tip of his strong, commanding, filthy tongue. There's no doubt about it.

"Maria?" His voice sounds far away.

I lift my head from where I've collapsed against the ground and am met with blue.

Bright, clear, mesmerizing blue.

I open my mouth to say something—anything—but am stopped short by a ringing from inside his hut.

"Fuck off," he calls without breaking my eye contact.

He pulls me up to a sitting position. My legs have turned to jelly, so I let him hold me by the waist and slide me into the water in front of him. I couldn't move by myself even if I wanted to.

The ringing inside stops, then immediately starts again.

"Fuck's sake," he hisses underneath his breath.

He turns, looking over his shoulder at the open door to his hut.

"What if it's the hotel?" I ask as the ringing stops again.

He turns to me, his eyes looking almost silver as they catch the glow from the moon in them.

"Then they'll call back."

I look at him, unsure of what to say. His lips, chin, half of his entire face is shining. I swallow down the flutter in my throat. It's me. *My orgasm.* He's made no attempt to wipe it off in the water. He's wearing it like a badge of honor on his sinfully handsome face.

The ringing starts for a third time and Griffin groans, tipping his head back to the sky.

"Stay right here."

His hands leave my waist, and he turns and swims over to his deck, lifting himself out of the water on strong arms. Each muscle in his back ripples and beads of water run down his skin as he stands.

He grabs a towel from the lounger and walks into his hut without looking back.

The ringing stops as he barks out, "This better be important."

The sound of his voice, all business-like on the phone, the one I'm so used to hearing at work when he's terse or short-tempered with me, slaps me in the face like cold air, instantly sobering me up.

What the fuck have I done?

I whip my head from side to side. The pool is deserted, as well as the beach behind me. I can't believe he booked all eight huts so he could have his privacy. Then again, it makes perfect sense. It's the kind of thing billionaires must do all the time. I'm surprised he doesn't have a holiday home here that he stays in. But the beach? Anyone could have walked past and seen us. *Heard* me.

Shit.

I just spread it all out for my boss on a business trip. If only I were his secretary, it would complete the cliché. I didn't work as hard as I have to ruin it all by being stupid enough to mix business and men together again.

My heart races in my chest. Griffin has switched a lamp on in his hut, and I can just make out his back to me as he talks on the phone in a low voice. I need to go now, before he sees me. If he comes back out here, I don't know what will happen. It's obvious I lack control when he touches me.

I cut through the water as quickly as I can and climb out onto my deck, making as little sound as possible. My heart hammers in my ears at the possibility of him coming back any second.

My bikini bottoms are in a crumpled heap on the floor, where Griffin threw them earlier. I scoop them up and tiptoe into my hut, closing and locking the door behind me and then I press the button on the wall until the white curtain slides all the way across, blocking out the stars, the pool... him.

"Good morning, Mr. Parker. How was your stay?"

The voices outside grab my attention and I walk to the door and peek through the spy hole. The guy who brought my luggage to my hut yesterday morning loads the same tan leather holdall I saw when I arrived, and a suit carrier onto his trolley.

"Just meetings, the usual," a voice I would recognize anywhere replies.

Just meetings?

My face burns with humiliation. He sounds so unfazed, whereas I've been up half the night wondering what to say to him this morning. What do you say to your boss the morning after a night like that?

We shouldn't have done it? We crossed a line? You made me come so hard I thought I was going to pass out?

I swallow as he appears into view, in full CEO mode. A pristine navy suit, shiny Italian leather shoes and a white shirt that looks even whiter in the dazzling sunshine. He takes a few notes from his wallet and hands them to the hotel porter, who dips his head in response.

"Thank you, Mr. Parker."

I turn and lean back against the door. How am I supposed to explain last night? How am I supposed to work with him again? I inhale, holding it inside for a few seconds, then exhale slowly. Well, fuck it. If he's not bothered, then neither am I. In fact, if he doesn't mention it again, it'll be much better. Leave it on the island where it belongs. A few too many drinks. A momentary lack of judgment.

A mistake.

"Will this be all?" the porter asks.

"No. Can you get next door's luggage, please?"

I glance at my watch. It's eight forty-five. He said we were leaving at nine. I'm ready; I just need to put my shoes on.

I reach down to grab them and take another deep breath, stealing myself for the knock at the door.

"Of course, Mr. Parker."

"Thank you. And tell my employee I will meet her in the lobby."

My mouth drops open, heat firing across the back of my neck. I resist the urge to open the door and hurl my shoe at him. *Employee?* Who the hell does he think he is? Pompous asshole. I bet he knows I can hear him from my hut. He's not even going to wait for me? He obviously had no intention of knocking for me.

I step into my stiletto pumps and grab my bag, casting my eyes around the hut one last time. Such a beautiful room. Such a perfect location. *Such a waste.*

I give my bag to the bellboy and then take my time walking to the lobby, snorting to myself as I pass the frangipani bushes. What an idiot I was, thinking that moment last night was romantic.

Griffin isn't in the lobby, so I check out at the desk and then walk over to the open fronted main entrance, lifting my head to the sun and taking a deep breath.

"Ms. Taylor?"

A driver calls my name as he walks around the front of a sleek black car. He smiles and opens the rear door for me.

I narrow my eyes at the vehicle.

Where's Griffin?

"How are you today?"

"Well, thank you." I give him a polite smile as I step into the car and slide onto the cool leather seat.

The scent of tropical air after rain fills the car, and despite last night and this morning, its scent is even more alluring in its assault on me as my stomach twists with a mix of anger and arousal.

I pull my lips into a tight line as the door closes behind me.

"Morning," Griffin says, his eyes never leaving the paperwork he's reading.

"Morning," I reply, looking at him out of the corner of my eye.

He looks perfectly well rested. Not a single hint of a dark shadow beneath his eyes. His dark hair is immaculately styled, and he's freshly shaven.

His Adam's apple moves as he clears his throat. He puts the pen he's holding between his teeth as turns the page on the paperwork he's holding and then reaches down to the seat between us to retrieve another document from a pile that's stacked there, his class ring glinting on his hand.

I force my eyes away from his lips as he takes the pen back out.

"Do you have enough space?" He makes some notes on the document he's holding, and then flicks to the next page.

I look at the middle seat and back at him. He lifts his eyes to mine, raising a brow as he makes the first eye contact of the morning with me.

"Do you have enough space?" he repeats slowly, as though I'm stupid.

My stomach twists again, but no longer in anger and arousal. This time, it twists in humiliation.

There's nothing in his eyes. No flash of recognition when he looks at me. No sign that anything happened last night. Just cool, calm Griffin Parker in full asshole mode.

It meant nothing.

I swallow down the acid in my throat. If he wants to pretend it never happened, then that's fine with me.

"Yes, plenty, thank you." I sweep my hair over my shoulder, and he snaps his eyes away from me and back to his paperwork, running one hand down over his tie as he frowns, his dark brows pulling low over unblinking eyes.

The car falls silent, and I reach down into my bag and pull out my notebook, turning to the last page I was working on yesterday. Since our meeting with Ken, I've been brainstorming ideas for new spa products using the cocoa butter he's going to provide us with. I have a few already, which I need to run by Todd.

I'm so engrossed in what I'm doing that we are at the airport the next time I look up. When I flew over, I came into Nassau first, and then caught a smaller plane over to San Andros. I look out of the window as we sail past the terminal building. Griffin seems unfazed. He's packed his paperwork away and has one elbow leaning on the car door, his fingers against his lips, and his jaw set as he stares straight ahead.

The car pulls up to a barrier and our driver says something to the guard on duty, who then presses a button, opening the barrier and waving us through as he says something into his handheld radio. I frown as we drive along the airfield and pull into an aircraft hangar.

"What are we doing here?"

"Flying back to New York," Griffin replies, not looking at me.

The car comes to a stop and the driver gets out, opening the door for Griffin first, and then coming around to open mine. I step out and look over the top of the car. There's a private jet with its door open, a smiling flight attendant standing at the top of the stairs.

I walk around the car, casting my eyes up and down the jet's sleek fuselage as our driver carries our luggage onto the plane and then returns, bidding us both goodbye.

"After you." Griffin holds his hand out, his expression unreadable as I look at him.

I frown, looking from him, to the jet, and back again.

His eyes darken and his jaw ticks. "Sometime today would be preferable."

I glare at him, pulling my shoulders back.

Jerk.

I climb the steps and say hello to the flight attendant and two pilots who are standing by the cockpit. Griffin boards behind me and shakes the pilots' hands, greeting them by name. I rein in my gasp as I walk into the cabin. It's all cream leather and mahogany, with large, individual seats separated by a narrow central aisle. It's like something from a music video.

"May I offer you some champagne?" The flight attendant appears beside me and directs me to a wide seat on one side of the aisle.

"Oh. No. No alcohol, thank you." I place my purse on the console table built into the side of the seat and sit down.

"Some iced water, then?" She smiles.

"Perfect. Thank you."

"You're welcome."

She turns to Griffin on the other side of the aisle, who's undoing the button of his suit jacket with one hand. He takes it off, revealing his broad torso in his crisp white shirt and hands it to her.

"It's a pleasure to see you again, Mr. Parker." Her smile for him is wider than the one she gave me, and her gaze roams appreciatively over his chest and back to his face.

"You too, Melissa," he replies, her name rolling smoothly off his tongue.

Ugh. Really?

He flashes her a charming smile as she walks away with his jacket.

I scowl and turn away, the muscles in my shoulders tensing. I roll them in circles and tilt my head from side to side as I try to loosen up. Melissa returns with my drink, and one for Griffin. She didn't ask him what he wanted. She must see him often enough that she knows him well and doesn't need to ask. I stare at her back as she walks to the front and closes the aircraft door.

"Why don't you get some sleep on the flight?" Griffin says without looking at me. Melissa walks by again and flashes him a smile. He keeps his eyes on hers, smiling back at her as he says to me, "You look tired."

Fire licks at my tongue as I consider hitting back with something that will tell him what a jerk he's being. It's a total contrast to the man I had dinner with last night. We're back to alpha boss-hole, a role he plays so well he probably created it himself.

Instead, I take a deep, calming breath and ignore him. I reach into my bag and pull out an aromatherapy roller-ball I made myself. It's got chamomile, rose and lavender oils in—perfect to help me get some rest on the flight.

I apply it to my wrists and behind my ears, then pull out a sleep mask. Despite it being Griffin's suggestion, I could do with the rest after the drinks and lack of sleep. Plus, it will mean I don't have to look at his face all flight or witness every time Melissa bats her eyelashes at him.

Perfect.

Chapter Thirteen

Griffin

"WHAT DO YOU MEAN, you don't have it? When you called the other night, you said—"

Excuses pour down the phone from the incompetent fucker on the other end in response.

"I don't want to hear it. Just ring me when you have something to tell me!"

I slam the phone down onto the desk and curse. Why is it so fucking hard to find someone who can do their job properly?

There's a knock at the door.

"Yes!" I snap.

"Mr. Parker?" Harley pokes her head around the door and then opens it fully, stepping inside. "I've got some sign offs I need for Friday."

"Of course, of course." I hold my hand out and she walks across the room and places a folder in it.

"Are you accompanying Emily again?" she asks as I flick through the pages and sign the necessary ones.

"Yes." I raise my eyes to hers. "Why?"

Her brows shoot up and she shakes her head. "No reason. Just wondered." Her smile returns as I close the folder and hand it back to her.

"Oh, and Harley?"

She turns back as she reaches the door.

"Make sure you get the outfits you borrow back to the boutiques on time. Not like the last gala."

She bites her bottom lip and nods at me. "Of course. Thank you, Mr. Parker."

I smirk as she closes the door. I may not know the single most important thing about what's been happening under my nose at the hotel yet. But I'm not stupid. I know enough of what my staff get up to. But sneaky tours of the penthouses for their friends when there aren't any guests staying in them, and borrowing outfits from the hotel boutiques are the least of my problems. Not when the person who stabbed me in the back is still out there. Unpunished. Or worse, still in here, working for me, waiting for another opportunity to threaten The Songbird.

I will drag them through hell myself before I give them that chance again.

"You mean I have to put up with your stinky shit in one of my apartments for longer?" I screw my nose up, flicking my gaze to Reed's sneakers across the room.

"The only stink in here is one of success, mixed with last night's pussy." He smirks as he hands me a glass of bourbon.

He's still running for LA Mayor, but Reed being Reed, has decided after hearing whispers on the politics circuit that there is something going on at the New York Mayor's office, he's going to extend his brief vacation here and find out what. Frankly, I'm pleased. He's my closest friend aside from my brothers, who live in other cities. It'll be nice having him around longer. But I'd pull out all my teeth before admitting that.

"Still making plenty of 'friends', then?" I snort as I take a drink and savor the fiery burn in my throat.

"Networking, yes. It's important for me to meet people. See what their concerns are. What issues the city is facing." Reed reclines onto the other couch and grins at me. "It's amazing what some of these chicks hear when they're at work."

"I don't see how underwear models can have a huge understanding of the inner workings of the New York Mayor's office."

"You'd be surprised, Griff. Besides, my friend last night works for one of the city's biggest defense attorneys. She had a lot of interesting things to say once I loosened her lips."

I chuckle to myself. "Is that what you call it?"

"True story." Reed lowers his voice. "I might need to apologize to your hot spa manager again, though. Attorney girl was a screamer."

I look over at him. He even looks guilty, hanging his head like a hound.

"Her name is Maria. Call her hot again and see what happens to you."

Reed's eyes light up. "What's that, buddy? You warning me off your chick?"

I shoot him a look that would make other men step back. "Second warning. And cut out the chick shit, too. She's not a bird." I tap my fingers against the side of my glass, then lift it to my lips and drain the rest of it.

"I knew something went down on that trip last week!" Reed ignores my warning and sits forward in his seat, his eyes focused on me. "You've been a moodier shit than usual since you came back."

"Thanks," I mutter, ignoring the waiting look on his face as I blow out a breath to calm the fire that's settled inside my gut since I returned from The Bahamas.

"So?" he probes when I offer nothing further.

"So, nothing. It was a business trip. We negotiated a new deal. A great one."

I run my hand down over my tie as I recall the way Maria spoke with Ken, engaging him in conversation about something he's passionate about. She's extremely astute. That entire trip cemented it in my mind. I need to loosen the reins a little and let her get on with it. The fact I haven't seen her in person since we got back, yet spa bookings are through the roof should tell me something—she doesn't need me. She's Maria. She doesn't need anyone. Another fact thrown in my face when I went back out to the pool and found it empty. If that isn't a huge fucking sign of regret on her part, then I don't know what is.

"Yeah, because it sure looks like business is thriving and you're ecstatic about it." Reed laughs.

I shake my head at him. "We had a moment, that's all. A short-lived one that won't be repeated. She's like me. We don't mix business with our personal lives—Don't look at me like that."

"I didn't say anything." Reed holds his hands up in front of him.

"You didn't have to. I can smell your friendly advice from over here. It stinks more than your sneakers."

He knows I'm joking. There's nothing further from the truth when it comes to Reed. Even as young men living together in college away from home for the first time, he was still a neat bastard.

His own version of control, I guess.

Just like I have my methods.

I knock back my drink, aiming to erase the memory of Maria's taste, which is still on my tongue if I merely think of her for more than a moment.

Reed drops his head and laughs. "I've known you years, Griff, remember that. You can't bullshit a bullshitter. I've seen you both together. She's under your skin." His shoulders shake as he continues to laugh. "Keep lying to yourself. But we both know the truth."

"Which is?" I reach for the bottle on the coffee table and fill my glass back up.

Reed's challenging eyes meet mine. "That she's holding all the cards right now. You can either be a pussy and let her avoid you at work, then be back here with your ugly pissed face when she starts dating someone, which she no doubt will."

My jaw stiffens as tightness spreads over my chest and down my arms.

"Or?" I knock back my drink again and reach for the bottle once more.

"Or you do what you do best." He raises his brows at me. "You go after what you want and make it yours."

I stalk into the spa the next morning with renewed purpose. Maria may think she can avoid me and forget about what happened. But no one has the last word. *Unless it's me.*

"Ms. Taylor," I bark as I approach the main desk.

It's early so only a few therapists are in, setting up for the day. They scatter when they hear me.

Maria glares at me. "Mr. Parker. Would you be so kind to explain why you're racing in here and making my staff jump with your excessive volume?"

I narrow my eyes at her. She's tied her hair up again, exposing her neck and throat. I swallow at the sight of her creamy skin.

I could wrap a hand around it again. Make her moan.

She looks back at me and sighs. "Mr. Parker?" A hint of regret laces her words as her eyes lose some of their fire.

"Griffin," I snap.

"You called me Ms. Taylor. I thought we were back on those terms." She holds my gaze, crossing her arms over her chest.

I keep my eyes on her face, even though I know crossing her arms has pushed her magnificent breasts up in her low-necked dress. *Damn.* She might regret everything about that night.

I only have one regret—taking that call.

"We make our own terms from now on," I say as she tilts her head and studies me.

"Okay." She releases her arms. "What can I help you with? Were you after an update on how things are?"

"Sure. Let's start with that." I thrust my hands into my pockets and walk to the desk.

She glances at my light gray suit, then taps into the computer bookings system.

"Bookings are up fifty percent on last month. I've spoken with Todd and Ken. The first batch of new products should be with us within two weeks, in perfect time for us to have trialed them and gathered feedback before Vogue writes their feature. Oh, and we've already beaten the month's target I set the team for new client intro-ductions." She fires off the list as though the quicker she can say it, the quicker our conversation will be over.

She looks back at me. "Did you want to know anything else?"

"You'll be coming Friday, won't you?"

My question must catch her off-guard as she blinks a few times before responding.

"To Emily's gala?"

"Yes. Will you be there?"

Maria purses her lips, looking far from happy. "Yes, I will. She wouldn't take no for an answer. She's been visiting the spa every time she's at The Songbird. In fact, I've seen her every day since we got back from..." Her eyes drop to the countertop.

"The Bahamas?" I finish for her.

She nods. And there's the first crack. The fact she can't even say the words means she's thought about it.

Maybe she's still thinking about it.

"Is anyone accompanying you?"

"Todd," she says, still not making eye contact with me.

"I see." My jaw aches as my teeth threaten to grind together until there is only dust left.

"It's not a date." She sniffs and busies herself with a small stack of treatment menus.

My hands ball into fists in my pockets. "Does he know that?"

She raises her chin, and her eyes meet mine, filled with a silent challenge.

"I don't date people I work with, Griffin."

I pull my shoulders back and they crack inside my jacket.

"Good. Neither do I."

Her eyes bore into mine and her pupils dilate as she parts her beautiful pink lips to speak. "Glad we've got that clear."

I jut my chin out, my eyes sweeping over her face one last time before I turn and leave.

Me too, Sweetheart, me too.

Chapter Fourteen

Maria

SINCE GETTING BACK FROM The Bahamas, time has flown by. The spa has been busy, and alongside running it and setting up things with Todd for the new products, I've barely had time to think.

Of course, there's that one thing which keeps knocking on the door to my brain. Forcing itself in, no matter how much I try to keep it out, adding a new bolt to the door each day. It just knocks louder until my head feels like it might explode with pressure.

Griffin Parker.

I should have known when I accepted this job that it wouldn't be easy working with him. I knew there was something that first time I met him in California. He was so restrained and in control. I thought it was because it was business. I should have listened to my instincts. Griffin Parker is a man who is not used to being told no. He's a man who craves being in charge. *To command. To control.* Heat fires in my core at the memory of his lips against my skin. It may make him invincible in business, and it may make him the most incredible, pantie-burning lover, but in terms of me and my personal life? It makes him the devil. I can't let a man control my future again.

I'm shoved back into the present as Will thrusts a long purple gown into my hands.

"Try this one, Maria."

I hold up the hanger and look down at the thin fabric of the gown.

"Wow, it's so light."

"It's silk. You'll look like a queen." He rummages around in the pile of garment bags he's brought over to my apartment and pulls another dress off a hanger, handing it to Harley.

"Ooh, I like!" Her face lights up as she eyes the pink fabric. "Thanks, Will."

"Don't thank me yet. We've still got to get all this back to Sylvia before opening tomorrow morning. Otherwise, she'll have my balls on a spike." He looks at Harley and raises a brow.

"Okay, point taken. I won't let you down." She gives him a small salute. "I can't believe Mr. Parker has us figured out."

"That man knows everything that goes on around he re... except..." He reaches into another bag and pulls out two deep blue velvet boxes. "About these!" He grins as he holds up the boxes like trophies.

"What are those?" Harley's eyes widen as she holds her hands out. "Please tell me they're shiny, Will? I'll love you forever!" she squeals as he pops the lid and reveals a glittering pair of diamond teardrop earrings.

Harley bounces up on her toes and kisses him on the cheek as she lifts them from the box and stares at them.

"They'll look amazing," Will says, before turning to me. "Okay, next!" He grins as he opens the second box and a necklace with a long diamond chain hanging down the middle catches the light.

My hand flies to my mouth. The diamonds look *very* real. And *very* expensive.

"I can't wear that. Where did you even get it?"

He shrugs my comment off with a light laugh. "A *friend* who happens to be a designer at Van Cleef and Arpels." He takes the necklace from the box and places it in my hand. "It will look amazing with the plunging neckline of that dress. Just guard them with your life, okay?" He looks between me and Harley, and we nod in response.

"You're the best, Will," Harley sings as she gathers up her dress, zipping it back into its garment bag. "Right, I'm off to deliver Suze's to her," she says, grabbing the other bag Will has prepared.

I kiss her and Will goodbye and then sink into the sofa.

I'm relieved Harley has asked Suze to be her plus one. It'll be nice to have some allies to talk to. Asking Todd to accompany me probably wasn't such a great idea. I've only spoken to him in a work capacity. The evening could be awkward if conversation dries up. And then there's Griffin. I've barely seen him since we got back from The Bahamas, since whatever the hell that was that happened between us.

My throat goes dry... *whatever the hell that was.*

No matter how hard I try, I can't get it out of my head. I almost had a one-night stand with my boss on a work trip. Because that's what it would have been. If he hadn't gotten a call, I know we would have ended up having full sex. It's obvious to me now that Griffin Parker, sun, and cocktails render me completely incapable of acting with any modicum of sense.

I practically rode his face and moaned like I was in a casting couch audition.

He's my boss.

So stupid.

Harley said he doesn't date anyone connected with work since all the drama with Gwen. And he even said it himself when he came to the spa the other day. He doesn't date people he works with. And neither do I. It's a recipe for disaster. The repercussions don't bear thinking about.

Besides, he made it quite clear the morning after, on the journey back to New York, that he wasn't giving it any further thought. He never mentioned a thing. If I hadn't been there myself, I would never have believed it had even happened by the way he was acting so cold and business-like. Maybe in his eyes, it never did. He probably has nights like that all the time and they all merge into one.

But I don't.

The way he... no! I must stop. I can't allow myself to indulge in memories of a night that should have never happened. But the memory of his deep voice growling out commands to me as he held me open and studied me with that look of pure, unfiltered desire on his face? That memory alone sends goosebumps coursing over my entire body. I should have known from the way he is at work—ruthless, powerful, downright brilliant at what he does—that he would be the same out of his suits.

Griffin Parker sure knows how to play dirty.

I need to forget. Push it to the back of my mind and carry on. I have a job to do, a spa to run and make even more successful than it already is. That's why he hired me. If he thinks I'm here for anything else, then he's mistaken.

That one night was just that—once only.

One mistake.

One lapse of judgment that would make things too complicated if ever repeated.

It was alcohol mixed with tropical heat and an incredible setting.

Nothing more.

"You look wonderful." Todd holds his arms out and cups both of my elbows as he kisses me on each cheek.

"Thank you. So do you." I smile at him.

The tension that's been following me around all day falls away as he launches straight into a story about his day at work and we walk from my apartment to the elevators. He's dressed in a black tuxedo; an easy smile on his face as he talks. I was worrying about nothing. This isn't awkward. I know he'll chat all night long, judging by how he's already slipped straight into a conversation with ease.

And he's a good-looking man. I only noticed when Harley pointed it out. He's got a youthful boyishness about him. Despite him being around thirty, the same as me, his dimples and blond curls make him seem younger. And I can relax in his company. Not like when I'm near Griffin, wondering what mood he's going to be in. He's the total opposite to Todd—dark, brooding, intense, in both personality and looks.

God, why am I even thinking about him?

Todd pushes the elevator button as he continues his story. I had zoned out. Led astray by thoughts of a man who should not be taking up any space in my head.

I look at Todd and try my best to give him my full attention and not be rude. I said I'd meet him at the gala, but he insisted on meeting me first, so I don't have to walk in alone. I didn't have the heart to tell him I've walked into many places alone. And rather than making me feel self-conscious, it's done the opposite—I've felt empowered. Large business dinners at my old hotel in California, regional and national management conferences—I've held my head higher for each one I've attended. I earned my right to be there and am proud of what I've achieved.

The Songbird's main ballroom is already filled with guests when we arrive. We each take a glass of champagne from a passing server and look at the chart near the entrance to see where we're seated. I could have asked Harley earlier today. I'm sure she would have seen it, as despite Emily organizing the galas, Harley told me Griffin has final say over everything. Including the seating plan.

"There we are." Todd points to the table on the front left of the chart and then places his hand on my back, steering me toward the front of the room. I spot Harley and Suze sitting at a table in the center as we pass. Harley gives me a grin and a wave as she talks to the man next to her, who I don't recognize. Meanwhile, Suze is deep in conversation with the lady next to her and they're laughing about something.

We reach our table and Todd pulls my chair out for me, sitting next to me once I'm seated. There are three other couples who are already at the table, so we say hello and introduce ourselves. They all know Emily and launch into stories about the other galas they've attended. Two of the men are trying to out-do each other by dropping not-so-subtle hints about how much they're planning to donate to tonight's charity, which is to raise money for the pediatric oncology department at New York Presbyterian Hospital.

Todd catches my eye and raises a brow, his lips curling. I bite mine to hide my smirk. At least the hospital will benefit from their public pissing match they seem intent on having.

"You made it!" a female voice calls out.

I look up as Emily approaches in a long, dark evening gown, her auburn hair in an elegant chignon at the base of her neck. She beams ear-to-ear and embraces each of the two loud men in turn. They exchange some words and Emily laughs, swatting one lightly on the chest. Then she greets everyone else at the table and comes to perch on the seat next to me.

"Maria, I'm so glad you could make it. That dress is beautiful, and that necklace..." She grabs my hand and squeezes it on top of the table. "... just divine. And Todd, how lovely to see you." She smiles past me, and her brows shoot up in greeting.

I can see why her galas do so well. She talks with everyone, and Harley said she knows half of Manhattan through her charity work and her father's business connections. She said he does something in corporate technology systems and I.T. Emily's been so kind, telling me about places I should eat and visit in New York. She's dropped into the spa every day since I got back from the business trip.

"Thank you so much for coming. I'm so glad Griffin suggested we sit at the same table. He's so thoughtful like that. We can get to know one another better," Emily says as she looks behind me. "Ah, here he is now. Griffin, you don't mind if we swap, do you? You are next to Maria, but you see each other every day at work. It's not fair that you should have her all to yourself." She laughs and looks back at me as a presence behind my chair makes the hairs on my arms stand up.

"Not at all."

The second the deep, gravelly voice reaches my ears, my nipples pebble into peaks and heat ignites low in my stomach. I turn in my seat as he greets the other people at the table, charm mode in full swing as he shakes hands, kisses cheeks, and pays compliments, causing many cheeks to blush. I look at Emily, who's watching him too.

"Handsome, isn't he?" she whispers, eyeing him in his tuxedo, his dark hair perfectly matching the immaculate black fabric. "Women always donate more when he comes. That's why I schedule the galas for when he's in town."

"Smart." I smile, because despite the gnawing in my stomach at the sight of Griffin spreading charm around like butter on hot toast, it makes sense now why Harley said Emily insists Griffin accompany her and doesn't bring a date. That way, he's able to network and drum up larger donations with ease using his blue-eyed charm.

"You've known each other for a long time, haven't you?" I ask, my eyes firmly stuck on Griffin and the way his eyes crease at the corners as he laughs. I remember those lines and that laugh. The way they sent shivers running up my spine when they were focused on me—and *only* me.

The gnawing in my stomach deepens as one woman from the table slides closer to him as he speaks.

"We have." Emily smiles in Griffin's direction. "Practically family. I grew up with the Parkers. Our fathers are best friends." She snorts and scrunches her face as something Griffin says makes the woman sidled up to him throw her head back in laughter and place her hand on his arm.

Emily's eyes stayed fixed on the two of them. "Always a long line of women ready to fall at his feet, but if they knew him like I do, then they'd know he'll never settle down. Griffin's wife is The Songbird."

The woman laughs again, stroking Griffin's forearm up and down.

"He's had relationships before, though, hasn't he?"

I don't know why I'm asking, it's not like I should care.

"Oh yeah, plenty. Most get fed up when they realize they'll always come second to work. And the ones that stick around longer? They're just after his money, like Gwen."

"Gwen?" My ears prick up, and I dart my eyes to Todd, who's busy talking to Reed and another unknown blonde on his arm who have joined us at the table.

"His last girlfriend," Emily mutters the word *girlfriend* as though it tastes sour. "She didn't deserve him. She tried to sell confidential spa formulations to a rival hotel in exchange for a higher position there once she realized Griffin would never marry her."

I frown over the table toward Griffin. As though sensing it, he looks back, locking eyes with me.

"I thought it was never proven who took them?" I say as I hold his darkened gaze.

Heat rises in my chest as he rolls his bottom lip between his teeth, and I see a flash of perfect white.

I know what that mouth is capable of.

I swallow and break eye contact, turning to Emily, who has leaned closer.

"It wasn't ever proven. But we all know it was her. Griffin does too," she whispers, straightening up and plastering a bright smile on her face as he finishes his conversation and rounds the table toward us.

He places himself behind my chair as he extends a hand to Todd, and they shake as Griffin's second-nature business charm persona stays firmly in place.

"Todd. Good to see you. I'm sorry to hear you had a family emergency. I hope everything is okay now?"

"It is. Thank you for asking." Todd looks at me. "I'm just so sorry that I couldn't make it."

"It was *unfortunate*, wasn't it, Maria?" Griffin says, leaning down over the back of my chair to greet me.

His expression is serious as Todd carries on spouting apologies. I turn my cheek, expecting him to graze the air next to it like he did when greeting the other female guests. But his warm lips make contact close with my ear, sending a bolt of electricity through me as he whispers softly so only I can hear.

"Beautiful dress... you look good enough to eat."

I swallow down the tiny gasp before it escapes my lips, but it's not disguised enough. His eyes flash as he stands. He knows he's affecting me. I swallow down the bubbles in my throat as he undoes the button of his dinner jacket with one hand and then takes a seat on the other side of

Emily. She immediately turns her attention to him, and he smiles, diving into a conversation with her without so much as glancing my way again.

The three-course dinner is soon over. Griffin hasn't looked at me once. But there are enough different conversations going on around the table that I have little time to think about it. Todd is good company, chatting to myself and Emily, and discussing city politics with Reed, whose date spends most of the night on her cell phone scrolling through social media and taking selfies. And Griffin has given most of his attention to the two wives of the men who were discussing donations at the beginning of the night, telling them about a friend of his whose child was treated at the hospital. Their wide sympathetic eyes soon turned into elbows in their husband's sides. I fight hard not to let my mouth drop open when one man pulls Emily to the side as we finish eating and tells her how much he would like to donate.

I look past the two of them as I stand from my chair, but Griffin has already disappeared from the table, his seat empty.

"Would you like a drink from the bar?" Todd asks as he makes his excuses to Reed and pushes his chair back.

"It's okay. I'll get them. You and Reed carry on chatting." I place a hand on his shoulder to stop him from standing and he flashes me a smile and wink as he reaches up and squeezes it.

"Okay, Babe."

My step falters. Maybe I misheard him? *Babe?*

He's already back in a deep conversation with Reed, so I make my way over to the bar and am pleased that Harley is leaning against it, her eyes bright with mischief as she sees me approaching.

"God, Maria. I wanted to tell you earlier, but girl, that dress..." She pulls me into a hug. "I want to rip it off you. No wonder Todd can't tear his eyes away." She inclines her head and I glance back to the table where both Todd and Reed are looking in our direction.

"No. He's just..." I trail off as Todd flashes me a slow, sexy smile. *Babe.* I swallow. "Okay, maybe he is."

I turn my back to him and face the bar, smoothing down the silky fabric over my hips. It's a close-fitting dress with a plunging neckline, showing off a larger amount of cleavage than I usually would, something which makes me feel rather exposed suddenly, especially because Will's addition of the diamond necklace drapes down right between my breasts.

"But we both know it's not Todd's eyes making you blush tonight." Harley stares straight ahead, a smirk on her lips as she takes a sip from her champagne flute.

"What are you talking about?"

The bartender takes my drink order. Harley's still smirking as I turn back.

"Harley?" I glance side to side, but the other people at the bar are deep in their own conversations.

"You don't have to be a genius..." She rolls her eyes and sighs at my blank face. "Okay. Don't look at me like that. It's perhaps not so obvious to anyone else, but this is me, remember?"

"You and your incredible man-reading?" I bump shoulders with her to show I'm kidding.

"Exactly." She grins. "That and the fact he had me re-arrange his schedule like there was a threat to national-security when he heard you would be in The Bahamas with Todd."

"You mean alone? Todd had to cancel, remember?" I thank the bartender as he finishes up with the drinks I ordered for myself, Todd, Reed, and his date.

"No." Harley widens her eyes at me, singing out the words. "Mr. Parker had me book all those huts the moment he knew you were going. One for you, and one for him. Todd's room was going to be on the other side of the hotel."

"What?"

I stare at her, not sure what to make of it. He knew he was coming all along. He had planned to be there? Booked us rooms next to one another? I pull my shoulders back as the muscles in my back tighten. So all that talk about him coming to assist as Todd couldn't make it was all a lie. A cover-up that I fell for, to disguise the fact that despite what he says, he doesn't trust in my ability to do my job properly.

"That bastard," I hiss, my eyes roaming the room in search of him.

"I don't get it. You're upset?" Harley looks at me with a confused expression. "I think you two would make a great couple. He's not as bad as you think, you know. You just get to him. He doesn't like to not be the one in control. I think you make him feel reckless. He's never made me re-arrange his schedule like that before. Not to take a trip. His brother was meant to have the jet in Boston. I don't know what favor he had to pull to get it." She pulls her shoulders up to her ears and gives an excited wiggle on the spot as she grins.

I continue my search for him as Harley carries on talking.

"No wonder he's been insufferable since you got back. I bet when he heard Todd wouldn't be there, he hoped something might happen."

There! Dark hair across the room. He's standing with a group of men, drink in one hand, the other casually slung inside his pants pocket as he laughs.

Damn him, why does he have to look like that?

I curse the way my stomach lifts. Like it's about to start a little dance, just for him. I avert my eyes before he sees me looking. That's all I need. For him to notice me watching him and think I'm hung up on him somehow. Hung up on a meaningless night that should never have happened.

"Maria?" Harley elbows me. "Why are you looking at him like that?" Her mouth drops open as I meet her gaze. "You didn't?" She narrows her eyes, studying me. "Oh, my God. You did!" She claps a hand over her mouth as her eyes dart between mine. "Okay. I need to know everything. Let's find somewhere quiet." She grabs my hand and pulls me.

"What about the drinks?" I point at the glasses on the bar.

"Oh, for God's sake. I deserve a medal for this patience I'm about to demonstrate," she says to the ceiling, before thrusting mine and her drink into my hands and gathering up the other three herself.

She marches over to the table, plonking the glasses down and sloshing some of their contents over the rims.

"Here are your drinks. Now, I'm stealing Maria for something very important. No one objects, do they? No? Good. See you later." She turns and grabs my elbow as Todd looks perplexed.

Reed smiles, his eyes eating up her curves in her pink dress as he runs his hand around his chin. "As long as you steal me next."

She shoots daggers at him before her eyes sweep over to his date, who's sitting looking bored with her arms crossed.

"Reed, you didn't introduce us to your friend." Harley waits, a satisfied smirk growing on her face as Reed shuffles in his seat, running his hand around the back of his neck as he laughs uncomfortably.

"Harley, this is... this is Felicia."

"Ugh... really?" The blonde next to him comes to life, throwing her phone into her clutch and flinging her chair back with a disgusted groan as she stands in her sky-high heels. "You know something? You're a total jerk, Reed Walker." She scowls at him. "Felicia is my sister. I'm Farah." She picks up the full glass of champagne Harley just delivered and throws the contents in Reed's face, then flicks her hair over her shoulder and stalks off.

"What the..." Reed grabs a napkin off the table and scrubs it over his face. "What the fuck was that, Harley?" He looks at her with round eyes, then dabs at his soaked shirt.

"That"—Harley clicks her tongue—"was Farah. Or do you have problems with your hearing and your memory?" She throws him a fake smile and then turns, propelling me across the room toward the main door with her.

"I can't believe she just threw that in his face!" I say, glancing back at Reed, who's staring after Harley with a *smile* on his face. *What the...?*

We walk out into the main lobby and find a quiet corner with seats, away from the other guests who are passing in and out to use the restrooms.

"From what you told me you've heard going on through the wall, and the fact he can't even remember a single woman's name, I would say it's the least he deserves," Harley huffs as we take a seat.

"Except he just used your name. Twice," I say, wondering why he looked pleased about getting a face full of champagne.

"That's different. I work for his best friend. He hears my name all the time when I transfer his calls." She brushes her dress down and then fixes her eyes on mine. "Enough about him. Tell me about The Bahamas." She leans forward onto her knees so I can keep my voice low.

"What makes you think there's anything to tell?"

She purses her lips and cocks her head to the side. "Don't play that game, or we'll be here all night... but fine… if that's what you want, I'm not going anywhere." She leans back in her seat.

"All right, all right," I mutter.

She jumps forward again like an excited puppy so our heads almost touch.

"Did you two have sex all trip?" she whispers.

"No!" I whisper back.

"Well, what then?" She taps her foot on the floor as she fidgets on the edge of her seat. I bet she was one of those kids that tore open all the presents on Christmas morning before their parents even woke up.

"We had a nice time. He was less… Griffin."

Harley nods. "And?"

"And we had drinks and dinner, then went back to our rooms and had a swim in the pool together."

"Please tell me you wore the bikini I packed for you, and not that hideous thing you put in?"

"What's wrong with my bathing suit?"

Harley raises a brow as if that is enough explanation.

"Yeah, I did."

She grins and claps her hands together as the back of my neck grows hot. I'm not sure why I chose that bikini when I got back to my room, and not the full one piece I had packed. Oh fuck, who am I kidding? I totally chose the sexy swimsuit after Griffin tucked that frangipani flower in my hair and I got all lust-drunk and stupid on the cocktails.

I drop my head into my hands. It was my fault it happened. I threw myself at him. And I definitely kissed him first. I remember that much.

"Oh, God," I groan.

Harley places a finger underneath my chin, tilting it up so I have nowhere else to look but straight into her eyes.

"What's wrong? Did he turn you down?" Two lines form between her brows.

"Not exactly." I look back at her, keeping my voice as quiet as possible. "He went down on me at the side of the pool."

"I knew it." She smiles as her shoulders relax and she exhales a long stream of air. "God, for a minute, I thought I had lost my touch." She laughs in relief.

"Did you hear what I said?" I hiss at her. "Harley, he's my boss!"

"I heard you. But I knew you were going to say something like that. It's obvious by the way he's looked at you since we met you. He totally wants to fuck you so much that your insides turn into a mold of his dick. What was the sex like?"

I don't answer, and Harley frowns at me. "Maria?"

"It never got that far, thank God." I place my hand against my chest, my heartrate increasing from talking about that night. "He got a phone call and went inside to take it. I went back to my room, and that was the end of it. It's not been mentioned since."

Harley looks at me like I've gone mad. "No wonder he's such a moody bastard this week. He's got a serious case of blue balls. Why would you leave him? Was it that bad? Was he like... slobbering all over you?"

"What? No, it was... it was..." I drop my voice. "I came so hard my legs were shaking for an hour afterward."

I catch her eye and giggle for the first time since this bizarre conversation began. Despite everything, I cannot deny, Griffin Parker sure knows what he's doing.

"I don't understand. What's the problem?"

I sigh. I've told Harley about my ex before, and about him and my dad both betraying my trust and stealing from me. She knows how hard I've worked to get to where I am, despite their setbacks. Maybe it makes little sense, but my job is me. It's who I am. It's what I love. I can't jeopardize that for a man. Especially one like Griffin Parker.

She grabs my hand in hers. "Look, the way I see it, you've both been betrayed by people close to you. You can take that shared history and turn it into something new and wonderful together. You both understand how the other feels."

Tension builds in my head, like someone is tightening it with a vise. Could that be true? No... it would never be that simple.

"I work with him, Harley. Besides, he hasn't mentioned it. It was just one night to him." I blow out a deep breath, rubbing at my temples. "He probably regrets it as much as I do."

Harley's eyes go round, and she straightens up in her seat, looking behind me.

"Why don't you ask *him* what he regrets?" a deep voice grumbles.

Chapter Fifteen

Maria

MY THROAT GOES DRY instantly, a lump wedging itself in there as the deep voice rolls over my skin like waves on the shore.

How long has he been standing there?

"Good evening, Mr. Parker. Oh! I think I see Suze looking for me." Harley springs up from her seat, giving me a 'talk later' look, and takes off before I can grab her and make her stay to help avoid whatever awkward conversation is about to take place.

The back of my chair shifts as weight leans on it. Every hair on the back of my neck stands to attention as I incline my head toward him over my shoulder.

"Come with me, Maria," he whispers in my ear, sending energy pulsing through my veins.

I stand and turn, but he doesn't look at me. He keeps his eyes focused ahead of us as he walks, one hand dropping to my lower back, leading me away from the lobby and down one of the hallways. We turn at the end and stop in front of a door. He pulls a card from his pocket, waving it over the sensor to unlock it.

"Inside."

"I don't—"

"Inside, Maria," he growls, making me jump.

What the hell is wrong with me tonight? Even though I'm sure he would never touch me unless I wanted him to, I'm still reacting like a rabbit entering the lair of a wolf.

I step inside one of the many meeting rooms the hotel has, one long table in its center, surrounded by gilded chairs with cream and gold fabric cushioning. It screams traditional elegance in here, not like some of the more modern offices on the higher floors.

Griffin closes the door behind us, and the sound of the lock being flicked echoes around the room, all the way to the high ceilings.

"Who were you talking about back there?"

I turn and face him, and his blue eyes appear darker than usual as they blaze into mine.

"You know who."

He strides toward me, and I step backward. The smooth edge of the table presses into my flesh as he comes right to me, stopping only when we are toe to toe, our chests grazing one anothers.

He pins me to the spot with his intense gaze.

"Don't play games with me, Maria. Tell me you haven't spent the night with Todd," he snaps, his eyes dropping to my mouth and his top lip curling as he says Todd's name. He's so close that the heat radiating off his broad body through his tuxedo seems hot enough to burn me. His scent reaches out, grabbing me, holding me frozen to the spot, just as his eyes have.

"Tell me he hasn't touched you," he growls.

"Of course not." I gulp and his eyes drop to my neck, watching the movement.

"Who then?" His tone softens.

He raises a hand, hovering it over my face as though waiting for an invitation, and I lick my lips as I stare back at him.

"Who?" he repeats, cupping the side of my neck, his thumb stroking up and down. The contact of his skin against mine has me sucking in a sharp breath.

"Why do you dislike Todd so much?" I ask, ignoring his question.

"Because he wants to fuck you. And he thinks he will," Griffin replies without hesitation. "Now tell me who you were talking about with Harley." He rolls his lips, breathing in heavily through his nose as his gaze drops. He reaches up with his other hand to stroke the diamond necklace, where it falls between my breasts.

"You," I murmur, my chest rising and falling with each heavy breath I'm struggling to take having him so close to me, having his hands on my body sending tingles dancing over my skin.

All waiting for his next move.

He shakes his head as he lays the diamond strand back down, leaving the back of his fingertips resting against the curves of my breasts.

"No."

"What do you mean, no?" My chest continues to rise and fall in exaggerated waves as his eyes roam over my breasts unapologetically, like he has every right to do it.

Like they belong to him.

"I mean, *no*, Sweetheart. You said he probably regrets it as much as you do. And I'm telling you that no, he doesn't." He follows the path of his fingers with his eyes as he slowly trails them across the neckline of my dress. The fabric is so thin that I swear each microscopic groove of his fingerprints are scarring my skin with their memory. "Tell me you don't regret it either, Maria. You can't regret something so *perfect*."

"What are you doing?" My voice comes out breathy as his fingers graze the underside of my right breast. But I don't move. I stand enraptured, gazing at the lines between his dark brows as he frowns in deep concentration, watching his hand near my breast. The other is still on my neck, cupping my jaw.

He looks at me from beneath his dark brows, his blue eyes lighter again, a breath-taking shot of opposing color to his black hair. *Dark and light.* Just like the two sides to him I've witnessed first-hand.

"I'm remembering your taste." He turns his hand and flattens his palm against my ribs, splaying his fingers out so they cover my skin like a web, immobilizing its prey. He lifts his head, jutting his chin toward me. "Tell me. How many times have you thought about that night?"

"Who said I've thought about it at all?" I look at his chin, and my eyes move upward to his parted lips—all soft, smooth... skilled.

"*I* am." His voice vibrates through my core as he closes the already tiny distance between us and places his lips against my ear, his warm breath licking at my skin like a flame as he enunciates each word slowly. "I'm saying you've thought about it when you've stroked that perfect pink cunt of yours."

I gasp and fall back onto the table.

He catches me, an arm sliding around my waist seamlessly as he holds me up against him.

"Don't act like you don't know what I'm talking about." He slides his other hand from my neck and runs his palm all the way down my body, over my breast, dragging the sheer fabric over my hardened nipple. He smiles to himself as I let out a tiny moan. *Why the hell can't I move?* I'm not a pushover, yet the moment his hands are on me, I'm under his spell.

"If I were to slide my hand inside your panties right now"—he runs his hand down and cups the area between my legs roughly through my dress—"we both know what I'd find."

My body tingles beneath his hand as I stare back into his eyes. He's looking at me with such intensity I can't even blink and break it for one microsecond.

"What?" I pant as he curls his fingers into the fabric and pulls me even closer to him.

He dips his head so his lips skim mine.

"A pretty cunt, soaking wet and aching for me to fill her."

"Griff—"

I'm cut off by his tongue as he licks my bottom lip, a low groan catching in his throat as I part my lips wider and allow my breath to entwine with his.

"Don't make me wait, Sweetheart," he says into my mouth, our faces pressed together. "I'm fucking starving for you."

The desire in his eyes burns like a blue flame as I allow my eyes to fall closed and surrender to him. He holds me around the waist, one arm wrapped around me tight, the other still holding me between the legs, and fuck, if it isn't the most aroused I've ever been in my life.

He pushes his lips onto mine, a deep moan coming from him as he kisses me with a depth that makes me rise to my toes. His lips, his tongue... they work together, exploring me, turning me inside out. Waves of pleasure crash through me and I slide my hands up into his hair, fisting handfuls, pulling him in deeper, letting him reach right inside me and take everything.

Take whatever he wants.

I'm powerless to stop him at this moment. And I couldn't care less.

Tiny whimpers escape me as he continues kissing me with such force that my knees suddenly go weak. If he wasn't holding me against him so tightly, I would fall to the floor, a puddle of jelly, all my bones crushed, kissed away by the sheer power of this man.

He pulls back, panting, his lips hovering over mine as he searches my eyes. "Tell me."

"Tell you what?" I pant back, our hearts pounding next to one another in our chests.

He flexes the hand that's cupping me, and then squeezes. I fall forward with a gasp as pleasure shoots through me.

"Tell me whose face you see when you make yourself come."

The material of the dress is so thin, I'm surprised my growing wetness isn't dripping down his fingers already.

"Who do you think?"

He's right. He could never be wrong about that. His face is etched into my soul forever.

"Say it," he growls, squeezing harder.

My pulse throbs between my legs. I bet he can feel it against his hand, it's that strong.

"Yours, Griffin. It's your face I see when I touch myself at night. It's your face that wakes me from my dreams and demands that I make myself come again before I can go back to sleep," I confess breathlessly as the heat in my core reaches a boiling point.

I might combust if I don't have his skin against mine soon.

His eyes darken again as both of his hands fly to my thighs, and he yanks my dress up around my waist.

"Fuck, Maria. You're mine. You're absolutely fucking perfect, and you're mine. All. Mine. You hear me?"

All I can do is nod as blood rushes in my ears and Griffin tears my panties down past my hips, sliding two fingers deep inside me.

"God!" I cry out, my hands dropping from his hair to grip onto his shoulders.

He pumps in and out of me, his thumb finding my clitoris and teasing circles over it. I'm so wet it's a miracle the guests in the ballroom down the hall can't hear.

"This cunt is mine, Sweetheart," he groans, his forehead pressed against mine as my body sucks him in like it's begging for more. "Don't ever disappear again when I'm in the middle of enjoying it. If you pull that shit again, I will fuck you so hard that you'll think you're going to break in two. Understood?" He sucks in a breath and then hisses out, pulling back to watch his hand work me.

He looks up at me and cocks a brow, waiting.

God.

I throw my head back as the first pulse threatens to explode. I would say anything right now to ensure he doesn't stop.

"I promise."

"Louder." He jabs his thumb into my clit and sends a shockwave of pleasure to me, and my face distorts as I cry out and squirm against him.

"I..." *Gasp* "... promise..." *Gasp*.

He grins a wicked grin. "Good girl. Now you can come."

I don't know what it is. Maybe it's his words, or the way he's looking at me like I'm the most beautiful woman he's ever seen—a goddess just for him—but his words act as a key, unlocking an invisible barrier inside me. I didn't think I was waiting for him—for his permission. But I should know better. Griffin Parker has told me himself that my pleasure belongs to him. My head might not be listening, but my body certainly is.

His eyes hold mine as my entire body tenses. I stare back at him, my eyes widening a split second before I'm thrown over the edge, racing through the air, desperately trying to grip on to something to ground me. The only thing is his eyes. Bright blue anchors that pin me to them as I come apart, shaking, contracting, moaning, screaming—every damn thing my body can do when it comes with a strength I've never known before.

"Again," he growls.

His fingers continue their assault on my senses, not giving me a moment's reprieve.

"I can't... I can't..." I swallow down giant gulps of air, grabbing at his shirt, his jacket, his hair—anything I can get my hands on as my body veers out of my control... and under his.

He watches me, his eyes holding mine, his deep voice sounding in complete control, a tenderness creeping into it.

"You can, Sweetheart. Let it go."

I pant, and he curls his fingers inside me toward my G-spot, his grip on my waist tightening as he holds me up. Then I come again, gripping onto his clothes, and pulling him up against me, my lips seeking his as I squeeze my eyes shut and moisture pricks in their corners.

"Fuck, you're so beautiful," he whispers. And then his lips are on mine again, their urgency growing, along with my own. I pull his shirt from his waistband and my hands dive inside to run over his abs.

"Griffin," I murmur between kisses, my hands exploring his smooth skin, delighting at every contraction and ripple of his muscles as he tenses at my touch.

I want him. I want him so badly. My ears are ringing and I can barely think straight. But I couldn't care less. All I'm thinking of right now is having more of his hot skin against mine, surrounding me, claiming me. I know I'm acting crazy, but right this second, nothing else matters. The world could be ending, and all I would be able to think about is having Griffin Parker's body inside mine.

His tongue dances against mine, driving me back into the table as he takes my hand and guides it to his hard cock, straining in his tuxedo pants. I wrap my fingers around his thick length, and he curses, diving back in to kiss me deeper. I run my hand up and down over him through his pants, as he lifts me and sits me on the table. He grasps my neck roughly and reaches for his zipper. The sound of each tooth coming undone cuts through the air, sending a moan of impatience from my lips.

"Griff—"

"Griffin?" another voice shouts over mine. "Griffin, are you in there?" The door vibrates as someone knocks on it.

I freeze, my breath catching in my throat. Griffin turns his head, and we both watch over his shoulder as the handle lowers.

My heart hammers in my chest and I press my hand to my mouth. If he didn't lock it properly—and the other person has a key card—then I'm about to get caught, with my panties literally around my ankles. I look up at his hair in panic. It's messed up from where I've had it in my fists. Both of us are panting, our faces flushed. There's no question about what we've been doing.

His jaw tenses, and the door remains closed. My chest sags, and I relax a little, taking my hands off his body and dropping them to my sides.

"Yes, Em. I'm in here," he calls back, his eyes returning to hold mine.

Emily. I couldn't recognize her voice. Not when my ears were still ringing from the strength of the two orgasms I've just had.

"What are you doing in there?"

I stare back at Griffin. A muscle in his jaw ticks.

"Just having a minute. I felt a migraine coming on." He rubs his thumb over my bottom lip, his dark brows pulling together.

"Oh, okay. Can I get you anything?"

"No, thanks. I'm good. I'll be out soon. Go back to the gala."

There's shuffling on the other side of the door.

Why won't she leave? I mouth to Griffin.

He tilts his head to the door to listen and I wipe underneath my eyes, hoping my make-up isn't too ruined.

There's more shuffling outside, and then a voice I recognize.

"Emily! Just who I was looking for. Please, you must introduce me to the most gorgeous man I've just seen at the bar. I know you'll know who he is. I think my ovaries might explode. He's just... well, come and see for yourself."

Harley.

I could marry that girl right now.

"Griffin? I'll see you back in there, okay? Let me know if you need anything," Emily calls through the door.

"Will do," Griffin calls back, his shoulders relaxing as the two of them walk away.

"Oh, my God." I slide off the table, pushing Griffin back so I have space to stand and pull my panties up and straighten my dress. "What the hell?"

"It's fine. The door was locked." He reaches for me, but I slip to the side, putting more space between us.

"It's not fine, Griffin. We were almost caught. *At work*." My stomach twists as nausea rolls through it. "I brought Todd with me, and I'm in here with you"—I glance behind me—"on a fucking meeting table!"

"Maria," he growls out what sounds like a warning.

"Don't." I hold up a hand as I take a deep breath. "Please don't. I can't talk to you right now. I don't trust myself when I'm alone with you."

My stomach rolls again, and I clasp a fist to my lips as I stare at the floor. What the hell am I doing? This isn't me. This isn't who I am. *This is where I work.* Where my team respects me. If Emily had walked in, or God forbid, another guest from the gala... I swallow down the bile in my throat.

"What's that supposed to mean?" he snaps, reaching for my wrist.

"Exactly as it sounds." I shake off his hand. "We shouldn't be alone together like this. It's a bad idea."

I walk to the door.

"Maria." His voice has a dark edge to it. "Don't walk out that door, Sweetheart."

A chill runs up my spine and I turn back to him, his eyes blazing into mine.

"I'm not your Sweetheart." My voice is thick with regret. "I never can be."

I unlock the door and open it, checking the corridor outside.

Empty.

I swear I feel the fire from his eyes burning into my back as I walk out into the corridor.

I don't look back.

Chapter Sixteen

Griffin

"WHERE THE HELL HAVE you been? You missed me getting a drink thrown in my face." Reed hands me a stiff drink as I join him at the bar. I knock it back in one, wincing at the burn.

He turns to the bartender and raises two fingers, signaling for him to bring more.

"Thanks." I take the second glass and turn, leaning back against the bar.

Reed quirks an eyebrow at me as he studies my face, which must look as grim as I feel. I straightened myself up in a bathroom away from the main ballroom so I wouldn't bump into anyone.

"Seems like both of us are having a fucking night tonight."

"Yeah." I take a gulp of my drink, welcoming the heat it brings with it this time. A bit more of the same, and the tension that has taken over my body might fuck off.

"What happened?" I ask, chasing the distraction his story could bring.

"Harley happened."

This time, I turn and quirk an eyebrow at him. "My PA Harley?"

"One and the same." He smiles. "She asked me to introduce her to my date, and you know..." He runs a hand around the back of his neck and winces. "... I couldn't remember her name."

I snort as I shake my head.

"Hey, I got the first letter right." Reed shrugs and takes another mouthful of his drink.

"Really? You want an award or something?" I'm glad I'm not the only one whose night isn't all plain sailing.

His eyes search the room. "Yeah, or something," he mutters.

I follow his gaze to where Maria is sitting at a table with Harley, another woman, and Todd. My eyes zero in on his arm draped around the back of Maria's chair.

What the fuck does she think she's doing? Running out on me again... and for what? To play happy fucking families with Tiny Tears over there.

"I never liked that guy," Reed says as Todd leans in and whispers something to Maria. "There's something off there. I heard he got his membership revoked from Seasons."

"Really?"

Seasons is a high-end, members only bar and restaurant on the upper westside where a lot of out-of-hours business meetings take place. I've been there a few times to meet clients.

"Yeah, I don't know what for, though." Reed swirls his drink around in his glass as he watches their table.

Maria jumps up suddenly, her head whipping side to side, one hand on her chest. I slam what's left of my drink down on the bar.

"Back in a sec, Reed."

I stride over to the table where they're all now out of their seats, pulling the chairs back, searching the floor.

"Will's balls will be on a spike! Remember what he said?" Harley blurts as she throws the edge of the table-cloth up in the air and peers underneath.

"What's going on?"

Harley looks at me, a guilty expression on her face. "Nothing, Mr. Parker. Suze just dropped her contact lens, that's all." The woman next to Harley nods and smiles at me apologetically.

"Maria? Can we talk?" I say to her back, seeing as she hasn't turned around since I walked over. She pulls her shoulders back and turns her cheek, the pulse in the side of her neck fluttering beneath her smooth skin as she looks back at me over her shoulder.

"Now's not a good time."

"It will only take a minute," I grit out.

"Can't it wait?"

My eyes fly to Todd, who has just spoken, and he falters as I glare at him, not even trying to disguise the fact I'm contemplating punching him square in the face.

"No. It can't," I snap.

He tips his chin and looks at me, his eyes glassy with one too many drinks. "Maria"—he turns and leans far too close to her—"I'll sort it, don't worry."

She glances from Todd to Harley, who nods at her. "Go. We've got this."

It takes a second or two before she turns around, like she's trying to think of a reason to refuse a second time. When she finally turns toward me, her brow is pinched, lines running across it as she chews on her bottom lip.

"What's wrong?" I ask, my stomach dropping.

I scan her body. She doesn't look hurt.

"I..." She looks into my eyes and her face clears as though something hits her. "I just need one second." She holds up a finger in the air and then darts past me toward the main doors of the ballroom.

"Maria," I call, but she's already gone.

"She did tell you she was in the middle of something," Todd says, a slight slur to his voice.

Harley looks between the two of us. She's known me long enough to know this fucker is skating on thin ice. Luckily for him, I don't have time to concern myself with his curly-haired drunken ass.

"Get yourself home, Todd. Bar's about to close." I blow out a breath in disgust and head toward the main doors after Maria.

Emily is coming through them as I get there.

"Griffin." She smiles at me. "How's your head?" She lays a hand on my shoulder as she looks at me. "All better, I hope? Migraines can be awful once they take hold. I didn't know you suffered with them." She looks at me as I search the main lobby over her shoulder.

Maria isn't there.

"Griffin?"

"No, no, I don't often." I glance at her. "I'm sorry, Em. I was trying to catch someone."

"Oh, forget them. They'll be back in a minute. Probably just gone to the restroom." She links her arm through mine. "Come, have a drink with me. I need to tell you about the donation that's just been pledged. You won't believe it." She pulls me toward the bar.

"No, Em. I really—"

"Ah! Here he is!" She smiles brightly at an older gentleman with a gray beard. "Griffin, this is Robert Turner. Tonight's cause is close to his heart."

Manners and business sense take over and I offer my hand. "It's a pleasure to meet you, Mr. Turner."

His kind face beams at me as he shakes my hand. "Likewise, Mr. Parker. Let me tell you, this woman here is a saint for what she's doing." He smiles at Emily. "That hospital deserves every penny."

Forty-five minutes later, I finally extract myself from Mr. Turner's story, about how the hospital helped his grandson—which, although very touching, could have been told in less than half the time. Emily could have handled him on her own, but she wasn't in any rush to move on faster and secure the next donation like she usually is. She was always the first one to do anything when we were kids. Beat me and my brothers every time. First without training wheels, first to get her license, first to secure her place at college. It was like life itself was one big competition. Maybe that's why she's a natural at fund raising. She treats it like a challenge.

People find it hard to say no to Emily once she sets her mind on them.

"Are you thinking of heading off?" she asks, following my gaze around the ballroom.

Most guests have left; it's so late. There are a few finishing long conversations, and those who had one too many of the complimentary drinks left, propping themselves up at the odd table.

I haven't seen Maria return. And Todd has disappeared.

"Go." She smiles at me. "You've got an early start tomorrow. I can stay with the team and make sure everyone is okay."

"If you're sure?" I look at her for confirmation, even though this is our usual routine. Emily always handles the last few stragglers, her energy never wavering even at the final hour. On more than one occasion, she's secured a generous last-minute donation from someone who's stayed late—especially if the reason of their late departure is the company they're enjoying without their spouse.

Emily's eyes land on a man I recognize who works in corporate finance. He's sat, running his hand up and down the leg of the red-headed woman next to him.

"His wife's a brunette." Emily raises a brow at the two of them and then turns to me. "As always. It has been a pleasure. Same again in three months?"

"Sure. Just give Harley the date. We'll work it out."

"You're the best, Griff." She slides her hands up to the back of my neck and pulls me to her, kissing me on the cheek.

"Do my brothers know you say that?" I chuckle as she narrows her eyes at me.

"Hey! The oldest siblings must stick together. Even though technically I'm also the youngest." She laughs and then gives me a small wave. "I'll call you tomorrow. Take you for lunch in the week to say thank you."

"There's no need."

"You say that every time. And I take you every time. So just say yes now and save us the breath," she says as she walks away, laughing.

"Fine." I exhale, knowing she's right.

I waste no time racing out of the ballroom into the foyer on the slight chance Maria might have stuck around and been chatting to someone. I need to speak to her. Find out what the hell is going on in her head. That's the second time she's run away from me. No one has ever run out on me once, let alone twice. *Why the fuck is she holding back so damn hard?* I get that she's been used and hurt by men in the past. But she can't deny whatever this is between us. If I can entertain the idea of getting involved with someone I work with again, then so can she.

I blow out a long breath. It only takes a second to realize she isn't here. I'll speak to her tomorrow. No more of that shit of avoiding me at work. I'll book out her entire schedule for the week to have one long meeting with me if she tries to pull that crap again. She won't escape me this time. Not without telling me to my face that she wants me to stop. I'm not an asshole. If she really wants me to stop, then I will. But only if I believe that's what she genuinely wants. And judging by the way her body bends to my will when we are together, I doubt that's the case. Our body, our desires, they're so innate, so primal—they never lie. She can tell herself that she doesn't want me. But I know the truth. I've tasted it seep from her body. I've felt it scream against my fingers.

She wants it as much as me, and she *will* be mine.

I head over to the main doors to go home.

"Good evening, Mr. Parker." Earl tips his hat in greeting.

"Good evening, Earl. You swapped to work the late shift?"

"I did. Lenny wanted to take the missus out for an anniversary dinner." He runs a hand over his silvery stubble. "Keep the romance alive, that's what I say. Happy wife, easy life."

"I can see your logic." I smirk.

"And know when they don't have eyes for you, too. I admire you young men for your persistence. But if a lady's heart isn't for you, it likely never will be. You can't force it." He holds a finger up in the air, waggling it as he frowns.

I shove my hands in my pockets and stare out into the evening air. "That's very true."

"Like that young gentleman with Maria tonight." Earl screws his face up. "Todd, is it? The one from the supply company, with the curls." He twirls his fingers by his ears.

I immediately tense, snapping my eyes back to Earl.

"Why? What's he done?"

If that fucker laid a finger on her, I swear he will be eating through a tube when I'm done with him.

"Oh, nothing. She's a strong one, Maria." His eyes glitter as he looks at me. "I like her. You did well bringing her here."

"What about Todd, Earl?" I press.

He waves a hand in the air. "Nothing she can't handle. Don't you worry. He was insisting on walking her to her door. But she soon got that idea out of him. Last I saw, he was trying to hail a cab."

I clear my throat. "Good."

Fucker, I hope it takes him to the next state over and keeps on driving.

"It's a shame she was in such a hurry to leave. Otherwise, she wouldn't have missed this." Earl reaches into his inner jacket pocket and pulls out a long, glittering strand, every part seeming to catch the moonlight and dazzle brighter than the last.

My eyes widen as I reach out. Earl drops Maria's necklace into my palm.

So that's what she was looking for.

"I was about to log it with security. It'll be kept safe and sound until she arrives in the morning."

I wrap the diamonds in my palm. "Thank you. But I'll save you the bother. I can give it to her on my way home."

"Good plan. It doesn't look like something you'd want to lose."

"No, it certainly isn't. Thank you, Earl."

I stare at my hand and the diamonds trailing out between my fingers. It's rare... exquisite. It needs special care and attention.

The type only I will give.

Chapter Seventeen

Maria

TONIGHT HAS BEEN A write-off. A total and utter—What word can I even use to describe what an absolute fuck up it's been? First Griffin and then...

"Oh God," I moan as I shake my clutch upside down and its contents clatter over the kitchen side. I don't know what I'd expected to find. It wasn't in here the first fifty times I looked. It won't have magically appeared now.

Will is going to kill me.

What if he gets fired? Or his friend from the jewelers gets fired?

I lean back against the counter and drop my head into my hands.

This is a disaster.

How can I have lost a diamond necklace that I only wore for a few hours? A necklace so expensive that the idea of telling Will makes me want to run to the bathroom and hurl. I had it on when I was in the meeting room with Griffin. I know I did because he touched it.

Right before his hands grazed my breasts. Right before I offered myself up on a platter for him—again.

"What the hell am I doing?" I whisper angrily, screwing my eyes closed. I can't think about him right now. I need to find this necklace.

Think. Think.

I definitely had it going into that room. And it was gone by the time I got back to the table and sat with Todd, Harley, and Suze. That only leaves the women's restroom, which I checked, and the meeting room, which I rushed back to after Griffin asked to talk to me. It wasn't in there either.

Maybe I can pay Will for it? I've got savings. How much can a thing like that cost? Maybe I can—

"Maria?"

There's a knock at the door as a voice calls from the other side. I walk over and open it.

"Todd? I thought you were getting a cab?"

"I was." He smiles at me and pushes off from the doorframe where he's casually leaning. "But trying to get a cab when half the gala guests are also leaving isn't going to happen. I thought I'd come see if you'd had any luck while it quietens down."

"Oh." I hesitate, shifting my weight onto my other foot.

"But hey, I can wait downstairs if—"

"No. Don't be silly. Come in."

I stand back and he saunters in, the scent of hard liquor accompanying him.

"Nice place." He walks into the middle of the open-plan kitchen and living area, his eyes casting around. He wanders about, then picks a book up from the bookshelf, raising an eyebrow as he reads the cover. "You like these, huh?" He turns, his eyes glinting.

The hairs on my arms prick up one by one, and I wrap my arms around myself.

"That's a gift from my Nan. She sent it to me."

"Hmm." Todd smiles to himself as he looks at the half-naked man on the cover of the romance book and puts it back on the shelf. "Some girls in the office read these books. They love them. Apparently, they're full of sex."

He looks at the other books on the bookshelf, running his finger over the spines.

"Like I said. It was a gift. I haven't read it yet." I tighten my arms around myself, a feeling I can't place creeping over me.

He purses his lips. "Shame."

I stand fixed on the spot as he picks my bottle of perfume up off the coffee table. He lifts it to his nose and sniffs.

"So? Any thoughts where the necklace could have gone to?" He turns to me, and something about the way he's looking at me, paired with the slur in his voice, makes my throat suddenly dry.

"No. But it'll turn up." I pull my shoulders back, hoping I sound convincing. Hoping I sound confident.

Todd casts his eyes slowly from my head, over my cleavage and to the side split in my dress.

"Maybe it slipped off inside your dress. Although there aren't many places it could be hiding." His glassy eyes come to rest on my breasts. "Not in a dress like that."

"I think you'll be able to hail a cab now, Todd." I turn toward the door to show him out, but he stays where he is. His eyes are still on me when I turn back around. "Todd. You need to leave now."

He looks at me and blinks, then presses the fingers of one hand into his eyes.

"Yes. Of course, sorry. I'm sorry, Maria." He walks over to me looking embarrassed, and my shoulders drop as I exhale.

"Good night, Todd." I reach for the handle.

His palm connects with the top of the door, slamming it back into the frame before I can open it an inch.

"Maybe we can do this again another night? Just you and me next time?"

He's so close that the sour alcoholic fumes emanating from him fill my nose and claw at my throat.

I swallow and turn away. "I don't think that's a good idea."

He sucks his teeth, dropping his head. "No. You're right. You're right. Sorry, I... one too many drinks. I just thought we had... a connection, you know?"

He looks at me from under his brows and it takes all my energy to swallow the burning lump down in my throat so I can speak.

"I'm sorry, Todd. I don't date people I work with."

He nods. "Of course, of course. Can't blame a guy for trying, though."

His eyes return to my breasts.

"Good night, Todd," I say firmly.

He takes his hand off the door and I waste no time reaching back for the handle.

"I've got it," he says as he wrenches the door open and straight into my face.

"Shit!" My hand flies up and I clutch my cheekbone, one eye on fire like it's about to bulge out of the socket.

"Maria! I'm so sorry! I'm an idiot... the door... I..." Todd reaches for me, and I take a step back, holding my other hand up.

"It's fine. It was an accident. Just go. I'm fine." I wince as each word digs the throbbing pain further into my skull.

"No. You need ice, you need..." Todd stumbles over to the refrigerator, opening it and grabbing an ice tray from the freezer drawer.

How much did he drink?

"Todd, really, I'm okay."

"You're not. Here." He grabs a towel and goes to empty the ice cubes into it, but his hands fumble and he sways, sending them flying all over the floor, along with the tray, which bangs loudly, making me jump.

"Just go! Please!" I cry as I hold my cheek.

He walks toward me, and I hold my breath as he pauses in the doorway. For one second, my heart stalls in my chest, and its beat is replaced with shards of ice-cold fear.

He isn't going to leave.

Then he steps over the threshold.

"Good night, Mar—"

I slam the door shut and lock it, pressing myself back against it as I suck in deep breaths, my heart hammering in my chest, my hands trembling.

I stay there for a few minutes, or maybe it's ten. I don't know. All I know is I can't make my feet move until my blood stops rushing in my ears like I'm caught in a riptide. Submerged beneath an unforgiving wave in a treacherous sea.

Whoosh. Whoosh. Whoosh.

The ice melting, forming small puddles across the floor. The refrigerator door is still open, so I go to close it.

A knock at the door has my heart leaping into my chest.

Shit!

I clutch my chest.

"Go home, Todd!" I shout, my voice betraying me and cracking.

"It's Griffin," a deep voice calls back.

Griffin?

I walk over to the door, pausing my hand mid-air over the handle. There is smeared blood on the back of it.

"What do you want?"

"I have your necklace. It was handed to Earl."

I fumble with the lock as my fingers continue in their shaking, cracking it open a fraction. Griffin's clear blue eyes pierce mine as I peer through the small gap.

"A guest must have found it." He opens his palm, and the glittery strand tumbles out, dangling from one long finger.

"Thank you." My voice comes out as a croak. I thought I'd be pleased to see that necklace again, ecstatic even. But I'm numb, like this is all a dream and not real.

I open the door wider and reach out for the necklace. Griffin's eyes widen and his brows shoot up his forehead.

"What happened?"

I stare at him like I've had a spotlight shone on me. "What?"

"Your face, Maria. What happened?" His dark brows draw together as he takes a step toward me.

I press my fingertips to my cheek. The tender skin is hot, and my cheeks are wet.

"It was an accident," I whisper.

Griffin looks past me into the kitchen, where the ice tray now lies in one large puddle of water and my clutch contents are strewn across the worktop.

"Did he touch you?"

"What?"

"Did he *touch* you?" Griffin repeats, his voice a low rumble. His gaze sharpens and intensifies with each word as he watches me.

I stare back, unable to form words, the throbbing kicking up a notch in my face.

"Todd," Griffin growls. "You thought it was him at the door when I knocked. Did he do this?"

His eyes roam over my face and then down my body as though he is checking for any other signs of injury. They come back up to my cheek again.

"I will fucking kill him." Griffin's eyes blaze, their incredible blue deepening, shining and dangerous. A fire crafted of shadows. I've never seen anything like it.

"No. It wasn't... he didn't... it was just an accident." My voice comes in pants.

Why can't I think straight? Why does my voice sound weird?

Griffin's eyes immediately soften, and he steps toward me.

"It's okay." He reaches up and cups my cheek, his large hand gentle against my skin as concern etches itself over his features. "It's okay."

My legs lose some of their strength and I crumple against his chest, relief flooding my body, easing the tension in each and every one of my muscles as I allow him to hold me to him.

As I allow his warmth and scent to soothe me.

His arms are strong around me, giving me what I so desperately need right now.

Someone I trust.

"I've got you, Sweetheart. You're okay." His lips are in my hair, whispering, calming, reassuring. "I've got you," he repeats. "I've got you."

"I'm sorry." I sniff into his chest, welcoming more of the warmth his broad body is providing. *When did it get so cold in here?* "I don't know where all this is coming from. He didn't touch me. He didn't *do* anything really... it's me... I just felt... I thought..."

Griffin tightens his arms around me, and I sink further into him, my palms held against my face as I suck in shaky breaths.

"He'd had a lot to drink, and he was saying things, looking at me... it didn't feel right. He sniffed my perfume, and I just wanted him to leave... I just wanted him to leave." My voice is so small, muffled by Griffin's chest. His heartbeat is strong against my temple as I turn my head to the side and rest it against his chest.

"And your face?" he coaxes gently.

"Todd opened the door into it. He didn't mean to. He was leaving, and I was standing in the wrong place, that's all."

Griffin pulls back and cradles my face in both hands, looking deep into my eyes.

"It's not your fault. None of it is your fault."

I stare back at him, my lips parted as he strokes my cheeks with his thumbs, wiping away the tears I didn't know had fallen. He brushes a loose strand of hair away from my cheek and dusts the back of his knuckles against my cheek.

"Let's get you cleaned up."

He closes and locks the front door, then takes my hand in his and leads me toward the kitchen, pulling a stool out at the small island and waiting as I sit up onto it. A frown mars his handsome features as he steps around the puddle on the floor and goes to the refrigerator, pulling out a bag of frozen peas and wrapping them in a towel.

"Keep this on. It will help the swelling." He places the bundle carefully against my cheek and the corners of his eyes pinch when I wince.

"It stings."

"It will. You've got a cut."

I nod, looking down at my other hand. I'm still clutching the diamond necklace, its intricate detail indented into my palm where I've been squeezing it.

"I can't believe I almost lost it. I don't deserve something so beautiful," I whisper sadly.

"It's only beautiful because of the person wearing it," Griffin says, taking his hand away from the pea pack as I take over and hold it up. His brow creases again as he studies my face.

I stare up at him, shivering as goosebumps pop up, spreading up my arms and over my shoulders.

"Thank you. For the pack."

He nods, extracting the necklace from my fingers and laying it down on the counter and looking at my arms.

"Do you feel cold?"

"I'm fine."

"It's the adrenaline. Keep that on your cheek and I'll turn the shower on hot for you. Just keep the water off your face." He strides off in the direction of the bathroom before I have a chance to object.

He returns a minute later. "It's warmed up, and I got you a towel out. I'll wait here. Call me if you get dizzy."

"Griffin, I'm fine—"

"Call me," he repeats, pulling the stool out so I can slide down to the floor.

His expression is serious as I turn and walk away.

"Wait." I stop and incline my face over my shoulder. "Can you get the zipper for me? It's hard for me to reach. Please?" I add as he frowns, making no effort to move closer to me.

His frown deepens as he steps forward. His warm hands skim the dip of my lower back as he unzips my dress all the way to the lace waistband of my panties underneath.

"Thanks," I mumble, looking back. He's already turned away, a grim expression on his beautiful face.

I shuffle off to the bathroom and close the door.

He looks mad. Maybe he thinks this *is* my fault. That I led Todd in when I shouldn't have. That I should have read the signs better. I drop the pack into the sink and take in my reflection in the mirror above. An angry red mark, which is rapidly turning a shade of purple, has settled itself across my cheek, and a thin red line covered in dry blood extends over my cheekbone toward the corner of my eye. Thank God it was only my apartment door and not something larger or heavier. I could have been knocked out cold.

I step under the hot jet and wash, layering the suds up over my body as I try to warm up and stop the shakes which have taken over my body. It feels like an eternity until I'm finally warm enough to turn the water off. I step out and dry quickly, pulling on a toweling robe before tackling my face at the vanity. I use my cleanser and remove every trace of make-up, then gently dab at the cut, cleaning off the dried blood. It's swollen and puffy, making my eye look darker underneath, but it's nothing some concealer won't cover once the swelling goes down.

No one will know.

I pull out all the pins holding my hair up, and it tumbles down around my shoulders. I look like I've had a dreadful night. There's no denying that. But the shower and freshening up has made the world of difference. My breathing and heart rate are back to normal, and the shakes have all but disappeared. All that remains on the inside is the lingering unease in my chest. I have a meeting with Todd scheduled on Monday. The thought of it makes my stomach roll with nausea and I gag before I can stop it. I grip the edge of the porcelain sink, taking in some slow breaths. Then I brush my teeth twice, trying desperately to scrub away the taste in my mouth and the tightness in my chest.

When I'm done, I leave and go back down the hallway. The kitchen floor is dry, no sign of the ice tray, and the contents of my clutch have been placed back inside, the necklace laid on the counter next to it.

Griffin looks up from his place on the sofa. He's sat, leaning forward, his elbows resting on his knees, still in full tuxedo. Mascara and tear stains smear across his once perfect white shirt.

"I'm sorry about your shirt."

He looks down as though just noticing. "It's only a shirt. Sit. I made you a drink."

He blows out a breath and runs his hands through his hair as I perch next to him. I reach forward and pick up the steaming mug on the table in front of me.

"You made me hot chocolate?"

He tilts his head to the side and gives me a slow, rueful smile. It lights up his eyes, and my stomach flips, forgetting the nausea that was lurking there ten minutes ago.

"I can't promise it'll be as good as one from The Songbird kitchen, but I figured it might help. Earl used to make it for me and my brothers whenever we got hurt... or into a fight with each other." He smirks, but it quickly falls from his face as he grows serious again.

I take a sip of the creamy chocolate, welcoming the warmth it sends through my body.

"You would tell me if he had touched you, wouldn't you?" He turns to me, and his eyes are full of something I can't place. *Regret? Anger? Guilt?*

"He didn't. I promise."

His jaw ticks. "But he made you feel threatened. Made you feel unsafe in your own home."

I struggle to keep my voice even as the image of the Todd's glassy eyes pushes to the front of my mind. The way he sniffed my perfume. "He had too many drinks, that's all. He's never made me feel like that before when I've been with him."

Griffin hisses out a breath, running a hand over his jaw. "You will never be alone with him again. He could have—"

"Please. I don't want to talk about it anymore tonight." The tightness in my chest returns as my voice cracks.

Griffin's eyes snap to mine, full of the same earlier fire once again. His gaze falls over my cheek and then back to my eyes, his own softening as I plead silently with mine.

"Okay."

"Thank you for bringing the necklace back. I thought I'd lost it in the meeting room..." I trail off, not wanting to go down the road to where that conversation might lead, either. I don't have the energy tonight.

"Someone handed it to Earl. I don't know where they found it." Griffin drops his head into his hands and rubs his temples as he exhales.

"Well, whoever it was, I'm glad they did." I smile.

He looks at me again, then stands, taking his phone from the coffee table and slipping it into his pocket.

"Will you call me if you don't feel well in the night, or if you need anything?" he asks, heading toward the front door.

"You're going?" I fail to hide the panic creeping into my voice at the thought of being alone.

He pauses and turns back to me. "You need to get some rest."

"Sure, but—" I try to stand, but my head spins and I fall back down again.

Griffin is on his knees in front of me in a shot, his warm palms cradling my face as his eyes search mine.

"I'm calling my doctor. You're dizzy."

"No, no, I'm fine."

I look back at him, relishing the sensation of his hands against my skin. I don't want to tell him I am one hundred percent sure that the head spin was merely a result of the night's champagne and the hot shower. I only hit my cheekbone. I don't need his concern. Even if I'm welcoming it, cupped around my cheeks.

"You're not fine. I'm not leaving you alone unless you agree to get checked out."

"No doctor," I whisper.

His brows knit together. "Then I don't leave."

"Fine." I stare back into his clear blue eyes.

He looks at the ceiling, taking his hands away from my face.

"Fine," he huffs like a petulant child who hasn't gotten their own way.

I stand again, and he jumps to his feet so he can hold me around the waist. I let him help me to the bedroom, one arm wrapped around me protectively as he tells me to take my time. Something inside me makes my feet slow, and I lean into him as we reach my bedroom.

"Thank you." I pull the covers back as we reach the bed. "Now, turn around."

"What?" He frowns at me.

"I sleep naked. Turn. Around."

"Maria, I'll get you some clothes. Tell me where they are."

"Turn," I repeat.

He stares at me, so I spin my fingers in the air. His jaw stiffens, and he glances at me one more time before he turns.

I don't sleep naked. That's a lie. But I don't fancy digging out some clean pajamas right now. And there's no way I want him going through my drawers.

I just want to get into bed and leave this night in the past.

I take the robe off and throw it past Griffin onto a chair. His shoulders straighten and he clears his throat as the robe sails past.

Then I slip under the covers and pull them up to my chin.

"You can turn back around now."

He doesn't move.

Did he even hear me?

Then slowly, he turns and undresses, holding my eyes with his as he shrugs his jacket off, laying it carefully over the chair with my robe. Next, he undoes his bowtie, his hand flicking out to the side as he pulls it free of his collar and it makes a whipping sound. Lastly, he removes his makeup-stained shirt and bends down to pull off each shoe.

He walks around the bed in just his pants and lowers himself down next to me, lying flat on his back on top of the covers, his eyes cast up to the ceiling.

I turn on my side to face him, trying my best to ignore the broad muscles of his bare chest and shoulders mere inches away from me. The heat from his body crosses the gap between us and the scent of his skin washes over me, bringing with it a calmness—a reassurance that I don't need to worry about anything else tonight.

Todd wasn't going to hurt me, I'm sure of that. But I'm still shaking. However, Griffin being here, his breathing filling the silence—it somehow makes it all seem better. His darkened gaze and knotted, thoughtful brow next to me gives me a sense of... peace. Maybe it's because he's always in control.

Whatever it is, I'm grateful he's here.

"Griffin?" I murmur. "Thank you."

He turns to me, his brilliant blue eyes holding mine. "Anytime, Sweetheart."

Sweetheart.

I smile at him as he turns his attention back to the ceiling.

"I'm telling you, though. It better not be baboon feeding time at the zoo." He reaches up and taps the wall above his head, which adjoins Reed's apartment. "No way can my ears un-hear that shit."

I look at his serious face again and laugh quietly. "You're funny."

"If you think that, you're definitely concussed. Now get some rest."

I bite my lip, sure that a ghost of a smile plays on his lips. I shuffle, about to get comfortable, the weight of Griffin's body on the duvet next to me making me feel something I haven't felt in the company of a man like this in a long time.

Safe.

Chapter Eighteen

Griffin

I PLACE THE GIANT bouquet on Maria's doorstep and leave it there. She was fast asleep with her hair sprayed out over the pillow when I left. The only thing ruining the angelic sight was the deep bruise which had developed through the night.

Fucking Todd.

I knew that asshole was trouble. I could tell by the way he looked at her. Couldn't keep his fucking eyes to himself. Well, now he won't have time to be looking anywhere, except maybe for a new job. One late-night, unwelcome phone call to his boss while Maria was in the shower last night, and our contract with their supply company was over. Like I would ever let him anywhere near her again. I was all set to race out of there and break his neck last night. But Maria? Seeing her like that... shaken, vulnerable. I've never seen her distressed before. There was no way I was leaving her alone.

I rest my palm against the closed door, drawing in a breath as I squeeze my eyes shut.

If that asshole had touched her...

I remove my hand and look at the flowers again. Then stalk off down the hallway.

I catch up with Reed and then head into the office. I spend the morning speaking to contacts about new suppliers and putting out some feelers. Then I log into The Songbird security system and bring up the footage for Friday night. I follow Todd from camera to camera, zooming in, witnessing the way his eyes drink in Maria's body whenever she isn't watching.

Asshole.

I bring up the camera for the hallway that leads down to the meeting room. Maria and I show up on it, heading into the room together, then around fifteen minutes later, Emily and Harley can be seen walking off together after our talk through the door. A little after, Maria exits, a deep flush over her cheeks. She turns and looks back at the closed door for a moment, before stalking off toward the women's restroom.

She isn't wearing the necklace.

I fast forward and Todd appears a minute after I leave, darting in through the door before it shuts behind me. A few minutes later the door opens, and he looks out, checking both ways before he walks out.

Son of a bitch. What the hell was he up to?

Further scrutiny of the night's CCTV brings up nothing interesting, so I stop for the day and head over to check on Maria on my way back to my apartment.

When I get there, the flowers are gone.

"Maria?" I call as I knock on the door.

She opens it with a bright smile. Her face is free of make-up, so the true extent of last night's bruising is clearly visible.

"Griffin. Come in. We need to talk."

She turns, her long dark waves tumbling down her back as I follow her into the open plan space.

"Thank you for the flowers. They're beautiful. But you really didn't need to."

They're in a vase on the coffee table and she smiles when I notice them, but quickly looks away as she sits on one of the kitchen stools and motions for me to join her.

I take a seat, and she pulls her laptop over the counter, placing it between us.

"I've found this company who can supply us. Well, Emily suggested I look them up. She called this morning to see how I was. Super early. She must not need sleep. Anyway, the guy in charge is one of her big donators. I was looking over their—"

"What are you doing?" I frown at her.

"What do you mean?" Her forehead wrinkles, but she keeps her eyes on the screen as she scrolls down the webpage.

"How long have you been up doing this? You should be resting, Maria." Irritation bubbles in my stomach.

She's ignored what I said.

"I'm not sick, Griffin." She glances at me, then back at the screen. "This won't sort itself. We need a new supply contract sorted ASAP."

"Says who?"

She sighs. "You canceled our contract with Todd's firm last night. I heard you on the phone when I got out of the shower. I knew you would do something like that."

"You think I want to do business with a guy like Todd?"

She side-eyes me. "I knew you would fly off the handle."

A fire erupts in my chest.

"You knew I would—Maria! The guy is a sexual assault waiting to happen." I slam my palm down on the counter. "You think I want him around you?"

"I could have still worked with him, Griffin. You didn't need to start making decisions about *my* contracts with *my* suppliers, for the spa that *I* run." She turns and faces me head-on.

"For the spa in *my* hotel!"

She rolls her eyes. "And there it is."

"What the fuck's that supposed to mean?" I glare at her.

"You know what? Maybe it's better I go back to California now. Because I don't know why you offered me this job if you can't trust me to make any decisions by myself."

I run my hands through my hair. What the hell is going on? Where is all of this coming from again?

"We've been through this, Maria," I grit out, fighting to maintain composure. This woman tests my last nerve.

"Yeah." She snorts, slamming the laptop closed. "Griffin-trusts-no-one-Parker. How great for the rest of us!"

I count to three.

"I came here to see if you were okay. How the hell did it turn into you attacking me?"

She looks at me for a long time.

"I don't know," she says, her shoulders dropping as all her fight leaves her.

I've been through the door all of five minutes and I'm already pissing her off. I thought we turned a corner this past couple of weeks, but maybe she does still hate me.

"I feel like no matter how hard I try, nothing will ever please you. Not unless you do it yourself. I wanted to come here and create something special."

"You are."

Even in the short time she's been here, the spa has soared. Bookings are up, it's being talked about every-where. We've got journalists queuing up to come and write pieces on the new treatment menu Maria created. She's completely transforming it.

"I'm not." She exhales, sweeping her hair over her shoulder. "You don't trust me to make decisions. You don't trust anyone."

I clench my jaw as sourness creeps over my tongue. She raises an eyebrow at me, the one above her good eye. The other eye looks smaller where her cheek is swollen underneath.

"You don't understand. I *want* to," I confess, my words heavy with meaning.

For you, Sweetheart... I want to.

"I do understand, Griffin. I've been let down by people I thought I could trust."

I exhale slowly. She's right. She knows how it feels to be screwed over by someone you thought you could rely on. But what she doesn't understand is how it feels to be looking around you at work, with some people you have worked alongside for years, and wonder, was it them? Was it them who fucked you over? Is it them who laugh about it now? *Stupid, idiot Parker. Can't even trust his own staff.* And knowing that even though it's been months, you're no fucking closer to uncovering the truth?

"Fine." I rest my elbows on the counter and drag my hands down my face. "You sort the new supplier contracts. Choose whoever you want. Just tell Harley when you decide so she can do the paperwork."

Maria presses her lips together. "Thank you."

I nod, my jaw set as I stand.

"Griffin?" Maria catches my hand and stands with me. "Yes?"

"I appreciate what you did last night."

I nod again, not sure how to respond. I would have done anything to help her last night. My primal urge was to take care of her. To protect her.

"It was nothing."

"Not to me." She looks down at our hands, where I've subconsciously entwined my fingers with hers. "You were there when I needed someone."

"I would do it again in a heartbeat." I pause and clear my throat. "Why did you run out last night?"

Now is not the time to ask. She may think she's okay. But she's throwing herself into work and setting up new contracts so she doesn't have to think about last night and how that scumbag made her feel.

But I still ask.

I have to know.

"Last night?" She drops my hand and crosses her arms over her chest.

"From the meeting room."

Her pulse flutters in her neck and she swallows.

"You're my boss. We work together," she says, as though that's all the explanation that's required.

"And?" I fire back.

"And haven't you heard the saying, don't mix business and pleasure?" She fixes her gaze to the side, away from me.

I cup her chin and turn her face back to me. "It's my hotel. I make the rules."

She looks at my lips, then away again. I will get nowhere today, trying to explain to her that I don't care about fucking sayings or rules. Not when all I think about is her. Her energy, her spirit... her taste. And after last night and Todd... today is not the day to think with my dick. I'm not a jerk, despite what she may think.

She turns her face out of my grip. "I'm going to keep working on this." She gestures to her laptop. "I'll see you at work."

My eyes roam over her purple cheek one final time. "You will."

She parts her lips as though she's going to say something else, then she gives me a small smile and walks over to open the door.

"Bye, Griffin."

"See you Monday," I reply.

I walk out the door and don't look back.

"Harley, hold my calls. I'm heading down to the spa before it opens."

"Okay, Mr. Parker."

I wait impatiently in the elevator as the floor numbers change on the display. Since when was the thing so fucking slow? It stops on the finance floor and Will joins me.

"Good morning, Mr. Parker," he says in a singsong voice.

"Morning, Will."

"How was your weekend? The gala was an enormous success, as usual. I swear Emily is a witch." He looks at me, his eyes widening. "No! I mean, in a good way. Like a white one, or a magic genie or something... Each one is better than the last."

"She knows what she's doing." My lips twitch as he pulls at his collar with one hand. "How is your friend, by the way?"

"Friend?" Will asks, looking confused.

"The one who lent you the jewelry."

His neck flushes and he clutches the files he's carrying close to his chest. "Oh, yes. He's fine. Thank you for asking."

The doors open and I step out into the lobby. "Good thing nothing went missing."

"No... of course. Absolutely." Will's words tumble out. "Very lucky. Blessed."

"Will?"

He straightens. "Yes, Mr. Parker?"

My lips curl into a small smile. "Leave his details with Harley, please. He might be able to assist me with something."

"Yes, sir." Will grins at me as I stride off toward the spa.

My fingers twitch the moment I round the corner of the corridor where the main spa doors are.

Blond curls.

"What the hell are you doing here?" I yell, zoning in on Todd, who is standing at the main desk like he has the right to be there. Like he has the right to be wherever the fuck he pleases.

Not in my hotel.

"He was just leaving," Maria's cool tone clips from the other side of the desk.

I look straight at her cheek. She must have covered it with make-up because all trace of the bruise is gone, like nothing happened.

"I came to talk to Maria." Todd turns back to her, dropping his voice. "I could lose my job. Do you think that's fair? All over a misunderstanding."

Red overtakes my vision as my pulse beats so loud in my ears my head might be at risk of exploding. I cross the room in three purposeful strides and grab the front of Todd's shirt, twisting it in my fist. A button flies off and skitters across the stone floor.

"You have the audacity to come in here and insinuate Maria misunderstood your fucking leery, pathetic ass?" I spit.

He tries to pull away from me, but I've got a tight hold on him, and he can't move anywhere.

"Consider yourself lucky it's only your career you're going to lose." I glare at him, our noses an inch apart.

His mouth twists into a grimace, and I drag in a rough breath, counting to three.

"Get the fuck out." I shove him away from me and he slams into the wall. "While you still can."

He recovers himself, glaring at me. "I'm telling you, that's all it was. A misunderstanding. I never touched her. And if she told you otherwise, then she's a liar as well as a cock tease."

Wham!

Pain courses across my knuckles as they connect with soft tissue and bone. Todd slumps to the floor, grabbing his face. I don't know how I got to him so fast, only that the feeling of my fist connecting with his face is the best release I've had in a long time.

"Get. Out," I growl.

He staggers to his feet, blood pouring from his nose. Someone must have called security, because two of my guys come running in and each grabs an arm. Todd snorts when he sees them.

"I'll get you for this, Parker!"

"No, Todd. You won't. Unless you want to be explaining sexual harassment and intimidation charges to the police, and adding criminal to your resume."

I stretch out my fingers by my side as my hand throbs.

"Now I get it." He looks from me to Maria, who is standing pale-faced, staring at me. "She's fucking you." He laughs, looking at Maria. "It makes sense now. That's what you were doing in that room Saturday night. Fucking your boss on the meeting table. Real classy."

"Get him out of here before I kill him!"

My heart's hammering in my chest as security escorts him away.

What the hell was he doing, thinking he could come here like that? Cause a scene, try to talk to Maria. To...

"Maria?" I rush over to her. "Are you okay, did he—"

"What the hell?" she hisses at me, shoving me in the chest. "You're lucky none of the team are in yet. They'd have seen you hit him. What were you thinking?" She glares at me.

I suck in air through my nose, my eyes bugging out. "You heard what he said about you. Jesus Christ! He can't speak about you like that."

"Of course he shouldn't. But you don't need to almost knock him out." Her gaze drops to the small droplets of blood on the floor. "I need to clean this up before anyone comes in."

"Maria." I grab her chin, forcing her eyes to meet mine. "I will never let anyone speak about you like that. *Ever*. And if they try, they'd better pray to God for a painless crossover when I kill them."

"But—"

Heat fires across my chest. "No! No fucking buts. Get used to it because I *will not* apologize for it."

"Why?" She glares, her head tilting back to look at me.

I take another step forward so our chests press together. Mine is rising and falling fast as I struggle to rein my anger back in. I'm about ready to explode from the way Todd spoke to her. If security hadn't arrived, it would have been paramedics taking him out.

How can she not see why? How can she not understand that the idea of anyone laying a finger on her makes me want to burn down the world if I had to, to hunt them down?

I stare deep into her eyes, daring her to look away as I catch my breath.

She doesn't.

She holds my eyes in defiance, her strong will glittering out in them.

I lift my throbbing hand and dust the backs of my fingers over the concealed bruise on her cheek. Her eyes pinch at the corners. It must still be tender, and that makes my anger ebb away, making way for concern as I lower my lips until they're hovering over hers.

"Because, Sweetheart, as much as you fight it, we both know... there's only one outcome between us."

Her eyelashes flutter as she blinks and looks up at me. The soft pink of her lips glistens where she darts her tongue out and wets them.

"Which is?" she whispers.

She looks so beautiful standing here, gazing up at me, her signature fire now subtle in her hazel eyes.

But I know it's there. I see it. I feel it. *I crave it.*

Her pupils widen as I stroke her cheek again. A smile spreads over my lips.

"The one where... You. Are. Mine."

Then I lower my lips down onto hers.

Chapter Nineteen

Maria

HIS WARM LIPS PRESS against mine. Everything about him surrounds me as he kisses me like he's starved—like he's not had human touch for an eternity. The solid muscles of his chest push against my breasts as my back is forced into the counter behind me. Large strong fingers wrap around my face, tilting it so he can kiss me deeper, and the scent of his skin reaches down into my senses and evokes a deep, raw urge to pull him closer and succumb.

Succumb to everything that is *Griffin Parker.*

"Griff—" I pant.

"Don't," he says, his lips still against mine. "Don't say anything. Just kiss me, Maria. Stop *fucking* fighting me." He strokes my cheeks with his large hands, and I oblige, wrapping my arms around his neck and kissing him back as fire ignites low in my stomach.

"Fuck, you're beautiful," he groans as he sucks my bottom lip between his teeth and then dives back into the kiss that's making every cell in my body tingle. I tighten my arms around his neck and allow my body to sink further into his.

God, this man. I never stood a chance.

"Um, Maria?" There's a giggle from over near the door.

I try to jump back, but Griffin has me pinned firmly in place, his hands never leaving my face.

"What do you need her for, Harley? She's busy," he answers, resting his forehead against mine, his eyes blazing into mine.

My heart is about to beat right out of my chest by the way he's looking at me.

"Nothing. I was just checking everything was okay. I got the security alert upstairs. But I can see it's all under control," Harley says.

"Yes. All under control," Griffin growls, his eyes dropping to my lips as his fingers caress my cheeks.

"I'll head back upstairs then."

"Goodbye, Harley," he says, then he presses his lips back onto mine and slides his tongue into my mouth.

I dive my hands into his hair as my tongue finds his and I kiss him back with an urgency that matches his.

He infuriates me, struggling to relinquish the tight control he has over everything. He's both my worst nightmare in business, and my heavenly daydream in pleasure. Because one thing is obvious—when it comes to the physical, Griffin Parker has complete and utter control over me. And what's more, I can't get enough of it. It's as though giving my trust to him with my body is the freest I've ever felt in my life.

"What did Todd mean?" I ask between kisses.

Griffin's shoulders tense beneath my arms. "Why are you thinking about that fucker?"

"I'm not... I..." His lips travel to my neck and kiss down to my collarbone. "He said he saw us in that room. Was he following us?"

"Following you," Griffin murmurs against my neck. "He'll never come near you again, Maria. I guarantee it." He pulls me closer.

What was Todd planning to do if I had been alone that night and not with Griffin?

He must feel my body stiffen, because his attention leaves my neck, and he pulls back to look at my face.

"I'm fine," I reassure him. "It's creepy. But he's gone now."

Griffin looks at me like he doesn't believe me.

"I'm fine," I murmur, pulling his lips back to mine so I don't have to talk about it.

He's more than happy to play along with my denial game, kissing me back deeply. I could get lost in his kisses. Come up for air days later and still want to dive straight back in for more.

How could anyone ever have enough of a man as passionate and sensual as Griffin Parker?

"The team, they'll be here soon," I whisper as his lips travel over my cheek, gently kissing where my bruise is carefully covered with makeup.

"I know they will. But every time I let you go, you run." His warm breath flows over my ear, and a shiver runs up my spine.

"You're a lot to handle." I look into his eyes as he brings his face back in front of me.

"I've been waiting my whole fucking life for a woman like you to handle me."

I gaze back into his clear blue eyes. His lids grow heavy, and he sucks in a breath as I slowly brush my lips back and forth over his, a smile growing on them.

"I need to start work." I press a last kiss to his lips and remove my arms from around his neck.

Despite how aroused I am with him being here, I am *here*. At work. About to be joined by my entire team for our morning meeting.

"And my boss is a total control freak," I add. "He'll have a heart attack in his designer suit if he thinks I'm using company time to—"

"To what?" Griffin steps back, but instead of moving away, he rests his hands on either side of me on the counter, leaning forward so I'm pinned between his arms.

Heat flushes my cheeks as I stand mute, locked in place by the gleam in his eyes.

"To make that pretty cunt of yours happy?" he rasps, looking down at my lips. "Using company time to spread her wide open so the man that's been dying to touch you since he first laid eyes on you can finally fill you with—"

I gasp and his gaze darkens with a sinful smile.

"Tell me you don't want that as much as I do, Sweetheart. Tell me I'm wrong." He slips a hand under my dress and one lone finger tucks inside my panties, swiping through my wet, swollen flesh.

"Griffin," I whimper, half of me shocked at what he's doing when anyone could walk in, and the other half battling the urge to grab his hand and sink myself down onto his fingers.

Amusement dances in his eyes. "You've run out of reasons. What are you doing tonight?"

"Tonight? I'm not sure yet," I say, my legs trembling as I force myself to stay still and not grind against the finger still inside my panties, stroking my clit in teasingly slow circles.

"The answer you're looking for is *me*."

Cocky bastard.

I look into his eyes, biting back my smile.

"Is it?"

He pulls his hand back and lifts his fingers to his nose, and his eyes hold mine, his pupils dilating as he inhales.

"Definitely."

My mouth waters as he slips the soaked finger past his lips and sucks the glistening wetness off, a deep groan vibrating his throat.

"I'll pick you up at six." He turns and strides off, leaving me staring after him. "Oh, and Maria?" He looks back from the doorway.

I arch a brow at him in answer.

"Pack an overnight bag. I'm not letting you out of my sight this time."

I smooth my hands down over my dress and take a deep breath as he leaves.

What the hell am I getting myself into?

Six o'clock takes years to arrive. Maybe it's because all I've thought about all day is Griffin. He told me he's been dying to touch me since he first laid eyes on me. All this time that I thought he was an insufferable moody jerk, he's actually been what? Lusting after me? Admiring me? It doesn't make sense. Just like the fact that I've packed my best silk lingerie in my overnight bag. No sense at all.

I always said don't mix money and business with personal relationships. I learned the hard way with my dad, and then my ex. When the two things cross, it rarely turns out well. Yet here I am, waiting for my boss to pick me up to spend the night with him. And we both know there won't be any going back or escaping for me this time.

He will have me exactly where he wants me.

And if I'm honest, it's exactly where I want to be.

There's a soft knock at the door and my stomach leaps into my throat. I take one last glance in the mirror, then rush to open it.

The expression taking over his handsome features as he drinks me in—first my face, then my fitted cream dress and stilettos—is enough to make me flutter with nerves. Forget the looks predators give their prey when they're about to sink their teeth in for the kill. They're nothing compared to the heat in his stare. It consumes me all the way to my toes.

"Where are we going, then?" I ask, studying his open-necked shirt and rolled-up sleeves. I was expecting him to be in full suit, like usual, for a restaurant for dinner.

"You'll see." He kisses me on the temple, his lips lingering long enough to make the hairs stand up on the back of my neck. Then he reaches behind me and picks up my overnight bag. "Ready?"

"I think so," I falter.

His lips curl into a breathtaking smile. "Don't worry. I'll take good care of you."

"That's what I'm afraid of," I murmur as I step out into the corridor and close the door behind me.

He laughs, a deep delicious sound as his eyes crinkle at the corners. He seems different tonight—looser, lighter.

"Come on. We should get there before sunset." He takes my hand and leads me to the elevators.

"Before sunset? How far are we going?"

He doesn't answer, just smiles in response. He lets go of my hand and swipes a key card against the panel, lighting up the highest two buttons and pressing the top one.

Figures. His apartment must be on the top floor. But if we're going there for dinner, then why did he say we need to get there before sunset? It only takes minutes to get upstairs.

The lift climbs and stops on the highest floor. The doors open and Griffin takes my hand again and leads me out into a smart hallway with deep cream carpets and fresh flowers. I look at him, puzzled, and he smiles, opening a door that says Roof. We climb a small staircase and Griffin opens the door at the top, bringing me out into New York's evening air.

"What are we doing up here?" The rooftop is so high it makes the sounds of the city seem miles away below us.

"I'm taking you somewhere."

"On the roof?"

It's then the sleek, black shape behind him comes into view.

"Somewhere on that?" I fight to keep my mouth from dropping open.

A helicopter.

He has a helicopter. On his roof. I should roll my eyes. It screams billionaire. The rest of us mere mortals hail a cab. But Griffin? Griffin has his own private helipad one staircase away from his front door.

As if a private jet isn't enough.

"Is it even safe?" I eye it warily, chewing the inside of my cheek. I've never been in a helicopter in my life.

"It's perfectly safe. Especially with the pilot we have." Griffin shakes the older man's hand, who's approached us. "Bruce, this is Maria."

The tension in my chest eases and I smile gratefully at him. He looks safe and dependable. He must have hours

240

of flying experience, probably an ex-military helicopter pilot or something.

Thank God.

"It's so nice to meet you." I shake Bruce's hand, clinging to it a second longer than is probably polite.

"Thanks for getting her ready for me," Griffin says.

"No problem, Mr. Parker." Bruce extracts his hand from mine with a reassuring smile and then steps back, away from the white markings on the floor.

"Where's he going?"

"He can't stand too close, or he'll lose his head," Griffin says, leading me over to the jet-black sky bird.

He puts my bag inside, next to the tan leather holdall he took to The Bahamas, which is already loaded, then turns to me and holds out his hand.

"I'll help you strap in."

I glance back at Bruce, who's waiting patiently. "Isn't he flying us?"

Griffin frowns, his brow wrinkling. "No."

I allow myself to be placed in the front seat of the helicopter as my head spins. Griffin fastens me in and hands me a headset.

"Put this on."

My mouth gapes as realization sets in. His lips quirk, and he places a kiss on my temple.

"I told you, Sweetheart, I'll take good care of you."

He rounds the helicopter and gets in on the other side, strapping himself in and putting on his own headset. I copy him as his lips move by the microphone. "Can you hear me?" His voice carries down my headphones, and I nod back.

"I think I might be sick."

He laughs and the moonlight catches his dark hair. I swear this is a side of him I've never seen before. Who is this smiling, laughing imposter? And where is the suited, ruthless businessman I'm used to? But as he flicks switches and carries out whatever checks he's doing, I realize—I have seen him like this before. That night in The Bahamas, at dinner on the beach. For a few glorious hours, we weren't Maria Taylor and her billionaire boss, Griffin Parker. We were just Maria and Griffin, two adults relaxing and enjoying each other's company. No work, no business talk. Just two people being open and sharing parts of themselves. The parts that other people don't get to see.

My stomach lurches and I instinctively reach out and grip Griffin's arm as we rise into the air, swaying a little as the rooftop sinks away below us.

He turns to me and smiles, before setting us on a course flying straight ahead. The life of the city buzzes below us as we carve our path through the sky.

It's probably a beautiful sight. But I barely notice any of it.

Nothing is as captivating as what is right in front of my eyes.

Griffin Parker.

Calm, strong, in control.

Him.

Chapter Twenty

Maria

"That was both the scariest and most exhilarating forty-five minutes of my life!" I laugh as Griffin places our bags inside the entryway of the beach house. "I can't believe you flew that yourself."

"I've been flying for years. A birthday gift from my dad." He smiles at me. "And you were in safe hands the entire time. I would never let anything happen to you." He walks into the huge open-plan kitchen and over to the fridge, pulling out a bottle of champagne and holding it up. I nod at him before allowing my eyes to roam around the space.

"This is your house?" I ask, walking into the living area, which is lined with white wooden bookshelves. I run my fingers along the spines of the sailing books, and local guides to coves and sea life.

"One of them," he says distractedly as he steps out onto the rear deck and pops the cork.

"One of them," I repeat, stopping in front of a picture of Griffin with Emily and two other men. The four of them are flashing mega-watt smiles, the sea behind them.

"Those are my brothers." Griffin smiles as he passes me, back to the kitchen to fetch two glasses.

I look at the photo again. They are a lot like Griffin. One has the same dark hair, but stormy green eyes, and the other has blue eyes like Griffin, although a shade darker, and shorter deep chestnut toned hair.

"You all look happy." I look at Emily's wide grin as I place the photo back down.

"It was the day Emily hit her first million in charity donations. We came up here for the weekend to celebrate." He comes to stand next to me, handing me a glass.

"Did you fly them all up here in your helicopter, too?"

He smirks as he clinks his glass against mine. "Are you making fun of my choice of transport, Ms. Taylor?"

"Wouldn't dream of it." I smirk and continue my perusal of the room. "Is the whole house like this?"

"Like what?" His eyes follow mine around the whitewashed wood furniture, and over the cream sofas and shutters at the windows.

"Like something out of Coastal Living magazine."

He tips his head back and laughs.

"What's so funny?" I look back at him and he shakes his head.

"The design editor for that magazine decorated the house for me as a thank you for helping her out once."

"Pays to have friends." I smile, looking around again. It really is a beautiful house. Calming, tranquil.

Griffin watches me closely.

"Let me show you around." His eyes sparkle as he takes my hand and shows me room after room of beautifully decorated spaces, all with the same light, fresh, coastal vibe.

"So, is this where you come when you take time off work?" I ask, setting my glass down.

He takes a dish of something out of the fridge and places it in the oven.

"I try to get here as much as I can. My housekeeper knew we were coming," he adds, noticing me looking at the pre-prepared meal.

"We?"

"I had Harley call her this morning."

"Oh." I lean against the counter as I remember the delight in Harley's voice when she caught us kissing. She visited the spa a couple of times throughout the day, but I was talking with a client each time, and so she went again, barely hiding the disappointment on her face. And now she knows that I'm here with Griffin tonight. I'm definitely getting grilled when we return.

"That'll take half an hour," Griffin says, walking over and standing in front of me.

I look around the kitchen, at the watercolor beach canvas on the wall, at the giant hurricane glass vase spilling over with fresh flowers... anywhere but at him. Because I know once I do, I won't be able to stop the fire inside me from engulfing me the moment he touches me. The moment he touches me and says all the things I love to hear spill from his lips as he shows me what I've been holding back from all this time.

What I've been missing.

The air in the room stills, until all that moves is our breath, slow and rhythmic, in time with one another.

"Maria?"

I take a deep breath and flick my eyes to his. Their bright blue grabs hold of me, and it seems fitting that we're at the ocean for this, because his eyes are the color of water I want to dive into. Dive into, drink from, bathe in... every damn thing possible.

"Yes?"

His eyes roam over my face and come to rest on my lips. "Say it."

"Say what?" I gaze up at him.

He lifts his hand and trails the back of one finger over the side of my face, then down my neck, his eyes following its journey as it comes to rest above the swell of my breasts.

He rolls his bottom lip between his teeth, watching my breasts rise as I take a deep breath.

"Give me permission to do anything I want to you."

The restraint he's exercising not to touch me any further without my consent has electricity coursing around my body, lighting up every nerve. I know once I say the word, that restraint will be gone. It will vanish, along with any chance of things ever being able to be purely professional between us.

There'll be no going back.

I wet my lips with my tongue, stalling for time, because as much as my body is vibrating with the need for him to touch me, my mind knows that once he does, I will just want more.

One night with this man will never be enough.

And there's the possibility this is all about the chase for a man like him. A man who is used to having his own way, getting whatever, or whoever, he wants. After my dad, I swore I would never gamble in my life. I've seen the destruction it leaves behind, the broken hearts.

But I find myself willing to take the risk, because in all my life, *no-one* has even come close to making me feel the way Griffin Parker does when he looks at me.

No one.

His eyes travel from my breasts and back to meet mine.

"You said you were starving for me. At the gala. You said you were *fucking* starving for me."

The muscles around his eyes twitch as he listens to me.

"I am."

The energy between us crackles in the air as I look at him. I knew what coming here meant. So did he.

But he's waiting for me to say it.

I part my lips and stand on my toes to whisper in his ear. "Maybe it's time I fed you."

He pulls back and the corner of his perfect mouth curls as his eyes flicker with the confidence of a man who always gets what he wants, sooner or later.

"About fucking time, Sweetheart."

Before I can react, he lifts me like I weigh nothing, and I wrap my legs around his waist to hold on. His eyes never leave mine, blazing like blue flames as he carries me upstairs to the master bedroom and throws me down on my back on the crisp, white sheets of the bed.

He crawls up over me and I sink my fingers into the hair at the back of his head and pull his mouth down to mine.

Our kiss is a hot, frantic mesh of lips, tongues, gasps, and moans. Every minute we've spent together up until this point creating an intense desire that we can only express by trying to climb inside each other, trying to intertwine ourselves in the fabric of one another.

He pulls back, panting, his eyes even more breathtaking in their fire.

"Come back." I reach for him, even though I need to catch my breath. But he sits back on his knees between my legs and shakes his head.

"Patience," he tuts. "I've waited a long time for you. You can wait one more minute." His eyes drink in my legs. "Keep the heels on."

It isn't a request. It's an order.

I shiver as he wraps one hand over my skin and then lifts one of my legs and runs his tongue across the top of my foot inside my shoe, and up to my ankle, the day's growth on his chin dragging against my skin. I wriggle and peel my back away from the bed. He smirks and pushes one large hand down on my stomach, holding me against the mattress.

"Someone's eager. Tell me"—he holds my other leg up by the heel of my stiletto as his tongue weaves a path up the inside of my calf—"can you feel your pulse in your cunt?"

I suck in a breath, biting my lip to hold in my moan.

The fact he's dressed in a shirt and suit pants with a Rolex on his wrist only makes his words even filthier. Even cruder. *Even more horny as hell.* I've never been spoken to with the language that Griffin uses. But each syllable that passes his devilish lips brings with it another wave of desire, another rush of heat, another clench in my core, followed by slick arousal coursing between my legs.

My hands scrunch up the sheets on either side of me, and he chuckles and places my leg down. "I thought so."

My body thrums with desire. I sit up and reach for him, but he grabs my chin in one hand before I can close the gap any further, halting my lips so they hover inches from his.

"Take it off," he hisses, squeezing my face so my lips pucker. "All of it."

He rises to his feet, his eyes holding mine as he unbuttons his shirt and throws it to the floor. My eyes rake over his toned, broad chest and stomach.

"Now!" he hisses again, unbuckling his belt, the sound of the clinking metal the opening credits to what's coming.

I reach around and unzip the back of my dress, letting it fall into a puddle around my feet. Griffin curses under his breath as he looks at my cream lace bra and thong. I wore this one specifically as the lace cuts low, causing my breasts to look like they're about to spill out over the top. Seeing his reaction, I'm glad I did.

He pulls his pants and boxers down in one swift move until he's standing gloriously naked. I swallow. His thick, hard cock with a vein running along its length hangs obnoxiously between his legs, taunting me with its arrogant confidence.

Even his cock knows I never stood a chance once I boarded that helicopter.

Now I get why he's such a dirty talker—he has the goods to more than back it up.

"You're getting distracted," he growls.

I bring my eyes back to his and unclasp my bra, my nipples pebbling as the air hits them.

"And the panties," he says, his eyes dropping to my hips.

I hook my thumbs under each side of the lace and wriggle out of them, letting them join my dress on the floor.

Griffin's jaw is set, his brows drawn together as he takes his time sweeping his eyes over my body. I stand on display for him, arousal burning low in my core.

"You're fucking perfect," he finally breathes.

He looks at me with an intensity that steals my breath, and then he closes the distance between us in one large stride and wraps a hand around my throat.

"One more thing, Sweetheart." His free hand reaches to the clip in my hair, and he yanks it out, sending my hair tumbling down my back. "Every time I fuck you, I want your hair down. Understand?"

I nod as I breathe in the air he's just expelled, growing drunk on the scent of him. He's everything I've never experienced—rough, controlling, commanding. Yet, I'm loving every second, despite knowing that I would never allow any other man to dominate me like this. *Especially* knowing I would never let any other man do this. Just him. *Only him.*

"Say it." His fingers tighten against my neck and he leans down and runs his tongue over my bottom lip.

"Hair down," I whisper.

He smiles, and then his lips are on mine, his hands fisting in my hair and forcing my head back as we kiss. I push my breasts into his chest, willing him silently to touch them. To relieve the heavy ache that's settled in my nipples since he knocked on my door at the start of the evening.

I whimper into his mouth as his hands finally leave my hair and slide down to grasp them, his thumbs rubbing over my nipples.

"Fuck," he groans into my mouth, pulling us down onto the bed as he tugs one nipple between his thumb and finger.

I hook my legs around his waist, trying to pull him even closer, but his mouth leaves me panting and writhing against the sheets as he dips his head and sucks a nipple into his hot mouth.

I moan and arch my back. Everything he does, every kiss, every touch, every word, has me loaded like a grenade that's had its ring pulled. I'm vibrating, every cell ready to explode.

"Griffin," I moan, grabbing his hair as he sinks two fingers inside me.

"You're so wet," he groans around my nipple. "So fucking *wet*."

He adds a third finger and pumps me hard as he sucks my other nipple and grazes it with his teeth. All I can do is roll around underneath his solid body, praying that he'll give me what I want soon. Because I know I'm not the one in charge. *He is.* It's always him.

He sucks my nipple one final time before leaning back on his heels and staring between my legs. He flexes his fingers, parting them inside me, stretching me wide open. The air is cold against the wetness that's seeping out all over his hand.

He bites his bottom lip and hisses, shoving my legs further apart with his free hand as he fixates on a spot deep inside my body.

"I can see right inside your creamy cunt." He closes his fingers back together and circles them inside me, rubbing my G-spot and making me cry out. "My cock's going to stretch you wide, Sweetheart," he growls as he fists his cock, the end of it dripping with wet beads of his arousal. "And it's going to feel fucking incredible... for both of us."

My mouth falls open as he swirls his fingers again, setting me trembling. He's so sure of himself, so confident, almost arrogant... and it has me moaning with the need to have him inside me.

To finally let go.

"Do you know what I want?" He pulls his soaking fingers out and holds them up to my mouth.

"What?"

As I part my lips, he slides his fingers inside my mouth and growls deep in his throat as I suck them clean. I swirl my tongue around them, hollowing my cheeks.

His curve of a smile tells me he's picturing me doing it to his cock.

"I want to watch your face as you bleed your orgasm all over my cock." He hovers over me, his eyes burning into mine. "Then I want to pump you so full of my cum that it's still dripping out of you next week."

I murmur around his fingers, wriggling beneath him.

I think I might be dead by the time he's finished with me. Killed by too much sex.

He removes his hand and reaches over to the bedside table. The next second, he's ripping a condom packet open between his teeth and rolling it down onto his cock, his eyes never leaving mine.

"But we'll start with the first one," he says as he holds my thighs wide open and pushes himself against me, the thick head of his cock pressing into me agonizingly slow.

I moan and pull my chin down so I can watch him bury himself in my body, inch by inch.

"Griffin."

He takes both of my hands in one of his and holds them over my head against the mattress.

"Yes, Sweetheart." He keeps pushing, his jaw clenched, until my body has accepted all of him and his balls are grazing my skin.

My eyes roll back in my head as I savor the stretch.

Fuck, he's right. It does feel incredible.

He circles his hips, forcing a deep moan from my lips as I clench my inner thighs and throw my legs around his waist, hooking my ankles at his back.

"You feel so good," I whisper.

"Lift your hips." His eyes sparkle at me as he slides a cushion beneath my bum, canting my hips up toward him and re-setting the angle at which he's entering me as he withdraws and then pushes straight back inside, holding my wrists above my head once more.

I cry out as pleasure rushes over every millimeter of my body, inside and out.

His other hand slides around my throat and his gaze darkens as he draws back and thrusts into me again, the sound of his balls hitting my skin echoing in the air.

"Again," I cry, squeezing my eyes shut.

"You feel even better than I imagined you would," he grits as he drives back into me.

He keeps hold of my wrists as he pumps his hips over and over, fucking me hard. I dig my heels into his back, holding him tighter, spurring him on as I arch my body against his chest. Heat and sweat cover our skin as I pant below him.

"Griffin... harder, please..."

"This sweet cunt is mine," he hisses, stealing my gaze as I open my eyes. "Isn't it?"

I nod, my breath turning to gasps as he thrusts, burying himself to the hilt and circling his hips, sending tension and heat racing to my clit.

"Say it." He slams in again, and I grind against his skin.

"Yours."

"All of it." He slams in again, circling twice this time before he draws back, every ripple of his fat cock rubbing the muscles deep inside me.

I swallow as a bead of sweat runs between my breasts. I don't care what he wants me to say. I will say anything to ensure he doesn't stop.

"This cunt is yours," I cry, bucking underneath him, my hands still pinned. Doing anything I can to get more friction against my throbbing clit.

"That's right. I'm the only one who fucks it." The sweat glistens on his chest as he leans down and drives his tongue inside my mouth, claiming it, just like he is with the rest of my body. He sucks my bottom lip as he pulls back. "Only me, Sweetheart."

"Only you," I pant as the tightness in my clit becomes unbearable. One more move and I will...

He circles his hips and I explode, coming around him in hard, fast waves.

"Fuck," he hisses, his eyes glued to mine as I moan and writhe beneath him. "Squeeze me, Sweetheart. *Squeeze*."

The crystal blue fire of his eyes brands me as he pushes his body into mine even harder, forcing me down into the mattress. He juts his chin forward, the muscles in his jaw tight as he groans and slams into me again. All the while his eyes burn into mine.

I will never be the same again.

He flexes his cock inside me, and it's enough to make my orgasm roll into another. My lips part and I hold his gaze as my muscles ripple around him again, spasming in hard waves.

He groans deep in his chest and his fingers tighten against my wrists.

"Tell me," he growls.

"I'm..." *Pant.* "... coming..." *Pant.*

"Good gir—"

"... all over your cock," I finish, moaning loudly as the pulsating continues, hugging Griffin's body tightly inside mine as I shake.

"Fuck, yeah," he growls, upping his pace as he watches me ride my pleasure out underneath him.

His cock feels incredible, every vein in it massaging areas inside me I've never taken notice of before, the rim of his head dragging over my G-spot on the outward thrust.

"Shit." I screw my face up as the final wave steals my breath.

He stills, grabbing my chin and forcing my eyes back onto his. Every muscle in his body tenses as he holds his breath.

Intense doesn't come close to describing the look in his eyes right now.

Then he thrusts again, and his cock swells inside me.

"You."

Thrust.

"Are."

Thrust.

"Mine."

Thrust.

Chapter Twenty-One

Griffin

I GRIT MY TEETH as my balls tighten and the heat rips out of them and up my cock.

"You. Are. Mine," I grit out as I empty. Empty everything I have into this woman who has invaded my head since I first laid eyes on her.

Her breasts rise and fall against my chest as she looks at me, catching her breath. Her hair is wild, her cheeks flushed, her eyes bright.

She's fucking stunning.

I release her neck, running my fingers through her hair and pressing my face against hers, kissing her sweet, pink lips—sucking in the taste of her.

Our kisses grow soft, and she whispers against my lips, "It was worth waiting for."

I kiss her again, releasing her arms from above her head. She wraps them straight around my neck, holding me close.

"It was. It certainly was," I murmur, dusting my lips all over her face. Kissing her forehead, her eyelids, the tip of her nose.

She looks into my eyes and frowns.

Shit. Was I too rough? Is she already planning her escape? Ready to bolt at the first given chance, just like the previous times?

"Griffin?"

My shoulders tense and I blink, stealing myself for the excuse she's about to give.

"I can smell burning."

"What?" My eyes widen. "Shit! The oven!"

Her cheeks are still flushed from her orgasm, her body still tightly holding mine inside her.

Perfect.

"Fuck it. Who needs food?"

She laughs and puts her hands on either side of my face, pressing a kiss to my lips. "Maybe not food, but you don't want to burn the house down."

"I'll build another." I catch her lips in another kiss.

"Go." She laughs, pushing at my chest. "I won't go anywhere... Go!" she adds, when I don't move.

"Fine," I huff, sliding out of her body and immediately hating the separation. I swing my legs over the side of the bed and pull the full condom off, tying it in a knot. "Don't even think about putting any clothes on before I get back."

Her laugh floats down the stairs behind me as I go to the kitchen and open the oven. Gray smoke billows out, so I open the kitchen window wide, coughing and wafting the air with a towel. I grab an oven mitt and chuck what was our seafood bake into the sink to let it cool off. Then I go back upstairs.

Maria is where I left her, on my bed, but with a white sheet over her beautiful body.

"No fucking cover-ups," I growl, pulling the sheet off and climbing over the top of her, catching a nipple between my teeth as she laughs.

"I don't know why you're laughing. I'm serious. I want you naked every second we're here." I suck her nipple into my mouth and flutter the tip of my tongue over it.

"We aren't at The Songbird, Mr. Parker. You don't get to make the rules."

She's biting her lip, her eyes bright.

"Sweetheart, you are mine. I *am* the rule." I suck the soft skin of her breast between my teeth, working my way up to her neck and then ear. "Dinner's fucked. Let me eat you instead," I growl, enjoying the way she shivers as my breath rolls over her skin.

"No." Her breath catches in her throat as I sweep her hair away from her neck and stroke it.

"No? Fucking *no*? Remind me why I hired you again? You're insolent." I arch a brow at her.

"Because I'm brilliant. And you need me." She arches a brow back.

I smirk at her and then jump up from the bed, pulling her with me.

"Come on. I'll fix us some food. You're going to need your energy."

"What time is it, Griff?" Maria turns over, snaking her arm around my waist as she lays her head on my chest.

After a picnic out on the deck last night watching the sunset, Maria passed out in my arms. I sat holding her for a while, studying the bruise on her cheek. It was taunting me for being so stupid to have not prevented it. To not have done something sooner when I should have seen it coming. That entire night, coupled with how hard she's been working at the spa, must have taken it out of her. She didn't even stir when I carried her up to bed.

"It's early, Sweetheart."

She tilts her face to look at me. "I fell asleep on the deck."

"You needed it." I dip my nose into her hair and inhale the heady, floral scent that is all her.

"Do you like it?" She reaches up to stroke my jaw. "It's a frangipani blend I made myself."

Now I know why it's so familiar. Those bushes in The Bahamas. The entire hotel grounds were fragranced by them. That was the first night I tasted her, and I've thought about that night every single day since. No one has ever disappeared on me mid-evening before. Until Maria.

"I do." I dip my nose and inhale again, recalling the jagged edge of disappointment that stabbed me in the gut when I returned to the pool that night and found it empty.

"What time do we need to leave?"

I cup her chin and lean down to kiss her. "Later."

She keeps stroking my jaw as she kisses me back, shuffling up the bed so she's level with me. I wrap my free arm around her back and roll her so she's lying on top of me. I don't try to hide the fact that my dick is sporting a raging hard-on between our bodies.

She breaks our kiss, her hair tumbling around her shoulders. I run my hands through it, stroking it back from her eyes as she talks.

"We need to get back for work. I've got to finalize the contracts with the new supplier and prepare for the reporter's visit that's coming up. And don't you have the filming schedule to look over?"

"Mmm." I exhale and close my eyes, enjoying the sensation of her hair running between my fingers.

"Griff?" she says again. The way she says my name in her soft voice does things to me. I smile as I open my eyes and look into hers.

"Yes, Sweetheart?"

"We need to get up. It'll take us nearly an hour to get back."

"I told you. We don't need to leave until later. It's all taken care of."

She shuffles in my arms, sending an excited false alarm to my dick as her soft skin grazes its tip. "What is?"

I reach up and stroke her face. "All of it. Harley, Will, the entire staff. It's all in hand. After the gala, and what happened..." I run the pad of my thumb over her bruise, which is visible again after she removed her make-up before we ate last night. "... I thought you would benefit from a day away from the hotel. Call today a training day if it makes you feel better."

"Training for what, exactly?" She smirks at me. "I find it hard to believe Griffin-control-freak-Parker would book the entire night and following day off work, unless it was of utmost importance."

"You're right. It's extremely important." A smug grin grows on my face.

Her eyes narrow at me. "Are you going to tell me what we're doing today, or do I have to suck it out of you?"

I smirk and her eyes widen as she realizes what she's said.

"Suck it out." I drop my voice low. "Definitely suck it fucking out."

"Griffin!" She laughs as I spin us so I'm on top of her, my cock weeping against her stomach.

I dive onto her, claiming her mouth as I kiss her forcefully, sliding my tongue in to taste her. She sighs. It's a tiny sound, barely audible, and it takes all my strength not to hitch her leg up, place one hand under her knee and then slide inside her wet heat.

All. My. Strength.

"Fuck, Sweetheart. You can't make those sounds and not expect me to fight the fucking devil on my shoulder who's telling me to slide inside you bare right now."

Maria bites her lip, her eyes sparkling. "I've got another idea. Let's take a shower."

I need a fucking iced one if I'm to get some of the blood back from my dick before I pass out.

"Okay." I kiss her again and pull her up out of the bed, walking her backward into the bathroom as I bury my lips in her neck and kiss her soft skin. "I can't control myself," I groan.

"I don't believe it. Griffin Parker out of control?" She narrows her eyes at me playfully as I lead us both into the shower and turn on the waterfall spray.

I back her up against the stone wall and lower my lips to hers.

"I've got you all day, to do with as I please. I will have you again, and again, and again," I say between kisses. "Remember whose cunt that is."

"Such a gentleman with words," she breathes against my lips, but there's no mistaking the smile in her voice.

"Don't you like it?" I move my lips to her ear. "Would you rather I not tell you how much I love the taste and smell of that sweet, pink heaven of yours? Not tell you that the sounds of her silky little hole, when she's coating me in her juices and I'm stretching her, is music to my fucking ears?" I growl, smiling as she sucks in a breath and whispers my name, letting it roll off the tip of her tongue huskily, like the mere feel of it there is enough to excite her.

"I do like it." She writhes against me as I kiss her again. "I like it so much that I want to give you more to talk about."

She places a hand against my chest and guides me around, so my back is against the tiles.

Then she drops to her knees.

Fuck.

I swear my eyes could burn her with the fire that ignites throughout my body.

She takes my cock in one hand and, keeping her eyes on mine, wipes the tip over her lips, spreading shiny pre-cum over them until they're wet. Then she runs the tip of her tongue over them, licking it all off.

I drag in a rough breath as she smiles and then opens her mouth and sucks all the way down to my base.

"Fuck!"

I drop my head back against the tiles as my balls throb. I swallow, my heart hammering in my chest as I drop my eyes back to hers. She's looking back up at me, her throat extended with my cock filling it.

She draws back slowly, then runs the flat of her tongue up and down my length as her other hand wraps around my balls and strokes. I bend my knees, sliding down the wall a little to brace myself. She takes me in her mouth again, sucking my head, and running her tongue around the ridge before sinking down over me again.

"God!" I hiss out, my eyes glued on hers as she fills her throat with me again.

She slides her fingers over my hands, interlacing them with my own, all the while keeping my cock firmly planted in her throat.

Then she draws back and guides my hands to her hair.

"Show me how you like it."

I flex my fingers in her hair, grinding my teeth.

"I like it just how you're doing it, Sweetheart. All the way down that perfect throat." I apply a tiny bit of pressure to her head, pushing her back down onto me.

She moans, sending the vibration around my cock and then draws back, sucking me back in again, increasing her speed.

"Holy..." I squeeze my eyes shut as my grip tightens in her hair and I lift my hips to meet her. "... fuck." I hiss out loudly as I guide her up and straight back down again, over, and over.

My balls tighten and I look down.

She's gazing up at me, her eyes watering as I hold her hair and fuck her throat. I would say fuck her mouth, but there's no doubt from the way my balls are slapping off her chin and she's gagged a couple of times that I'm slipping right down her throat.

Right down her perfect, smooth, tight throat.

"Fuck, I'm going to come," I groan, pulling my cock out of her mouth. I may be a selfish bastard at times, but there's no way I want her to choke with the load of cum I'm about to shoot.

"On my face," she moans.

I search her eyes, which are glittering up at me.

"Come on my face, Griffin. I want you all over me."

She's serious.

"Shit!" I grit my teeth together, one hand jacking myself off at lightning speed, the other holding a fistful of Maria's hair as I hold her head still. "Open your mouth, Sweetheart," I pant.

She drops her chin and parts her lips. My balls pull in, loaded and heavy against my legs as the first white spurt fires out, coating her smooth pink tongue.

"Fucking hell," I growl.

How am I still standing?

Spurt after spurt fires out, covering her lips, cheeks, chin, and running down her neck. It keeps coming until I'm physically shaking from the force of it.

Euphoria floods my body as the last wave leaves me, and I slide down the shower wall, pulling her onto my lap as my chest surges, sucking in much-needed oxygen.

"God," I pant, pulling her face to me and kissing her.

I don't care that she has me all over her face and inside her mouth. I fucking love it. I'm all over her, just like she wanted. I hold her and kiss her over and over as the water falls down on us.

There's no one in this world who can deny it now.

She is mine.

All.

Mine.

Chapter Twenty-Two

Maria

"How about over there?" I bounce up on my toes and point to a stretch of beach.

"I told you. I've got the perfect place in mind." Griffin smiles over at me as I lean on the side of the speedboat and watch the ocean whizzing by underneath us.

"Fine. I trust you." I grin back before looking out over the water again.

This day couldn't be any more magical. After Griffin insisted on matching my efforts in the shower this morning, and making my legs turn to jelly with the power of his tongue, he made us breakfast, which we ate out on the deck watching the ocean. Then he grabbed a picnic basket his housekeeper prepared and took me on the short walk to the marina where he keeps his boat.

I'd heard from Harley and Will that Griffin loves to be out on the water, and his boat is his real true love in life, after The Songbird. But I wouldn't have believed just how true that was if I weren't seeing it with my own eyes. At The Songbird, he's calm, focused and in control, which he is here too, I guess. Only it's different. At the beach house, and on the water, he's lighter, younger... more carefree. He's wearing black trunks and a white t-shirt with a baseball cap... and he's barefoot! He's the complete alter-ego from Griffin Parker, Manhattan's youngest billionaire hotelier with custom-made suits and a fresh-shaven jaw each morning. He didn't even bother to shave today. But the biggest contrast is his eyes. Here, they're bright, buzzing with energy... with life. In New York, they're more clouded, intense. He's always thinking of the next big business deal, and what the hotel needs. He doesn't switch off there, and now I understand more than ever why he loves it here so much.

"Are we nearly there yet?"

"Almost." He steers the boat toward the shore and around some rocks that extend out into the ocean.

I crane my neck, trying to see around the rocks faster, and Griffin shakes his head with a chuckle.

"Patience, Sweetheart. It'll be worth the wait."

He catches my eye and warmth blooms in my chest as I recognize both of our words from last night. *It was worth the wait.* I don't think there's ever been something truer.

The sun is shining down on Griffin's muscular forearms as he turns the steering wheel. *He* was worth the wait. Each one of my thirty years, including the ones living with my father's gambling addiction, and the ones with my ex's lies and deceit—I would do them all again if it meant meeting him. To feel the way I do when he looks at me is worth every tear I've ever cried.

He's my reward for never giving up.

He kills the engine and reaches over to grab me around the waist.

"Okay, my beautiful, perfect woman. We're here."

"We are?"

It's a small, secluded cove. Griffin is busy putting down an anchor for the boat as my eyes run up and down the pale sand. It looks the same as the last four coves we passed on the way here. Maybe he fancied more time on the boat. It makes sense. He loves it so much. I'll happily pass one hundred identical coves if it means him being so happy and relaxed.

"Let's go." He steps into the water, which comes up to his mid-thigh.

I look at him, then back at the water. I didn't pack a bikini, as I had no idea we would do this. Luckily, I had a light, floaty dress in my bag, which should dry quickly if it gets wet. But I only have lace underwear on.

He laughs at my expression, then grabs me around the waist, hoisting me over his shoulder and carrying me the short distance to the shore before setting me down gently.

"Thank you."

The firm muscles in his broad shoulders are visible through his t-shirt as he wades back to the boat and grabs the picnic basket, carrying it above his head as he comes back to me.

"My pleasure. Can't go having you getting all wet and needing to take all your clothes off, can we?" He winks at me as he grabs my hand and walks us up the sand.

Yes, I am definitely with alter-ego Griffin today. I have never seen him wink. Ever. But the butterflies in my stomach are evidence that despite it being a new side to him, it's one that I'm more than happy to be spending time with.

Griffin picks a spot and spreads a picnic rug out on the sand. He opens the basket and starts taking out dish after dish of tasty-looking food—olives, dips, crackers, a baguette, fresh fruit, tiny little cakes that have chocolate frosting. I raise an eyebrow at him, and he grins at me from underneath his baseball cap, his blue eyes squinting in the sun.

"After last night's dinner was well and truly fucked, I can at least give you a proper lunch." He continues unpacking the food and then pulls a bottle of champagne out and two glasses.

"Someone's trying to win serious points." I laugh as I watch him pop the cork. It flies over the sand, so I run over to pick it up. Something glinting in the sand catches my eye.

"Hey, Griff, look." I hold up the tiny, perfect hermit crab shell I've found as I walk back over to him. It's perfectly pink on the outside, but it's the empty inside that catches my eye. It's bright, crystal blue. I've never seen anything like it.

"It's kind of like you," I say as I give it to him to look at.

His dark brows knit together, and he gives me a look like I've gone mad. "How do you figure that?"

"Well, most people just see the hard exterior, but once you get past the pinchy crab, there's something unique and quite beautiful underneath." I smile at him as he hands it back, then I drop it into the picnic basket to take back with us.

"I think the sun's gone to your head."

I smile as he hands me a glass of champagne. "Your secret's safe with me. I won't tell anyone there's a caring guy who spends all night sleeping in half a tuxedo to make sure someone he works with is okay."

He comes to stand next to me and we look out at the ocean. "Not just someone I work with, Maria. *You*."

"I'm only me, Griffin." I let out a contented sigh as I breathe in the sea air. It really is beautiful and relaxing here, away from the city.

"I happen to think only you is pretty fucking impressive. Why do you think I flew from one coast to the other to persuade you to come to New York? It had to be you."

Heat blooms in my chest as his words sink in. I know he chose me specifically after hearing about my spa in California. It's something I'm so proud of, and the fact he recognizes that means a lot to me. He's the first man in my life who's really appreciated how hard I've worked to get to where I am. And I'm realizing he's also the first man since my father left whose opinion I've cared about, too.

"I know how important the hotel is to you. You can trust me to give it everything."

"I've never doubted you," he says, keeping his eyes fixed on the water. I turn to him as the torment falls over his face like a curtain at the end of a show. "I doubt myself. My own judgment."

"Griff—"

"Let's not talk about it now. We came here to take a step back."

I look at his profile, his short, dark hair, his perfect cheekbones, and soft, kissable lips. And then there are his eyes—piercing blue windows to his soul. A beautiful man with a beautiful, complicated soul. I couldn't be any more in danger of losing my heart to him than I am at this moment, hearing the uncertainty in his voice, questioning himself, even when he's achieved more than most people ever do in a lifetime.

A gull flies past overhead as I take a deep breath.

"I know why you wanted to come here now. It's perfect." Griffin's eyes are on my face as I turn to look at him. "What?"

His eyes move over my face, coming to rest on my lips. It makes my stomach flip.

I know that look.

"This isn't what I wanted to show you. Come on." He sets my glass down and takes me by the hand, leading me along the small beach to the cliffs at one side. "This is what I wanted to see."

We walk toward a gap in the rocks, hidden from view from the shoreline. We go through a tunnel, ducking our heads in places to fit through.

"What the...?" I let out a delighted gasp as I try to take in what I'm seeing.

Griffin just smiles at me as tingles run through my body and my head grows light.

We are in a cave with one small arch leading directly to the ocean. Sunlight streams in from a tiny gap up above us in the rocks, illuminating the small shallow pool of aquamarine water. Its mesmerizing color reflects off the surrounding rocks and bathes them in a blue aura.

"This is incredible! How did you find this place?"

I step forward until my bare toes are immersed in the water. It's like a mini beach hidden inside the cliff.

"It's a Parker family secret. My grandfather used to bring my grandmother here to escape her parents."

"They didn't approve?" I turn to him in interest. I love when he shares stories about his family.

He smiles. "I'm told they took a while to warm to him. My grandmother was a Broadway actress, and they thought he was a distraction. He was only just starting at the hotel then, an entry-level position. It was a good job, but not for them. She was catching the eye of every leading male actor on the circuit. Her parents saw my grandfather as having the least to offer her."

"That's harsh."

"That's life." Griffin shrugs. "He did have the least to offer. But he loved her, and he proved it day after day, working his ass off at the hotel until one day he was made manager. But he wanted more. My grandmother helped him buyout the owner. She had more money than him."

"She sounds amazing. They both do." I smile, stepping forward into his open arms. He wraps me inside them.

He clears his throat. "They were."

I tighten my arms around his waist. "I'm sorry. I didn't know you'd lost them already."

He dips his nose into my hair and inhales slowly.

"It's life. And now I get to carry on for them. The Songbird was what the press called my grandmother. Her singing voice brought people from all over the world to hear her."

"Wow." I tilt my chin up to look at him. "So that's where the name comes from."

"It is." His eyes sparkle down at me. "Now enough of the history lesson. Time for some biology."

I laugh as he lowers his lips toward mine, pausing before they touch.

"You're fucking perfect. Have I told you that?" He breathes against me, sending tingles throughout my body.

His arms tighten around me and then he kisses me, pulling me up onto my toes as he grips my waist. I snake my arms around his neck and allow myself to become lost in him.

The real world might be going on outside this cave, but I have all I need right here.

"I'm never letting you go," he whispers against my lips before kissing me harder, deeper, moving me until my back presses against the cool, damp rock of the cave wall.

"I never want you to," I whisper in response, stroking the back of his neck.

His damp clothes press against me, making us stick together. I would dive right inside him if I could. Nothing feels close enough.

His hands slide up my legs, underneath my dress as his tongue commands my mouth. I let out a small whimper as he bites my bottom lip and his lips curve into a self-satisfied smile against mine.

He knows exactly what he does to me.

He lifts one of my legs behind my knee and wraps it around his waist, his other hand roughly tugging my panties to one side so he can sink his fingers inside me.

"Griffin." I shudder and clench around him as a rush of wetness covers his fingers.

"Jesus, you're so wet whenever I touch you," he groans into my mouth as he finds my G-spot and strokes. "So, so wet."

He slides his fingers out of me, and before I process what's happening, he's shoving his wet trunks down and rolling a condom onto his hard cock.

Where did it even come from? I never saw him get it out of his pocket. Trust him to always be prepared, Mr. Loves-to-be-in-control.

"Turn around."

I lean back against the wall, panting as I look down. He's stroking himself, one hand wrapped around his thick cock.

It's primal and sexual... and damn if it isn't making my pulse beat hard, low in my core.

He squeezes as he gets to the tip and sucks in his breath, his lower abs clenching.

"Don't make me ask again." He tilts my chin up with his other hand and fixes me with a dark look.

I glance down again, and then turn around. His lips are on my neck the second my back is to him, one hand reaching around to palm my breast roughly, the other diving inside my panties and stroking my swollen clit.

"You're mine, Sweetheart."

His kisses trail from my ear down to my shoulder. Then he grabs my hips with both his hands and pulls me back toward him, so I'm bent forwards with my hands on the rock.

"Mine," he repeats as he pulls my panties to one side and drives inside me like he has every right to.

Of course, he does. My body, my heart... this man has the right to it all. He knows I want him, and it only seems to fuel his desire for me more.

I'm thrown forward with the force, but before my head reaches the cave wall, Griffin clasps one hand around my shoulder and pulls me back, so I sink onto him again, every inch of him pushing inside me, spreading me wide around him.

"Fuck, Griff," I pant, my legs trembling with the delicious burn of his possession.

"Tell me what it feels like when I'm deep inside you," he groans.

The pleasure coursing through me has stolen the words from my lips, so instead I clench hard around him. He hisses out a low and extended "*Fuck*" as he stills inside me, his cock pulsating.

"It feels like that for me, too," I whisper breathlessly, finding my voice.

He flexes the fingers on my hip. "That was a mistake, Sweetheart. Don't try to tease me." His voice is laced with amusement.

I clench again, drawing another curse from his lips.

"I'm only trying to please you, Mr. Parker." I smile as he growls low in his chest.

"That shouldn't sound as filthy as it does," he groans as he moves again, thrusting into me over and over, building up speed. "Jesus, your cunt is tight. I'm going to enjoy fucking it bare when we get back to the city."

"What makes you think you will?" I pant out as tension builds in my core and I slide back and forward over his cock, which is soaking wet, covered with my arousal.

"Oh, I will, Sweetheart. Mark my words." He takes his hand off my shoulder and buries it between my legs, rubbing my clit in tight, fast circles. "Now be a good girl and cover my cock with your cream as you come. I love feeling you squeeze me when you let go."

I screw my eyes shut, insanely turned on by his crudeness. I don't even swear most of the time, yet here I am, flooding over him like a waterfall, and quivering with each word that passes his sinful lips.

He is a filthy-mouthed God disguised as a man.

"God!" I plant my hand more firmly against the rock, its coolness a direct contrast to the fire that is taking over my core. "Griff!" I gasp in a breath, holding it for a second, then let it out in one long cry as I come hard around him, my legs shaking. "I can't... I can't..."

"I've got you," Griffin groans as he holds me up and stops me from crumpling into a spent heap at his feet. "I've got you," he says again, the telltale swell of his cock inside me drawing a deep groan from him. It's as though it gets even harder the moment before he comes.

"Fuck... fuck..." he hisses, slamming into me, pulling me back against his strong thighs as he buries himself deep. He groans one final time, holding himself still, deep inside me, flexing his fingers against my skin as he finishes pumping out. "You make me come so hard, I worry my balls might explode," he pants.

I take some deep breaths, the thundering in my chest slowing as he pulls out of me, straightening my panties and pressing a kiss to my shoulder.

I turn around as he's taking the condom off and my eyebrows shoot up.

"Told you they might explode." He smirks.

I tear my eyes away from the volume of white liquid at the end of the condom and up to meet his. He's smiling at me in a way that makes my heart catch in my throat. I could get used to this version of him—the relaxed one who makes jokes, albeit rude ones, and smiles at me like I'm the most special person in the world to him and there's no one else he would rather be standing with right now.

He steps forward and cups my cheek, his eyes lingering on mine before he kisses me gently. "Let's go eat, before I dine on your pretty cunt again."

I smile against his lips. Yes, romantic and crude all at once. Who knew that would be my biggest turn-on? Griffin Parker did, so it seems.

He takes my hand and leads me out of the cave.

"I'm famished. You're quite an appetite builder, Sweetheart." He grins at me, but his eyes widen as I clap a hand to my mouth.

He snaps his head across the beach to our picnic. The entire rug is covered in around twenty gulls, all flapping and pecking and squawking at each other. Two are fighting over the baguette and there are crumbs and sand being flicked up all over the place.

"Oh, my God." I don't know where to look first. It's carnage.

"No, you don't, you feathery bastards!" Griffin yells, ripping his hand from mine as he races over the sand, clapping his hands and then waving his arms around. The gulls hop further down the sand and then fly up over his head and back to the picnic.

"Griffin, it's too late!" I call after him. But it's no use. He's fixed on the target, like a missile.

"This is our food!" he shouts as he grabs the baguette off one of them and holds it in the air above his head. "Ah-ha! It's gone now, you little shit."

Another gull flies up and knocks his baseball cap off his head as it snatches the bread out of his hand and flies off with it.

Griffin grabs a cupcake and launches it into the air after it.

"Did your friend send you? The one that keeps shitting on my fucking carpet!" he roars.

I run over to help, and then stop short, my eyes raking over the chaos. Our entire picnic has been decimated. It looks like a food fight gone wrong, remnants of it scattered along the sand, all the way to the shore where some birds have tried to fly away with their stash and dropped bits during their escape.

"Griffin." I stand with my mouth open. It's like he's finally snapped. All that stiff, in control, business persona he usually holds together so well is coming careering down in front of my eyes.

But I can't look away.

He needs this.

"Feather-brained bastards!" He grabs another cupcake and hurls it out into the sea.

"You tell them, Babe." I smile because this is going to be good for him, even if he doesn't realize it yet.

He turns to me, eyes blazing as another gull runs past him, flapping its wings, knocking over the champagne bottle.

"That's a two grand bottle, you little fucker!" he cries, making a dive after the gull, which darts out of the way at the last minute, leaving Griffin face down in the sand. He roars as he jumps up, sand flying everywhere, as he chases the final stragglers away.

He's panting through his nose when he comes back to me, his jaw set in a tense line.

"It's just food." I bite back my smile at all the sand in his hair and on his face.

"*Our* fucking food." He shakes his head and sand flies everywhere, breaking my reserve as I erupt into giggles.

"I'm sorry," I say as he looks at me, unamused. "It's just—" I struggle to talk as I laugh... "—it's birds again. They must have a thing about you." I slam my hand over my mouth.

Griffin narrows his eyes at me. "Fucking birds. And my hotel is called the fucking Songbird!" He throws his arms wide and looks at the sky. "You're shitting me, right?" he calls up to the clouds.

I laugh and he looks back at me, his eyes softening at the corners.

"I'm glad *you're* happy." He scoops his cap off the floor.

"I am." I walk over and wrap my arms around his waist as he puts his cap on.

"Argh! The fuck!" He rips it off and throws it on the ground where the sun catches the giant dollop of bird shit that's inside.

I snort, my shoulders shaking.

"This isn't funny." He rakes his hand through his dark hair, which only smears the gloop over a larger area.

"Oh, it is." I grin at him, then pull him in for a slow kiss. "It really is."

He grumbles and then kisses me back, wiping his hand on his trunks before grabbing each side of my face. The next second, I'm looking at sky as he throws me down on the sand and climbs over me.

"What are you doing?" I laugh as he hovers over me, shielding my eyes from the sun with his muscular torso.

"Those fuckers may have taken our picnic, but I'm still eating." His eyes darken as he slides my dress up. "And I'm starting with dessert."

Chapter Twenty-Three

Griffin

"Good morning, Mr. Parker. How was your trip away?" Harley asks with a huge grin on her face.

I roll my lips to hide my smile. She and Maria have grown close. They may not have had a chance to catch up since we got back last night, but Harley knows Maria went with me. And after working for me for five years, she knows me well enough to work out that this isn't some short-lived, meaningless hook-up.

"It was just what I needed. Thank you, Harley."

She raises her brows and smiles as she plucks a large bag from the floor and deposits it on top of her desk.

I look at her in question.

"You can decide how much my bonus will be later!" She drums her fingers together excitedly as she looks at me and then the bag.

"You got it already?" I ask, impressed.

"Will helped. But yes! I peeked, you know, to check it. Gah! It's gorgeous." Harley's smile grows as she takes the silk handles of the bag and holds it out to me. "She will love it, Mr. Parker."

My smile matches Harley's as I take hold of the soft handles. I hope Maria is going to like it. God, I would get her anything she wanted, a realization I came to long before the Hamptons. That time together merely cemented it further for me. She might be mine now, but I'm most certainly hers, too. She's got me like a dog, pining after her.

We landed back late last night, and I hid my disappointment when she wanted to go back to her own apartment. Alone. The idea of pounding her into my mattress all night long was much more appealing.

"Thank you, Harley." I lift the bag off her desk. "I'm very grateful."

"Oh, you're welcome." She smiles at me.

She's thinking about going to the spa to see Maria the minute I go into my office.

"Maybe you could go grab us a coffee from the place you like?" I raise a brow at her. "The last couple of days have worn me out a bit."

"Yes, Mr. Parker."

I don't miss the small squeak she makes as she jumps up from her desk.

"Oh, Emily called for you. She said she's on her way in."

"Okay. Thank you." She almost runs to the elevator, and I chuckle.

I head into my office and get to work for an hour, returning emails and calls that have come in overnight. I stayed up late after we got back last night playing catch up, so I'm pretty on track with what we have going on.

Later this week is the filming of *Steel Force*. We've got the production crew and actors staying in the hotel for a few days. They only have a couple of scenes to film in the hotel. The rest will be out in the city, so won't require any input from me. But the ones at The Songbird, especially the one outside at street level, will take some preparation. I've already increased security to keep members of the public who come to watch safe. And I've placed Earl in charge of the front of house presentation. Everything looks to be under control.

There's a knock at the door.

"Come in!" I call, getting up from my chair and rounding my desk.

"Griffin!" Emily beams at me as she rushes over and wraps her arms around me, pressing a kiss to my cheek. Her eyes sweep over my face as she places her purse down and shrugs out of her coat. "You've caught the sun."

Harley's head pokes around the door behind Emily and I wave her in.

"Here you are, Mr. Parker... Emily," Harley adds as she places down a coffee for me and one for Emily, too.

I smile at her. She is a great PA, and the fact she thought to get Emily a coffee as well just highlights how thoughtful she is. Why Reed seems to have a stick up his ass if I even mention her name is a mystery to me.

"Thank you, Harley." I wait until she's gone before I join Emily, who's sitting on one of the sofas.

She casts her eyes over me again, her lips twisting in thought.

"You've definitely caught the sun, Griffin. Been taking outdoor lunch meetings this week, have you?"

"No. I went to the beach house. Spent yesterday out on the boat." I take a sip of my coffee.

Her eyes light up. "Oh, I love it there. Why didn't you say? I would have come and kept you company."

"I wasn't alone."

"Oh?" Her brow creases at the same time as she spots the giant Louis Vuitton gift bag I placed at the side of the sofa earlier. "I see." She turns to me with a smile. "Have I met this new friend?"

I smile as I lean back on the sofa and have another drink of coffee. "Perhaps."

"Oh, come on, Griffin. Don't go acting all coy." She reaches out and shoves my leg. "How long have I known you?"

"Long enough to know I don't like to kiss and tell."

I adjust my back against the sofa cushions, the skin still tender where Maria's stilettos scratched my lower back. It's a gratifying pain, though. One I gladly welcome as a reminder of a fantastic night. *God, I want her again.* That first night... the beach the next day... the times back at the beach house before we flew back to the city... They aren't enough. No number of times will ever be enough.

I'm addicted.

Emily sighs and purses her lips. "Suit yourself. You know I'll get it out of you. But if you prefer to think you've won for now, then I'll let you believe it. We all have our secrets."

I smile as one corner of her mouth curls.

"Okay. On to business. I have some things to run by you." She glances at me as she pulls some documents from her bag and lays them out on the coffee table.

I nod and lean forward over my knees to look. She likes to come and talk business with me. She's perfectly capable of running her charity by herself, but it seems to make her happy to come and run things by me and get my opinion.

I'm probably the only male she has in her life who shows an interest. I feel bad for her, the way her dad ignored her most of her life growing up. He had more time for me and my brothers growing up than he did for Emily. Some men don't see daughters and women as equally capable, or maybe even more so, than a man at running a successful business.

Emily looks away from me, her eyes casting back down to the documents she's brought with her. "This gala was an enormous success, one of the best yet. Thank you, Griffin."

"Don't thank me, Em. You're welcome to host them here anytime you want."

She reaches over and lays her hand on my arm. "Thank you. We make a good team."

"It's all you. You're doing an incredible job."

"That means a lot coming from you, Griffin." She looks at me for an extended time, studying my face, and I get the feeling she's going to tell me something. Instead, a frown passes over her lips, and she turns back to the documents, drawing us back into talk of benefactors and publicity for when she hands over the very sizeable donation to the hospital.

The rest of the morning passes, one call after another, until I finally get a moment to myself.

I blow out a breath and stretch my arms up behind my head as I lean back in my chair and stare out at Manhattan. It's one of the best views in the world, knowing that this entire building, and at least six others in my eyeline down the street, are all mine. The Songbird is my only hotel, but I own buildings housing luxury penthouses, offices, and retail spaces running all the way down Park Avenue. They're leased off me. The only one I run myself is The Songbird. This place is where my heart lies. Here, and at the beach house and my boat.

The beach.

My cock twitches as I recall the way Maria came so hard on my face in the private cove that she was too dizzy to get up afterward. We laid next to one another on the sand on our backs instead, looking at the sky, holding hands. I was covered in sand, food, and bird shit. But all I noticed was the way her hair smelled, and that her taste lingered on my lips like honey.

Sweet as fucking honey.

I sit up, sliding my chair back to my desk, and grab the phone, hitting speed dial.

"Hello," she answers on the second ring, her voice soft and breathy. It makes me want to grab my dick in my pants and squeeze.

"How's your morning been, Sweetheart?"

There's a smile in her voice. "It's been great."

"You're not feeling... like you're missing anything?" I lean back in my chair, my hand stroking over my tie as I wait for her response.

"Something like?"

"My tongue."

I smile as I imagine her down in the spa, leaning her beautiful curvy hips against the counter as she talks to me.

Are her cheeks blushing that beautiful pale pink? The one that turns darker, dusky in color when she comes.

"Well, I guess it has certain redeeming qualities."

I chuckle, leaning forward and looking at the word Spa lit up on the cradle display. She's all those floors below me when she should be here, next to me, on me... around me.

"I've got a packed afternoon. But I'm sending you something."

"Sounds intriguing."

There are voices in the background, and someone says her name.

"Listen, Griff. I've got to go. I'll speak to you later."

There's a pause and then the line goes dead.

I run a hand around my jaw. She's the only department manager who's ever been the one to end a call first on me because her team needs her. It's not just a job for her. It's a passion. And I love that.

I *understand* that.

I pull out my wallet and retrieve the business card Will gave me, turning it over in my fingers.

Then I pick the phone back up and make another call.

Chapter Twenty-Four

Maria

"TELL ME EVERYTHING," HARLEY hisses as we move along the line in what has become our favorite coffee and lunch place to go to together whenever we get the chance.

"I told you this morning when you came into the spa." I smile at the cashier as I take out my wallet.

Harley frowns and pushes it away, handing over a bill. "Keep the change," she tells the cashier.

She ushers me over to our usual table by the window and points at the chair. "Sit."

I laugh as I place our drinks down on the table and take a seat. Harley sits opposite me and hands me a bagel.

"Thanks." I take it from her and swap it for her drink.

"You might as well have told me nothing this morning. It was a watered-down PG-rated version." She fixes her eyes on me as I raise the bagel to my lips.

I roll my eyes and place it back down. She won't let me eat until I give her more. And knowing how busy my afternoon schedule is, there will be nothing to gain from holding back.

"Okay. What do you want to know?"

"Um, everything!" She waves her hands in the air like I asked the stupidest question in the history of all stupid questions.

"Okay..." I look around the deli. It's busy, as usual. Everyone is too caught up in their own lives to be interested in me confessing to having sex with the boss.

Incredible, scorching hot, multiple orgasms sex.

"So?" Harley's eyes light up as she leans over the table and makes herself comfortable.

"So, he asked me to pack an overnight bag. I thought we were going for dinner, and then back to his place. I kind of liked the idea of him being there all night again, you know, after he stayed the night of the gala."

Harley nods in understanding. Griffin still wants to kill Todd, and Harley comes next in line for people who have him on their hit list.

"So, he picks you up and takes you riding in his huge chopper instead." Her eyes twinkle and I laugh.

"Something like that."

She leans closer, her eyes trained on mine. "Come on, Maria. Give me more than that. I only meet married sleazebags when I'm out honeying. I need the details!"

"How's that going? Have you had many clients?"

"Yes. It's going great. I'm fab at it. They always cave when I show some tit or ass. Don't change the subject," she says quickly, eyeballing me.

"Fine." I roll my eyes with a smile. "We go in his helicopter—which he flew by the way—thanks for warning me he had a license. I thought I was going to hurl for half the journey."

Harley laughs as I continue.

"Then we... got close, you know." I tuck a loose strand of hair behind my ear. "And ate out on the porch. I fell asleep, so he carried me up to bed. Then the next day we went out on his boat, and he took me to a secluded cove that has an amazing cave with a secret miniature beach hidden inside it."

Warmth spreads low in my stomach. It felt amazing to go away with him, to see him outside of work. Now that we're back, the shine is still well and truly there. It hasn't worn off like when you look back and realize it wasn't actually that good, or you enjoyed it more than they did. That they were just playing along, pretending, or wishing they were there with someone else and not you. The way everything I did with my ex used to feel.

I've been fighting it since I arrived in New York, but I can't deny it any longer. Griffin does something to me. I've spent so many years being independent and not letting anyone close again romantically. And I was happy that way. Truly. But since him? Seeing how he not only accepts but applauds and encourages my ambition and passion in work—it has me thinking... maybe business can co-exist alongside pleasure, after all. Maybe it doesn't have to be one or the other. Not when it's with the right person. And right now, nothing feels closer to right than Griffin.

"What was the sex like? I bet it was hot. Is he as bossy as he is at work? I bet he likes to be in control. Like a Dom? Ooh, are you a Sub? I mean, just role-wise. I don't mean wear a collar or anything. Unless you're into that kind of thing. Are you?"

I look up at Harley wide-eyed and we both burst into giggles.

"Okay. Don't go into that much detail. He's still my boss."

"Mine too." I sigh as I blow the steam off the top of my latte and take a sip.

So much of this feels right. But why he couldn't own another hotel? I could have met him in a bar on a night out and not had to work with him. It would make it much simpler if things go wrong.

"He said he was worn out." Harley winks at me, and my cheeks heat.

"Did he?"

"Yeah. You must have fucked all his energy out of him."

"I think he was the one who did that to me." I bite my lip and she zeroes in on it like a bloodhound.

"I knew it!" Harley drops her voice. "He's good, isn't he? Like stupid, porn-star sized dick and knows how to use it good. I mean, he must be. It can't *just* be his face and billions in the bank that women are attracted to. The amount that call the office for him, using some stupid business ruse to try to snare a lunch meeting with him, you would not believe." Harley leans back and crosses her arms. "I think I should put it in my job description. Horny bitch blocker."

"Really?" The latte is bitter on my tongue suddenly. I grab a sugar packet from the table and stir it in.

Harley watches me, her lips curling in amusement. "You don't need to worry, Maria. None of them get anywhere. And ever since you started at The Songbird, I haven't even seen him go on a date with another woman. And that's saying something. I couldn't keep up with them all before."

"I'm not worried." I sip my latte again and wince. It still tastes off. Maybe they've made it differently today.

Harley reaches over and grabs it, taking a sip and licking her lips as she pushes it back to me. "Delicious. You know what that means?"

"I'm getting sick because my taste buds are off? I don't know." I look at her.

"It means you've got it bad. And I don't blame you. He's a good guy beneath the grumpy boss-hole exterior. Plus, he's totally only had eyes for you since like forever, so you don't need to concern yourself with all those other women. He never saw them more than a few times each. Maybe Gwen. But that was different. They worked together, until you know, she left after stealing all the secret formulations. Although it wasn't proved, she's still suspect number one." Harley chews on her lip, her eyes darting to me. "I talk fast on caffeine, okay? It's a problem and I'm handling it." She takes a huge sip from her cup. "Starting tomorrow."

I smile and push my cup away as sourness well and truly sets in. I can't be jealous of him being with other women before I even moved here and began whatever it is I'm beginning with him. A relationship? An arrangement? I don't even know what to call it. I'm being ridiculous thinking about his hands on other women's skin, his lips whispering in their ears, him calling them *his*.

Completely ridiculous.

"Come on, eat up. I've got to head back in five." Harley motions to my untouched lunch.

"Oh, yes, of course," I reply absentmindedly as I pick the bagel up and bite into it.

Nothing. I taste nothing.

Actually, that's a lie.

What does jealousy taste like?

"Oh, my God! It's divine." Will runs his hand along the cream leather piping, leaning down and inhaling. "It even smells all luxurious."

I shake my head with a smile as he carefully wraps the Louis Vuitton overnight bag back in its tissue paper and places it inside the bag that was waiting for me when I got back from lunch. The note left with it said,

Sweetheart, you'll be needing this. G.

What does that mean? That he wants to take me to the beach house again? He sees us having nights away together?

I haven't seen Griffin since we landed last night. I headed back to my apartment as I promised to call my nana. And I needed a little breathing room. I had an incredible time, seeing him away from work, looser and happier, was wonderful. But the closer we flew back to the city, the more his business mask slipped firmly back into place. I love that side of him, too. The driven, brilliant man who runs his own empire. But I needed some time to get my head around the previous forty-eight hours and what had happened. The gala, Todd, Griffin staying the night, full of concern for me. Then flying us away and me feeling like I'm living that part of a romantic movie together where everything is perfect. I'm not used to it.

That isn't my life.

That wasn't my life.

Until him.

The more time I spend with him, the deeper he sinks into me. The further he penetrates. We are so similar in some ways. And so different in others.

My ex and my dad, and the mistakes they made have made me wary. Made me put a shield around my heart. They were both selfish, weak men. And their deceit cut deep. *So deep.*

Griffin is nothing like them. He's generous, and brilliant, and he respects me and my work. I don't want to keep away from him. However, I'm not sure I could survive a man like Griffin Parker if he took a knife to my heart.

I chat with Will while the spa team finish up for the day and start leaving, one by one, until it's just the two of us left.

"You coming? I can carry this beauty for you?" Will grins, eyeing up my gift. Either he's been talking to Harley, or everyone in this hotel really does know everyone else's business, because he hasn't even asked who it's from.

"Not yet. I need to finish up some things first."

"Okay, gorgeous. I'll see you tomorrow. Have a fun evening packing and unpacking your new overnight bag." He grins at me as I look at him. "That's what I would do the night I took that work of art home."

I laugh as I wave at him.

I work for another hour, not realizing how late it's gotten, until the spa phone rings, making me jump.

"Hello?"

"How's your afternoon been, Sweetheart?"

My heart flies into my throat at the sound of his voice. The second call in one day.

"It's been great. I got a gift." I look over at the beautiful gift bag.

"Did you?" He sounds amused.

"You didn't need to do that, Griff." I lean my hip against the counter as I talk to him.

I bet he's sitting at his desk, running his hand over his tie. He does it whenever he's thinking.

"I wanted to."

"Well, it's beautiful. Thank you."

"Don't *say* thank you."

"Why not?"

"Show me instead."

I pause, heat pooling in my cheeks. If I don't cut him off now, then I will spend the night with him in any way he chooses he wants me. But saying no isn't even an option I'll consider. Just the sound of his voice has my entire body aching to be close to him again.

"I'm locking up now."

"Perfect."

"Why is that so perfect?" I bite my lip as his deep chuckle sends goosebumps scattering along my spine.

"Because now you can show me your gratitude instead." His reply is confident.

He knows he has me.

"I—"

"You'll wait for me downstairs, Maria. I've got plans for us tonight."

Five minutes later, Griffin strides through the spa entrance and straight over to me, his determined eyes locked on mine. His lips twitch into a ghost of a smile before they crash down onto mine, and his hands wrap around the back of my neck.

"Fuck, Sweetheart. I've waited all night and all day to see you and kiss you again. Are you trying to torture me?"

He strokes his thumbs along my jaw as he kisses me again, sliding his tongue between my parted lips. I sink into him, pulling him closer as I put my arms around his waist and my hands against his back. His muscles ripple beneath my fingers and he growls against my lips as he tugs at the band in my hair, which stays firmly in place.

"What did I tell you?"

"We're not doing anything on my counter, Griff," I pant between kisses, "so I don't need my hair down."

He grumbles, his chest vibrating, and then presses his tongue back inside my mouth, kissing me in the way I've been thinking about non-stop since we landed last night.

This man is dangerous. But like all things dangerous, he sends a thrill running through my body that makes me feel more alive, more present, than anything else in the world.

I didn't realize quite how much I craved seeing him again today until this moment.

"Spend the night at my apartment with me, Maria. I've thought about you all fucking day."

He tilts my head back so his blue eyes can gaze into mine.

"Okay." I smile. "I guess I should give my new bag its first outing."

He smiles, his eyes softening, giving me a glimpse of beach house Griffin, as he presses another kiss to my lips. "Great idea."

He carries my bag for me as I lock up and we head out to the main entrance. Earl sees us, tipping his hat in greeting.

"Beautiful evening."

"It is." Griffin's eyes dart to mine.

"And Dandy seems to be playing ball." Earl looks up above where the white and gray pigeon stares down at us from a ledge.

"Who's Dandy?" Griffin follows his gaze, a scowl covering his handsome face. "Don't tell me you named the bird, Earl."

Earl looks at me. "Ms. Taylor did. I think it suits her."

"Suits *it*," Griffin says. "You can't know it's a girl. It's a fucking pest, is what it is."

I press my lips together, fighting the fluttering sensation in my gut as Griffin's eyes scan my face.

"You named the troublemaker Dandy?"

"It's a nice name. I thought you might appreciate it."

He narrows his eyes at me as Earl pipes up, "The seed was a brilliant idea."

Griffin whips his widening eyes to Earl. "You're *feeding* it?"

Earl and I exchange a smile as Griffin rakes a hand back through his hair.

"Fuck's sake. Why the fuck would you do that? That little asshole's shit is literally costing me thousands in carpet cleaning!"

"Was." Earl holds up a finger. "Ms. Taylor suggested feeding her seed around the corner down the alley. She's started spending more time there now she's come to expect it. The carpet hasn't even needed the usual extra clean today." Earl sweeps his arm over the immaculate sidewalk carpet proudly.

I lay a hand on Griffin's arm.

301

"It makes business sense. This way you're spending a fraction of the amount on seed instead. And the carpet looks better than ever."

He looks at me, a glint in his eyes, which I can't read. "You're still feeding the flying rats."

"Everyone's a winner, Sweetheart," I sing sweetly as he narrows his eyes at me.

My heart is pounding in my chest.

He will make me pay for this later.

"Have a good evening, Earl," Griffin says, placing his hand on my lower back.

I wave goodbye and Griffin steers me around the corner to the residence's entrance, his hand never leaving my body. When we reach the elevators, we step inside one and he scans his key card and presses the button. His jaw is set, his eyes dark. He says nothing.

Maybe taking on the bird problem with Earl myself was a mistake.

The doors slide open as the elevator chimes, and we walk out into a plush carpeted entryway.

"We can fetch your things later," Griffin grunts. "Right now, I need you in my apartment."

He scans his card again, opening the ornate double doors in front of us, and guides me in.

Maybe he wants to show me around first before I get my overnight things.

"This is beautiful." I barely have time to finish my sentence, my eyes taking in the incredible open-plan penthouse with views over Central Park, before two strong arms spin me and slam on either side of the wall next to my head, caging me in between them.

"Do you do it on fucking purpose?" His voice is a low whisper.

"I—" My breath catches in my throat as I look up into his blazing eyes. I struggle to speak as my mouth goes dry.

"I said, do you do it on fucking purpose?" he rasps, leaning closer to me so his breath mixes with mine.

The warmth of it hits my lips, making them part.

I don't understand. Why does he look so pissed?

"It's just seed," I whisper, licking my lips instinctively as he leans even closer.

"You think that's what bothers me?" He chuckles softly, the sound making the hairs on the back of my neck stand up.

"It's not?" I breathe.

He's standing so close that every time I take a breath in, my chest rises and my breasts brush the front of his shirt.

Touch, retreat, touch, retreat, touch.

"No, Sweetheart," he growls, making me shudder as he removes one hand from the wall and uses it to hold mine and guide it to his pants. "What bothers me is how fucking crazy you make me when you show me just how smart you are."

He holds my hand against his unmistakable erection, which is hot beneath my palm. I wrap my fingers around it, drawing a sharp hiss from his lips. I love that I affect him as much as he affects me.

Keeping my eyes on his, I reach up and pull my hair loose from the band, giving him a small smile.

His gaze darkens and he sucks his bottom lip in between his teeth as he takes one strand from near my face and twirls it slowly around his fingers.

"Do you want to know what's happening tonight?"

"What?" My eyes are on his lips as my breasts graze his chest again with my breath.

"I'm fucking you bare." He says each word slowly, so slowly that just the sound of them alone slipping over his tongue has my pulse coursing blood between my legs.

A deep, consuming rhythm, just for him.

All for him.

"Griff—"

"Tell me you don't want it, Maria."

He moves quickly, pushing my dress up around my waist and tearing my already wet panties down my thighs until they drop to my ankles. His lips claim my mouth with a searing fire as he rips open his belt buckle and pushes his clothes down, pressing me into the wall.

"We can't yet, it's—"

"We're both clean, Maria. And you're on birth control. You had a medical report from when you accepted the job."

My mind spins as his lips pepper kisses along my jawline.

I had to have a full medical before accepting the job. And Griffin's seen it?

"That's supposed to be private," I pant as his fingers find my clit and apply the lightest pressure. I grab hold of the back of his hand, relishing his skin against mine as he locks eyes with me.

"I would never disrespect your privacy. I haven't read it."

My mouth drops open as his fingers curl against me.

Fuck, it feels so good.

"Then how?"

He watches me as I shiver from his touch.

"I know nothing came up because you would have stopped me by now. And I saw your pill packet at the beach house." He groans deep in his chest as he dips his fingers lower, and they get covered in slick wetness. "Accept it, Sweetheart. You. Are. Mine. And you belong to me in every sense of the word." His lips graze mine, and I struggle to breathe steadily as he whispers against them. "I will have you any way I want. And you'll beg me for more."

He's right. Of course he is. He's always right.

My body's been bonded to his since the first time he touched me. Like an unbreakable contract written in blood. *Mine and his.*

"What about you?" I roll my hips, rubbing my clit against his palm, my chest shuddering with each delicious pulse of arousal exploding inside me.

"What about me?" He slides two fingers inside me and we both gasp as my body accepts them greedily.

"How can you know you're clean?" My eyes roll back in my head as he swirls his fingers inside me, and I fight off the unwanted images of him with all the other women before me that Harley mentioned.

He dusts the side of my face with the knuckles of his free hand.

"You're the only woman I've ever wanted to fuck bare. There's something real between us. I know you feel it. I'm not fucking around with you, Maria." He flexes his fingers inside me, causing a rush of wetness to meet them as I stifle the moan in my throat. "You're who I want. Only you. I can't fucking think straight when you're near me."

His eyes bore into mine, making everything else in the room disappear.

Intense should be re-written in the dictionary to say 'Griffin Parker'.

I can't tear my eyes away from his and the way he's looking at me like I'm the only woman he's ever seen. Ever *cared* about.

"I—"

He presses his fingers to my lips. "I got tested before we went away. The results came back today. They're on the counter if you want to see."

He slides his fingers out of me and takes a step back.

I grab his tie, pulling him back to me so I can dust my lips over his.

"I believe you," I murmur.

He gives me a wicked smile and then traces his tongue along the inside of my lips. I lean in for a kiss, but he moves away.

"No more reasons, then?"

I shake my head, blood coursing through my veins, my pulse rocketing.

"No."

"So I can fuck this pretty cunt bare, like I've been dreaming of doing since I first tasted it."

His words are strained, as though he's holding himself back. Him fighting to control himself because of me steals my final reserve and I pull him closer.

"Yes."

He bites his bottom lip and lifts one of my legs, holding the back of my thigh.

"You're mine," he grits out, his eyes dropping to where the head of his broad cock is pressing against my skin.

I gasp as he nudges forward and I stretch around the smooth tip of him.

"Yours. Only yours."

"Fuck, Sweetheart," he hisses, pressing my leg back toward the wall so I'm spread open for him. "Fuck."

He snaps his eyes up to meet mine and the heat in them sears into me as he drives forward, pinning me to the wall as he fills me completely.

"Griff," I gasp, my mouth dropping open as he groans and juts his chin forward.

"Mine," he murmurs, "you're so fucking wet and tight, and you're mine."

We stay like that for a second, staring at each other, me wrapped tightly around him, him shaking as he digs his fingertips into my flesh, sweat beading along his hairline in anticipation. His balls press against my skin as every thick inch of him claims me.

I've never wanted to be owned before.

Not like this.

But he's right about what he said before.

He can have me any way he wants me.

And I *will* beg for more.

No doubt about it. Griffin Parker owns my body, and what's more... I want him to. I want to give him everything. Because looking back into his crystal blue eyes now, our bodies pressed as tightly together as they can be, his breath mixing with my own, I know...

This man is going to mean everything to me.

And more.

"Give me everything," I whisper.

His pupils dilate at my consent. He looks between my eyes, then presses a gentle kiss to my forehead.

"Good girl," he breathes.

When his eyes meet mine again, they're dark with lust.

I suck in a breath. And hold it. Waiting.

He watches me as he pulls back, smiling as he slams into me, forcing my back to climb up the wall. I cry out in pleasure as he sets a steady, unrelenting pace. Fucking me hard and deep, his brow pulled into a look of deep concentration as his gaze drops and he watches where his body disappears inside mine.

"My good girl," he growls, forcing my leg higher and driving deeper.

I surrender completely to him, gasping and panting as he drives into me over and over. I come hard for him, twice, before the perfect moment he loses control, cursing and squeezing his eyes shut as he spills deep inside me, filling me with everything he has.

Owning me.

Claiming me.

Like there was ever any danger of me being anyone else's ever again.

I welcome his wet heat inside me, tears pricking at my eyes as he pushes as deep inside me as he possibly can.

It's still not enough.

"I'm making you mine forever, Sweetheart," he pants, his orgasm subsiding as he opens his eyes again.

His breathing is labored as he rests his forehead against mine and holds the back of my neck with his other hand. His intoxicating blue eyes fix on to mine and he smiles at me, one side of his perfect mouth curling, until a sinful flash of perfect white teeth show.

He looks like sex.

If earth-shattering, orgasmic sex was packaged up in one body. Then it would be him. *Griffin-mind-and-body-commanding-Parker.*

And I'm his follower. The one who comes to worship at his feet.

If I ever thought I could escape this man once he had his sights on me, then I was so undeniably mistaken.

I was his the moment he decided he wanted me.

I never stood a chance.

Chapter Twenty-Five

Maria

"TIME TO WAKE UP, Sweetheart."

Warmth caresses my face as the gentle whir of the remote-controlled shades being raised at the windows echoes in my ears.

"Five more minutes." I sigh sleepily as I inhale the scent of my lavender pillow spray mixed with the aroma of Griffin on the crisp sheets.

He leans over me from behind, inhaling the same spot as me.

"My bed smells so much better with you in it," he whispers in my ear, pressing his warm, hard body against my back.

"Good. I'm glad." I smile, keeping my eyes firmly closed.

"Sweetheart." He plants soft kisses against my bare skin from my shoulder all the way up to my ear. "We have the filming to prepare for."

"Mmm." I let out a half moan, half groan.

He's right. The crew are arriving tomorrow, ready to start shooting the day after. The Songbird needs to be ready. It's come around so quickly. The last week has flown by. Since that first night I spent in his apartment, I've barely left. We've gotten into a routine. Concentrate on business all day. Concentrate on each other all night.

I swear every staff member in the hotel suspects something is going on. But they don't seem to care. I was worrying over their reactions for nothing. The Songbird is Griffin's hotel, and I've discovered through Harley that he has an open policy about employees dating. I guess when the boss allows it for everyone—so long as work isn't affected—then it doesn't raise so many eyebrows when he does it himself.

"Kiss me good morning first." I turn my face so his lips can reach mine.

He holds my chin between his fingers and gifts me with the softest, most perfect kiss I could ever hope to wake up to.

"What's that look for?" He smiles at me, his eyes sparkling before he presses his lips to my forehead and kisses me there.

"I was just thinking about how I love waking up next to you."

"I see." His voice deepens as I wriggle in his arms, knowing exactly what's coming.

The same thing that's come every morning since I came home to his apartment with him that first night. The same thing I crave in my dreams and yearn to wake up for.

"You know how much I love sinking myself inside that pretty cunt when I wake up," Griffin whispers, nipping at my ear with his teeth. "I guess this morning shouldn't be any exception."

I sigh happily, rolling onto my back and wrapping my arms around his neck as he kisses me.

He lines up the head of his cock and then he's sliding inside me, causing our kiss to stop as we both open our eyes and gaze at one another. The same we do every time he first enters me. Ever since that first night we had sex without a condom, and he looked so deep into my eyes that it was as though he was seeing my soul.

And I was offering it up for him to take.

His eyes search mine, the skin around them softening as I smile up at him. It's like the removal of the physical barrier between our skin removed the invisible one around our hearts as well.

I'm falling in love with this man.

And the way he looks at me, I swear he feels it, too.

"Griff," I murmur, stroking my fingers down the side of his face as I look into his eyes.

"I know, Sweetheart. Me too." His eyes pinch with emotion, and then his lips find mine again and he sinks back inside me.

I let my eyes fall closed and wrap myself around him as he rocks us both to a slow, awakening orgasm.

This.

This is what I love about him.

At night, he fucks me like he owns me. Hard, dominating, unapologetic. Like I'm his plaything, designed for his pleasure. And I love it. I love every toe-curling, hot sweaty minute as he whispers pure and utter pantie-melting filth in my ear and makes me come un-done around him again and again.

But in the mornings... it's different.

That first time his eyes find mine, they always bright-en. Lift with an undisguised pleasure that I'm still here. That I stayed to welcome another new day with him. His words are still pure filth and sound so perfect tumbling from his beautiful lips. But they're always spoken differ-ently. Softer, sweeter. Whispered to me as he holds my eyes in his and makes love to me.

Yes.

Griffin Parker makes love like a God, too.

I am well and truly fucked if this ever ends.

"You're so beautiful," he murmurs, stroking my hair back from my face as he stays firmly rooted inside my body. "I'm so glad you're mine. You were made for me, Sweetheart."

God, this man.

I gaze up at him, pressing my fingertips to the corners of his eyes, tracing the creases there from when he laughs. I stroke them with a featherlight touch as my eyes search his, looking for any lingering doubt he might be hiding.

There's none.

"I could never be anyone else's. You were made for me, too."

He smiles at me, and then his lips are on mine again, his tongue sliding into my mouth as he rolls me on top of him.

"After work tonight. I'm fucking you like this, with your incredible tits on display."

I laugh as I look at him, my romantic morning Griffin slipping away for another twenty-four hours as domineering Mr. Parker returns.

"If I'm on top, doesn't that mean I'm in charge?" I flex around where he is still inside me and a groan vibrates his throat.

"You might get to be on top later. But never forget who owns this perfect fucking body."

He spins us again until he's hovering over me with my wrists pinned to the mattress.

We look at each other with matching energy buzzing behind our eyes. He's right. Even when I get on top, it's always him in control. He always knows just how to hold my hips and lift me like I weigh nothing, dragging me up and down onto him to get us both off at the same time.

That's him. My perfect, skilled man.

Always in control.

Always gets it right.

"Right, my beautiful girlfriend." He leans down, kissing me again as he slides out, separating us. "Shower time."

I close my eyes, pretending to relax back into the pillows. I love the way it sounds when he calls me his girlfriend. He never asked, exactly. But that's Griffin all over. He decided. His choice. His rules. He called me it one morning, and then made love to me so tenderly that by the end of it my head was spinning as I realized how deep we'd both gotten so quickly. But I've adored every second of this journey with him.

His large hand grips mine and pulls me up from the bed. My eyes fly open as he pulls me against him.

"Don't fucking toy with me, Sweetheart."

A sting flashes over my skin, sending a ripple of electricity following it as Griffin slaps me on the behind. I suck in a breath, my cheeks flushing as he watches me.

"Fuck, get your ass in that shower now." He palms his now hardening cock as he pushes me along in front of him. His eyes cast down to my ass, where the skin must be reddening. "Why can't you do as you're told?"

I glance back at him over my shoulder, knowing exactly what it does to him when I don't do what he wants straight away. It messes with his control-freak nature and usually ends up with him needing to gain it straight back in the best way he knows how.

"I have to be inside that perfect cunt again," he growls.

I bite the inside of my cheek to hide my smile as I step under the hot spray of the shower and welcome his mouth onto my neck and his hands onto my breasts.

He's in control, physically. There's no doubt about that.

I have no intention of fighting him on it. I know where I crave control, and that's at work.

But here? Wrapped in the arms of the most brilliant man, naked, with his adoring words pouring out over me, and his earlier adoration seeping from me...

I can't think of anything more perfect.

"Look what great sex does for your skin," Harley says as we join the end of the line.

"I'm looking." Will assesses me with a grin.

We've joined the line for coffee at the new deli which has opened in The Songbird's retail lobby. Harley couldn't believe Griffin had been keeping it a secret for months while the plans were finalized.

"I can't believe you knew about this and didn't tell me." She raises her brows at me.

"I only found out a couple of days ago. We barely talk about work."

"No, too busy with your mouth full, I bet." She smirks at me as I give her a playful look of horror.

"Well, whatever it is. That man has it bad. Were those the third bouquet of flowers he's sent this week?" Will asks, referring to the frangipanis that arrived at the spa this morning when he was dropping down some paperwork for me.

"Fourth." I tuck a strand of hair behind my ear as I move along the line.

"Fuck me." He exhales. "Louis Vuitton and the entire New York flower market. And here's me thinking my diamond cock piercing was extravagant."

Harley catches my eye with a smirk. "Van Cleef and Arpels man?"

"The one and only." Will smiles to himself as we reach the head of the line and order.

Harley gets one for her and Griffin and I take a pen and draw a small bird on his before handing it back to her.

"It'll make him smile," I explain as her brows pull together.

"Good. He needs it. He's driving me nuts barking out orders for the film crew's schedule. It's all in hand. Been planned for weeks. But he's still on the control train making sure it's all perfect. He'll have us all out cleaning the sidewalk carpet with our toothbrushes soon."

I laugh. She's got it. That's my man to a tee. Mr. Every-thing-Must-Be-Perfect.

"Anyway, I better get this back upstairs to him, pronto. Please come blow him under his desk at lunch or some-thing, Maria. Get him to chill the heck out."

"Bye, Harley." I grin as she stalks off toward the eleva-tors.

"You getting lots of use out of that gorgeous bag?" Will asks as we walk across the lobby.

"Yes, I suppose." I smile.

The truth is, I used it once to move my make-up and small items to Griffin's penthouse that first night, and because I haven't left, and have grabbed a new outfit for the next day each evening on my way home from work, it's not been used since.

"Well, make sure you do. Not everyone gets bought a gorgeous Louis Vuitton like that, you know."

"Who has a Louis?" I turn and find Emily grinning.

"Hi, Em." I smile back and kiss her on both cheeks.

She drops into the spa so much now that we speak most days. I wouldn't say we are friends, exactly. But well on the way, perhaps.

"Maria does," Will says. "And a fine beauty it is, too."

Emily looks at me, her brow quirked in question.

"It was a gift from Griffin. For all the work I've done in the spa."

I ignore the wide eyes Will's giving me at my blatant lie and smile at Emily instead.

It's not completely dishonest. He is very vocal about my work at the spa. Maybe it's because Emily has known him her whole life, but I don't feel right telling her about his dating life. The fact that she's not mentioned the two of us to me yet, despite how many times I've seen her, tells me she doesn't know. And that's Griffin's call.

"Oh, I see. Well, that's lovely. He's always been so generous. He bought Gwen a diamond necklace after her first month here."

"Exactly. So generous," I agree.

My eyes meet Will's as Emily waves at someone across the lobby. He shakes his head at me, pointing at his neck. I have no idea what he's going on about.

"Thank you again for all of your help," I say to Emily.

"What for?"

"The new supplier contracts. I was so grateful to get your call after the gala. It's all been set up now. It makes me more comfortable knowing you recommended them."

"Oh. Don't worry about that." She waves a hand in the air. "It was nothing. You would do the same for me."

"Well, I appreciate it," I repeat as we part, and she and Will head off to the elevator bank together.

I make my way to the spa. The sight of the frangipanis greets me as I enter through the main doors. I walk over and touch a delicate petal.

Should it bother me that Griffin bought Gwen a diamond necklace? I mean, they were dating.

I shake my head as I push the thought to the back of my head. It's done. It's all in the past.

I open up my calendar on the computer.

My day is far too busy to even worry about it.

Chapter Twenty-Six

Griffin

"MR. PARKER, A MAN called twice for you while you were at lunch, but he wouldn't leave his name."

"Thank you, Harley," I say, passing her to walk into my office.

I close the door and shrug out of my jacket, throwing it onto the arm of the sofa as I head to my desk. There's only one man who would ring and refuse to leave a name.

I glance at my watch. I was at lunch with Maria for less than an hour. It must be important if he's tried twice in that time.

I pick up the phone and dial the cell number I have memorized.

"We've got something," the voice says the second the call connects.

About fucking time.

"And?" I sit down in my chair and lean over my elbows on the desk.

"There was a woman trying to sell recipes in exchange for a position."

"Formulations," I mutter.

"Yeah, yeah, those." The guy coughs out a wheezy breath. If he hadn't come so highly recommended, I would have fired his ass by now. *Fucking recipes.*

"This woman. What did she look like?" I press my fingers into my eyes as I picture Gwen and her dark chestnut hair.

Everything pointed to her having stolen those formulations. After she left, she went to a rival hotel, as Head of Client Experience. A role with more overall responsibility than Spa Manager at The Songbird. It all seemed convenient. We break up. A few days later, it's discovered the paperwork for the new formulations has been stolen. Then she leaves and takes up a position elsewhere. She said she thought it was better not to work together anymore.

God, I'm such an idiot to trust her. To trust anyone.

"Brown hair." The man sniffs. "Our source says they have photos."

"Send them over."

I run my hand down my face. The thought of handing them over and pressing charges against Gwen, someone I used to date, makes me feel nothing, apart from satisfaction. I can finally get closure, look at my other staff and know it wasn't them who betrayed me.

Move on.

"We will. We will," the man's voice is hesitant.

I roll my shoulders and they crack as I try to loosen them.

"Now," I hiss. "You have my email."

"The source. They're, um... proving hard to get hold of."

Fucking hell.

I clench my fist against the cool glass of my desk. I swear this guy thinks I'm an idiot. The amount he's charging me. For what? Months of nothing. *Fucking nothing.*

"So get hold of them," I force out, wishing I could get hold of his neck right now and do some forcing of my own.

"We will."

The skin on my knuckles has turned white. He always says 'we'. As far as I'm aware, he works alone. But I guess all those years in the police force and then heading into private investigating after early medical retirement means you know people in the right places.

"Do whatever it takes," I grunt, my eyes drawn to my cell phone on the desk as the screen flashes with a new message from *Sweetheart*. I smile as I pick it up and open it.

Sweetheart: Thanks for lunch. Missing you already.

I miss her, too. Fucking sap that she's turned me into. I grin as I tap out a reply.

Me: Thanks for sitting on my face. I'm missing your taste already.

Sweetheart: What are you talking about? I did no such thing!

My grip tightens on the other phone.

323

"Whatever it takes," I repeat. "I want this over." I don't give him a chance to reply before I slam it back into the cradle and lean back in my chair with my cell in hand.

I'm wound tighter than a fucking sprinter at the blocks waiting for the pistol. My girl is the only thing that'll relieve that pressure. She doesn't even know how much I need her to stop me having a coronary at the age of thirty-three. She's my fucking escape from all of this.

Me: Not yet. But you will, tonight. I'm starving for you, Sweetheart. I know you won't let me down.

I smile as she types a reply.

Sweetheart: I'd never let you down, Griff.

I inhale, filling my lungs until they sting and force me to blow it all out.

Despite all this shit, I have her.

I can *trust* her.

"Is everything in place?" I bark, scouring the sidewalk for signs of trash or bird shit. It would be just my luck that 'Dandy' and her little posse all came down with some kind of avian diarrhea and shitted up a storm right where filming will take place in a few hours.

"Everything's fine, Mr. Parker. It's all in hand. Your lovely lady was on the case this morning, checking our feathered friends were going to be on their best behavior."

I nod at Earl, my lips curling at his mention of Maria. I kept her up half the night working out my frustrations from yesterday's phone call. Her silky skin and breathy moans of my name were the best fucking therapy. I'm almost one hundred percent chilled and calm this morning. *Almost.* The knowledge we are expecting hundreds, if not thousands of fans lining the sidewalk later, trying to catch a glimpse of Jay Anderson, Steel Force's lead actor, has me on edge. Just the right amount. Enough to make sure everything is perfect. I don't want any unforeseen surprises.

"Thanks, Earl." I pat him on the shoulder as Emily heads toward us.

"Good morning, stranger." She grins and sweeps me into a hug, kissing me on the cheek.

"Sorry, Em." I give her a weak smile.

I've been a shit friend the last couple of weeks. Apart from a rushed lunch, where I had a phone call and had to head back to work early, I've barely seen her. I've spent every spare second with Maria. Something I also need to tell Emily about now that she's here.

"I forgive you, so long as you don't make a habit of it. We're childhood friends, Griffin. Nothing can affect that." She winks at me as she wraps a hand around my arm.

"You look nice."

My eyes drop over the cream fitted dress she's wearing. It's a lot like one Maria wore last week. The night I took her for dinner and then dropped to my knees and sank my tongue against her needy flesh before my apartment door had even closed behind us when we got home. I can't get enough of that woman. It's insane how much I want her. I've never felt like this before in my life.

"Thank you. I have a lunch date." Emily cocks her head to the side as she watches the security team setting up the barriers on the sidewalk.

"You do?" My brow quirks in interest.

She looks at me, smiling. "I do. I think he might be the one."

"Em. That's incredible! I'm so pleased for you." I look at her with interest. I've known her my entire life, but I didn't see that coming. She hardly ever mentions any men. I know she must date. But I've never known her to have anyone serious. "When can I meet him? Make sure he's good enough?"

She avoids my gaze and smirks. "No one will ever be good enough for you, Griffin."

"Probably." I laugh as we walk into the hotel and across the lobby. "But I just want you to be happy, Em. I care about you."

Her hand tightens on my arm, and she smiles. "That means a lot to hear you say that."

"Have you told Maria?"

Emily frowns. "I wasn't going to bother her today. I'm sure she's busy."

"Don't be silly. She'd love to see you," I say as I lead us in the spa's direction. "Actually, I wanted to tell you, but I haven't seen you in a while. Maria and I are dating."

"Really?" Emily's voice lifts in surprise, but her face remains unchanged.

"You knew already?"

"I've known you a long time, Griffin." She exhales with a smile.

"Yes. I should have guessed." I chuckle as she stops walking and turns to face me, her brows furrowed.

"Just be careful, Griffin. I don't want to see you hurt again. Look what happened with Gwen."

My shoulders stiffen and I clear my throat as her eyes narrow, studying me.

"That was Gwen. This is Maria. It's completely different."

"Is it?" She looks at me like I'm an idiot led only by his dick.

"Completely," I say, my jaw clenched. I know Emily cares as a friend. But the idea that she is suggesting Maria could be anything like Gwen is ludicrous. "I'm in love with her."

Emily's eyes widen, and she visibly swallows before nodding. "Of course you are. I meant nothing by it. Maria's wonderful. I just want you to be happy. I've known you long enough to want that for you more than anyone else."

The concern in her eyes makes me drop my shoulders. "I'm sorry, Em. I didn't mean to snap."

"It's fine." She gives me a small smile and takes my arm again. "Come on. Let's go say good morning to Maria. Then I want you to introduce me to Jay. Apparently, he's even more of a hunk in the flesh than on screen."

I smile as we walk. "So I'm told. Lucky fucker."

"Maria. It's so great to see you. How are you doing?" Jay Anderson's eyes crinkle at the corners as he leans forward and kisses my girlfriend on both cheeks. I swear if she blushes, all hell will break loose.

He has a broad frame. I'm an inch or two taller than him, but he makes up for that in width. The sleeves of his FBI costume are straining against his biceps. Still, I'm sure I could take him.

"You two know each other?" I look at Maria in question.

"Oh, not really. Just in passing. But I know Jay's brother, Blake, and his fiancé, Daisy. They live in Hope Cove, and Daisy worked with me at my spa there." Maria slides her arm around my waist and smiles up at me. She's the first woman I've seen who's completely unaffected by the all American sandy-haired hunk in front of us. Even Harley was tongue-tied meeting him this morning.

"You're not missing Hope Cove, then?" Jay asks, checking his costume and tightening the strap on his bullet-proof vest as he chats.

Maria's eyes dart to mine and she strokes the side of my ribs through my shirt.

"Not so much. I love the new challenges New York is bringing me."

She smiles at me, and I want nothing more than to grab her chin and kiss her right now. Smear that red lipstick she's wearing all over us both as I devour her. I look at her red nails as she places her other hand on my chest. She smirks when she sees my eyes on them. She knows how much I got off on watching those bright red nails wrapped around my cock in the shower last night.

I narrow my eyes at her and give her a knowing smile as Jay continues chatting away.

"Hey, I gotta go, guys. I want to video call my wife, Holly, before filming starts. She's pregnant and couldn't fly over with us."

He flashes a show-stopping smile at us, and I suddenly understand what Emily meant. This guy looks like a walking ad for airbrushing. Is he even real? How can a man look so... perfect?

"Dreamy, isn't he?" Maria laughs after he's gone back inside the suite the film crew have taken over.

I turn to her, and her eyes are bright as she bites her lip, watching me.

"What did you say, Sweetheart?" I lift my hand and tug her lip free, swiping my thumb between her lips and running it along the lower one, grazing her teeth with the pad.

"Nothing." She gazes at me as I take my thumb back.

"It better be fucking nothing." I dip my head to her ear. "Remember whose good girl you are," I whisper, before pressing my lips against her skin. The scent of yellow and white tropical flowers in her hair evokes memories that instantly speak to my dick. "Fuck, Sweetheart, you'll be the death of me."

She grins as she leans into my lips, her hands resting on my chest where my heart is beating out a strong, deep pulse.

"I hope not, Mr. Parker. I'm growing quite fond of you."

I pull back and grab either side of her face between my hands, causing her to suck in a breath. We don't say anything as we stare at one another, our faces growing serious.

We don't need to.

Her words, and the heat carrying between us, says it all.

We've passed the point of no return.

We are each other's course now. And we are sailing it together.

Unchartered territory never looked so damn beautiful.

A couple of hours later, I am standing outside the main entrance as a team of around twenty people film Jay and his co-star screeching up to The Songbird in their car, then flying out, drawing their guns as they run to the main doors. It's a few seconds' worth of shot, but it's taken over an hour so far because of the sheer size of the turnout.

I cast my eyes over the sea of people, squeezed shoulder to shoulder behind the barriers. Most are women, but there are some men, too. Even some children. There are signs with 'We heart you, Jay' on them. And one that says, 'I wish I was Holly Anderson!'

There's a buzz in the air. Excitement crackling it to the point you can almost see it. It's taken this long to calm the crowd down enough to be quiet during the filming. Jay and his co-star spent ages signing autographs and having selfies taken with fans. They've finally won over their cooperation, and the sidewalk is silent as the set team counts down to another take that's about to begin.

I look over at Maria, who's standing with Harley and Emily watching it all unfold. She's grinning, her hands clasped together underneath her chin as she watches. She wants this to be a success as much as I do. If it goes well, they may film more special episodes here in the future, and it's great publicity for the hotel.

They call action and pull off the practice shot without a hitch. Then they film it again for real.

I miss every second.

My eyes are glued firmly on her.

As if she senses it, Maria looks over at me and smiles. My heart swells in my chest and I look away with a stupid school-boy grin on my face. *What the fuck has she done to me?*

I shake my head with a chuckle and look back up, but she's gone. Instead, a crowd of excited fans, whooping and cheering, have taken her place. They have flattened the barriers and piled through them, spilling all over the front entrance to the hotel.

I look up and catch one of the security team's eyes and tip my chin at him. He raises his arms and calls out, herding the crowd away from the main doors. They're chanting something about Jay, but I miss it as I swivel my head around, looking for Maria.

"Earl!" I call over the chanting. "Have you seen Maria?"

He looks at me from his position by the main door. He rises to his toes, to call back over the gaggle of chanting heads which have now enveloped us.

"She was here a moment ago, Mr. Parker. She hasn't come past me, so she must still be outside."

I dart my eyes around again. This is crazy. The fans are jumping up and down now, singing and dancing. It's like fucking Mardi-gras on my front steps. Harley and Emily have disappeared as well. They better all be together and not getting squashed into a wall at the back or something.

It takes another forty-five minutes after Jay and the team say goodbye and go inside before the fans finally quieten down and realize that they will not see him again today. Forty-five minutes of my blood pressure going postal as we bring one end of Park Avenue effectively to a standstill.

Eventually, most of the crowd disperse, and I leave security with the hardcore stragglers, who would probably set up tents and camp to have the chance of another glimpse of Jay if they thought they could get away with it.

I head back inside. Maria is there looking flustered as she talks to Harley on the far side of the lobby, holding her hands up in the air and motioning around.

"What is it?" I hurry over to them as Will appears and hands something to Maria.

"Maria thought she saw—"

"What it must be like being famous," Maria cuts in, looking at Harley. "I can't believe how crazy those fans were." She smiles at me as she clips her ID onto her dress.

"Really?" I frown looking between her and Harley.

I'm missing something.

"Uh-huh," she murmurs. "Right. Better get back to work. I've got the spa booked out for the film crew to use for the rest of the day."

"It's all go in the crazy nest!" Harley says, motioning to Will to follow her to the elevators.

"You sure everything's okay?" I ask once they've gone.

She seems on edge. Her lips are pursed, and the earlier excitement in her eyes has dimmed to something that looks a lot more like unease.

"I'm fine, Griff. I just have a lot to do, that's all." She looks side to side, then rises on her toes and places a soft kiss on my lips. "I'll see you later."

She turns, but I grab her hand and yank her back to my chest. "Give me a proper fucking kiss."

"Griff—"

"No one's looking." I pull her around the corner so we're less exposed. "And even if they are, it's my hotel."

She smiles at me properly, one hand reaching up to stroke along my jaw.

"A proper kiss?" She arches an eyebrow.

"That's what I said." I wrap my arms around her waist and hold her tight.

She tilts her chin, offering her lips to mine and I breathe in her sweet breath as I dip my head and take her mouth, sliding my tongue between her parted lips until she moans softly. She sinks her hand into my hair, and I press her against the wall, losing myself in her until she's panting in my arms.

When I pull back, her lipstick is smudged, and her cheeks are flushed.

"Now that's a kiss, Sweetheart." I smile at her, pressing my lips lightly against hers one last time. Then I stalk off toward the elevators and back to my office.

Chapter Twenty-Seven

Maria

THE NEXT COUPLE OF weeks pass by in a blur. Everything is perfect. The spa is thriving, and I make it out a few times with Harley and Suze for drinks and a catch up when Griffin has late work meetings.

Griffin.

The best piece of the perfect puzzle that my life has turned into. He's incredible. There's simply no better word for him and how our relationship has developed. I've practically moved into his penthouse. He threw a fit when I suggested going back to mine for one night, thinking he might need some of his own space back. The next day he sent Earl up with a bundle of flatpack boxes and told me to text him when they were full. Then he came, shirtsleeves rolled up, muscly forearms out, and carried each one up to his place himself. One by one, until everything except the odd item, like my suitcase and some paperwork I need to sort through, was at his place, piled up proudly in the master bedroom for me to unpack. I don't know why he didn't send anyone to help, as there were a lot of boxes. But the way his smile grew with each box he moved, and the intense way he made love to me on his bed, surrounded by them afterward, I would say he wanted the moment for himself.

To be in charge of it.

My gorgeous, control-freak.

"Griff?" I call as I enter the penthouse with my key card and step out of my heels in the entryway.

I pause at the hallway table. There's a piece of thick cream card with my name written on it. I turn it over.

Meet me on the balcony.

A stupid grin plasters itself to my face as I walk through the apartment, across the living area, and over to the open door leading out to the terrace style balcony which overlooks Central Park. It's a large space with beautiful, giant potted plants, giving it a real roof garden feel. Griffin's housekeeper tends to them all. I'm not sure he has a green fingered gene in his body.

I step out onto the cool tiled floor, my eyes casting over the fairy lights which are strung over every available branch and wrapped around every plant. Against the dark evening air, they cover the entire balcony. It's like being under a magical spell.

"Roma's been busy," I say as my eyes fall onto his broad, shirt-clad back standing with his hands thrust into pockets as he looks out at the view.

"She had a good reason to be." Griffin turns to me, and the lights catch his eyes, illuminating them as they drop appreciatively over my body.

I shiver in delight, goosebumps dancing up my spine. No matter how many weeks we've been together, the first time he looks at me after being apart always sends my heart racing in my chest, and butterflies fluttering everywhere else.

He looks at me like he needs me to breathe.

"She did?" I walk over to him and wrap my arms around his waist as he presses his lips to my hair and inhales. "Why is that?" I look around the balcony. There's an ice bucket with a bottle of champagne inside and two flutes next to it.

"Why do you think, Sweetheart?"

I gaze up at him, biting my lip.

What is he talking about?

He brings his lips down to mine and kisses me, murmuring his next words against my mouth. "It's three months since your first day at The Songbird."

His mouth curls in amusement as I do the math. He's right. Three months ago, today I walked through those doors to begin my first day as Spa Manager.

"I see." I run my hands down his biceps, the fabric of his shirt smooth beneath my fingertips. "So, you did this for me?"

"Of course, I did. You're mine."

He leans in and kisses me again, dropping his hands to cup my ass through my pencil skirt. His fingertips dig into my skin as a deep rumble rolls through his chest.

"I love you in these tight skirts, Sweetheart. And I love sliding them up even more."

I laugh as his mouth moves to my neck and he fists the sides of my skirt, inching it up my thighs.

"Fuck," he hisses as his palms connect with the bare skin on my thighs. "God, you don't know what you do to me." He presses his body against mine so I can feel exactly what it is I'm doing to him. "I promised myself I wouldn't fuck you until after."

"After what?" I sigh as his lips leave my neck and he draws back.

"After I gave you this." He reaches to the table and lifts a black velvet box.

"What's this?" I search his face as he looks at me, but he just smiles at me with his crystal blue eyes.

"Open it."

I take the box from his hand and flip the lid. Inside are the two most dazzling stud earrings I've ever seen in my life.

"Griff." I don't know what to say.

I stare at them in the box as Emily's words echo in my ears.

"He bought Gwen a diamond necklace after her first month here."

He frowns as he looks at me. "Don't you like them?"

"I do, I..." I swallow as I meet his eyes. "Is this a thing you do? For everyone? I mean, they're beautiful, but you don't need to. I do my job because I love it. Not because I expect..." I trail off as I look back at them twinkling in the box.

"For everyone?" He tilts my chin, so I have to meet his questioning gaze.

He knows. He always knows when I'm holding something back.

I take a deep breath. "You bought Gwen a diamond necklace. You don't need to with me. I do the job because I love it," I repeat.

Where exactly am I going with this?

"Who told you that?"

My stomach twists. I shouldn't have said anything. I'm a grown-ass woman getting jealous over an ex because of some jewelry. An ex who he didn't date for more than a few months, and who—by all accounts—caused a huge amount of scandal and lost income to The Songbird when she stole the spa formulations and took them with her to a competitor.

"Maria." Griffin shakes his head as he looks at me. "Never compare the way I am with you to anyone or anything else. Do you hear me?"

He's caught me in his intense gaze, the one I'm unable to break free of. It's like an anchor fixing me on the spot.

"Okay," I whisper.

"Yes, I bought Gwen a necklace." His hands go to my ear, brushing my hair away as he gently removes my current gold studs, one at a time. "But that's only because she lost hers after a client fainted on her and pulled it off as she caught them. It was too broken to easily fix."

His fingers linger on the sides of my face before he takes the new studs from their box and slides them through my ears.

"Thank you." I reach up and touch one.

"It wasn't a present to her, Maria. Not in the way you think. The hotel paid for it."

Something about the way his eyes soften at the corners as he looks at the new studs in my ears has my stomach doing somersaults.

"Oh. I see."

I could kick myself for sounding so jealous and insecure. I've spent most of my adult life not needing reassurance from men. It's who I am. Yet, with Griffin, the idea of all this ending, or not being real, has my heart in my throat and my mind running away with me.

"They're blue diamonds," he says softly, wrapping me back in his arms, the topic of Gwen obviously over in his mind already.

"They're the same blue as your eyes." I look into them, the close match stealing my breath.

"Then it will be like my eyes are always on you." His gaze drops to my lips, and he runs the pad of his thumb over my bottom one, pulling it down so my lips part. "Just like my thoughts are."

I barely have time to register what could be the most romantic thing anyone has ever said to me, before his lips are on mine, full of urgency as his hands push my skirt up around my waist.

He hooks his thumbs underneath either side of my lace panties and drops to his knees as he slides them down to my feet.

"Fuck, your scent is the stuff of dreams."

He leans his forehead against my lower stomach and grasps each of my hipbones tightly as he inhales. His breath dancing against my skin has arousal flooding between my legs and I lean back against the tall Perspex guard rail as my hands drop to his hair.

No matter how many times he goes down on me, the sight of him down there, the anticipation of what's to come, has me ridiculously wet within seconds.

"Good girl," he murmurs as he swipes his tongue through me slowly and gets covered in slick wetness.

"Griff?" His blue eyes look up and lock on to mine.

He smiles at the way my voice raises, as though asking a question as I say his name. I don't know why I do it. Maybe it's my way of telling him I trust him. That I am giving him complete control over my body.

Whatever it is, it always causes his eyes to darken with a wicked glint.

"Lean back, Sweetheart. I'm going to fuck you with my tongue until your sweet cum is all over my face."

Oh, God.

My eyes roll back in my head as he begins his assault on my body, easily whipping me up into a frenzy that has me panting out his name and shuddering at lightning speed. He knows just what my body needs. He knows it better than I do. Like I was designed just for him to be able to pleasure me in a way no one else can.

"Griff," I moan, grinding down shamelessly onto his face the way that drives him wild.

"Sweetheart," he growls in warning before he sucks my clit. "Give it to me. Right in my mouth."

I clench his hair in my hands as he pushes and pushes me closer to the edge. My thighs shake on either side of his head as the pleasure in my body climbs higher and higher.

"Fuck," I cry through clenched teeth, every muscle in my legs trembling.

If it weren't for the barrier behind me, and Griffin's firm hand pinning one of my hips in place, I would have collapsed to the floor by now.

"Let it go," he urges as he removes his mouth and uses his fingers to tease my clit.

He likes to pull back like this sometimes so he can watch. Watch the moment I start to twitch and my muscles spasm, sending my pussy contracting into waves and pushing out extra wetness.

He likes to watch, all right. Almost as much as he loves to taste me.

"Griff!" I cry out as I explode.

He's on me like a shot, his mouth covering me to catch the squirt of wetness that's firing out. I shake against him as cum shoots out of me and he drinks it down with a deep, delicious growl.

"Fucking hell!" he groans as I writhe and wriggle all over his face, riding my orgasm down. "Your cunt's the sweetest thing in the world... Jesus," he hisses, as my body slows.

My head is spinning, and my legs are shaking as he stands and takes me into his arms, pulling me against his solid, fully dressed body.

"You're mine, Sweetheart. Don't ever forget that. I'm never letting you go."

His eyes bore into me, and then his lips are on mine, sharing the taste of my release with me as he unbuckles his pants and frees his cock. He lifts one of my legs and is inside me in one swift thrust, trapping me between him and the barrier.

Thank God we are high enough that no one on the ground can see.

"Mine," he repeats, driving into me with a force that knocks the air from my lungs. I reach around and grab the clenching muscles in his tight ass as he fucks me only the way he can.

"Yours," I whisper, relishing every stroke, as he drives himself further into my heart with every hit. "Always yours."

"Ooh, what's all this?" Harley plucks a jar from the box I'm unpacking and unscrews it, taking a sniff.

"It's the first delivery from the new suppliers." I pull out one of the facial oils and admire the deep golden glass of the bottle.

"Fancy." Harley smiles as she rummages in the box some more. "I like the packaging. Better than the old stuff Todd used."

My face must give something away as Harley frowns at me. "Has he tried to contact you again since the gala, and the filming?"

"No." I shake my head as I place the bottle down onto the counter. "I think I got it wrong, Harley. It was a split second."

I think back to the day of the filming when the crowd surged forward through the collapsed barrier. We were swallowed up in the sea of bodies and I'd been bumped into and jostled around. My ID somehow came off, and then I thought I saw blond curls moving away from me in the crowd. But the more I think about it, the more I think I just imagined it, or got it wrong.

Why would he have been there?

"What did Mr. Parker think?"

I look at her and smile. We've been openly dating for weeks now, and it's still odd that my friend doesn't call him Griffin when she's talking to me. But I know Harley likes to be professional.

"I didn't mention it to him. The more I thought about it, the more I realized it probably wasn't him. And Griff gets so mad at the mere mention of Todd, I didn't want to give him extra stress he doesn't need."

"Yeah, I get that." Harley tilts her head in understanding as she takes the last jar out of the box for me.

I knew she would understand. She told me she had to take the final account settlement to Griffin for him to sign to release us early from our contract with Todd's company. Apparently, he broke the nib right off the pen with the force of his signature when Harley said Todd's name. The idea of mentioning him when I was probably mistaken is just a bad idea. I hate seeing Griffin so stressed about something that's over and in the past.

"How are things with you? Have you seen Suze this week?"

I've loved being able to catch up more with them both recently. But this week I'm getting ready for the reporter from US Vogue to come and do her feature piece in the spa, and so I'm pulling late nights, making sure everything is perfect. She's coming to use the gym, pool, and saunas first. Then she's coming for a full body massage and our deep cleansing, age-reversing facial. It's got one of the new products I developed with the suppliers using Ken's cocoa butter. I'm so excited to read her piece on it. Me and the team have all tried it, and it's worked for all of us. Soft, dewy skin that's bursting with moisture and glowing like an angel. It's going to have the spa booked up for months.

"I'm seeing her tonight. It was supposed to be tomorrow, but I got a last-minute honey booking."

"How's that going?" It's so interesting that Harley earns all this extra cash trying to help catch out unfaithful husbands.

"Great. Cheating, lying pigs keep me in business." She grins at me. "Actually, tomorrow's could be an awkward one."

"Really?" I begin arranging the new delivery of products onto the display shelving.

"Yeah." She rolls her eyes with a snort. "I always get a client brief first. Who they are, where they work, etc. It's to help me strike up a conversation. This guy is from one of our largest competitors. I will have to be careful I don't let anything slip."

Harley's told me she has an entire other persona, name, job, the lot, that she gives to clients so they don't know who she really is, and that she works at The Songbird. The last thing she needs is for a client who's whacked with a huge divorce case to realize she works for an agency and come after her looking for payback.

"The one Gwen went to?"

The thought of her makes me uneasy. Not just because she's Griffin's ex, but because I've seen just what her lying has done to him. It eats away at him that his trust in his staff has been compromised because of her. Emily is convinced it was her, as are the rest of the staff. And I'm inclined to believe it as well. It all makes sense. But Griffin can't let it go without evidence. That's what he's waiting for. Something concrete. Maybe then he will be able to move on and forgive himself for trusting the wrong person.

"No. That's another one. I still need to watch what I say, though. Most of the time they're too busy thinking with their dicks to have a meaningful conversation. But can't be too careful." She folds her arms across her chest and then nods in approval as I finish arranging the display. "Looks good. What time is the reporter coming?"

I glance at my watch. "She should be with us in an hour."

"Well. Good luck. Not that you need it. You'll smash it, Maria." She bounces off toward the spa doors. "Meet you tonight to de-brief?"

I narrow my eyes at the new bottles and turn one a miniscule amount until they're all straight. "Sounds good. Griffin's meeting Reed later before he heads back to LA."

"He's going back?" Harley whips her head back around, pausing mid-step.

"That's what Griff said."

"I thought he was staying awhile longer?" Harley's face clouds over with something I can't read.

"You know as much as me." I smile at her.

She purses her lips and then turns. "See you later."

An hour later, Josanna Frederick swoops into the spa. Swoop being the best word to describe her, in her immaculate white trouser suit, matching cashmere coat, killer heels and sleek platinum hair, that she wears like a glinting cape of ice around her head.

"Josanna, it's so lovely to meet you." I extend my hand to her and give her a warm smile as one of the team takes her jacket.

She shakes my hand firmly. "Maria Taylor. It's a pleasure. I heard about your spa in California, and your new facial here in New York, and had to see for myself."

"Of course." I smile at her as she looks around the spa reception area.

I've heard rumors that she sometimes does this—comes to review some places herself. The magazine never gave us the heads up their editor would attend instead of the features reporter I was expecting. But I prepared for this just in case.

"Would you like something to drink? We have aloe vera infused coconut water."

Her glossy lips twitch in the corners at the mention of her favorite beverage. "Lovely, thank you."

I signal one of my team, who darts off toward our kitchen.

After a tour of the facilities, I settle her in with Caitlin, my most experienced therapist, for her full body massage and facial. Josanna made no notes at all during the tour, but I wasn't expecting her to. She won't have gotten to her position as editor for US Vogue without a killer memory. And killer instinct, too, I imagine.

I offer her assistant, a young man who's been sitting on his laptop in our lounge area, another drink to refresh the never-ending ones my team has been supplying. He smiles at me quickly and then goes back to tapping on his keys with lightning speed, cursing under his breath as he stops and hits delete.

"Deadline?"

"Always." He gives me a tight smile as I pick up one of the room scenting mists from the new display and spray it in the air.

"Here, this has grapefruit in. It's great for concentration and mental clarity."

I wrinkle my nose up as the mist spreads in the air, then turn the bottle to read the label. *That's funny.* It says 'Focus' on it, but the mist in the air is clearly not the blend we usually have. In fact—I sniff again to make sure—it's not even one of our usual blends at all. This one smells... well, it barely smells of anything, except a trace of an artificial fragrance oil that is making my throat scratchy. We only use the purest essential oils in our fragrance sprays. *What the hell is this?*

"Maria!" Caitlin runs toward me from the walkway that leads to the treatment rooms flying over the smooth floor and narrowly missing one of the Jerusalem stone pillars the spa is so famous for.

"What is it?"

Her eyes are wide, her face ashen as she grabs my hand. "Something's wrong. You need to come now!"

She keeps hold of my hand and I race along beside her, followed by Josanna's assistant, who's abandoned his laptop and looks as worried as Caitlin.

She pulls me into the treatment room where Josanna is sitting on the bed in her white robe, clutching at her chest, wheezing. Her shoulders rise to her ears with each labored breath she fights to take.

"What happened?" I rush over to Josanna and loosen the top of the robe away from her neck.

"I don't know. She was fine one second. And then she said she felt itchy and started to breathe like that," Caitlin cries.

"Josanna, it's okay." I rub her arm, trying to reassure her as my eyes land on her lips, which are rapidly swelling like a bad filler job.

"Caitlin." I turn to her, keeping my voice calm. "Call an ambulance. Tell them we have a severe allergic reaction, and they need to get here now."

She nods, all color drained from her face before rushing to the phone outside where her frantic conversation with the emergency operator bounces off the walls.

"Does she have any allergies we weren't told about?" I ask Josanna's assistant as he stares at her wide-eyed. Her entire face is red and blotchy and swelling by the second. "Any allergies?" I snap as I rush to the sink and soak a pile of washcloths in fresh, cool water.

"N-no! I don't think so, I..."

He stares at me as I use the first cloth to wipe over Josanna's face, taking as much of the facial product off as I can before throwing it on the floor and grabbing a clean one and repeating the process.

Caitlin would have gone through the treatment questionnaire with her beforehand to make sure the products were suitable for her.

Josanna's eyes are wild as she shakes with the effort of trying to draw in a full breath, the wheezing racking up another notch.

"They're on their way," Caitlin pants as she comes back into the room.

"Okay. Great. Caitlin, tell Earl. Make sure he's looking out for them and grab someone from the front desk to show them here once they arrive."

She nods her head fast, her face crumpling as she slaps a hand over her mouth and runs out again. I shout out into the hallway after her, where the rest of the team has come to see what is going on.

"Helen! Ring the front desk! Ask if they have any Epi-pens in their medical kit."

"I'll call upstairs, let them know what's happening," someone else pipes up.

I turn back to Josanna's assistant.

"Has anything like this ever happened before?" I ask, as the skin around Josanna's eyes seems to inflate and they are forced into two tiny slits. Her breathing has slowed to an almost inaudible crackle. A slow, labored rasp that seems to be taking every ounce of her energy to take.

Shit!

"I don't know... I... her hand swelled up once!" Her assistant's eyes light up at his sudden memory, bringing with it a nugget of information. "She shook hands with someone who had just applied cream with, um... shit." He squeezes his eyes shut. "... Lanolin! With lanolin in it!"

None of our products contain lanolin. There's no way it can be that. I look back at Josanna. Her torso is tensing, every muscle straining as she fights for air.

If that ambulance isn't here soon, then...

Time stills as she grasps my hand in hers, squeezing it until my fingers are numb.

No...

My mouth goes dry and my other hand flies to my chest as two paramedics flood the space around Josanna. She lets me go and I step back, my head light as one of them places an oxygen mask over her nose and mouth and the other jabs her leg with what looks like a large marker—an Epi-pen that is used in extreme anaphylaxis cases, or severe allergic reactions. I only know because my nana booked us both onto a first-aid course once when I was visiting her in England. She said I might need to revive her if she had a heart attack from some of the steamy books she reads. She was joking, of course.

But as Josanna is strapped down to a stretcher and whisked away, her swollen face barely recognizable, I couldn't be more thankful that I recognized it and knew to call for medics straight away.

"Maria?" Harley's panicked voice calls to me as she rushes over and grabs my arm.

I've somehow made it into the main hotel lobby. Josanna's assistant runs alongside the stretcher as Earl and the other door staff clear a path through a crowd of people congregating on the sidewalk outside.

"Where did they all come from?" I stare at the growing mass of people outside, many now holding camera phones in the air and recording the paramedics as they put Josanna in the back of the ambulance and her assistant climbs in next to her.

"They're here for Jay. Him and the film crew check out in an hour."

I turn to Harley, my mouth dropping open, before I drag my eyes back to the scene outside. The ambulance has switched its lights and sirens on and is weaving a slow route through the city traffic.

All those people saw everything. They filmed every-thing.

"What the hell happened? We got a call upstairs." Griffin's deep voice washes over me, grounding me. Just knowing he's here helps to calm the hammering in my chest.

He rushes over toward us from the main entrance, his suit jacket flying behind him. He must have been outside seeing the ambulance off with Earl.

"An allergic reaction. It must have been something personal one of the team used that she came into contact with. She didn't have any allergies to anything in the products we use."

My words fall out of my mouth faster than I can fully process them.

How can this have happened?

We are so careful about cross contamination for this very reason. All my team know not to use their own hand creams and lotions when they're working. They can use as much of the spa product as they like when they're at work instead.

"Are you okay?"

Griffin places his hand on the small of my back, steering me away from the center of the open lobby toward one of the quieter hallways that leads off. His dark brows furrow as he glances around at the crowd of guests the incident has attracted. He tips his head toward the staff at the front desk, and they smoothly spread throughout the lobby, reassuring people, and dispersing them back to continue with their own days once more.

"Yeah, I'm..." Tightness grips at my chest. "She could barely breathe. What if they got here too late?"

"It'll be okay. I'll call the hospital, see what I can find out," Harley says from where she's followed us.

"Thank you." I give her a weak smile and then let out a huge breath, pressing my palms to my face.

"Hey, it's okay." Griffin pulls me into his powerful arms and wraps me inside them, his lips resting in my hair.

I inhale his scent—that air after a tropical storm—and my heart rate slows further as I settle into the warmth and safety of his chest, somewhere I've become so at home in these past couple of months. I stroke my hand down his tie as my other hand grips the fabric of his shirt around his back.

I wish I could stay here forever.

"Come upstairs. You need to sit down and have a strong drink." His arms move from around me, and one hand slips inside mine, threading our fingers together. "Maria?"

"No." I look back into his eyes. "I need to check on my team." I slide my hand from his grasp and swipe my fingers under my eyes. Then I straighten my shoulders and clear my throat. "I'll call you once I've made sure they're all okay. Then we'll see if we can work out what happened."

I don't give him time to answer before I stride off in the spa's direction, my stomach a tangled ball of nerves.

I could easily have seen a person die for the first time today. Nothing could be worse.

The rest of the day passes by in a blur of team meetings, taking witness statements, and making sure everyone is okay, including arranging extra support for Caitlin and any of the others who may need it. I re-arrange all of today's appointments so that I can send the team home early.

By the time they've gone, I'm completely exhausted. I sit in the empty spa reception for a while, listening to the running water which flows beneath the glass floor in a make-shift stream. It's a beautiful design, and the sound of the water running is just what I need to help calm my nerves after such a stressful day.

I can't believe it happened. I need to understand what went wrong. But I also need to make sure Griffin is okay. Harley called down to say he had been over to see the management board at Vogue this afternoon. I don't know what's going on. He was still there when I last spoke to Harley, but she said she had managed to speak to a doctor at the hospital, and Josanna will make a full recovery.

Thank God.

I collect my thoughts and head up to Griffin's office. It's late, but he's usually always here later than me, either still working at his desk, or leaning back in his chair, staring out at the skyline as he waits for me. His blue eyes always look over and catch mine the moment I walk in, like he can sense me before I say anything. The way his

brows lift, and his eyes sparkle at me when he sees me....
God, I live for that part of each day.

But now?

Nothing.

The office is deserted, and all the lights are off. Even the cleaning crew isn't here.

I head up to the apartment and let myself in. But I don't need to walk around its vast interior to know that Griffin isn't here, either. The emptiness is louder than any sound he could make when he's home. He was planning to meet Reed tonight. But after everything that's happened, I expected him to be here. Or to have left a message.

I pull out my phone and call his number. It rings once and I'm sent to voicemail.

Did he just reject my call?

Acid rises in my throat as my tongue turns to sandpaper in my mouth. I look around the apartment for signs that he's been here.

Nothing.

Maybe he's still over at Vogue. But this late? No, he would have left hours ago.

I pace up and down in front of the glass doors that open to the balcony.

God, what if something has happened at the hospital and Josanna got worse again? Could that be where he is? But surely he would text.

I drop down onto the giant couch and stare at my phone. He's never not told me what time he will see me later. Or text me to tell me if he's gone to a last-minute meeting. Ever since the jokes about checking my schedule when I first began working here, he has always been completely transparent about where he is and wants to know where I am in return. It just doesn't make sense. There must be something wrong at the hospital.

I call him again, leaving a voicemail telling him I'm going to the hospital. Then I text him to tell him the same. I can't do anything there. But she got ill at my spa. I need to at least see how she is, see if there's anything I can do to help.

My phone rings in my hand before I even make it to the front door.

"Griff?"

"Don't go to the hospital. She won't see you." His voice is sharp, cutting into me.

I freeze mid-step.

"What? Why? Isn't that where you are?"

"It's best you keep away."

My eyes sting at the coldness in his voice. It's not unkind exactly. But it's the tone he uses all the time whenever he has business to take care of. When he's in full Griffin Parker boss-hole mode. Unemotional. Detached.

The tone he's never once used with me, even before we were dating.

"I don't understand. Where are you?"

He mumbles something. It's muffled, like he's covering his phone with his hand.

"Griff, are you on your way back?" I hate the giveaway in my voice. The slight break in pitch that hints at the lead weight that's dragging down my stomach.

Something isn't right.

"Don't wait up," he mutters.

And then he's gone.

Chapter Twenty-Eight

Griffin

"WHAT?" I SNAP AT Reed as he raises his brows at me.

"Was that Maria?"

He slides a glass of bourbon toward me and nods at the bartender. "Two more."

"Yes." I drop my head into my hands and scrub them down my face.

"What did she say?"

I lift the glass and swirl the deep, amber-colored liquid around inside it before knocking it back in one hit. Reed passes me another wordlessly, taking a mouthful of his own as he rests one arm on the bar.

"She was about to head to the hospital."

"Ah." He shifts on his bar stool, getting comfortable, probably sensing we might be here awhile.

"That's the last fucking thing this shit-show needs."

I place my glass down, my eyes fixing on a stain in the deep brown wood of the bar. This is the place Reed and I come when shit gets serious. The small bar attracts a different clientele. The kind who all have something to drink about. And it isn't rainbows and candy. No one bothers us, and we don't bother them.

I side-eye Reed, who's frowning into his glass.

"Why do you look so fucking glum? You're not the one getting sued."

"It won't come to that." He fixes his eyes on me as I slam my glass down on the bar, attracting a glance from the bartender.

"It's already fucking come to that! They're going for the whole fucking lot. Actual bodily harm, negligence... you fucking name it, it's on those papers." I hiss at the burn in my throat as I knock back the rest of my drink.

"That's what they do, Griff. They wave some enormous balls around to scare you a bit, and then they settle. And that's if The Songbird was at fault. How do you know this woman hadn't eaten some weird superfood or some shit that made her swell up?"

I shake my head, cursing under my breath as I remember the unrecognizable face of Josanna Frederick as she was wheeled past me on a stretcher. Although, I don't need my memory. It was plastered all over social media before she even got to the hospital.

Fucking fans and their cell phones.

"It doesn't matter. No one fucking cares. All they see is the editor of US Vogue almost dying at The Songbird."

"She swelled up a bit, so what?" Reed shrugs. "It happened to a guy I knew back in LA. Had his dick sucked during lunchtime by his mistress, who'd eaten a peanut butter sandwich an hour earlier. Poor bastard was more worried about his wife finding out than the state of his dick and face where she kissed him. I reckon the quick trip to hospital was the least of his worries."

"This isn't some guy who pushes papers around a desk, Reed. This is Josanna Frederick." I meet his eyes as he looks at me, rubbing his fingers over his lips in thought.

"Your legal team is handling it. There's nothing more you can do tonight. Why don't you go home? Tell Maria what's going on. She deserves to know."

"Since when did you grow a conscience?"

He smirks at me before his face falls serious again. "It's not her fault. Don't ruin what you've got with her over this."

"That's not what I'm doing."

Reeds raises a brow at me, his silence saying more than words can.

"I'm not," I mutter, clenching my fist and releasing it again as the familiar twitch of feeling like I'm losing it prickles in my fingers.

"It's all under control. Don't worry. It'll get sorted and be old news by the end of the week."

I snort as I clench and release my hand again. It's not under control. It's fucking so far out of control that it felt like the ground was moving with every step I took out of Vogue's offices this afternoon. The head of our legal team accompanied me. He knew what was coming. Fucking assholes. They're going to drag The Songbird through the courts over this if they can. They don't care about the money. It's the story they're after.

The Songbird is headlining the papers again, for all the wrong reasons. We only just got past the stolen formulations scandal, and now this.

And to think it happened in Maria's spa, of all fucking places.

I'm too pissed to decide what to make of it yet. All I can focus on is proving that it wasn't The Songbird's fault. Avoid a fucking media circus. I've called an emergency meeting with the entire legal team at seven in the morning. We need to cut this off before it grows.

"Go talk to her," Reed urges as the bartender takes our empty glasses.

I look around the bar. We are the last two drinkers. *How the fuck did that happen?* Another glance at my watch tells me it's much later than I originally thought.

Looks like I will be running on extra coffee tomorrow morning.

I nod at Reed. He pats me on the shoulder, and we leave the bar and head home.

"Maria?"

I stomp into the darkened living area, yanking my tie off and throwing it onto the back of a chair, along with my jacket.

The dark outline on the sofa doesn't move.

"You're back, then?" Her voice is monotone.

"Yeah, I am." I reach down and pull off my shoes, dropping them to one side before I stretch my neck side to side, cracking it.

"Why are you sitting out here in the dark?" I turn to her but can only make out the outline of her long hair falling around her shoulders.

"I was waiting for you. You sounded different on the phone. I thought something must be wrong."

Wrong is an understatement.

"It's—"

"Of course, I couldn't ask you, because you hung up on me before I had a chance," she snaps.

My skin prickles and I roll my lips. "Right, and you're pissed about that." I let out a sarcastic laugh. "I'm the one who spent the afternoon in Vogue's head office explaining how their editor almost *fucking died* in my hotel. And you're pissed because I didn't take the time to talk to you on the phone!"

I walk over to the lamp and flick it on, bathing the room in a dim light.

"That's not my point."

"Well, what fucking is?"

I look over at her. She's glaring at me, her eyes like deep brown crystals shimmering in the light. She's still wearing her work dress, and it hits me—she's been sitting here all evening. Sitting here getting pissed at me for not taking the time to engage in small talk on the phone when I was in the middle of handling a crisis.

"You don't have to be an asshole." She stands from the sofa, jabbing a finger in my direction. "Did you ever think I might want to know what was going on in those meetings? It happened in my spa, for God's sake. I have a right to be involved!"

I stride over to her, blood rushing in my ears as I stop inches away, so our bodies are almost touching.

"It's still my fucking hotel," I hiss, my eyes holding hers as she stares back at me.

Her eyes drop over my shirt and back up. She tips her chin up, before whispering softly, "Fuck you."

The way she says it makes it almost sound like something sweet. But the dark, dangerous hue her eyes have taken on tells me she meant it to hit me like a missile. Leave a huge fucking crater in all sense of reason that I might have had and taking all my restraint away with it.

"What did you say?" My eyes bulge in their sockets as I lean toward her.

She stands her ground, quirking her brows at me. "I said Fuck. You. Would you like me to spell it out for you? F. U—"

My jaw tenses. "Don't *fucking* push me tonight, Sweetheart. I've reached my limit."

"Oh? You've reached your limit? Well, maybe I'm sick and tired of you and your limits. Did you ever think about that? Hmm? What about me and my limits? I'm a part of this hotel as well. Something you can't get through your thick skull."

"They're suing us."

Her eyes go wide, but she doesn't move.

I expect her to react. To gasp, ask questions... something.

I don't expect silence.

"Did you hear what I—?"

"You blame me." She stumbles back a step, her shoulders slumping like all the air has left her lungs.

Her statement stabs me in the gut, cutting through the foggy haze the long day and hard liquor have created.

"Of course not!" I snap back, screwing my face up.

"That's why you spent the night out at a bar instead of coming home." She looks to the ceiling, shaking her head. Her eyes are bloodshot, like she's exhausted, emotionally, and physically.

"No, Maria, I don't, I—"

"It's okay. I'd be asking myself how it happened. *I am* asking myself how it could have happened. I keep wondering what I missed. There's nothing I can think of. I went to housekeeping to check what they launder the robes and towels in, what they mop the floors with. I spoke to maintenance to see if they made any changes to the air filters. I can't understand it."

"That's what you did this afternoon?"

Despite everything, I can't help the swell of pride in my chest, impressed with the lengths she's gone to trying to make sense of what happened.

She glances at me, and then away again. "Yes. It's what I did. And I was going to tell you when you got back from Vogue. Harley told me you were there. Only you chose to keep me out, deal with it yourself, feel like the one *in control*. Like usual." She snorts, crossing her arms over her chest.

"I'm telling you now, aren't I?" I take a step toward her, aching to touch her suddenly. We've never been alone in private like this, where she can't even stand to look at me. "Jesus, Maria, what do you want from me?" I almost shout, my head spinning.

I grab a cushion that's fallen from the sofa and hurl it across the room.

She watches it hit the wall, knocking a frame off center, then snaps her eyes back to me, something igniting in them.

"I want you to stop trying to buy me. Stop sending me flowers! Stop buying me designer bags! Stop spouting off romantic crap and giving me diamond earrings that make me think of you every time I look in the damn mirror!" Her eyes are wild as her chest heaves. She's on a roll. "I don't care about any of those things!"

"Then what do you fucking care about?" I step forward so I'm almost nose to nose with her. Her perfume washes over me, sending blood racing through my body. I flex my hands at my sides, itching to reach out and pull her to me.

She steps back again, distancing herself from me.

"You! This hotel! My job! I want you to stop shutting me out at work. I don't know how many times I need to tell you."

As my heart races in my chest, my control slips further through my fingers.

Pain... in her eyes. Pain I put there.

366

"Maria." I reach for her, but she steps further away. "I get it, okay? You're pissed. I was just trying to get my head around this fucking mess. Trying to think of some way I can stop them from suing the hell out of the hotel and turning everything to shit."

"We can handle it."

"No." I squeeze my eyes shut. "*I* will handle it. I'm meeting the legal team in the morning." I need to get control of it. Of everything. Before it's too late.

A huff of air escapes her lips as she rolls her eyes.

"What?" I grit, blood coursing through my veins.

"Nothing." The disdain falls from her voice like water through a net. When her eyes come back to mine, they're dull, their usual brightness extinguished. "Consider this my notice, Griffin. I think we both know it's time I went back to California."

"What? No!"

I'm on her before I even register what I'm doing. Forcing her back down onto the sofa seat as I hover on my arms above her, my lungs sucking in giant mouthfuls of air.

"You can't fucking leave! I won't allow it!"

"I can't stay, either!"

She pushes at my chest, but I don't move. I *can't* move. The idea of her leaving has me paralyzed.

"You will never give up control. It's like Emily said, this hotel is your wife! No one will ever be good enough to be trusted."

My lips are inches from her as I hiss, "You know why I'm this way. As soon as I find out who stole from me, then I can—"

"You'll what? Be magically cured?" She laughs quickly before her voice turns icy. "You'll never be able to get over it."

My eyes drop over her neck and her pulse beating out a powerful rhythm against her delicate skin. I've kissed that neck, felt that pulse beneath my lips so many times now.

She can't leave me.

She can't.

I've never wanted to change so badly for anyone. To let someone in. *Until her.* And now she's threatening to leave me?

Anger courses in my veins as bile rises in my throat. Maybe that's why the words race out of my mouth before I can stop them.

"Like you can't get over your dad and your ex stealing from you, you mean? Always having to account for every cent, keep *every* fucking receipt. I've seen your purse. You're living in the past as much as I am, Sweetheart." I sneer.

Slap!

My head snaps to the side as her palm connects with my cheek. My skin stings from her touch. I pull my eyes back to hers. The fire has well and truly returned to them.

"You're an asshole," she hisses.

I glare back at her, my rage mixing with lust at how much fight she has in her.

It's that fucking spirit that I love so much.

She can't leave.

Arousal drowns my muscles as the strength in her voice breaks the dam, and I know beyond doubt what I need tonight. It's not drinking my self-fucking pity away in a bar.

It's her.

She's my fucking lighthouse in a storm.

I should never have pushed her away tonight. Just breathing the same air as her now...

Fuck. Pushing her away was a mistake.

We are both panting, a mix of fury and something else in our eyes as our hot breath mixes together.

"I'm sorry."

She turns her face to the side.

"I'm sorry," I whisper again, moving my head so she has to look at me. My eyes hold hers, *pleading* with them.

She stares back at me.

Her eyes shine as she finally speaks. "That was really low."

My heart plummets in my chest.

"I know... you're the last person on this earth I want to hurt." My eyes pinch at the corners as I stroke her hair back from her face. "*I am sorry.*"

I stare deep into her eyes, hating myself for the hurt that's reflected. She's done nothing but be incredible since she arrived in New York. She only wants what she deserves, what she's earned—my respect and trust at work. Something I am so close to giving. *So close.* I thought I was there. But my actions tonight prove otherwise.

She doesn't deserve this.

"Never disappear on me like that again." Her eyes burn into mine, her chest rising as she sucks in wild, angry breaths. "*Never* again," she repeats.

"I won't," I breathe, staring back at her.

She means so much to me. I want her more than I ever have. My cheek stings, but it only makes my already hard cock stiffer.

She glares at me a second longer, her chest rising and falling with angered breaths. Then she grabs the back of my head, pulling my mouth to hers in a desperate kiss.

I push my body into hers, one hand curling around her neck, holding her in place underneath me as I dive into her, devouring every soft moan she makes against my mouth. Each one speaking directly to my cock as I push against her.

We kiss until we are forced to pull apart to breathe.

"Fuck, I need you, Sweetheart. I need you so bad, I will explode if I can't be inside you," I gasp against her lips.

She gazes back at me, her beautiful hazel eyes captivating me, just like every time she looks at me like this—like I'm everything she was searching for.

"Show me." Her words are stained with an undercurrent of hurt... and anger. But the fact that she's still here, her hands holding my face to hers, tells me all I need to know.

"Don't leave me, Sweetheart. Don't ever leave me," I murmur, my voice unsteady.

I unbuckle my pants, pushing them down as I yank her dress up around her waist.

"Griff?"

I stop, searching her face as she runs her fingers over my cheek. Her brows pull together as she traces the hot skin on my cheek.

"Yes?"

"I'm sorry I slapped you. But don't push me away. *Please.* Never push me away."

I hold her eyes. "I'm sorry. I'm sor—"

She grabs me, pulling my mouth to hers again, a whimper fighting its way from her throat as I drive my tongue inside her mouth and she grabs at my shirt, our bodies in their own hot, desperate fight to connect. To join together.

Desperate to just be.

I don't even bother trying to remove her soaked panties; I just rip them to the side before sinking my cock deep inside her.

A deep, guttural groan leaves my lips as I drive forwards until my balls meet her skin.

"Fuck, Sweetheart. Fuck." I hiss, one hand still on her throat, the other dropping to grasp her hip as she parts her legs wide.

Her eyes lock onto mine and her lips part. She clenches around me, hugging my cock inside her as I fight to maintain any semblance of control. She thinks I have it all the time. But she doesn't realize she's the one person who can unravel me. Her body, her scent, her touch... her words.

Threatening to leave me.

"You're mine. You'll always be mine." I pump into her.

She tilts her head back and peels her spine away from the sofa, pushing her body up to meet me. I rotate my hips each time I drive down so her swollen clit rubs against my body.

"Look at me."

She brings her eyes back to mine, lust flashing in them as her hands grip the back of my neck.

"You're such a good girl, taking my cock so well."

My words draw a deep moan from her lips as she wriggles underneath me, opening herself up further so I can sink deeper. I hold her eyes as pleasure bathes itself over her face. She loves it when I praise her. Despite all her fire, and me knowing I've met my match in her, I still have *that*. That one power over her I could so easily abuse, but *never* would.

She wants to please me.

It's in her eyes, it's the taste on her skin. Even when she fights with me, she can't deny it. She needs it as much as I need to control. It fulfills some twisted part of each of us, planted there firmly from our pasts. We can both fight it. Deny it. But it will always be there. Like a scar that we wear. Only together, it can be something beautiful, worn like a mark of survival.

"Harder," she cries, dropping her hands to my ass and pulling me into her. "Please, Griff... harder."

I lean over to grab the arm of the sofa behind her head with both hands, using it to drive my body forward with everything I have, losing myself inside her.

She moans, shaking underneath me, covering me in her wetness.

"Fuck. Such a good, tight... Such a fucking tight—"

Her moans turn into gasps, and she screws her eyes shut, grabbing one of my shoulders and sinking her nails into my skin.

I know her body, her sounds.

She's about to come.

"Look at me," I growl.

She peels her eyes open, her pupils dilating.

I bite my lip and thrust into her once more, circling my cock inside as I'm buried to the hilt. It's the final touch that sets her off and she bucks and writhes around below me.

"Fucking beautiful," I murmur, as she comes undone and her wetness soaks my straining cock.

I thrust into her harder, her orgasm loosening her up so I can push even deeper. Even my balls grow slick from how wet she is. She watches me, her mouth slack as the familiar heat grows in my groin.

"You're amazing, Sweetheart. Now watch as I fill you with my cum. Remember who this cunt belongs to."

Her gaze never falters as I groan, then suck in a sharp breath, my cock going wild, pumping out my heat inside her.

Our eyes lock on to one another as I growl, "Mine."

I'm clenching my ass cheeks. My cock threatening to cause me to take off, like a rocket. The strength of my release has me panting, searching her eyes.

"You're mine," I whisper, all strength from my voice deserting me.

Leaving me.

She nods, sucking in a breath, then pulls my face to hers, kissing me. Holding me against her. Being everything I need right when I need it most.

Right after I left her alone and then hurt her with words.

I screw my face up as we kiss.

She's right. I am an asshole.

The biggest asshole in history.

"I love you."

She freezes, and I hold my breath as she looks at me, her face serious.

She strokes along my jawline. "I believe you." She kisses me again, her lips soft against mine. "Griff?"

"Sweetheart?" My chest shakes as the final parts of me leave, filling her body, giving her everything.

Including my heart.

The way she looks back at me steals my breath.

"I love you, too."

She smiles.

And then her lips are back on mine.

Chapter Twenty-Nine

Maria

WHEN I WAKE UP, Griffin's already gone. He'll be heading into the meeting with the lawyers any minute now. He'll be running on adrenaline. Certainly not sleep. We stayed up making love until two hours ago. Not like the first time when he came in, when it was all anger and hurt fueled. This was different. This was him showing me he was sorry. Showing me he loves me. Neither of us has said it again since that first time last night. But we haven't needed to. We spent the night wrapped in each other's arms, our eyes never leaving the other. No words were needed. We said everything we needed to with the way we looked at each other.

And now my handsome, complicated, passionate man is heading into a meeting he's worried about. *Really worried.* This could be bad for The Songbird. We could face criminal charges if they can prove neglect or malicious intent.

I shower quickly but have missed four calls from Harley by the time I check my phone. I call her back as I'm grabbing my bag and walking out the door. *Damn it.* It goes straight to voicemail.

I ride the elevator down, waiting until I'm heading out into the street, where I have a better signal to ring back. Despite having an internal entrance from the private residences wing to the main hotel, I like to come this way. I get to say good morning to Earl and check on the pigeon situation.

"Harley, what's going on?" I ask the second the call connects.

"Maria. Don't go through the main entrance!" She's flustered, her breath loud down the phone as though she's rushed to answer.

Maybe she's just got in. It's early for her to be there already. Maybe Griffin asked her to be there before the meeting to take notes.

"I'm already there, what are you—" My words stick in my throat as I round the corner. A group of journalists are huddled around The Songbird's entrance. There must be around thirty. Some have cameras set up.

"Ms. Taylor?" one shouts, causing all their heads to whip in my direction.

"What do you have to say about the claims that it was your spa products that put Josanna Frederick in hospital?"

"Do you feel guilt over what happened?"

"Is there any danger of anyone else being harmed?"

"Ms. Taylor?"

"Do you have any comments?"

"Ms. Taylor?"

I push through the gaggle of microphones and cameras being shoved in my face. Earl holds out his arm and scoops me along and in through the door. I look back, giving him a grateful smile. He nods at me with a wink. His face is so warm and kind that I could cry. He turns back to the crowd and puts his hands in the air, motioning for them to step back.

"Maria? Maria? Are you still there?"

"I'm still here." I put my phone back to my ear and Harley blows out a breath.

"It's going to be a crazy day, Maria. Prepare yourself. They're in the spa. I wanted to warn you before you got there."

"Who are?" Coldness creeps over my skin as I rush across the lobby and head toward the spa. My heels click loudly on the marble floor and attract curious glances from guests.

"The police," Harley says. "Vogue insisted they launch a criminal investigation after one cream used on Josanna was found to have contained a high level of lanolin, along with other known allergens."

"But that's not possible. We never use it as an ingredient. *Never.* Wait! How do they even know? How have they tested it so fast?"

Harley lowers her voice. "Josanna's assistant swiped it on the way out yesterday. I'm so sorry, Maria. Look, I have to go. It's going nuts up here. But I'll be down to see you as soon as I can. I just wanted to warn you. I think they'll want to talk to you."

"Okay, thank you." I end the call and walk into the spa.

It's unrecognizable. Uniformed police officers questioning the spa staff have replaced the usual calm serenity. Others, in plain suits, are packing the reception computer into a box.

"What are you doing? Why are you taking that?"

The one packing ignores me, but the officer with him looks up from his notebook.

"We need it to help with our enquiries, Ms—?"

"Taylor." I frown as the last of it is packed into the box and the quiet officer walks off with it.

"Maria Taylor?"

"Yes." I bring my eyes back to the officer in front of me. He's older, tall, dark-brown hair, wearing a charcoal suit. He would probably look friendly and approachable if it weren't for the circumstances. "What's going on?"

"Ms. Taylor, I'm Detective Field. I'm leading the investigation into the incident that happened here yesterday."

I stare at him, my mouth open.

Incident? What is this? An episode of CSI?

"Look. We don't use any synthetic ingredients in our products. Or ones known to be common allergens. There must have been a mistake. I'm extremely relieved that Ms. Frederick will be okay after experiencing something so frightening. But I can assure you, it was nothing to do with The Songbird, or my staff." I glance to the side where Caitlin is ringing her hands in front of her as an officer questions her. "Is this really necessary? My staff have done nothing wrong. In fact, their quick actions yesterday probably prevented the situation from being much worse."

"It's just routine." Detective Field gives me a forced smile. "I would appreciate it if you could answer some questions for me though, please?"

"Of course," I mumble, looking around again. The spa products on the glass display shelves I unpacked yesterday are all being gathered into a box and carted away. It's like watching everything you've built be slowly taken apart around you, piece by piece. And there's not a single thing you can do to stop it.

I squeeze my eyes shut, pressing my fingertips to them. The sooner this is all cleared up, the better.

I spend the next forty-five minutes going over yesterday's events with Detective Field as he makes notes on his pad. He nods and makes the odd sound to encourage me to go on. But other than that, he says very little.

Odd. Shouldn't he be asking me questions? Gathering evidence?

He must know this is all a freak accident. Josanna must have come into contact with something before entering the spa. Maybe a guest in the hotel? She's well known in her job as editor of Vogue. It's quite possible that someone stopped her on the street or inside the lobby before she arrived and spoke to her. Shook her hand, kissed her on the cheek. *Something.*

I give Detective Field all these avenues to consider, but he just hums a non-committal response and looks at me from under his brows until I continue. By the time my chat with him is over, and he and the other officers leave, I'm drained. And the sparse scene around me tells me we won't be opening today.

"Cheer up. It's never that bad."

I look up from where I've sunk into the spa reception sofa.

"Hey." I smile as Harley plonks herself next to me, wrapping an arm around my shoulders.

"I brought you a latte." She squeezes me into her side, and I stare at the two takeaway cups she's placed on the table in front of us.

"Thank you." I exhale slowly, a deep groan leaving my lips. "This all feels so surreal. How are things upstairs?"

Harley grimaces and passes me my cup.

"Great," I mutter, picturing the chaos going on up there as I take a sip. She's put extra sugar in for me. Probably thought I could do with all the help I could get.

"It's not the best day, I'll say that." She drops her chin into her hands.

"Griffin?"

She gives me a kind smile. "He's okay. He's in full damage control mode with legal. It's quite impressive, really. He sure knows how to command a floor. The entire office is running like a well-oiled machine up there doing what needs to be done. And then some."

My chest swells at him coordinating everything and taking control—*a breathtakingly handsome force to be reckoned with.*

"God." My voice trembles. "I feel like I've let him down. Let you down. Let everybody down. How could this have happened? We're so careful."

"Stop right there." Harley fixes her eyes on mine, gripping my hand. "No one blames you. This isn't your fault. Vogue are just swinging their dicks about in a piss-ing competition. It's all for show. As soon as Josanna's swelling has gone and she feels less like she should be featuring on a show for facial fillers gone wrong, then they'll probably drop it."

"I doubt it. They took all the products and the spa computer. They're going big guns."

"Meh." She waves a hand in the air. "That's only to make a point. Josanna's embarrassed because her face got splashed all over the news when she was put into the ambulance, that's all. It's crazy upstairs right now, as they've got to react and plan. But I spoke to Will, and we both think this will be done by the end of tomorrow."

"But they found ingredients in the cream that should never have been there."

I wrack my brain for how that can be. Someone must have got samples mixed up, or the test results switched. There's just no way it was the spa's fault. I personally went over every formulation with the new suppliers be-fore they sent us our first batch. And we all tried the test batch they sent over. It was all fine. I had no concerns. At all.

"Yeah, in one jar. One jar that her assistant swiped. He could have easily done something to it to make it look like the cause. Or maybe he even laced it himself. Think about it. Demanding boss, underpaid, underappreciated assistant. I bet there was a grudge there that had been building for years." Harley's eyes light up.

"You sound like you're planning a movie script." A small laugh shakes my shoulders as I snort.

I don't know why I'm almost laughing. Maybe it's the mention of a demanding boss. Just like Griffin when I first began working here. I would never have believed back then that we would be where we are now. Or maybe, which is more likely, it's the fact that if I don't find something to laugh about today, I might lose my mind.

"I'd have to have a smart, upcoming actress play me. You know, discover a new star, launch their career." Harley lifts her cup and clinks it against mine, giving me a wink.

I smile and shake my head at her. I'm glad she's here, trying to ease my worry. But it's there in her eyes—she's worried, too. Yes, maybe it will all be sorted before we know it. But there's a part of my gut that tells me it won't be so easy. Something just doesn't add up, and Vogue won't give up easily.

It's like I'm missing a single word that can change the entire meaning of a sentence. That one word that will explain everything.

Truth.

The next couple of days are strange. There's no better word for them. The spa remains shut, so I busy myself with cleaning it from top to bottom, even though the cleaning crew does it. I can't sit and do nothing. I barely see Griffin as he is in meeting after meeting, coming in late at night. He curls his arms around me when he climbs into bed, and we end up having sex. It's hot and heavy. Not that I'm complaining. He needs that control when it probably seems like he has none at work right now. But I miss my other Griffin. The gentle, tender one who makes love to me in the mornings with his eyes locked on mine.

That Griffin is gone.

I wake up in a cold bed now.

Alone.

I'm about to head out the door when there's a buzz on the apartment intercom.

Who would be calling at this time for Griffin? Surely, they'd know he would be in his office already.

I press the button.

"Ms. Taylor?"

"Yes?" I frown as my mind scrambles to place the familiar voice.

"It's Detective Field. I wanted us to have a talk."

My chest deflates as I let out the breath I'm holding.

Finally! They've got to the bottom of what happened.

God, I'm so relieved. Now we can clear this whole mess up and move on.

I can get my Griffin back—every version.

"I'll come down right away." I'm smiling as I rush to the elevator, fidgeting with one of the earrings Griffin gave me as I will it to hurry up.

Detective Field comes into view, standing in the residence's lobby the second the elevator doors slide open. My smile grows as I approach him. But something about the grim look in his eyes and the way his mouth stays set in a firm line has my step faltering.

"Is everything okay?" I glance between him and the uniformed officer with him.

"Ms. Taylor, we're here to inform you we are arresting you on suspicion of causing grievous bodily harm, and for theft of funds—"

"What?" My stomach lurches into my mouth and then plummets to the floor, setting my head spinning.

Detective Field continues his spiel, *"You have the right to remain silent. Anything you say can be used against you in court."* But the rushing of blood in my ears drowns him out.

"There's been a mistake," I murmur. "You've got it wrong."

Grievous bodily harm... theft?

The uniformed officer takes hold of my wrists, cuffing them. Detective Field's face remains impassive.

"This is wrong! I don't... have you spoken to Griffin?" I ask, my eyes searching down the sidewalk toward The Songbird's main entrance as I'm escorted over to a waiting squad car and pushed down inside it. The same sea of journalists head in our direction like a tsunami, cameras flashing, voices yelling out questions.

I screw my face up and turn away from the window as they bang on the glass and run alongside the car as we drive away.

What the hell is going on?

I sit in silence in the back of the car, too stunned to say anything.

Where's Griffin?

When we get to the precinct, I'm put in an interview room, and my cuffs are removed. I wait alone for thirty minutes until Detective Field and another non-uniformed officer I haven't seen before enter the room.

I glance between the two of them. She's younger than Detective Field, probably only a few years older than me. I look at her hopefully, but she remains emotionless as the two of them take the seats opposite me.

I lean forward onto the cold metal table. It stays rooted to the spot where it's bolted to the floor. Everything about this room is grim. The dark gray walls, the cold, damp floor... the smell—musty and stale.

The stench of injustice.

Detective Field opens the folder he has placed on the table in front of him and clears his throat.

"Could you please state your full name for us?"

I swallow, but the thick lump in my throat remains firmly lodged. "Maria Vera Taylor."

Detective Field glances at me, and then back at his open folder. "Ms. Taylor. We are required to inform you that this interview is being recorded on camera."

"Okay," I acknowledge, my mouth dry.

Why am I here? It doesn't make any sense.

"Ms. Taylor. How long have you worked at The Songbird?"

"Coming up for four months now." I glance between the two of them again.

What does that have to do with anything?

"We understand you had an incident with a Mr. Todd Ackerman while working there. Can you tell us more about that?"

What?

"It was just a misunderstanding. He was interested in a romantic relationship with me, and I didn't feel the same."

"And his supply contract with The Songbird was canceled as a result?"

I nod.

"Please answer for the audio." The female detective sniffs.

My eyes stay on her for a moment before I drop them to the desk. "Yes, that's correct."

Detective Field nods. "And Mr. Parker asked him to leave rather forcefully when he came to the spa to discuss it with you?"

Shit. My stomach churns as I recall the way Griffin punched Todd in the nose and security carted him off—bruised and bleeding.

"He asked him to leave, yes."

My mind is running at a million miles a minute trying to make sense of all this.

Did Todd report Griffin to the police? Is this what this is all about? Some vindictive ploy to get back at us both?

"Are you in a sexual relationship with Mr. Parker?"

"I'm sorry, what?" I snap my eyes back up to Detective Field, who stares back at me, waiting. "Why are you asking—"

"A yes or no will do at this stage." He sighs.

"Yes," I splutter, "but I don't see what that has to do with—"

"And when did this relationship begin?" He fixes his eyes on me and my chest grows hot, perspiration beading between my breasts and causing my shirt to stick to me.

"Um..." My mind flashes to the pool in The Bahamas, then the night of the charity gala. "... I'm not sure I could tell you the exact date."

"Was it before or after the contract was canceled with the company who employs Mr. Ackerman?"

"Before," I say, my voice unsure.

"I see."

The female detective leans over and whispers something in Detective Field's ear, and he makes a sound of agreement.

"Okay, Ms. Taylor. We would like you to look at the following emails and call logs, please." He lays documents out in front of me across the table. "Please confirm that is your work cell number at the top there, and that is your work email."

I frown as I scan the document. They look like mine, but they can't be. There's a call to the new suppliers with a chat transcript typed out below, detailing how a new revised ingredients list is being sent over. Then there are several emails confirming the same, the new, much lower costings mentioned in one.

"Ms. Taylor?" Detective Field presses, boredom creeping into his tone.

"Yes... they... they are my number and address, but I never made this call... and the emails, those weren't sent by me."

I press my hand to my mouth as I read the documents again, nausea creeping over me.

"You have passwords for your work email, correct?"

"Yes."

"And all company computers where you have access to these systems, along with your spa's accounts, are in areas where a staff ID card is required to gain entry, correct?"

"Um... yes."

The sickness rises in my throat. The only computers that can access my work emails, and the spa accounts, would be ones connected to the main management servers, either on Griffin's floor, or the one in my office in the spa.

"Thank you." Detective Field nods to his colleague and she gathers the papers into a pile. Then he places a fresh set down in front of me. "Can you please tell me what these are, Ms. Taylor?"

I frown at him, shaking my head. "I don't know what you mean."

"Read them out, please." He points to the top line of text on the first sheet of paper.

The blood in my veins turns to ice.

"Um..."

He leans back in his chair, waiting.

"The Finance Corporation of Bahamas Bank," I mumble, my eyes dropping to the next line. "Account Holder, Ms. Maria Taylor." I look up at him. "Why do you have overseas bank accounts in my name?"

"Please look at the amount in the account, Ms. Taylor."

I gulp as the figure swims into focus.

"It's not mine. It must be another Maria Taylor. There's been a mistake."

Detective Field ignores me, spreading more documents out over the table.

"We have multiple statements and invoices here, showing that funds were sent from you at The Songbird hotel to this account. Including the large, returned portion of the contractual payment when you changed the product ingredients and reduced your cost of supply significantly."

The pages swim out of focus as my eyes sting and my throat burns.

"This wasn't me. I swear! I love The Songbird, I would never—"

"Are you in financial trouble, Ms. Taylor?"

The question catches me off guard, and all I can do is stare at the two detectives, trying to make sense of what's happening.

"No... I'm not... why—"

"Have you ever been in debt before?"

"No!" I screw my eyes shut.

This is ridiculous. Surely they can see that?

"Our records show you once amassed a substantial debt from missed loan payments." Detective Field places another piece of paper down.

"No!" I glare at him. "I told you. I've never been in debt."

"Explain this." He taps the sheet of paper on the table.

I wish more than anything I could tear them all to shreds. Lies, each and every one. Thin white lies, ripping my composure apart.

I snort as I look at the sheet.

"That was my ex, Damien. He forged my signature on the loan. It was all sorted years ago."

"We don't have any record of a Damien."

"You wouldn't. He was an ex-boyfriend I wanted to get away from. I paid off the debt and he agreed never to contact me again as long as I didn't report him." I tip my head back and look at the ceiling, my chest tight as I remember thinking that would be the end of it. That he would be a stripper called Mercedes' problem from then on.

"Money discrepancies and men seem to collide in your life frequently, Ms. Taylor. Would you agree?"

I bring my eyes back to Detective Field and stare at him as I brace myself for the next shit cannon he's no doubt about to launch.

"Your father was a gambler with poor control of his finances."

Sparks fly in my stomach, and I lurch forward in my seat.

"That was years ago. And last time I checked, it's not a hereditary condition."

Detective Field remains fixed to his seat, his eyes locked on mine as I exhale, following my small outburst, and lean back.

"No, no, it's not. But it goes some way to explaining why you have issues with men and money. Were there any witnesses to Mr. Ackerman's inappropriate advance toward you?"

"What?" My forehead screws up as I shake my head at him. "Why?"

He presses his lips together and shrugs a shoulder. "It could be said that you invented the alleged behavior in order for Mr. Parker to cancel the contract and allow you to enter into a new one with a company of your choosing. A company that has no prior history with The Songbird, or Mr. Parker, and wouldn't find it strange that the spa in such a prestigious hotel would want to substantially reduce the quality of the products they are using."

A crazed laugh leaves my lips as the sweat beneath my shirt turns cold.

They really think I did this. They've got the entire thing mapped out.

Motive, method, and means.

What's next?

"Entering into a relationship with Mr. Parker was a clever move. Gain his trust. Allow him to give you more responsibility. You were able to keep it all out of his sight."

I suck in a sharp breath as I stare daggers at the female detective speaking properly for the first time. I've never wanted to rip the hair out of someone's head before—tear it clean out from the root—until now.

"No!" I snap, forcefully. "You're wrong. My relationship with Griffin has nothing to do with any of this!"

The two of them say nothing, just exchange a look that has me wanting to scream until the whole of Manhattan hears me.

God, if they think this, then what does—

"Ask him! He will tell you all of this is complete crap! You've got it wrong. Someone's setting this all up to look like I did something when I didn't." I press my fingers into my temples and take a deep breath.

I thought they were coming to tell me Josanna Frederick had dropped her complaint. That there was some other explanation for her allergic reaction.

Not this.

Not arresting me for causing bodily harm... not arresting me for stealing... from The Songbird... *from Griffin.*

"Please. Call him." My voice breaks.

He must be worried. If he even knows I'm here. Would anyone have told him? Maybe he's at work, so busy, and doesn't even realize what's going on.

"We have," Detective Field says matter-of-factly. "He's helping us with our enquiries."

Hope blooms in my chest.

Griffin is so calm when he has to be. He'll know what to do. He'll see this for what it is—a huge misunderstanding.

"He is? Well, can I talk to him, can I—"

"No." Detective Field gathers all the papers up and shuts the folder.

There's a knock at the door and a young, uniformed officer pokes his head in. Detective Field walks over to him and the two exchange hushed words. The female detective sits with her arms crossed, watching me.

He returns to the desk and whispers something to her before addressing me.

"Ms. Taylor. We would usually have to see a judge before this happens, but it seems in this case, alternative arrangements have been made, and you have been granted bail. Please do not leave the city. We will need to speak with you further during our investigation. We would also suggest you instruct a lawyer."

With that, they both stand and wait for me. Detective Field goes first, and the female detective's eyes burn into the back of my head as I exit the room and am led to the main waiting area.

"Maria!"

Harley flings her arms around me, and I hug her back tightly, my head spinning, so grateful for her warmth and familiarity.

"Harley. They think—"

"Shh. Not here."

She looks over my shoulder at the detectives and then bundles me out of the door and down the steps onto the street. There's a cab waiting, and she pushes me in gently, following straight behind.

"Teller apartments, please, the address I gave you earlier," she says to the driver, before sitting back next to me.

"Why are we going to your place? I need to talk to Griffin."

She grabs my hand and squeezes it, her pretty face masked with worry. It's one of the rare times I've seen Harley without a smile.

"Now's not a good time. He's got a lot on. But he'll come round, Maria. I know it. He loves you. He'll see this for what it is."

I look at the seat next to her.

My Louis Vuitton holdall is there.

A sob catches in my throat.

"What do you mean? I need to speak to him, Harley. I need to see him, I—"

If that wasn't enough, the tears in her eyes tell me everything else.

He's gone.

I've lost him.

"No!" I choke out, squeezing my eyes shut as hot tears sting at their corners. "He doesn't believe it, does he? He can't. He knows me, he... we..."

I swallow down an ugly cross between a cry and a snort as I picture his face—his hurt face, thinking I would do this to him.

Thinking that this is real.

But I also know him.

I know he has to be in control. He looks at facts. He takes emotion out of it when it comes to business—when it comes to The Songbird. If Detective Field showed him all that evidence, all those statements, the emails, the call logs...

"Oh, my God, he thinks I did it. He believes I did it." Realization stabs me in the gut.

Harley wraps an arm around me as my chest burns and I shake.

Can I blame him?

It sure looks damning, even from where I'm sitting, and I *know* that I've done nothing wrong. He's been lied to before. Deceived by someone close to him. Someone unknown. He's never gotten over it, never...

"I need to speak to him, Harley."

Her arm tightens around me as Manhattan passes by in a blur out of the window.

She doesn't say anything.

She can't.

We both know Griffin.

Once he makes his mind up, that's it.

Game Over.

The End.

Chapter Thirty

Griffin

"Okay, thank you, detective."

I throw my cell onto the desk and sink my head into my hands.

Shit.

Fucking shit.

Fucking... fuck... fuck... fuck!

I groan into my hands, screwing my face up.

If I screw my eyes tight enough, maybe this won't really be happening.

She wouldn't have deceived me.

Made me fall in love with a lie. Fall for someone who isn't even *fucking* real.

Every muscle in my body is heavy. Weighed down like I have boulders tied around my ankles and have been thrown into the Hudson.

Drowning.

Drowning in deceit and lies.

More fucking lies.

Detective Field said Maria just left. The bail went through and now she's free while they build their case.

Build their case against the woman I love.

Thought I loved.

Fuck it, she's not even real. *Is she?*

I have no idea who Maria Taylor is. Maybe that's not even her real name.

There's a knock at my door.

"Griffin?"

I sniff as I lift my head up and pull myself together.

"Come in."

"It's true, then?" Reed says, after taking one look at my face.

"Seems that way."

"Fuck." His eyes widen and he glances down the hallway that leads to my office before coming all the way in and closing the door behind him. "So, the emails, and the—"

"All legitimate."

He comes and drops into the chair opposite me, leaning back as he rubs a hand around his jaw. "Wow."

I roll my lips, sucking in a breath as I look at him.

"She must have planned this from the beginning. From the first day she stepped foot into The Songbird, if not before."

Acid rises in my throat. All those times she was lying to me. All that time she was planning against me behind my back.

Laughing about me behind my back.

"No." Reed shakes his head. "No, I don't believe that. This is Maria... I just don't... you headhunted her, Griff. She didn't target you. This is..."

Yes.

I headhunted her.

This is on me.

"You know. I thought I was a good judge of character. It's never let me down once in business. Then I realized. It's women and my personal life I've no control over. First Gwen, now Maria."

My chest constricts just saying her name.

"I should just turn celibate. Because my dick obviously renders my brain unable to function with any fucking logic!" I clench my hands, relishing the cracks my knuckles make.

"It's not you, Griff."

I snort.

"It's not," Reed says more forcefully, pinning me with his gaze. "There's nothing wrong with your judgment. You could never have predicted this would happen."

"Twice!" I snap. "I've been screwed over by someone close to me twice. I thought not knowing for sure who stole the formulations was the worst thing. But it's not." I look at the ceiling as my heart races in my chest. "It's the fucking knowing that hurts most. It's the knowing that stings like a motherfucker."

I meet Reed's gaze, my eyes dry and scratchy from where I've rubbed them raw.

"I told her I loved her. Can you believe that? I'm a fucking idiot. And part of me still hopes this isn't real."

"Griff. This. Is. Not. On. You. No one could have suspected. God, I thought you were going to marry her!" Reed's eyes are wide. "I thought she was the one. I really did. Do you think there's been a mistake? Do you think—"

There's a glimmer. But I extinguish it. I don't need false hope.

"No!" I bark, glaring at him as the back of my neck burns. "No mistake, Reed. She set up an offshore account in The Bahamas, for fuck's sake. It's like she's laughing at me. Rubbing in what a fucking idiot I am for crossing that line for the first time with her there. She knew she had me then, playing the innocent."

Fire licks at my core.

She resisted me until that point. Kept telling me she didn't mix business with pleasure. Kept me fucking drooling after her like a dog until she had me just where she wanted me.

Hooked.

I played right into her hands. Thinking she was different. That she was strong and determined, but delicate and sweet too.

Delicate like those fucking flowers I've been sending her nonstop.

I thought she was everything I have waited my whole life to find.

My Maria.

My lighthouse in a storm.

No.

She *is* the fucking storm.

"What are you going to do?" Reed leans forward over the desk, scanning my face.

He's concerned. We've known each other for years and he's rarely seen me lose my shit like this. I don't mean me being angry. He's seen that a billion times. I mean the fact that my eyes are as bloodshot as a wasted addict's right now.

And my heart is hurting.

My *fucking* heart is heavy in my chest, like a full sponge barely holding on. Water dripping out.

That's my fucking soul right there. Dripping out and washing away down the drain.

She's fucking ruined me.

"Move on," I grunt. "The police are handling it. I'm helping them. And the investigator thinks they're almost there at gathering the evidence against Gwen. Both will be out of my life for good. Finally."

Kill two birds with one stone.

"I'll deal with all this shit and then I'll get on with work... and employ a *male* spa manager." I snort as Reed shakes his head.

"Griff, you don't have to throw yourself straight back into work. It's okay if you need time to process this."

"When did you turn into a therapist?"

Reed holds his hands up. "I'm just saying. You need time to process, that's all."

"What I need is the fucking investigator and police to do their jobs."

End this shit.

As though a higher power has heard me, my email pings. I recognize the sender. It's from the burner account set up by the PI.

I click on the attachment, loading the first image up to full screen.

"Fuck's sake!" I hiss. I turn the screen so Reed can see. "You can't even make out her face!"

I bang my fist on the table.

This day just keeps getting better.

Reed squints at the grainy image of a woman holding a large brown envelope. She's wearing a baseball cap, so you can't see her face.

I click through the other images. They're all the same.

Useless.

"It could be Gwen." Reed frowns, tilting his head and inspecting the one image that captures her face. But it's too grainy to make much out at all.

"It could also be fucking Santa Claus as far as proving anything goes!" I click out of the email in disgust. "That could be anyone. I'm no closer to finding out the truth. No closer to fucking anything."

His hand lands on my shoulder and squeezes. "It'll happen, Griff. Trust me. The truth always comes out."

I look into his eyes.

He sounds so certain.

So sure.

I take a deep breath and stand, buttoning up my jacket with one hand.

"In the meantime. It's business as fucking usual," I say.

First thing on today's list—deal with the press camping on the sidewalk since the Josanna story hit. No doubt they'll all know about Maria and the arrest now.

Fucking brilliant.

Chapter Thirty-One

Maria

THE CELL TONE ECHOES around the corridor. Each individual beep like another knife to my heart.

He's blocked me.

He can't even speak to me.

I tried the first time in the cab back to Harley's place, even though she told me not to. The sound cut through me then, just like it has each time since.

Although, over the last two days, something else has grown with each rejected call, each bounced email I've tried sending him.

Rage.

A rage so strong it's like nothing I've ever felt before. Not even when Damien racked up thousands of dollars' debt in my name. Not even when my father stole from me.

This is a rage that's kept me up all night on Harley's couch. Firing my determination to discover the truth.

Someone set me up.

Someone threatened my integrity. Made me out to be a criminal.

The media has had a field day, pulling up all my history and spreading it around like vomit after a night on cheap liquor for everyone to gape over.

Even going to the local store at the end of Harley's block caused stares. Eyes that tried to penetrate the cap I wore to avoid being recognized.

I'm on every newsstand.

The headline: **From Songbird to Jailbird.**

My face. My past. My soul.

All there, laid bare for the world to judge.

But that's not what's feeding this rage. It's not what's accelerating it to a point that my body might explode if I don't let it out.

No.

That's all *him.*

The man I gave my heart to. Who has so easily dismissed me. Dismissed everything we had together.

Gone.

Just like that.

Like I meant nothing to him at all.

Maybe I never truly did.

I stride around the corner, my steps heavy and determined.

I wore my red dress for this. The one he seemed to disapprove of so much on my first day at The Songbird.

And I wore my hair down.

Fuck him.

I attract worried glances from some of the staff as I sail past them out of the elevator. I'm not supposed to be here. The police told me to stay away.

I don't care about any of that right now.

Harley's desk is empty as I approach Griffin's door, and I'm glad. It will make this easier. She will only try to stop me. She's told me Griffin's thrown himself into work even more since I was arrested. Apparently, he's barely left the office, so my chances of him being here are high.

I don't knock.

I push the door open with such force that it bangs back against the wall; causing the blinds to shake against the glass.

He's standing with his back to the room, staring out the window. He doesn't even flinch when I slam the door behind me and it trembles in its frame.

I glance around.

His office is immaculate.

His suit is immaculate.

Everything about him is immaculate and screams *you meant fucking nothing to me.*

It took me an hour to do my make-up to cover up forty-eight hours' worth of puffy eyes from all my tears.

He's not even affected.

"What took you so long?"

He makes no attempt to turn around. He just lets the ice in his voice portray the hatred that's probably burning in his eyes right now.

A cold burn that could freeze over hell.

"I have so many things I want to say to you." My heart hammers in my chest as I walk over to his desk, surprised at how calm my voice is.

How *strong* I sound.

I look over his broad back. I was once wrapped inside those powerful arms. Held like the most precious thing in the world.

And then discarded like trash.

Not even given the respect of a chance to explain.

I stop on the other side of the desk, fixating on the back of his head as I continue.

"Then I realized... You're not worth my breath."

He bristles and then turns, his crystal eyes piercing mine, causing my heart to threaten to stop unless I keep going... Finish what I came here to say.

His face is emotionless. I can't read him at all.

I don't know him at all.

Not like I thought I did.

The Griffin I fell in love with wouldn't cast me away like this.

The only reaction to me glaring at him is the slightest pinch at the corners of his eyes. The eyes that used to hold mine while he buried himself inside my body.

Inside my heart.

The eyes that are looking at me now with such detachment, I swear my soul tears clean in half. But despite the pain he's causing, I still wish more than anything he would come to his senses.

Pull me against his chest and call me his.

How can I ever be anyone else's after this man?

I suck my stomach in and straighten my shoulders, steeling myself for what I came to say.

I have to do this.

He doesn't get to hurt me the way he has and not have to look me in the eye when I tell him.

I take a deep breath.

"You are so self-obsessed in your own warped little world where everyone lies to you and you can't trust anyone that you can't see what's going on."

I don't give him a chance to speak before I continue.

"Someone has set this all up! How can you be so stupid that you don't see it? Why would I *ever* jeopardize my career, my reputation, for money? If you think that's who I am, then you don't know me at all!"

My voice rises as I grab at my earrings, taking them out and slamming them down onto his desk. I can't stomach seeing them reflected back at me every time I look in the mirror anymore.

Vibrant blue diamonds—two painful reminders of what's gone.

Griffin doesn't flinch, just holds my eyes with his icy stare.

"Just like I never really knew you," I hiss, pulling my hand back and leaving them there, glinting. "Did it ever occur to you that there are people out there who want to see us fail? Like Todd, for example? He has the knowledge and the contacts to somehow change the supplier's order. And he sure as hell hates you enough."

"The emails were sent from your account, Maria."

It's the first time he speaks, and his deep, calm voice makes my chest tight.

So many memories I wish I could erase. So many memories that hurt too much right now.

407

"I lost my ID on the filming day. Anyone could have snuck in that day and not been detected. There was so much going on."

"Funny, you never reported it to security." His voice bleeds sarcasm as he keeps his steely gaze on me.

He's thought about this. He's really fucking thought about this.

And he still thinks I'm guilty.

"I didn't think. Will found it minutes after I realized it was missing. I thought I must have just dropped it. But maybe it was gone longer."

"It was a woman who phoned the suppliers to authorize the change."

Griffin takes his hands out of his pockets and places them on his hips. I can't help glancing down at them. I swallow away the memories the sight of them provokes.

All these fucking memories.

That's all they will ever be now.

In the past.

"So is half of the world! Almost four billion other women! That proves nothing and you know it! You're just far too quick to believe what you want to!"

I lean over the desk toward him, and he shifts on his feet, inching closer to me.

"And what is it I want to believe, Sweetheart? You tell me, seeing as you can read my mind so fucking well," he hisses.

My breath catches in my throat, and it burns.

Oh, it burns!

"*Sweetheart.*"

That one word that carried so much weight. Now used against me. The most painful ammunition.

He's made himself judge, jury and executioner.

I look into his eyes and know I've lost him for good.

No matter what I say.

No matter what I do.

Griffin Parker has shut me out of his heart.

Forever.

"Fuck you," I whisper. "You think you have to push people away to survive? You think I would really do this to you? You know nothing, Griffin. You'll die a lonely old man, trusting no one."

The corners of his mouth turn down and his nostrils flare as he leans toward me, his face inches from mine. His eyes fall over my hair briefly before he looks back into my eyes, locking me in place.

"Don't you worry your pretty head over me. I won't be lonely."

My eyes sting as I hold his and picture him with someone else.

His arms around someone else. His hands on their face. His body driving into theirs.

Maybe he's even been there already. Erased me physically, the same way his eyes tell me his heart has closed to me, too.

I force myself to ignore the warm mint of his breath, the scent of his skin.

That clear air after a storm.

"Oh, you'll be lonely, *Griff.*"

His eyes flash as I attempt to wound him with my choice of words, the same way he did to me moments ago.

"You'll be lonely. Because no matter what you do, or who you meet. You'll never trust anyone. And that means you'll never truly be whole. I know what that's like. I've been there. But I still chose to trust you."

I search his eyes, my anger making way for something else.

Sadness.

Overwhelming, consuming sadness that this beautiful, infuriating, complicated man will always be a slave to his closed off mind.

A man who can love with so much passion that he'd steal the breath from the entire world.

If only he would allow himself.

"You'll never trust anyone," I say again. "You'll always be that one step away from true happiness. No matter what lies you tell yourself."

"You'd know all about lies," he hisses, looking back into my eyes.

I wish more than anything I could lean forward and brush my lips against his. That this wasn't happening. That we weren't here like this.

How did we even get here?

I sigh, grief settling in my chest. Grief for what we could have had. For what we so nearly *did* have. It pulls me down with a heaviness that I will try my whole life to shake off after today, and probably never succeed.

I look at him as my heart dims, like someone blew the candle out.

Puff. Gone.

"I will prove to you I didn't do this. I'll find evidence. Because that's what you need. My word, anyone's word, will never be enough for you. And if that's what it takes to help you, then I'll do it. Because despite what you think, Griffin, every second that we spent together was real to me. None of it was a lie. None. And you know what?"

His pupils dilate as he looks at me, and I swear there is the tiniest crack in his armor. Beneath it, the tiniest fragment of who I know he is fights to shine through. The man underneath the suit, behind the corporate desk.

The man he's showed to me.

The man I wish would come back to me.

"You've destroyed my heart. You knew they were going to arrest me, and you did nothing. You packed my things and gave them to Harley. You shut me out without even giving me the respect of seeing me and telling me to my face that you believe I did all those things they're accusing me of. But despite all of that... I wouldn't change a thing. Because for me, what we had was real. I trusted you in a way I haven't trusted anyone in years. And I'm grateful to you for that."

I search his face one last time, my chest burning with emotion, my legs somehow still holding me up.

"So, thank you," I whisper.

Then I turn and walk out of his office before he has a chance to reply.

I walk until I reach the elevators.

Until I reach the main hotel door.

I don't stop walking until my final tear dries, and by that point, I seem so far away from where we once were that I know...

I've just walked myself out of his life.

And I don't think there are any paths that lead back.

I look up at the gray sky and pull my cell phone out of my bag, taking a deep breath as I wipe my cheeks dry with the heel of my hand.

I dial and wait for it to connect, a small smile of hope on my lips as she answers.

"Harley? It's me. Listen. I need your help. I need everyone's help."

Chapter Thirty-Two

Maria

"I can't believe it. How's he going to handle this?"

Harley's eyes shine at me as I drop my head, my chest heavy with emotion.

I never expected this.

"I don't know. Maybe it will help him in the long run. We both know the not knowing was eating away at him. He was always looking over his shoulder, wondering who had deceived him." I squeeze my eyes shut and rub my temples with my fingertips.

Two weeks.

If I could go back in time, this wouldn't have happened yet. I wouldn't have this sickening pull deep in my stomach, knowing what this might do to him.

Griffin.

My heart still squeezes in pain every time I think of him. I haven't seen him again. He hasn't tried to call me. He hasn't asked Harley how I am.

He hasn't cared.

He's gotten on with his life like I never existed.

But I can never be so lucky to be gifted with the freedom of not having a broken heart. Because that's what it is—broken. Some days it beats so hard in my chest when I see a pigeon or something blue. A commercial for a beach holiday did it yesterday. Another day's make-up ruined from another fresh wave of crying.

That it even still beats is a miracle.

I open my eyes and lift the envelope from my lap, smoothing my hand over it. His name, which is written so clearly on the front swims in front of my eyes.

Despite knowing this is for the best, the idea of what opening this envelope might do to him had me lying awake all night. I contemplated not telling him, letting him believe it was me. Maybe it would be easier for everyone that way. But Harley wouldn't hear of it.

"He'll finally have the truth. It's only Griffin that needs to be told now," Harley says, her eyes shining with unshed tears.

Vogue has agreed to drop the charges against me and against The Songbird now that they know who the real blame lies with.

Everyone knows the truth now.

Except Griffin.

I look over at Will and Suze, who nod in support.

It's taken all four of us two weeks of round-the-clock, head-wracking, document sifting work to get to this point. After I called Harley, the wheels were set in motion. She called Suze, and Will, and even Earl. I thought I had cried enough. But seeing how these people who haven't known me long at all were so willing to give up their evenings, weekends, sleep, *sanity*, in order to help me—I swear I cried enough tears for Griffin to sail his boat in an ocean of them.

Maybe they were doing it for me.

Maybe they were doing it for him, too.

Either way, I'm eternally grateful, because five heads are better than one.

And now we know who stole the formulations from Griffin all those months ago.

And who set me up.

I almost wish I didn't.

I'm not sure if it will help him.

Or break him.

Harley said he's buried himself in work and looks the perfect billionaire businessman every day. But she sees the dullness in his eyes. She hears the monotone voice he uses.

She said he didn't even react when Detective Field came to his office late yesterday with the news that they had new evidence and were releasing me from their enquiries.

He did nothing, except carry on with his day and ask her for the notes for his next meeting.

Nothing.

He really has pushed me so far out of his mind.

But he's always on mine.

He's never left.

Everything I've done this last two weeks has benefitted me, cleared my name.

But I already knew I was innocent.

This is for him.

My hands shake as I stand, envelope in hand.

"You sure you're ready for this?" Will asks.

Suze smiles at me as Harley wraps an arm around me.

I pull my shoulders back and nod. "I am. It's what needs to be done."

"Can't you stay, though? We're going to miss you so much!" Harley squeezes me tighter, her voice cracking.

I reach up and hold her hand in mine, the waver in my voice betraying me and laying my feelings out bare.

I'm going to miss them too. So much.

"I'll come back and visit in the future." I sniff, holding tightly to Harley's hand. "But right now, it's best this way. I need to be away from all reminders of him. I need to remember who I am. And heal."

Tears run down her face as she holds me. Suze and Will join in and we all hold onto one another in silence.

There's nothing left to say.

"Hey, Earl."

He turns and watches me walk across the sidewalk carpet and up the steps to the main door.

"Maria!" He throws his arms wide, his cheeks glowing in the cool air as he pulls me into a hug. He draws back to look at me, holding my shoulders as his kind face looks over mine as though he is committing it to memory.

"Don't." I sniff with a small smile. "I've not stopped crying all morning, saying goodbye to everyone. And now that I'm saying goodbye to you, I'm about to start all over again."

I wipe at my eyes as he rubs the top of my arms.

"You've never looked more beautiful to me."

I giggle. "Softie. You'll take care of them for me, won't you?"

He nods, letting me go.

"Only the best seed. Now that they're behaving themselves and we have an understanding over the carpet, we'll do fine. You can call me the pigeon whisperer."

I smile at him, straightening my bag on my shoulder.

"And I'll keep an eye on him, too," he says gently.

My chest squeezes. "Thank you," I whisper.

His eyes drop to the large brown envelope poking out of the top of my bag.

"I'm taking it up to give to him now."

Earl smiles. The warmth in it almost sets a fresh round of tears off. My friends have been amazing. They've all worked tirelessly to help clear my name. I have no idea how they came by some of the evidence they gathered.

And I didn't ask.

I'm just so grateful that they did it all to help me.

To help him.

"You can do it. You're strong," Earl says, handing me a key card.

"Then why do I feel like I could shatter at any moment?" I choke out, swallowing back a sob as I take the card and smile sadly.

He puts his other hand over mine. "That's the beauty of strength, my dear. It grows in the moments we think we have none. You're wonderful, Maria. I wish you every happiness in your life. I know you will make it remarkable, whatever comes next."

I nod at him, swallowing down the giant lump in my throat and fighting back tears.

"Bye, Earl. Thank you. For everything."

He kisses the back of my hand and then tips his hat to me, his kind eyes crinkling as he holds the large gold door open.

I step inside and take a deep breath.

I walk straight to the elevators, not looking around, not marveling at the ornate lobby, the giant crystal chandelier above me, or just the atmosphere The Songbird has. It's like nothing I have ever experienced before in my life.

It's special. Magical.

I ignore all the things I loved when I first walked through those gold doors months ago.

It's the only way I will do this. Blinkers on.

Memories are the most painful torture.

The elevator doors slide shut and I scan the key card. The button for Griffin's office floor lights up. I press it and stand in the middle of the space, grateful that I'm alone so that I can compose myself.

I haven't seen him since that day in his office.

Haven't heard from him.

Nothing.

He hasn't tried to contact me, and when I asked Harley, she looked heartbroken to admit he hasn't even asked her about me.

Not once.

Even though he knows I have been staying with her in her apartment.

I guess that tells me all I need to know.

Griffin Parker might be the love of my life.

But I'm not his.

The elevator reaches the top and I step out into the familiar corridor.

It's deserted.

Everyone has left for the day, just as Harley said they would have done at this time. Griffin will be here, in his office. Harley said he has a conference call overseas to make, so he would be the only one here.

It's better this way.

I'm not even planning on seeing him. My heart can't handle looking into his eyes again. Not when he looks at me like he doesn't even know me.

I'm going to leave the envelope outside his door. He will see it when he leaves. And then he will know.

He can close the book.

Just like he has on us.

I reach the corner near his office door and the sound of voices makes me freeze in my tracks.

Griffin's and another...

He's talking to a woman.

They must be by the doorway to his office because their voices are clear, carrying down the hallway.

"I just needed you to know. It's taken me all this time to get the courage to come and tell you. But with the baby due any day, I knew it was time. I couldn't put off coming to see you any longer."

I stand back against the wall, leaning as close as I can to the corner without them seeing me.

"I understand, Gwen."

Gwen?

"I couldn't be happier. This is incredible news, it really is. After everything that's been going on recently—"

Griffin sucks in a breath.

Is he running a hand down over his tie, the way he does when he's thinking?

"Well, after everything that's been going on, this is..."

Their voices stop for a moment and there's a rustling of clothes as though they're embracing.

"I just had to come to you, Griffin. You had to know." Her voice is heavy with emotion. "And now it's time for a new start."

"You're going to be a great mom, Gwen."

"And this baby is going to have an amazing father."

"And a wonderful mother." The smile in Griffin's voice is obvious.

I swallow, fighting to keep my breathing quiet. He tells Gwen his meeting is about to start. And then there is the unmistakable sound of lips kissing skin.

My heart plummets to my feet.

A baby?

Footsteps come up the hallway and I step inside a meeting room, out of sight as Gwen walks past.

She's beautiful.

Long auburn hair flows around her face.

Griffin liked my hair down and would hold it in his fist as he thrusted into me.

And run his fingers through it when he made love to me.

Did he do the same to her?

Does he do the same to her now?

Because they sure sounded close just now.

My eyes drop to her large bump, screaming at me like a beacon.

"But with the baby due any day."

"You had to know."

"The baby is going to have an amazing father."

They broke up not long before I joined The Songbird.

They were dating.

Nine months ago.

I hold my breath as Gwen walks off toward the elevators, carrying a baby inside her.

A baby whose father is the love of my life.

My hands shake as I take the envelope out of my bag. I can't stop them, despite taking slow breaths to try and calm myself.

Griffin's door is closed. I walk over to it.

Maybe this is how it's supposed to be.

Everything he needs to know is in this envelope. Everything that's been holding him back from being able to trust anyone, let anyone in.

It's all in there.

His ticket to a fresh start.

And judging by Gwen and what they were talking about, it couldn't have come at a better time.

"That baby really will have the most amazing father," I whisper as I lean the envelope against his door.

I stand back and look at it, brushing a tear off my cheek.

"The best."

Chapter Thirty-Three

Griffin

THE ENVELOPE FALLS ONTO my shoes as I open my office door. I know it's from her. I don't even have to read her writing on the front to know.

The way my heart lifts when I open the door and catch a trace of her perfume tells me—*delicate yellow flowers*—she was here.

It's been two weeks of hell since I last saw her.

Two weeks of hell waking up without her every day.

Two weeks of questioning everything I thought I ever knew about myself.

I take the envelope over to my desk and grab a bottle of scotch from the minibar in my office before sinking down into my chair.

I yank my tie loose with one hand, and raise the bottle to my lips to take a huge gulp with the other.

There's no need for a glass.

Not tonight.

Whatever is in this envelope is going to sting like a motherfucker. I know it.

It's the evidence she told me she would get. Proving her innocence. And cementing what everyone around me has been trying to tell me.

She didn't do it.

But if that's true, then it means I fucked up and lost the best thing in my life. I lost *her*. The only woman to ever make me feel like I was both flying and drowning at the same time.

I hope to God this envelope contains a confession instead. Something... anything that means I haven't screwed up.

But that's a load of bullshit.

I *have* screwed up. Either way, I have royally screwed up. I've either allowed myself to be betrayed again, or worse... I've betrayed myself by letting her go.

Pushing her away. Blaming her.

Not *trusting* her.

Because despite everything, I wanted to. God, did I want to trust her, more than I've ever wanted to trust anyone in my life.

I take a swig from the bottle again, embracing the burn all the way down my throat.

Then I rip the envelope open and start reading.

"Come on, come on, for fuck's sake," I hiss under my breath, pacing the floor in front of my office window.

It goes to voicemail, so I hang up and call back immediately.

"Mr. Parker?" a voice finally answers, stifling a yawn.

It's not even that late, it's only—Fuck. I glance at my watch. It's after midnight.

I've spent hours reading the contents of that envelope, drinking more scotch, and reading it all again. Over and over until my eyes have blurred.

"Where is she, Harley?"

"Gone," she says without missing a beat.

She was expecting my call.

She knows.

Everyone knows.

They could all see what Maria tried to tell me herself. She didn't do it. She didn't do any of it.

"Where?" I bark.

"Um..."

"Look, I know I'm an asshole. But I need you to tell me where she is right now!" I squeeze my eyes shut and pinch the bridge of my nose, my head swimming with the half bottle I've drank. "Please, Harley. I *have* to see her."

"I'm not trying to stop you." She sounds more awake, and there's rustling as though she's sitting up in bed. "But she didn't actually say. Just that she needed to get away, and she has a flight tonight from JFK. I assume, back to LA."

"Thank you!" I go to press the end call button, and then take a deep breath and bring the cell phone back up to my ear. "Harley?"

"Yes, Mr. Parker?"

"How was she? Did she seem...?" I run a hand down over my loosened tie, which looks like a string of shit dangling around my neck, all screwed up. "Will she forgive me?"

There's a pause before Harley exhales a long breath. "I don't know. She was heartbroken when it all happened."

Was? Is she over us already?

"Harley?" I press.

"I just... I don't know. There's a lot of hurt there. You really did a number on her."

Fuck.

I fall into my chair and sink my head into my hands.

"But—"

"But?" I spring upright, pressing the phone hard against my ear.

Harley sighs. "But she loves you. *Really* loves you. You've read what's in the envelope, right?"

"Yes." My eyes cast over to the brown envelope sitting on my desk. Everything placed neatly back inside it.

Bullets in a casing, ready to fire out their truths on the world.

"She thought about not giving it to you."

"What?" I screw my face up as my mind races, knowing what's inside, what each of the documents proves.

"Yeah." It sounds like Harley's smiling, a sad smile, the sort that doesn't reach your eyes. "She was so worried about what it would mean to you, what it might do to you. She considered letting you continue thinking it was her. She would have done that for you. That's how much she loves you."

I squeeze my eyes shut as they sting and fire claws at my throat.

That's how much she loves you.

I nod, swallowing down nails, dry rusty nails that scrape all the way down to my core, shredding me to pieces from the inside out.

"Thank you, Harley."

I hang up the call, grab my jacket, and race out of my office. If only I hadn't been such a fucking sorry-for-myself idiot and drunk half a bottle of scotch, I could have taken the helicopter to JFK. It would be so much quicker.

I race past Earl who calls "Go get her!" after me as I sprint into the Manhattan traffic. I let my driver go home early, not expecting to be going anywhere tonight.

Another stupid mistake.

A car blares its horn and I jump back to the sidewalk, scanning the street. It's after midnight and it's still busy. But maybe someone is looking down on me for once, because a cab with its light on, indicating it's available for a fare, sees me and pulls up to a stop.

"Kennedy Airport!" I yell as I dive into the back seat and slam the door. "I'll pay double. Just get me the hell there as fast as possible!"

The driver doesn't bat an eyelid, just nods at me in the rear-view mirror and then steps on the gas.

Despite his best efforts and me breathing down his neck the entire way there barking out orders on which route to take, it still takes almost fifty minutes to get there.

Each one sets my blood pressure climbing.

I can't be too late.

Please say I'm not too late.

I grab a wad full of bills—enough to buy the damn fleet of cabs—and thrust them at him as I throw the door open wide, practically tripping over myself as I stumble out and get my jacket snagged on a latch inside the door.

I yank at it as I scan the outside of the terminal for any sign of her.

Who am I kidding? It's been hours. She will be inside by now, if not worse.

"Fucking come on!" I yell as I tug at the base of my jacket.

What the fuck is it stuck on?

"Hang on, I can—" The driver opens his car door.

"Forget it!"

I perform a ridiculous semi-drunken spin, which attracts giggles from a couple of young tourists taking their cases out of the cab next to us, and manage to extract myself from my jacket, slamming the door shut and leaving it hanging there like a dead bit of skin as I tear off through the doors and into the departure terminal.

My head spins from side to side as I search the check-in boards.

There!

There's a flight leaving for LA in thirteen minutes.

I race to the desk, which is deserted. Everyone must have checked in already. I spin on my heels, panic rising in my chest as I fist my hands in my hair.

Boarding gate!

She will be boarding now, if they haven't finished already. I race to security and am stopped by a sullen looking female officer.

"Passport and boarding pass please, sir."

"What?" My eyes widen.

My heart is pumping so hard in my chest as I try to look past her toward the boarding gates.

Looking for a glimpse of her.

Her favorite red dress.

The bag I bought her—if she even kept it.

Her long, dark hair.

My Maria.

"Sir?" The officer looks me up and down and inhales slowly. "Have you been drinking?"

"Look, my girlfriend is about to board the flight to LA. I have to stop her. I have to—"

She raises an unimpressed brow.

I meet her eyes. "I fucked up, okay? I know I did." I point behind her in desperation. "But if she gets on that plane, then she's gone before I can tell her I'm sorry. Before I can tell her I love her and that I need her!"

The officer seems to ponder as she looks at me again.

"Please?" I plead. "She's everything to me. She has to know that. I have to tell her! I've been an idiot. A fucking idiot. She's all I want. She's all I will ever want." My voice comes in pants as my heart hammers in my chest.

Maybe my sorry ass pulls at her heart strings. Or maybe—unlike me—she's just a decent human being who believes people when they're telling the truth, because she nods and tips her head toward me.

"Okay, but you can't come through without a ticket."

I stare at her, and she clicks her tongue and points. "Go! Go buy one and get your girl!"

I nod frantically and follow her direction to an open ticket counter.

"Thank you!" I cry, wanting to kiss her.

Thirteen hundred dollars later, one ticket to Cleveland—it was the first one available—and I'm racing through the boarding gate lounge, sweat making my shirt stick to my back.

I reach the gate for the flight to LA as the gate staff are chatting and closing up.

"Wait! The flight to LA?"

But they don't need to answer me.

I follow their gaze out of the window, which overlooks the runway. The wing lights of the Atlantic Airways' flight shine brightly as it takes off into the night sky.

With Maria on it.

No.

Nausea rolls in my stomach, and I fall to my knees and stare out of the glass.

I stay there until it's only a tiny glimmer in the sky.

She's gone.

My cell beeps in my hand, but I'm too busy staring out of the car window to look at it.

I've thought about this day a million times. Played it out in my head.

What I will say. What I will do.

But now that I'm sitting here, I'm numb.

You always think knowing the truth will set you free. But I feel more trapped than ever.

My cell rings and I glance at the screen before answering.

"What?"

"Mr. Parker. What do you think?"

He sounds pleased with himself. Pleased that he finally worked out what the fuck's been going on. It only took him the best part of a year.

Maria did it in two weeks.

My amazing, incredible love did it in *two weeks*.

I always knew she was capable and tenacious. And she's proved it time and time again.

Why the fuck couldn't I have trusted her before it was too late?

"Mr. Parker?"

"What?" I ask again, scanning the building beside me for signs of life.

"The email I just sent you. You can clearly see their face this time. Along with the other evidence I have, I think we can say without a doubt that—"

"I know. I know who it was. I'll have your account settled by the end of the day."

Before he can say anything about using his services again, I end the call.

I open his email, already knowing what it contains.

There it is, clear as day.

The face of the person who has caused so much shit in my life.

The face of the person who made me into the mistrusting asshole I am today.

The asshole who sent the only woman I've ever truly loved away.

I needed concrete evidence before I believed Maria. And she provided me with it, in spades. How she managed it just astounds me.

She has always amazed me.

I should have known she was telling the truth.

I should have done better.

I run my hand down over my tie as I look out at the building again. It's early, so they won't be expecting me. It's the last place I expected to be today.

Harley has arranged for the jet to take me to LA this afternoon. Maria might have gotten away from me last night, but I'm not letting another night go by without telling her how sorry I am.

How much I screwed up.

How much I love her.

But first, I need to do this.

I signal to my driver that I'm heading out, then I exit the town car and head into the building. The concierge tips his head in greeting, and it doesn't take long before I'm standing on the other side of the door.

Behind it, the truth about what's been going on all this time.

It opens before I can even knock.

"Griffin!"

Arms embrace me, and lips graze my cheek. The light in their owner's eyes fades as she looks at me.

"What is it? You look like someone died."

I look back at her.

Maybe that's because it feels like someone has.

"I know what you've done, Em."

She frowns, jerking her head back as the tone of my voice slaps her in the face.

The color drains from her skin. She looks like when a wave hits you when your mouth is open and you aren't expecting it, saltwater forcing its way down your throat, making you gag.

433

Knowing it was her all along makes me want to gag. Throw up my entire past and all I've known, right here by her door.

Everything I ever knew was a lie.

She stands back, closing the door behind me as I walk inside.

I don't even wait for her to face me again before I shout, causing her to jump.

"Why, Em?" My anger flies out like a missile. Of all the people, I never expected it to be her. "You're like fucking family to me. What the fuck?!"

I wish I was wrong. God, how do I wish this wasn't real. But it was all there in that envelope.

My friend.

The person who has stood next to me all these months, watching what the deceit has done to me.

One of the few people in my life who I have trusted.

It was her all along.

And for what?

Why would she do this?

Emily's eyes meet mine, and there's a harshness there I've never seen before. She stalks past me into the kitchen, and I stride after her, needing answers.

Desperate for them.

"Tell me, for fuck's sake! You're the last person on earth, Em!" I slam my fist on her kitchen counter, making the mug on it jump up and clatter back down. "Did you need money? Is that it? You should have just asked. I would have given it to you."

She snorts and looks at me in disgust.

"Don't give me that, Griffin! Like you don't know why." She rounds the counter, placing herself on the opposite side to me.

"I don't!" I roar. "How in the ever-loving fuck could I possibly know why you, of all people, would do this to me? How *could* you?"

Rage burns in my heaving chest as I stare at her.

"Please," she says, her voice laced with venom. "Don't play the victim. You're perfect, remember?"

My mouth drops.

She's gone mad.

Raving fucking mad.

"What?!"

"Perfect Griffin, with his line of tarts," she mutters to herself.

"What the hell?" My eyes bulge in my head.

She sounds nothing like the Emily I grew up with. The detest in her eyes, the poison pouring from her mouth... she doesn't even look like the Emily I know.

"Who the fuck are you?"

"Someone you've never even seen!" she shouts, her eyes wild. "Someone you've never even noticed. Too busy with your cock out, sticking it in your staff!"

Blood rushes in my ears as I glare at her, my fists twitching by my sides. Fuck, if she was a man, I would have torn her limb from limb by now, childhood friend or not.

"Don't you dare talk about Maria."

She laughs, a crazed sound as she rolls her eyes and tilts her head back.

"Does it hurt? Knowing the person you love will always look at you with disappointment in their eyes?"

"What?"

I search her face for a sign of the Em I know. But as she wrings her hands in front of her body, fidgeting, chewing on her lip and alternating between frowning and smiling, I can't even make out a ghost of that Em anymore.

She looks batshit crazy, and I'm treading on water, struggling to keep my head above the waves as they threaten to drag me under.

Em? What's happened to you?

"You were the one who stole the spa formulations and tried to make it look like Gwen did. Tried to sell them to a competitor in exchange for a job offer for Gwen. Why?"

She focuses again and meets my eyes.

"You weren't supposed to find out yet." She shakes her head to herself, curling her arms across her chest.

No shit!

"Well, surprise! Because I did! I know everything. Harley spoke to someone who you approached. He didn't take you up on your offer, but he sure remembered you."

My blood boils in my veins as I recall the sound of his voice on the memory stick recording Maria had put in that envelope. Smug as shit that one of my closest friends was going behind my back. Being in the business I'm in, it's easy to not have many friends, especially from rival hotel chains. Always competing. Always wanting to come out on top. Always happy to see you fail.

Emily sighs as though it's an effort to talk.

She's put me through almost one entire year of hell, and she can't be bothered to speak to me.

"She was wrong for you, Griffin. So wrong. The spa was never going to go anywhere with her running it. And you were too blinded by lust to see it. You were better without her. Trust me."

"Trust you?" I splutter, making Emily bristle and stumble back a step. "I don't even fucking know who you are! You let me think one of my staff stole from me?" I can't keep my voice from rising as I press my palms into the counter and lean over it. "You even told me you thought it was her!"

"She was never good enough for you. I knew you needed some help to see it."

"My personal relationships are nothing to do with you! That wasn't your call to make!"

God, I'm shaking. Every muscle in my body is tense to the point of fucking shaking. This is deceit on another level.

"I knew you'd do better, and that The Songbird would do better without her managing the spa. Then you chose Maria. And she seemed great. But then you had to go and stick your dick in her, too." Emily rolls her eyes and I almost pounce across the counter to wring her neck.

"Don't you dare fucking speak about her like that!"

Emily snorts back a laugh.

"I even told you I had met someone. Wondering if it would make you jealous. But she already had her claws in you by then. Figures that you'd choose her over me, someone you've known your whole life. All because she spread her legs for you."

"Enough!" I yell, slamming both hands down onto the counter. "Is that what this is about? It's all because you're jealous? You set her up? You were going to let the police think that she almost poisoned someone to death? That she was stealing money, syphoning it off to an offshore account?"

I lean over the counter, dragging big breaths deep into my lungs.

I cannot believe this. Emily, who I have known my entire life, was the one behind it all along. Because what? She's jealous?

"I was so careful. You weren't supposed to find out like this. Not before..." She screws her eyes shut. "How did you work it out?"

Her shoulders slump in defeat as she stares at me, and for a moment, a glimpse of the Emily I thought I knew emerges. The kind one. The one who raises thousands of dollars for charity. The one who thinks of others first.

"I didn't." I grit my teeth.

Her brows shoot up her forehead. "You didn't—"

"Maria did."

Emily stills, then nods, dropping her eyes to the floor.

"I had a private investigator working on it for months, and Maria still worked it all out before him."

I'm still so amazed by how she did it. I know she had help and wasn't doing it entirely alone, but still. She's diligent. I know her. She said she was going to prove her innocence, and she did. She looked for the flaws and found them, just like she found in the contract with the grower on her very first day at The Songbird.

And she exposed my flaws at the same time.

My glaring, ugly flaws that cost me her.

"It's all on here." I take the memory stick out of my pocket and place it on the counter. Emily's eyes land on it. "It's a copy, before you get any ideas."

"I see." She sniffs and folds her arms across her chest.

"Everything is on here, Em." I jab my finger over the stick. "The CCTV footage from the night of the gala. I know Todd went into that room after me and Maria and found her necklace. Only his drunk, stupid ass lost it. Then you found it and handed it to Earl, saying you'd found it in the ladies' restroom. But that was a lie, wasn't it? You didn't want Earl to know that Todd had told you about finding it in the meeting room. I saw the two of you chatting on the cameras and him showing you something. I just couldn't make out what."

Bile rises in my throat as I recall reading that piece of evidence in my office last night. It makes sense now why Emily insisted to Earl that she found the necklace in the ladies' restroom. She didn't want him, or me, knowing that she knew Maria and I were in that room together. She wanted us to think she didn't know about our relationship at that point.

Even then, she was already planning something.

"Then you called Maria the next morning to ask if she had found it. And when she told you about Todd and that I had canceled his contract, you suggested the new suppliers to her. She even fucking told me you had called her and recommended them!"

I shake my head in disgust at myself. She told me. I had that piece of evidence right in front of me the whole time, but I was too distracted by what Todd had done to her. I didn't listen. It's only afterward that I now remember her saying it at all.

I'm an idiot.

A fucking idiot.

"True. I recommended them. I know how they work, how their systems operate."

She's not going to deny it. At least she's going to give me that. At least she's not going to lie to my face.

Not anymore.

"You emailed them during the filming, asking them to change the ingredients to lower quality ones. You took Maria's ID and used her log in. Earl remembers you going inside."

Earl has always had an incredible memory. He remembers the exact time Emily passed through the main doors. She was gone when the emails were sent. Their time stamps prove it. Maria was still outside, caught up in the enormous crowd of fans when the crowd barriers gave way.

"You knew exactly what you were doing. You have cyber knowledge from your father's business. You had the skill to hack into Maria's account and send the emails. And you made the phone call to back them up. You told them you were Maria, and they believed you. I just don't understand why. Maria did nothing to you. Neither did

Gwen. The Emily I know would never do something like that."

She stays mute, staring at me.

"God, Em! Fucking say something! Do you hate me? Is that it? Do you hate me that much that you wanted to ruin everything I care about? Josanna could have died, for fuck's sake!"

"I didn't know she had an allergy, okay? That was never... I never planned that."

"So that makes it all okay?"

She winces. "I just wanted Maria to leave. I could have run the spa for you. We could have been so good together," she whispers.

"Jesus Christ!" I fist my hands in my hair. A vein in my neck pulsates hard, threatening to explode.

Good together? Me and Em?

"We grew up together. What the fuck are you talking about?"

Her eyes fill with tears, and she shrinks into herself, her shoulders rounding in over her chest. I'm struck by how small she suddenly looks.

How broken.

"You know me better than anyone, Griffin," she whispers. "You're the only one who really knows me. I'm not a bad person. I was just protecting you! I... I... I want what's best for you. What's best for both of us. I thought if we were... but then I saw the way you looked at her and I knew. You have never looked at me like that in all these years. Not once."

She looks to the ceiling, tears running down her cheeks.

"My father... he loves you... I've seen how proud he is of you and your brothers, but mostly you. You're the golden boy, Griffin. You heard him say it yourself. He always wanted a son. But he got me."

"What?" I screw my face up. "What has your father got to do with any of this?"

"I was never going to be good enough for him on my own. But you... he loves you..." Emily's voice cracks as she topples, and before I know what I'm doing, I race around the counter and catch her in my arms as she falls.

"I'm sorry, Griffin!" she sobs, giant, wracking breaths taking over her body. "I'm so sorry. I just thought that... I thought that if we were together, if I was with you... that he might... he might..."

"He might notice you?" My voice betrays the anger that's still fizzing inside my chest and comes out flat, dull, and lifeless, just like my heart.

"That he might *love* me," she whispers, clawing at my shirt and collapsing into me. Her sobs turn into full-blown wails against my chest. "I was never good enough. He looks at me like I'm this enormous disappointment."

I hold her in my arms, all the years of friendship stronger than the hurt and anger I have for her right now.

And I understand.

Her shaking body, weak in my arms, tells me.

It was never about betraying me.

It was all about feeling worthy of him.

"He's a complicated man. He doesn't show his emotions well."

I don't know why I'm defending him.

It's all true. Every word she said.

He has said he wanted a son in front of Emily. He has praised me and my brothers when we are all together, and played down Emily's achievements, as though they mean less, as though a woman can't possibly reach the same levels in business as a man. But she's always laughed it off, bounced back, worked harder at her charity as a result, poured herself into her work. I thought she loved it, that it brought her fulfillment.

I never realized she was doing it for him.

To prove to herself she was worthy of his love.

"You don't know him, not like I do," she whispers. "Nothing I did was ever enough. But you? He thinks the sun rises with you. I thought if we were together, he would finally take me seriously. I would finally be enough. The two of us could have been perfect. You were always the one who was there for me. But then Gwen appeared, and you started dating her. The spa wasn't thriving with her running it. I just wanted her gone. I didn't think the formulations were a big loss. I knew you'd make new, better ones. And you did. Well, Maria did. I didn't count on you falling in love with her. I was hurt and angry that you've never looked at me the way you look at her. Never spoken about me the way you speak about her... *no one ever does*."

"This is all because of your father?" I draw back to look at her tear-stained face and she lifts her hands to pull me back to her. Her sleeves ride up and something white wrapped around her pale skin peeks out.

"What's this?"

She tries to take her arms back, pulling her sleeves down.

"Em?" A warning tone creeps into my voice as I take her arm in my hand and push her sleeve up over her wrist. "Jesus."

I suck a breath in through my nose as I check her other arm. It has a matching white bandage tightly woven over it as well.

"I thought you'd all be better without me. I've caused so much pain. I've seen what all this has done to you. I never meant to hurt you. I thought my charity work would repent me for my sins. But I'm beyond redemption, Griffin. I shouldn't be allowed to live anymore." She breaks into sobs again and I tighten my arms around her, looking up at the ceiling as my eyes burn.

I've known Emily my whole life. She's like a sister to me. Despite how livid I am at her for what she's done, to me, to Gwen, *to Maria*, I can't stop the helplessness creeping over me.

She's sick.

Her father's lack of love and attention has changed who she is.

It's warped her beyond recognition.

It's turned the kind, fun friend I've known for years into someone who will lie and cheat, and prevent other people's happiness, all because of her own pain and bitterness.

It's turned her into someone who's hurting so much that she wants to end her own life.

She's *attempted* to end her life.

All because one stupid man didn't know how to show love for his daughter properly and couldn't be a better man.

"You must hate me so much, Griffin. I'm so sorry. I would never have let Maria go to jail for it. I had everything written down. All of it. My confession. I had it ready to be found when..." She breaks into a fresh round of sobs, her slender frame feeling weak and fragile in my arms. "I couldn't even get that right."

I reach into my pocket and pull out my cell phone.

"What are you doing?" Emily cries as she clings to me.

"I'm calling my doctor."

"Why?"

I look down into her eyes, the depth of the sadness in them enough to swallow me whole if I let it.

"Because you're like family to me, Em. And I'm getting you the help you need."

Chapter Thirty-Four

Maria

THE FIRST WEEK AFTER I leave New York, I barely eat.

The week after that, I survive on the sugar in my coffee and a few slices of toast forced upon me.

I can't. I just can't.

Everything has lost its flavor. Nothing will ever taste anything other than bland ever again. Not now that I've lost him.

I think about him.

All day.

All night.

I picture him going to prenatal appointments with Gwen. Decorating the nursery. Stroking her bump.

Maybe they've already had the baby. I wouldn't know. I've kept away from the internet and haven't switched my cell phone on since I boarded the flight at JFK.

I've shut myself off from the outside world and just... *existed.*

If I can even call it that.

It's more like endurance.

Endurance of soul-crushing torture.

All those years learning not to let anyone in to stop me from getting hurt. And now? Now there's a giant void where my heart used to be. He took it when he couldn't trust me. When he left me to fight alone. But more than anything, it's gone because I know he's hurting, too. He knows now. He will know everything about Emily.

And that makes the empty hole in my chest where my heart once was bleed for him.

He will be hurting.

My Griffin.

No. Not my Griffin. Not anymore.

We were so close to being each other's one. That one person who you can open up to and bare your soul.

So close.

If only he had had more faith. Hadn't been scared to be vulnerable. We could have gotten through this. We could have been together. Where I thought we belonged.

But now Griffin Parker will just be a memory to me.

A memory that fades as the years pass.

And he has Gwen now, and a baby. It's a new start for him. I hope he grabs it with both hands and holds on tight.

Because one thing I've learned about love. Even if they break your heart, you still want theirs to be full. If you truly love them, you still want them to love and be loved.

Just like I want Griffin to live a life full of everything I wish we could have had.

Together.

I stare out from my place on the window seat, my feet curled up underneath me, a book resting on my legs. There's a young girl with her mother in the street outside. She has a bag of seed and is scattering it onto the ground, bouncing on her toes in delight as a flock of pigeons surround the two of them and peck greedily.

The sight brings warmth to my chest, but with it, a pang of pain. It's a welcome change from the dull heaviness that's like a lead weight around my neck.

Never gone, never easing.

Just there.

Always.

At least I can still feel. I'm still alive. Because most days, I would believe that I'm not. That I am stuck somewhere in the in-between. A kind of purgatory for the broken-hearted. And if that were true, would that make Griffin God or the Devil?

I lean my head back against the wall and exhale.

I need to move.

I need to get up and do something.

Anything.

I drag myself over to the mirror, wincing at what two weeks of heartbreak and lack of self-care has done to me. Then I scrape my unwashed hair up into a bun with my chipped fingernails and grab my purse, heading for the bookstore.

Chapter Thirty-Five

Griffin

"How's she doing?" Reed asks as he walks into my office and drops into the seat opposite my desk.

"Not great."

"Shit, man, I'm so sorry. You did the right thing, though. Even though it might not feel like it."

"It sure as fuck doesn't feel like it." I drag my hands down face, knowing my eyes are bloodshot and I look like hell.

After seeing Emily two weeks ago and witnessing her breakdown, I knew I had to do something. I couldn't leave her like that, knowing she had made an attempt on her life. The second I left, she could have tried to finish the job.

I called my doctor, and he admitted her to a private mental health facility right away. We found all sorts of things in her apartment. Photographs of Gwen and Maria. Small items that belonged to them. She was stalking them, obsessed with them. She had let her pain mutate into something dark and consuming.

When I called her father to tell him what had happened, his response was: "What's the silly girl gone and done now?" He only grew quiet when I explained everything, including the slashes on her wrists.

Then he broke down.

And in that moment, he sounded so much like his daughter that I had to hold my hand over the phone so he couldn't hear me cry.

So many mistakes.

So many wrong decisions, misplaced affection, poorly directed attention.

He loves Em. That much was clear by how distraught he was. He's had the world's harshest wake-up call, realizing the pain he's put his own daughter through. The scars he's given her that she's spread onto those around her like a disease.

Infected everyone.

Including me.

The one small positive is that Josanna Frederick and Vogue decided not to press charges. It likely has more to do with their mental health awareness campaign and the bad publicity it would cause now that Emily has been admitted. She's sick, and Josanna's allergic reaction was an unintended effect of that sickness.

Just another casualty joining the list.

"It's not your fault, Griff," Reed says, pulling me back to the present.

"You seem to be saying that to me a lot recently."

"Because it's the truth." He looks at me sadly. "You still haven't heard from her?"

I blow out a breath, leaning back in my chair as he addresses the elephant in the room.

"No."

I've tried calling, texting, emailing.

Nothing.

I flew to LA and went to her spa in Hope Cove. Her manager, Daisy, was there. She said she hadn't heard from Maria in a week and that she hadn't come back there.

I have no idea where she is.

Staying with family or friends, I expect.

Only, the realization that I have no idea where that would be cracks open my heart like a nut in a vise. She told me about her parents being back together. But I have no idea where they live. And I know she has family in England.

But that's it.

I was too busy doubting her to really listen and discover who she is. And now I'm paying the price.

I have no idea where the love of my life is. Or if I will ever see her again.

"You could always hire the PI to find her?"

Reed's shoulders shake as I give him a look that tells him what a shit idea that is.

"Sorry." He holds his hands up. "Just trying to lighten the situation."

I smirk back at him. "Jerk."

"Hey, it made you smile, didn't it? You could consider it, though? Use a different firm, obviously."

"No." I shake my head. "I can't do that to her. I've caused her enough pain. I'm not the man she deserves. God, even Gwen took nine months to have the courage to come and see me and tell me to my face it wasn't her who stole the formulations. I was such an asshole that she couldn't bring herself to face me in person for all those months."

"Yeah, you can be one hell of a stubborn and scary bastard when you want to be." Reed chuckles.

"Thanks," I mutter.

"Listen." He rubs a hand along his jaw. "Gwen had her reasons. And it's all good now. She's all shacked up and having a baby with her childhood sweetheart. *Who*"—he arches a brow—"she only reconnected with as a result of running back home after all the scandal broke. So really, she has you to thank for her fairy-tale ending."

I snort. "You figure?"

I was so happy for Gwen when she came to my office that night. She's moving on with her life. And she deserves it. We were never right for each other, and the way she looked that night—she was glowing. She looked happier than I've ever seen her.

Happier than I ever made her.

She deserves a new start with her old flame she reconnected with when we broke up. I don't care if it was straight after. We were over long before that. We both knew it. I wish them all the best. Lucky them. Finding each other.

Being free to love one another.

"Griff. I've known you years." Reed leans over my desk, fixing his eyes on mine. He can be a joker sometimes, but when he's serious, he's intense. "You love Maria. She's it for you. I can see it. You think you don't deserve her? Because you hurt her?" He screws his face up. "That's a load of shit."

"I fucked up—"

"Yes! You did. But you can fix it. Be the best man you can be. Do better. Find a way to show her. Do something that speaks to her. Show her you deserve her forgiveness. Fucking beg for it at her feet if you have to! But I swear, if you let a woman that makes you look as happy and alive as you did when you were with her go, then you're a fucking fool who will regret it until the day he dies."

"When did you turn into a romantic?" I snort.

He shakes his head with a soft chuckle. "Since I saw the light... and it was pink."

I narrow my eyes at him and his cryptic answer. "What—"

"Um, Mr. Parker?"

A soft knock on the door—which Reed left open—interrupts us.

"Harley, everything okay?"

She falters in the doorway, her eyes drifting over to Reed and back to me.

"Yes, sorry. I didn't realize you had company. I just need some signatures. It can wait until later."

I'm about to tell her not to worry about it and to bring the paperwork over, but she looks at Reed one more time and then disappears before I have the chance.

"You think she heard us?" Reed looks at the empty doorway after her.

"Probably. But it doesn't matter. She doesn't know where Maria is."

His eyes linger on the space where Harley was just standing, before he nods, bringing his eyes back to me.

"Worry about finding her after."

"After what?" I run my hand down over my tie as I look at him.

"After you've worked on yourself. Done things, made changes. Become the man you know she deserves. The man I know you already are."

He stands and gives me a smile.

"You know what you need to do, Griff. Now fucking believe in yourself and do it."

Chapter Thirty-Six

Maria

Three Months Later

"HAPPY NEW YEAR, LOVE."

"Thanks, Nana." I smile at her.

I could almost fool myself with the glimmer of genuine peace in my smile. It's been good for me, this past three months with her.

Like coming home.

"Here." I bring out the gift I hid by the side of the sofa earlier and hand it to her.

"What's this? We've had Christmas?" Her eyes light up as she tears off the paper.

"I know. But this is something to enjoy in January. You always complain it's so long, cold, and dark."

"Oh, Maria, love!" She grins and strokes her hand over the half-naked male on the book cover. "You know I love TL Swan. She's my favorite."

"I know." I smile back. "Look inside."

She turns to the first page and her mouth drops open.

"How on earth did you—? Did she send this all the way from Australia?" Nana turns the book over in her hands, her face glowing.

"She was doing a signing in New York before I left."

New York.

I swallow the lump in my throat, forcing it away. I need to be able to speak about New York and not immediately think of *him*.

"Oh, love. This is wonderful! Thank you so much! A signed copy! And done in person for my granddaughter. This really is the best gift."

The joy on her face warms my chest, thawing a small chip away from the frozen lump that's lived there for the last three months.

"And there's another one on the way. To replace the one you sent me."

Nana reaches over and grabs my hand. I felt so guilty when she told me she had sent her favorite signed copy for me to read when I was in New York. Only, it didn't arrive before I left and it's never been returned to sender, despite having her England address on the packet. It must have gotten lost somewhere.

I smile sadly.

She told me it was a love story about two troubled souls who find one another. Now it's lost somewhere between here and New York.

Oh, the irony.

"Well, it just so happens, I have something for you, too." Nana grins at me and produces a small box from beside her.

"What?"

She chuckles. "Like Nana, like granddaughter. I have some tricks up my sleeve too, you know?"

I shake my head with a smile as I take the box from her and lift the lid. She was always doing things like this when I was a child. Surprising me with the most thoughtful gifts. She has the biggest heart I've ever known.

"I don't understand. What is all of this?"

My fingers graze the envelopes, a giant pile of them, all with the same mailing stamp.

New York.

Nana reaches over and pats my arm. "This is your story, love. I waited until you were strong enough, and now I see you are. It's the new year, and it's time for you to decide how the next chapter goes."

"I don't understand." I look at her and her eyes are misty, filled with all the wisdom and knowledge only living a life as full as hers can give.

"You will." She pats my arm again. "Read them all in order and you'll understand."

Then she stands and smiles at me once more before leaving the room and closing the door gently behind her.

I look back into the box and take out the first envelope. They're all in date order. This one being the oldest, sent a few days after I left New York.

I pull out the letter and something drops out, landing in my lap. I laugh out loud at the words on the paper napkin from The Songbird's new coffee deli.

Latte sisters—they taste better with you.

I unfold the letter and read Harley's words. It's addressed to Vera, my nana. Harley says she found her book delivery when she was sorting out my old apartment. It obviously made it there, after all. She says how she misses me, and that Will, Suze, and Earl all do too.

She wouldn't have known I was here when she wrote this. I never told her where I was going.

The thought makes warmth swell in my chest. Harley wrote to my nana just to make a friend. That's Harley all over. A sweet chatterbox.

She talks about things being quieter without me, but that she understands why I needed to leave. She doesn't mention Griffin, only to say that when he read our envelope with all the evidence about Emily in, he went to see her, and it all came out. She confessed to everything and is a lot sicker than any of us realized. She's getting the help she needs now, though. Griffin has seen to it and is paying for the best medical care for her.

I move to the next letter. It's obvious my nana has written back, as Harley asks her what she thought of the big twist in chapter twenty. I smile. Harley's been converted to the steamy books Nana reads and is enjoying the one she sent over. This letter, though, contains a printout from a small, local paper outside of New York. There's Gwen, and a man called Rick holding a newborn baby, their wide grins bursting with happiness for the camera.

I clasp my hand to my mouth as tears blur my eyes.

The rest of Harley's letter says Gwen came to Griffin and they had a talk, and that Gwen has just had a baby with her childhood lover that she reunited with.

Harley knew I saw Gwen with Griffin that night. I left her some garbled, emotional voicemail on my way to the airport about how he was moving on and I was happy for him. She must have told Nana in the hope she would pass the news on.

Maybe she thought I needed to know that he wasn't moving on?

My shoulders drop. It changes nothing. I still had to leave. We would still have been over, whether or not the baby had been his.

My stomach squeezes. A part of me is happy he isn't starting a family with Gwen. But a larger part sinks.

He isn't having a new start. How is he really doing?

I put the letter back into the envelope and move on.

The next one has a photograph inside.

A laugh escapes my lips and I shriek out loud at the photograph. A fancy state-of-the-art pigeon coop has been erected down the side alleyway of The Songbird. Earl is standing proudly underneath it and the words 'Dandy Residences' are on a brass plaque above the little entry hole.

I clutch my chest as a wave of emotion rolls through it.

He did this.

Only he would call it that.

I grab the next envelope and whip out the letter, scanning it as fast as I can.

Broken, withdrawn, thrown himself into new projects.

Harley's talking about Griffin. How he's working longer and longer days, pushing himself to do everything and more. He's hired a new spa manager, a man who comes highly recommended from another hotel in

Boston. And he's been investing heavily in new partnerships with The Songbird and a new charity.

Maybe he thinks he needs to replace all the lost funding Emily's galas used to provide now that she's no longer running them.

I move on to the next letter, and it contains a press release detailing an exciting new conservation project backed by The Songbird hotel in New York. There's a picture of Griffin standing in front of a coconut palm shaking hands with Ken.

I scan down the text and almost faint at the amount of money which has been pledged to *protect and breed The Bahama Oriole birds.*

He's done all this?

I move on again. Harley's excitement leaps off the page in her words as she tells my nana about a team building day the staff went on. The theme was trust, and it was all about trusting one another and trusting yourself.

There are photographs of Griffin again, all suited, dark hair styled perfectly, looking every inch the handsome billionaire hotelier that he is.

I bite my lip at the stunning image he makes.

He's smiling, his blue eyes bright. But I know those eyes. They're not glittering the way I know they can.

Like two blue diamonds.

He's still hurting, I just know it. And seeing it here in front of me has my fingers trembling, tears racing down my cheeks as I continue reading.

Letter after letter, Harley talks about Griffin. About how she's never seen anyone look at me the way he did. Never seen him as happy as when I was there. And never seen him as lost as he has been since I left. She says she eventually admitted to him where I was once my nana confessed I was staying with her, but that he said some cryptic spiel about how you can't cage a bird.

Am I the bird? Does he think coming after me is caging me? Is that why he hasn't come?

There are more letters and photographs. All incredible achievements that The Songbird is making.

All incredible things Griffin has done.

The next letter has me choking back a sob.

Griffin posted my bail.

Harley says he even got Reed to help pull some strings at the New York Mayor's office to apply some pressure to get me out quickly. The police wanted to keep me in, question me further. But Griffin wouldn't hear of it.

He did everything he could to get me out of there.

Even though he thought I was guilty, he still held on to a tiny thread of hope, whether consciously or not.

And he helped Earl. Gave him money—a lot of money—to help gather evidence to prove my innocence.

He did it all.

He knew I was innocent.

Deep down, he knew. He just needed to allow himself to believe it.

He needed to *trust*.

I look inside the box. There's just one envelope left, dated yesterday.

Once I open it, that's it. All of them gone.

My final peek into his life is over.

I open the thick padded envelope.

It contains a small packet and a note.

This one is in different handwriting... handwriting that the sight of alone is enough to make my throat burn.

I open the note first, unfolding it carefully.

Maria, no amount of I'm sorrys will ever be enough. But I will say it until my tongue bleeds if that's what it takes for you to believe me. I was stupid. Fucking stupid. I should have trusted my heart, Sweetheart. It will only ever be you. Forgive me... please. Be mine forever, because I've been yours since the first moment I saw you. Griff.

I tip the packet upside down, and something drops into my palm. A small, perfect shell, so unique because of its ocean blue center.

The same color as his eyes.

He kept it.

I sob, letting every tear carry out a piece of hurt with it as I stare at the shell I found that day at the cove with him. That was the first time I saw him for who he truly is, underneath the suits, behind the cool, calculated businessman.

My Griffin.

The man who owns my heart and soul.

The man I don't know if I can live without.

Survive, yes, but live? *Really* live?

I stopped doing that the second I lost him.

"Maria?" Nana pokes her head around the door.

"Nana," I sob, looking back into her kind eyes. "All the things he did before I left... and since... he—"

"I know, love." She smiles at me, and I want to run to her, feel her familiar, comforting arms around me.

But I can't.

I'm glued to the spot as she holds out another envelope to me.

"I'm not sure I can take another one." I sniff, smiling sadly at her.

"You're strong, Maria. You can do whatever you set your mind to. You always could. And I will support you in whatever decision you make. But no one's perfect. We all make mistakes. And I know genuine remorse when I hear it. That man is haunted by his regrets, my love."

"You've spoken to him?" My voice shakes.

"More than once. He's a stubborn so-and-so." She chuckles. "The number of times he wanted to come over here once Harley finally admitted this was where you were. But I told him no."

"Griffin wanted to come here?" I stare at her as my heart lifts in my chest.

I said before there was an empty hole there. But time with my nana has slowly made me realize, my heart wasn't gone. It was just bruised so badly that it was hiding in the shadows. Her love and time helped coax it back a little at a time, back into the light.

"He did. But you weren't ready."

She sits next to me and wraps a warm arm around my shoulders. I lean into her familiar scent—lavender and sugar—and allow her to hold me.

"He's a man who knows what he wants. But I needed to be sure that you were healed enough to know what you want. I saw your pain." She squeezes me tighter. "I knew you wouldn't speak to him until you were ready, and he had to accept that. You're just as stubborn as him." She chuckles again.

"And now?" I ask as I hold the piece of paper from inside the envelope between my fingers, its tiny form seeming like the heaviest weight in the world.

Holding so much promise and so much hurt in the few words held inside.

The words that begin the next chapter.

The one only I can write.

"And now, it's your decision to make." Nana rubs her hand up and down my arm, over the goosebumps that have covered my skin.

I unfold the paper, pulling my bottom lip between my teeth as I read the words.

This is it.

My decision.

Chapter Thirty-Seven

Maria

I TAKE ONE MORE look at the piece of paper with the hotel name on and step out of the taxi, smoothing down my clothes.

Dress—red.

Hair—down.

I need to feel confident for this.

I pay the driver and walk into the hotel, through the sleek marble foyer and past a giant art piece of an airline engine, toward the bar. Images from that night in The Bahamas flood my mind as I walk into the dark space. But where the bar at Hotel Atlantica was lit with fairy lights and warmed by the Caribbean sunset, this one is dark with its low lighting, deep green velvet seats and marble-topped tables. It's sexy and sensual, just the same, but different.

This bar is older, wiser, and not tinged with strong tropical cocktails.

Just like me.

Every tiny hair on my body stands up, my skin tingling.

He's close. He must be. My body can sense him. As ridiculous as that sounds, it's the truth. I know his eyes are on me.

I just can't see him, I can't—

He's sitting at the bar.

The second my eyes meet his, my whole body vibrates with anticipation and denied longing. After all these weeks, these past months... it just takes one look, and it's like no one else in the room exists.

Damn him for still having such an effect on me.

His piercing blue eyes are fixed on mine, stealing the breath from my lungs.

I swallow.

I've missed them.

I've missed *him.*

His eyes drop over my body and back up to my face, sending a shiver up my spine.

"I've never seen anyone look at someone like he looks at you."

That's what Harley said. That he looks at me in a way that makes everyone else around us know we are meant to be together.

I push down the rising flutters in my stomach and walk over to him.

His eyes never leave mine.

Meeting him here, like he asked me to in that final note... it means that whatever happens tonight, I will never forget his crystal eyes. They are a symbol of my future staring back at me.

I just have to decide if it's a future they're a part of, or whether they'll only ever be a memory from now on.

He rises to his feet as I get closer.

I open my mouth, ready to greet him, but words escape me as I struggle to make sense of what is happening.

He's really here.

He should be in New York.

I stop an arm's length away from him, and already the heat radiates off his tall, broad body, calling out to mine as he studies me.

It's been weeks. Months.

But now he's standing here, looking even better than I remember. His dark hair is softer, his eyes bluer.

Everything about him screams at me to take notice.

To really *see* him.

He's wearing a suit, a deep gray one, with a charcoal tie. The pattern catches my eye as he runs his hand down over it. The tiny silver specks are birds. Hundreds of tiny birds flying free.

"You came." His voice is calm, deep, the perfect mix of breathiness and rasp that makes him sound like sex.

I always loved his voice and the things he said.

I shake the thought from my head as I draw in a slow breath and look at him. The corners of his mouth lift and I stare at his mouth, at his lips, before whipping my eyes up again.

"What are you doing here?" I whisper, the pressure making my throat ache as tears threaten my eyes.

His eyes light up, and then lines appear around their corners as he smiles at me. A smile that is tinged with sadness. I know because it's just like the one reflected in my bathroom mirror every day.

"What are you doing here?" I ask again, searching his face as the anger I thought I would feel doesn't come. I've been through every emotion since leaving New York. Anger, disbelief, grief.

Now that he's here, all I feel is relief.

And hope.

Relief that he's still in one piece and he's okay. Everything with Emily will have hit him hard. I know that. I was scared about how he would take it. Scared he would close himself away even more. But he's here, looking even stronger and more intense than I remember.

It didn't break him.

I look over his face again—dark brows furrowed as he watches me, soft lips, which whispered so many things to me through all our days and nights. I glance down at his hands, the hands that know every curve of my skin.

Then I look back into his eyes and it's there again. Poking me in the heart and making me take notice.

Hope.

Most of all, there is *hope*.

Because despite everything, I only need to look at him to understand that time apart has done nothing to reduce my pull to him. The lift in my chest when he looks at me. The flutters in my stomach, from the heat of his body being close to mine. The rush of energy flooding my veins from breathing the same air as him.

Breathing in something so familiar—*tropical air after a storm.*

This indescribable urge to be with him, near him, surrounded by him, hasn't gone away. It hasn't faded. If anything, it has grown, intensified in its power.

Surely if my instincts are telling me that this is right. That *he* is right. Then there's still hope?

"Griffin?" I whisper as the two of us stand, unable to look away from one another.

He clears his throat and parts his soft, skilled lips. Lips that I have kissed a million times.

"I came for *you*. I was always going to come for you... It will only ever be you." His eyes shine as he looks at me.

And there, before me, is the inside of the crack that I saw that final day in his office. Only now it isn't a crack. It's a giant ravine.

Griffin Parker is standing in front of me with his heart laid bare.

It's in his eyes.

It's in his voice.

He looks like the man I last saw, but he's not. Not exactly. Something about him *has* changed.

I can sense it.

I hold my breath, my chest burning. His shoulders rise and fall as he waits—waits for me to say something.

I finally take a deep breath.

"How's Emily?"

He holds my gaze, unblinking. "You want to know how Emily is?"

I nod as I slide onto a bar stool. He hovers for a moment, his brow furrowed, then he sits on the stool next to me and runs his hand down over his tie.

"I shouldn't be surprised that the first thing you do is ask about someone else. Even after everything she did. You're an amazing woman."

I gnaw on my lips, dropping my eyes from his.

What do I say to that? How can I possibly answer that?

You think I'm amazing, but you still let me leave? You still couldn't trust me enough, trust yourself enough, to make me stay?

"She's doing okay. She's making progress. At least, that's what her doctors say."

I glance at him, brushing my hair over my shoulder as he watches me. "That's good. I'm glad she's getting help. Harley said in her letters that she had a lot to talk about with her dad?"

He clears his throat, his eyes fixed on my face as he shifts in his seat, causing our knees to touch. I stare at where we connect and then slowly slide my legs to the side, away from him.

"It was in her letters," I add, glancing back at him, "the ones she wrote to my nana."

"I know about the letters." He signals the bartender, who appears moments later and places two glasses down in front of us.

"Of course you do."

I lift the glass to my lips and take a sip, more as a distraction than through thirst, despite my mouth being dry. I've no idea what it is, but it's alcoholic enough to send fire blazing a trail down to my stomach.

"I didn't, to start with." Griffin leans both elbows onto the bar and turns his face toward me, but not before gifting me a perfect side profile of his dark, brooding looks.

I saw it before, I always knew, it's so obvious, but it's like I'm noticing again for the first time just how *beautiful* he is.

My stomach tightens and I look down into my glass. "You didn't?"

"No. I had no idea where you were. Harley never told me she had found you. Not in the beginning. I don't think she wanted me to know. After everything with the police and them questioning you... she didn't think I *deserved* to know."

"Hmm." I smile as thoughts of Harley standing up to Griffin dance through my head. "What changed her mind?"

He shakes his head. There are faint dark shadows beneath his eyes. But they don't detract from his beauty. *Nothing can.*

"I don't know. I think she took pity on me." He laughs and takes a gulp of his drink. "I've been a shitty person to be around lately, so Reed tells me." He glances at me and then exhales a long breath. "I think everything with Em and her dad—they've been having therapy sessions together—coupled with everything that has been happening at The Songbird, just made her think. Made her want to believe in a miracle. Made her need to have that.

Plus, she misses you. Everyone does. They all blame me for you leaving."

"I did leave because of you."

His eyes shoot to mine, the blue in them brilliant—alive and crackling, like electricity.

Silence cocoons us for a few seconds, before his eyes pinch at the corners, regret swirling in them.

"I know. And I deserve every shit word you want to hurl my way."

I search his eyes. There are people around us, but their presence does nothing to dampen the energy passing between us as though we are the only two people here.

It was always like this with him.

He's intoxicating.

Heady, captivating.

When I'm with Griffin, nothing else seems real. The world is a whisper, a faint image fading into the background.

Leaving only us.

He leans closer.

"I deserve all of it. And I will fucking take it, drink it up, fucking *live* off it like it's my air for the rest of my days, if it means you'll be able to look at me for more than a few seconds without turning away. I've been in hell since you left."

He places one hand on my knee, grasping my skin, and spins me on my stool so I am facing him head-on.

"Look at me, Maria. *Please.*"

I raise my eyes to his and try to ignore the burning that is taking over my throat as he holds my gaze.

His brows flatten over his eyes as he looks deep into me with an intensity that touches my soul.

"I'm *sorry. So sorry*. Sorry for everything."

He's so goddamn beautiful. Like a dagger made of crystal. Deadly and sharp if used against you, but breath-taking and fragile at the same time.

My eyes sting, and I blink, fighting to maintain composure. "It's not okay. What you did... you broke us. You said you'd never let me go, that you would never leave."

"I know." He drops his head and sucks a breath in through his nose. When he looks back up, his eyes are shining. "I *know*. I fucked up. I've never wanted this before. I've never met someone who made me feel so out of control before. Until you."

He takes my hand in his and I gasp as electricity shoots up my arm.

"I promise you I will make it up to you if you come back to me. I will fucking *worship* you until my dying breath. And I will *never* doubt you ever again, I swear."

I swallow hard, darting my eyes from side to side. Our intense conversation is attracting looks from interested guests further along the bar.

"Fuck them," Griffin hisses. "Look at *me*, Sweetheart." *Sweetheart.*

I snap my eyes back to him and yank my hand free.

"You don't get to call me that anymore."

His brows pull together, darkening his eyes as he looks between mine.

"Please. Just talk to me. Come upstairs where it's just us and talk to me. I'll stay here another week if I have to. Fuck! I'll stay for eternity until you give me a chance. *Please.*" He fixes his eyes on mine, the intensity flowing from them as he looks at me as though my answer means everything to him.

Maybe it does.

"*Another* week? You've been here a week already?"

The corner of his lips curl and he nods. "Knowing I was closer to you... I needed it... It felt..." He presses his lips together, his shoulders tensing. "I will do anything for you, you have to know that."

"I don't have to know anything. You couldn't trust me when it mattered. You..."

I am about to say he left me at the police station, but that's not strictly true now. He posted my bail and did everything he possibly could to get me out of there as fast as possible. He's the reason I didn't spend the night in a cell. Something I only found out from those letters.

"You left me when it mattered. Instead of talking to me, you chose to believe I was capable of doing all those things to you, to The Songbird."

I glance around again. The couple down the bar aren't even trying to hide the fact they're leaning closer, abandoning their own conversation to listen to ours. And why wouldn't they? Front row tickets to our horror show must be entertaining. Like a morbid fascination in watching something you can almost certainly tell is headed for disaster.

"Maria." Griffin follows my gaze. "Come up to my room. We can talk there."

I look back at him and nod, allowing him to guide me from my stool and through the lobby to the elevators with his hand resting on my lower back. When we step inside and the doors close, he presses the button with his other hand.

"Are you doing all your work from here? A week is a long time for you to leave. I know you. You hate leaving the hotel for long."

"The hotel isn't the most important thing in my life."

"That's not true." My voice comes out quiet, my throat still dry, despite the drink I had moments ago.

The Songbird is his wife. Just like Emily said.

His jaw stiffens, and he holds out an arm, indicating for me to walk out first as the doors slide open. We walk to a large, ornate door and he unlocks it with his key card, holding it open for me. I slip past him, my dress brushing against his shirt.

He catches me, curling one hand around my forearm as I pass, and his warm breath dusts my neck as he dips his head.

"I've made mistakes. But I have *never* lied to you. Not once. When I tell you it's not the most important thing in my life, I mean it."

He lets go and I move all the way into the hallway as the door falls shut behind us.

"Just to yourself, then? Not lied to me, but lied to yourself?"

I spin and glare at him. Maybe it's the drink downstairs, or the freedom to speak with no-one listening, but anger ignites low in my stomach. A fierce flame that is licking at me, drawing up all the pain I've felt and pulling it into a mass inside me. A giant, fiery mass so great that I can't hold it in any longer.

"Tell me. What *is* the most important thing in your life? What are you even doing here? You don't trust me, remember?" I shout, willing the pounding in my chest to stop. To stop and let me rest.

I can't keep doing this.

He stiffens, closing his eyes, screwing them shut. The anguish pouring from him steals the strength from my legs. They're weak as my stomach twists into knots.

He may be the one who pushed me away.

But *I* ran.

I could have stayed until he had read the evidence I found.

We could have had this conversation weeks ago.

I ran, and the scars it slashed into him are shown all over his face, clear as day.

I did that to him.

But I had to.

As much as it destroyed me to leave, I had to.

How can you stay when the man you love looks at you like he doesn't even know you? When you have never felt more like yourself than when you are with him, but it's still not enough for him?

I thought I would never see him again, that even after he read the evidence in that envelope, it would be too late.

But now he's here.

And my head is spinning.

"I'm here to say I'm sorry!" He rounds on me, pinning me in place with his eyes as his chest expands and he sucks in a breath, his energy matching mine as he raises his voice. "I'm fucking sorry! I want you to know that I've spent every miserable fucking day regretting pushing you away, regretting doubting you. I *knew* deep down that's not who you are. But I was too fucking self-absorbed to see it! I was too concerned with being lied to again by someone that when I thought it could be you, I shut down, okay? I fucking shut down! Because nothing in this world is worse to me than the idea of *you* lying to me." He points at me, his finger shaking, before he drops his arm to his side and curses again. "Nothing is worse. Not Gwen, not Em... not even my own mother could be worse to me."

"I never lied to you."

He paces in front of me and rakes his hands through his hair.

"I know. I was a fucking fool, all right? I know that now. I knew it then, too."

"I don't—"

He turns back to me, slamming both hands against the wall on either side of my head and leaning toward me. If I didn't know him better, it would make me jump.

But it doesn't.

His passion is one of the first things that drew me to him.

All it does is make me ache for him more.

I used to be on the receiving end of all that passion.

Me.

His breath caresses my lips as he leans closer.

"I love you, Maria. You know I do. I love you with everything I have. *Everything I am.* You've seen me. The real me. Fucked up, paranoid, the lot."

My breath mixes with his and our bodies hover inches apart as we pant, emotion coursing out of every pore into the surrounding air until it's thick and hard to breathe.

"You're not fucked up, Griff."

His eyes hold mine, a wild, haunted depth to them. "I am. I'm the worst kind of fucked up. I let you go. I pushed you away. *My lighthouse in a storm.*"

"Your what?"

He reaches up and ever so slowly traces the back of one hand down the side of my face, his knuckles dusting the curve of my cheek.

I fight from leaning into his touch as his hand moves to my chin and then to my hair, stroking it between his fingers as his eyes follow.

"My lighthouse in a storm. It's always been you. You're everything to me. You make me a better man."

"You don't need me for that. You are a good man."

He drops his eyes and his lips curl down into a scowl. "I'm not. I'm far from it."

"You are! You get your friend the best medical care possible when she needs you, even after everything. You start conservation projects for endangered birds. You build pigeon houses!"

I can't help smiling as he looks up.

Dandy residences.

"You built them a house, and you named it."

"Because it made me feel closer to you. As ridiculous as that sounds, those scrawny little fuckers remind me of you. Remind me of when I saw you every day, and you believed in me. When you *trusted* me. Before I lost you. When you were still *mine*."

The smile falls from my face, and I hold my breath, not trusting myself to speak, remembering the time outside my apartment all those months ago when I accused him of cheating on Emily, thinking it was Griffin I heard next door with all those women, night after night.

"If I was dating someone, she would be everything to me. All mine."

"Yours?" I whisper.

His hand pauses over my heart where he's holding a strand of my hair between his fingers.

"Yes, Sweetheart. Mine."

I stare back at him.

His?

Is that what I want? Of course, I know I want it. But can I handle it?

"What happens next time you don't trust me? What happens, then?" I shuffle against the wall. I have nowhere to go unless I put my hands on his chest and push him away.

But I don't trust myself to touch him.

"There will never be a next time. I promise you." He removes his hand from my hair and draws his arms back, freeing me. "I trust you with my life, Maria. If I've learned anything from this, it's that you are the *one* person who I do trust. You were there for me even when I didn't deserve it. After Josanna... with Em... Harley told me you thought about not telling me it was her."

"I did." I swallow the lump in my throat. "I hated knowing that she did that to you after all your years of friendship. I know what it's like to be betrayed by someone who is family."

"Sweetheart." Griffin's voice softens as he looks at me.

"Look, I don't want to talk about my dad again." I swipe at my stinging eyes with my fingertips. "This isn't about him. That's in the past. I've moved on."

"You learned to trust again?" Griffin's eyes burn into mine.

"Yes," I whisper.

"So you know that it's true when I say I have, too. You know it's possible."

"I—"

"*Please!*" The crack in his voice makes me freeze. "Please let me prove it to you. Let me earn your trust again."

"What about the next time something happens that you don't like, Griff? You put me on a pedestal. You made it so impossible to live up to your standards. You want to control everything. But people being real, *being human*, is something you can't control. What if I do something you don't agree with, then what? You'll fly off the handle again? Blame me? Tell me not to worry myself as you 'won't be lonely'?"

Shame claws at my chest as the words leave my mouth, tearing open my insecurities about what he said. That he wouldn't be lonely.

That I was replaceable.

His eyes widen and he shakes his head, jabbing his fingers into his chest. "Okay, I have lied to you! Because that is a lie! The only lie I've ever told you. I will be lonely. *Fucking lonely!* Because no one can penetrate this *bastard heart* of mine, except you. No one has even come close. Does that make you feel better? Knowing that you are the only person in the world who makes me cry in the shower?"

Makes him cry?

I open my mouth to speak, but he continues, his eyes wild, his arms flailing in his designer suit jacket.

He's a man teetering on the edge.

"I used to jerk off in the shower thinking about you." His eyes drop over my body. "That dress! Your hair, your eyes, your lips... fuck! Everything about you. Your drive, your determination... your fucking brilliant mind! I had to! Just so I could function when you were near me. I used to jerk off every morning picturing you. Imagining you were mine, that you would want me as much as I wanted you." He inhales sharply. "And now I cry. Does that make you happy? Does that tell you just how *fucking lonely* I will be if you don't give me a chance to make it right? You own my thoughts, Maria. You own *me*."

He stops, resting his hands on his hips, sucking in deep breaths as his jaw ticks and his eyes reach mine once more.

"*Only* you, Sweetheart. *Always* you."

We stare at each other until his breathing has slowed and my heart has stopped pounding against my ribs. His eyes never leave mine. Never stop holding mine, blazing into mine with an intensity that could burn the world.

"What will you do if I say no?"

"Jesus." He looks to the ceiling and then scrubs a hand down his face. "Don't, Sweetheart. Think about it for longer. Take as long as you need. I'll wait."

"But if I do say no? What will you do?"

"I'm not leaving without you," he grits out. He draws in a breath, blinking rapidly as he stares at me. "Fine. I would have no fucking choice... I'd have to open a bird sanctuary."

"What?" I laugh for the briefest second as his lips twitch. Then he falls serious again and the despair on his face kills the sound in my throat in an instant.

His eyes shine as he looks at me. "I don't know. Curse myself every day for being such a fool? Wonder what you're doing? If you're happy? If you've fallen in love? If someone else is treating you better than I did?"

"If someone else is touching me?" I whisper.

He screws his face up and his teeth grind together. "Fuck, yes," he hisses. "Just know that if anyone ever..." He clenches a fist in the air, a vein bulging in his neck. "If anyone ever hurts you, I will cut them up into so many pieces and burn them so there is no hope of ever putting them back together. You understand?"

My lips part as I breathe. The power in his words is reflected in his eyes.

Those beautiful, blue eyes... so intense, so passionate.

"You understand? I will come for you in a heartbeat. Promise me. Promise me you would call me?"

"No." I shake my head forcefully, my voice raspy. "No!" I say louder.

"God." Griffin's face crumples as he bends at the waist and drops his face into his hands.

"I can't call you! I can't live a life without you where I would call you if I needed help. It doesn't work like that!"

He lifts his head and straightens up. Tears are pooling in his eyes.

I take a step toward him, the strength growing in my voice with each word.

"If you want to be the man I call, then you need to be the *only* man I call. The one I call when I can't get a cab. The one I call when I see something that makes me think of you. The one I call when I just want to hear your voice. The one I call to tell you I miss you, even though I saw you an hour ago. The one I wake up with every day. The one I *love* with my heart, body, and soul. You have to be *that* man."

He looks at me, and the hope in his eyes has me sobbing, giant tears coursing rivers down my cheeks to match the ones shining in his eyes. I said I had already cried enough to make an ocean for him to sail in. Now I see we've both cried enough for the other to drown in.

Unless we save each other.

Hold on together and keep one another afloat.

"You have to be that man, Griff. No one else can even come close to being him. If it's not you, then it's no-one."

"It's me," he answers immediately, moving toward me. "It's me. Fuck, Sweetheart, it's me! I will prove it to you."

He takes another step forward, his hard, broad body encasing mine, pinning me against the wall as he looks down at me.

"It's me," he says again, and then he snakes his hand around the back of my neck and pulls my lips to his, whispering against them.

"Me."

Chapter Thirty-Eight

Griffin

"ME," I BREATHE AGAINST her lips as their heat warms mine. "I swear to you, Sweetheart. No one can love you as hard as I can. No one can feel like he's fucking dying every day without you, like I do. You are everything to me. The most important thing in my life. I will sell The Songbird to prove it to you. You and me, we can sail the world on my boat. Be together always."

"No," she whispers against my lips.

Pain lances through my chest. I thought my heart was shredded. Shredded and then mashed to a bloody pulp by now. Unable to feel any more pain. But I was wrong.

That one word tears my world apart.

No.

No?

"I swear to you, I'll make it up to you, I'll—"

"You can't sell The Songbird. I won't let you. You love that place. *I* love that place. It's in your blood. It's who you are."

She lifts her delicate hands to my shirt and balls it in her fists, pulling me up against her so our chests press together.

"Who I am is nothing without you." I flex my fingers on the back of her neck, looking down at her. Her eyes drift closed, and her pulse flutters beneath her skin. "Sweetheart?" I brush my thumb around the front of her neck, pressing it gently over the vein, her life pumping beneath my skin, grounding me in a way nothing else can.

She parts her lips and looks up at me. I hold my breath. Hold my breath while I stare at the woman I love.

Helpless.

At her total fucking mercy.

I have never been at anyone's mercy in my life.

I only know winning.

Being the best.

It's what I craved, what I worked so hard to maintain. Everything had an order, a place. Everything had to be perfect.

Until I met her and realized just how empty I really am.

How fucking *imperfect* my entire existence was.

Because standing here, looking at her, I know.

Nothing will ever matter to me as much as her.

"Griffin." Her lips graze mine as she rises on her toes. "I want it to be you. I want it to be you more than anything."

"Just say it, Sweetheart. Say the word and it's done. I swear on my life, I won't give you any reason to regret it."

"Griff?"

I pull her closer, resting my forehead against hers. "Say it."

"Yes—"

I don't wait for her to finish. Smashing my lips against hers, I curl my free hand into her hair and tease her mouth open. Tasting her, remembering her.

Three long fucking months.

I'm so stupid. I could have lost her forever.

"Thank you," I whisper as I kiss her with everything I have, and she sinks into me. *"Thank you."*

I push forward, trapping her against the wall as I deepen our kiss. A small moan falls from her lips, and I relish it, swallowing it down so it's mine forever. I press into her harder, deeper, unable to get close enough.

If I could pull her inside me, I would.

Merge us together forever.

"I love you," I pant, our kisses growing more urgent. "Fuck, Sweetheart. I love you more than anything."

Her hands tighten on my shirt, and she pulls me closer, our faces squashing together as we kiss away months of separation.

"I love you, too," she pants, and I freeze, pulling back to look into her eyes.

"What's wrong?" Her eyes dart between mine, her lips red and swollen. She tries to pull me back to her and frowns as I stand firm.

"Say it again."

"I love you," she whispers.

"Louder."

She moves her hands, placing her palms on my cheeks, instantly transporting me back to the mornings where I would bury myself deep inside her body and lose all sense of time whilst staring into her eyes.

God, I miss those mornings.

"Louder, Sweetheart," I growl, needing to hear her say it, needing to know that she still feels it. That we still have that.

Everything else will be okay if we still have *that.*

If I haven't fucked up so badly that we've lost it.

She looks at me, her eyes searching mine. "I love you."

"Again."

"I love you, Griffin Parker!" Her lips lift into a small smile, and it's the best fucking sight in the world.

"I love you, fuck, do I love you," I groan against her lips as I grab her behind the knees and lift her into my arms. "I can't say it enough. Even if I said it in every breath for the rest of my life, it'll never be enough. I love you with all I have. You are mine. You were destined to be mine. I know it."

I carry her to the bedroom, enjoying the sensation of her fingers snaking through my hair and the softness of her lips floating kisses along my jaw as she whispers about missing me, loving me, wanting me.

Forgiving me.

Every touch from her is like a firework in my chest. Bright, dazzling colors, erupting into something that makes me feel invincible.

She thinks I have the power.

But I don't.

It's her. It was always her.

I place her on her feet in front of the bed, my hands going straight to the zipper at the back of her dress and pulling it all the way down.

"I need you, Sweetheart. I need to be inside you. I need to feel you on me everywhere."

I need to erase the emptiness from the last three months. Fill it with her. Her scent, her moans, her wetness.

I pull my tie off and she pushes my jacket off my shoulders, her fingers going to the buttons of my shirt.

"Griff," she moans as I swoop onto her neck, gathering her hair and pulling it to the side, exposing her soft skin. I suck on her pulse. It flutters against my tongue.

"You're stunning. Everything about you is fucking stunning," I growl in her ear.

She quivers in my arms as I push her dress down so it drops to the floor.

I love this about her. She's strong. She's determined and driven, and so fucking capable. But when it's just us, just me and her, she knows what I need.

She knows I have to be in control.

That it turns me on to be the one in the lead.

She gives it to me willingly, handing over her body and her pleasure to me.

But she's the one who can bring me to my knees with the power she holds over me.

And she doesn't even realize.

Her love is what powers me.

Without her...

"God." I steal a breath as I pull back and look at her curves in her lace bra and panties. The swell of her breasts strain against the sheer fabric, and all it takes is one gentle flick of the clasp on her back to release them into my palms and guide her nipple into my waiting mouth.

"Griff," she moans, sending blood rushing to my throbbing dick.

Every sound she makes is like waving a red flag to a bull. Every breath, moan, sigh, whimper—especially the whimpers—feed straight into my overwhelming desire to claim her, own her.

Make her mine.

Over and over again.

Her hands continue to fight with my shirt as I lift my mouth from her nipple and dive back into her mouth, seeking out her tongue with mine.

"I need to feel my skin on yours."

"I know," she pants against my lips, undoing another button. "I need it too."

"Now!" I pull away and grab my shirt, ripping it open and tearing the fabric, yanking it from my arms and launching it across the room.

Maria looks at me, her eyes sparkling as I unfasten my belt and pull my pants off, pull everything off until I'm naked in front of her. My body presses into hers as I drive my tongue inside her mouth again, my hands holding her face in the perfect angle. Exactly where I want it.

Only the lace of her tiny panties stands between us.

"Lie on the bed, Sweetheart."

She moves back, panting, her neck flushed. Then lies back as I climb over the top of her.

"Do you remember our first time together?"

I hook my thumb inside the crotch of her panties, hissing as it grazes her wetness. She whimpers, tilting up toward me, her nipples drawing into tight peaks as her chest trembles.

"Do you remember the way I ate you? You have the most delicious cunt. I would die if you told me I could never taste it again."

I ball the fabric inside my fist and drag her panties down her legs as she writhes against the cool sheets.

"This..." I bring them to my nose and inhale deeply. Her pupils dilate as she sees what I'm doing. "... This is what I fucking live for. For you. Every drop of you."

"Griffin."

I throw her legs over my shoulders and angle my face down, spitting on her already glistening skin. I rub it in, pushing it inside her with a finger as she arches her back off the bed.

"You're mine, Sweetheart. I'm inside you. I'm all over you. Just like you're all over me."

I grab her hips and dip my head so I can lick all the way from her sweet, pink, puckered asshole to her clit. I smile as she cries out and threads her fingers into my hair, pulling it hard and grinding herself against my face.

"Yessss, put me where you want me." I press my face into her, sucking, kissing, licking. "You're so fucking wet. I've missed your cunt... your body. I've missed *you*."

"I've missed you, too." Her voice is breathy as she gyrates against me, her skin growing hotter.

I recognize her sounds, the way her breath hitches each time my tongue presses down on her clit, the way the muscles of her inner thighs clench when I suck it into my mouth.

She's close.

"No." I stop and move up the bed so I'm lying over her. I stroke the side of her face, staring into her hazel eyes. "Your first orgasm back with me is going to be on my cock."

I lift her leg, spreading it wide, and we lock eyes, groaning in joint ecstasy as I push inside her.

Fuck.

My groan deepens, vibrating low in my chest as her tight wet heat stretches around me. "It's going to be on my cock while I watch you take it."

She moans as I pump in and out slowly, my eyes never leaving hers as she cradles my face between her hands.

"You are everything to me, Sweetheart."

Her lips part as I thrust deeper, driving into her, forcing her down into the mattress.

"Tell me you love me again. I need to hear it. I need to know I didn't lose that. That I didn't fuck up everything."

"You could never fuck that up, Griff." Her fingers stroke my cheeks. "I could never stop loving you. My heart wouldn't know how."

"Tell me." I plead with my eyes as I thrust into her, her hot wetness pulling me in, embracing me with all that she has.

Giving me everything.

"I..." Her mouth drops open, and she moans as I circle deep inside her, rubbing my cock over her sweet spot as I pull back out.

"You...?"

"I... Oh, God, that's intense."

She clenches around me as her thighs shake.

"Sweetheart?" I growl, quickening my pace as my loaded balls draw up to my body.

"I do," she murmurs as I slide in deep again, my body pressing tightly against hers as I fill her up to the hilt. "I love you. Every part of me loves you."

My chest swells along with my cock as I soak in her words, bask in them as I push into her.

"I can't believe I almost lost you." My voice sticks in my throat, thick with regret as I hold her gaze. "I don't deserve something so beautiful."

She gasps as I circle my hips again, her eyes rolling back in her head before coming back to rest on mine again.

"That's what I said after the gala when I thought I lost the necklace."

"I know. I remember."

I remember everything about that night. How I saw beneath her armor, her strength. I glimpsed the vulnerable side of her. And it only made me want her more. Made me *need* her more. I ached to hold her in my arms and never let her go. I knew then that we were both the same. We both thought we didn't need anyone else.

And we didn't.

Not anyone.

Just each other.

Only each other.

"I love you," she whimpers against my lips as I pump into her faster.

"I love you too, Sweetheart."

I catch her lips in mine as she cries into my mouth, coming hard around me, squirting her wet orgasm all over my cock, her cum pouring out of her, down the sides of me as I thrust.

"Fuck, it's incredible when you do that. I love it, I fucking love it!" I thrust harder. "The next one's going in my mouth. I want to drink you up all night. I want your cum all over me. I want to fucking bathe in it," I hiss as my cock throbs deep inside her.

"Yes." She widens her legs further so I can fuck harder, a deep blush spreading over her neck. "Please, Griff... fill me up," she breathes against my lips as she pulls me closer. "I love you. I need you to fill me. Give me *you*."

I look into her eyes, the woman who knows me better than I know myself. Who, despite my fucking stupidity, is willing to give me another chance.

"You have me, Sweetheart. You've had me since the first second I saw you."

I hold her eyes as my jaw tenses and the first hot spurt fires from my body into hers. I rise above her, growling like a sex-starved lunatic as my balls explode and I drive myself deep inside her, coming with a force that leaves my lungs wrung out and gasping for air.

Every searing drop leaves my body, and she sucks it in. Accepting it, welcoming it.

Just like her heart has with the rest of me.

"I love you," she pants. Her eyes are bright, and the flush has spread to her cheeks.

She looks fucked.

She's every incredible dream I've ever had.

She pulls my lips to hers and kisses me, sighing as I wrap my arms around her.

And I swear in this moment, my heart grows fucking wings.

Chapter Thirty-Nine

Maria

Epilogue – Six Months Later

"It's in the bag, I know it. There's no way that award is going anywhere else." Harley grins as she links her arm through mine, and we walk toward our table.

The men stand as we approach, and Reed pulls the chair next to him out for Harley. She smiles at him. The last time we were all together like this at a big function, she took delight in instigating the events that led to his date throwing her drink in his face. And now she's smiling, no, make that smiling *and* giggling at something he whispers in her ear as she sits down.

I definitely need to find out what's going on there.

"Sweetheart?"

I turn and gaze into intense blue eyes focused on me.

"We've only been gone a little while." I laugh, warmth blooming in my chest as Griffin wraps an arm around my waist and pulls me to him.

"Too fucking long," he murmurs, his eyes glinting as he flexes his fingers against my lower back, the edge of his pinky lightly grazing the top of my ass.

I smirk at him. "You're thinking about it again, aren't you?"

He leans forward, his lips grazing my ear as his scent surrounds me. "I'm always thinking about it when you're involved."

I laugh again and lean into him, shimmying a little, so my long silk dress flows over my bare skin.

"Sweetheart." Griffin's voice takes on a warning tone. "If anyone in this room looks at your perfect ass, which I know is bare under that *fucking sexy* dress"—his eyes roam down over the red fabric appreciatively—"then I'm going to have to remove their eyeballs from their skulls. Don't make me get blood on my tux."

"Spoilsport." I press a kiss to his lips. "It's your fault, anyway. Don't soak my panties as we're about to leave if you don't like the consequences."

His eyes darken as he dips his lips to my ear, his voice husky. "Not going to happen. That cunt? I can't get enough. It's my daily vitamin."

His expression is serious. The only small giveaway that he's amused is a slight curl at the corner of his mouth.

"Daily, huh?"

"It's a multivitamin, meaning *multiple* times a day."

"Oh." I nod, my smile stretching. "That explains it, then. For a minute, I thought you'd been overdosing."

Griffin tilts his head to the side, a dark-haired vision in his black tuxedo. "No. In fact, I think I may be deficient. I've been getting these cramps."

He strokes the base of my back, sliding his hand a touch lower and sending goosebumps racing up my spine.

"Really?"

"Yes. Enormous ones. In this one muscle. The fucking thing is tense all the time."

I laugh again, placing my hand against his chest as I gaze into his eyes. His dark brows rise in question.

He's been amazing ever since we came back to New York together. Every day, more and more of the funnier, lighter Griffin sneaks out. It's the side I see when we are away at the beach house or on his boat. Where he feels relaxed and free.

But small parts of that Griffin have started emerging when he's in Mr. Parker mode, when he's suited up and running his empire like a dark-haired ruthless God.

And I love each one that finds its way out into the light.

He smiles more, he makes jokes—sometimes. He looks *happy*. There's a change in him that everyone has noticed. And The Songbird is thriving as a result.

He's no longer looking over his shoulder, suspecting everyone, not trusting any of his staff enough to relax and let them do their jobs without breathing down their necks.

He's changed.

We both have.

"We'd better give you another dose when we get home, then," I say.

"You better." He smirks, before kissing me.

We sit down at the table. The others are all having their own conversations—Harley, Reed, Will, and Mr. Van Cleef and Arpels—who is lovely, and called Fraser, and thankfully still doesn't know that I almost lost one of his ridiculously expensive diamond necklaces. Suze has brought someone with her, a guy who has hung off her every word all evening, and then there's Earl and Mrs. Earl, Diana.

Everyone is here at the Met for the Annual New York Business Excellence Awards. They're prestigious and old school. I'm surprised Griffin is as calm as he is. Harley said that during the run-up, he usually starts marching around The Songbird like they're on a military maneuver, uptight and serious, fretting over how many awards The Songbird will pick up.

They win every year.

Best hotel in New York. Best location. Most romantic honeymoon suite.

They clean up.

But this year, he's also got his eye on another award.

The one for best hotel spa.

It's been doing so well. The man he brought in from Boston to run it, Daniel, has been doing an outstanding job. I glance over to the table next to us where he's sat and catch his eye. He widens his eyes, giving me a mock 'oh shit' face, and I smile and shake my head. He doesn't need to be nervous. I told him earlier, his achievements speak for themselves far more than any shiny glass award ever could.

But he wasn't in one hundred percent agreement. He strives for perfection, just like Griffin. No wonder they get on so well.

"Right, ladies and gentlemen. Well, isn't this exciting? Another year."

The room breaks into applause as the mic is turned up and all eyes turn to the front of the room. I turn to Griffin, who has his arm wrapped around the back of my chair and he gives me a panty-melting smile—*if I were wearing any*.

He's been acting extra attentive today. I mean, he's always intense and possessive, and all those things that I shouldn't love, being an independent woman, but yet, I can't seem to get enough of. But today? Today he's been watching me and smiling at me when he thinks I don't notice. I swear he's plotting something, although Harley swore earlier when I asked her that I had nothing to worry about. Yet, she also seems extra smiley tonight. I mean, she's even laughing at Reed's jokes.

Something is definitely amiss.

I turn my attention back to the stage where Josanna Frederick is standing, looking incredible in a black beaded evening gown. Vogue always covers this event. It makes up their special summer issue, and Josanna has been presenting the awards for the last few years.

Everything with the reaction and her hospital visit is all in the past now. Once she heard about Emily's treatment and all the investment into mental health charities and wildlife conservation that The Songbird has been involved in—all set up by Griffin—she extended an olive branch, and they've even met multiple times since for business. I'm sure he even said he was meeting with her earlier today.

Griffin's thumb lands on my shoulder, stroking my bare skin as Josanna introduces the awards and talks about life in New York and the elections, which will be happening in the next few months.

After a scandal that's been kept under wraps so far, the current mayor is terminating his position early, and so an entirely new election campaign has begun. Hence why Reed only returned to California for a short while and then changed his plans from running for Mayor of LA, to snagging the Mayor of New York title. Griffin is loving having him around, even if he claims that he's a giant pain in the ass most days.

Over the next hour, The Songbird scoops up award after award. Griffin makes a speech, standing up on stage looking delicious in his tuxedo, and more than a couple of women glance my way with envy in their eyes.

Daniel jumps out of his seat so hard that it flies backward, tipping onto the floor, when they win Best Spa. His delight is infectious, and draws extra loud cheers and whistles from our table as he goes to collect it.

I look over at Harley and smile as the final award winner leaves the stage. She beams at me. In fact, Reed, Earl, Suze, Will... *everyone* is grinning at me.

I turn to Griffin and lower my voice, leaning close to his ear. "What's going on?"

"What do you mean?"

His eyes are creased at the corners, and they're glittering.

"You're not telling me something! What is it?" I laugh nervously, glancing around the table again, and at all the eyes that are on me.

He leans forward and brushes his lips against my temple, pressing a soft kiss there. "Show's not over, Sweetheart. Turn back around."

I narrow my eyes at him as he inclines his head toward Josanna, who is talking about an extra award that has been introduced for the first time this year.

"This is extremely exciting. Especially for myself, as I am a vigorous advocate for women achieving recognition in business. We live in a changing world, and for many years, it was a man's world. And sometimes, it still is. But women are strong. We are capable. We are fearless. We are brave. And we will not be quiet anymore. Women are holding more top positions in business, in politics, in running our own companies than ever before. And this year's new award is to highlight just that. So, it is with great pleasure I present the award for Manhattan's Businesswoman of the Year."

I glance back at Griffin, who's watching me closely. His dark brows lift over his crystal eyes and penetrate deep into me as Josanna talks about a new company this woman has set up; a supply company that sources ingredients ethically for salons and spas, and produces award-winning products, which have amassed cult status and multiple celebrity followers.

My lips part and I stare back into Griffin's eyes as tingles run up my spine.

"And so, I would like to invite the founder of Phoenix, Maria Taylor, to please come up and accept her award."

Harley whoops, and our table erupts into a raucous applause. Then the rest of the guests join in. It echoes around the giant space, off the walls and ceilings, thundering around us. But it's muffled, like I'm not quite in the same room.

I'm locked in one the color of diamonds.

Blue ones.

"Griff?"

He leans forward, placing his hands over mine in my lap.

"Sweetheart?" His brow quips in amusement as his perfect, sinful lips curl into a smile.

"You knew about this?"

"Maybe." His smile grows. "Now go. Everyone's waiting."

I glance around the room at the other guests clapping and smiling in my direction, and then I stand on shaky legs.

"Maria?"

I look back at Griffin.

He leans back in his chair and brings his hands together, joining in with the applause. "You've more than earned this, Sweetheart."

I look into his eyes and the tiny lingering doubts leave.

Fly away.

And I turn and walk.

"I think I did pretty well for my first time in full control." I grin at Griffin as I slide my key into the lock on the beach house door, the small shell with the blue center dangling from my key ring, my other hand holding my award.

"I think you did exceptionally well." He sweeps my hair to the side and dusts his lips down over my neck as his hand slides down to my ass. "I don't know what was sexier tonight. Watching you win that award"—he taps it with the fingers of his free hand—"or watching you fly the helicopter in this dress, knowing your cunt's bare underneath." He snakes the hand on my ass around to my front and cups me through the thin fabric.

I laugh, leaning back against his chest.

"And I don't know what's a bigger thrill, winning this award, or piloting that beast."

I look over to the sleek black helicopter set down away from the house. Griffin organized flying lessons for me when I came back to New York. He told me he wanted me to feel the rush of flying, and being in control in the sky, as long as I promised to land back into his arms.

He's a romantic when he wants to be.

"You want to take another beast for a ride?" His fingers cup me tighter as a growl vibrates up through his chest against my back.

And the rest of the time... he's...

"Mr. Parker?" I tease as he snakes one hand up round my neck, pressing his hard cock against my ass as he gives my throat a gentle squeeze. I sink back against his muscular chest, loving everything about when he takes command of my body.

Loving him.

"Fuck, Sweetheart. Call me Mr. Parker in that voice again and I'll take you right here against the door," he rasps, angling my jaw toward him. "Do you want that?"

I bite back my moan as his tongue darts out and licks along my jaw and up the side of my face to my ear, setting my legs trembling with uncontained arousal.

"I said, do you want that?" His fingers flex against my throat as he growls, pinning me in place.

Heat pools between my legs as my breathing quickens. I nod, tilting my head to look back at him.

His eyes blaze into mine.

It's a sight that never dims, never fails to take my breath away.

The way he looks at me... the way he's always looked at me.

He is beautiful.

Heart, body, and soul.

This man is everything.

I lick my lips, wetting them, smiling as the action causes a muscle to tick in his jaw. My heart is hammering in my chest as I look back at him, his pupils dilating as he hears my words.

"Yes... Mr. Parker."

Griffin pulls me over the sand toward the shore.

"I thought you wanted to get an early night?" I grin as I allow him to lead me barefoot over the soft sand.

"That was before."

My feet sink as we walk, and I falter a little. Griffin's hand tightens around mine instinctively, and he steadies me. "Before what?"

"Before the front door of the beach house became my favorite place." He smirks back at me and I laugh.

"I thought the kitchen table was your favorite place?"

He cocks a dark brow as if in thought.

"And the shower."

He opens his mouth.

"And that spot on the stairs where the sunrise first lands in the mornings?"

His eyes glitter as he smiles at me.

"Fine. The entire fucking house is my favorite. Every floorboard, carpet fiber, inch of tile, wall, you name it, where you've been mine, okay? Every single one. *All* my favorite."

I bite my lip as he turns back around and continues to lead me to the water's edge. A contented sigh leaves my lips as the water laps around my feet, immersing them in a cool pool with each swell of the tide.

"It's a beautiful night." I tip my head back and look at the sky.

You can see the stars here. I'm not sure I've ever seen the stars in Manhattan. But here, where the sky is so clear, they dazzle like gemstones on a deep midnight blue quilt.

"It sure is."

Griffin has tilted his head back to the sky, one hand still wrapped around mine, holding it snugly inside his. Protecting it.

He looks calm, happy. I love coming out here with him and seeing him like this. Things have been hard for him—the lies, the betrayal, finding out it was all Em, losing me, finding me again—but when he's out here, all trace of that is gone, like a distant memory.

He looks younger, like a man in his thirties should, his jaw smooth, all tension gone. And his eyes are bright, with a smile that actually meets them.

He looks incredible.

"I'm so glad we came here tonight." I let go of his hand and slide underneath his arm, holding him around the waist as he inclines his head toward me and kisses the top of my head.

"Me too."

We were going to go back to the apartment after the gala tonight, because we are due to visit Emily tomorrow. She's been discharged now and is continuing her therapy at home, from her parents' house. They wanted her to move in with them for a while and it seems to have been the best thing for her. Griffin said he sees her growing closer to her dad each time he visits. Which he does. A lot.

I don't go often. Emily is his friend. I'm not sure I ever really knew her. Not the real her, who Griffin grew up with. Maybe I will in time, as she finds herself again.

"It's fine. We have time, Sweetheart. We can fly back in the morning." He tightens his arm around me. "I wanted us to be here for this."

"For what?" I turn to look at him and he catches me in his piercing gaze.

"For—" He turns to face me, one hand going inside his jacket pocket.

A shadow appears overhead, and as it passes, Griffin jumps, grabbing at his neck.

"What the fuck?" He swings around in the direction of the seagull that's cawing as it sails past us. "Ugh." He raises his hand and pulls something dark and thick off the back of his neck.

"Is that—?"

"The fucker dropped it on me! Ugh!" He peels the dark clump of seaweed off his neck and throws it into the water, where it lands on the surface with a dull *splat.* "What's it even doing out in the dark? Shouldn't it be roosting or whatever the fuck it is they do?" He stares after it, scrubbing at his neck, his nose wrinkling. "God, I stink!"

I lean toward him, plucking an errant slimy green strand from his shoulder as I try to hold my laugh in.

"Oh, I don't know. If anyone can pull off salty slime and fish pee, then it's you."

"Sweetheart," he growls, looking at me darkly.

I bite my grin back. "I should call you the bird whisperer."

"Not funny," he huffs, straightening himself up and reaching into his jacket again.

"He's coming back." I point at the seagull, which has turned and is slowly gliding along the air back in our direction.

Griffin's eyes go wide and his jaw ticks. "He better not be."

I point behind him, and he turns.

"Get outta here!" he yells, attracting the bird's attention more and causing it to fly closer to us.

Griffin waves his arms in the air, ducking as the bird swoops over his head and lands a couple of meters out on top of the water, where it bobs happily, beady eyes trained in our direction.

"Fuck, you made me drop it, you little bastard!" Griffin hisses as he bends down and retrieves something from the water, shaking it dry as he mutters under his breath.

"Drop what?"

He looks at me, and then back at the bird who is watching us.

"You're going to be our fucking audience now, is that it? Jesus Christ," Griffin tuts as he turns his attention back to me.

I roll my lips together, my shoulders shaking with a silent laugh.

"Don't." His lips finally curl into a trace of a smile as I grin at him.

"It is a little funny."

"Not even the slightest bit." He shakes his head, looking down at his hand.

"Okay." I press my lips together again, but my eyes must give away the giggle I'm trying to hold in.

It vanishes the second Griffin drops to one knee on the sand in front of me.

"Griff?"

"Don't say anything. Not yet. Not until you've heard what I have to say."He takes my hand and squeezes his eyes shut, kissing my fingers. When he opens them again, they burn into mine.

"Maria, I love you. You know I love you. I tell you every single day. But I want you to *feel* it. I want you to feel it and understand just how much you coming back to New York six months ago means to me. I will hate a part of myself for the rest of my life for what I put us through. For the *gamble* I took. I chose wrong, Sweetheart. I dealt the wrong hand, and I lost."

My chest tightens at his choice of words.

His voice is heavy with emotion as he holds my gaze.

"I gambled. I played it safe and only listened to my fear. Instead of believing and trusting my gut. I will never be so stupid again."

"I know," I whisper, my throat growing tight as I look at him on the ground by my feet.

He has done everything and more since I came back to New York. To start fresh. To make me feel secure and loved, and *trusted.* He wanted to loan me the money to start my new company, Phoenix. It seemed fitting to have a bird name, especially one that rises from the ashes and is reborn.

Just like us.

Him and me.

Reborn into something even greater, even more beautiful, even stronger than before.

I didn't take it. He knew I wouldn't, and that I would want to do it myself, but he tried anyway. He will always try. But he doesn't get his own way all the time. A fact he is starting to accept.

A little.

Occasionally.

"I want you to be mine forever, Sweetheart."

"I am."

"No." His eyes search mine as he holds up what's inside his hand. "I want to say it in front of our family and our friends. I want everyone in the world to know and be witness to it. To the fact that you agree to be mine, and in return, I agree to be yours and to love you with everything I have. For eternity."

He flips open the small wet box and inside is a perfect single stone.

A bright blue one.

"Hold out your hand."

He places the large diamond in my palm and closes my fingers around it.

"When you're ready. When you truly trust me again, then Fraser will take this and put it on a band for you, any design you want. A circle of trust, worn on this finger."

He dips his head and kisses my wedding finger.

I look at him, and then slowly uncurl my fingers. The perfect sea-blue diamond sits there, like a droplet of the ocean shimmering in my palm.

The color of his eyes.

A little circle of trust.

"When you've forgiven me. When you've really forgiven what I put us through, then put this back in *my* hand. And I will do the rest."

"Griff?"

I pull him to his feet, clutching the diamond in one hand as I hold the side of his face with the other, dusting my fingers over the dark five o'clock shadow that's settled along his jaw.

"I forgave you before we came back to New York. I wouldn't have come otherwise."

And I mean it.

I forgave him before I even walked into that meeting in the hotel. I forgave him when I was reading Harley's letters and hearing about everything he did.

For me. For Emily. For everyone.

Maybe I even forgave him before that. Because I knew. Despite his ruthless, sometimes harsh exterior, Griffin Parker is a good man.

He has a *good* soul. And when he loves you, you feel invincible.

Cherished, protected, worshipped.

Loved.

And that's what matters.

He loves me. And I love him.

That's what I told my nana after the hotel. That we have love, and that everything else will be worked out. That when your soul burns so bright for another, that it has to work out. Nothing else matters. She looked at me like I'd just spoken the closing words to one of her favorite books, pulling me into the tightest embrace as the emotions caught up with us both. We stayed there for a long time. Knowing that this new chapter for me, meant the end of one spent with her in England. It's bittersweet as I miss her so much being so far away, but she's already flown over twice since I left, bringing a case full of books for Harley with her.

"I forgave you a long time ago," I say again.

Griffin's jaw softens and his eyes shed another tiny glimmer of guilt that lives there in them.

It's there every day, but it's shrinking. With every kiss, every I love you, every love making session in the morning, every epic, wild all-consuming time we devour one another.

It shrinks.

And my love for him grows, filling the gaps it leaves.

One day, our love for one another will have filled them all.

"No, Sweetheart. I need to *earn* it. I need to know you trust me again." The weight inside him pours out in his words.

My beautiful man has gotten it wrong.

So wrong.

"I do trust you." I stroke his cheek as I speak softly. "I never stopped trusting you. You bailed me out at the police station. You gave Earl money to help us gather evidence. Those aren't the actions of someone who doesn't deserve another chance. I never stopped trusting you. *You* stopped trusting yourself."

"I broke us, Maria. You said it yourself in England." He searches my eyes, and more than anything, I wish I could take the last ghost of his guilt away, pluck it out of his body, throw it in the ocean and watch the tide carry it away.

"But we aren't broken anymore." I smile at him. "Some of the strongest things are those that are tested. They bend and sway. But then they're rebuilt on new foundations and are stronger than ever."

He looks at me, holding me tightly against his chest.

"That's us. Stronger than ever."

"Yes," I breathe against his lips as I rise on my toes and kiss him. "That's us. Our pasts are both stormy in places. But we don't give up. We use the air and we let it carry us, like we're flying."

"Flying?" He smiles at me and sends warmth blossoming through my body.

"Yes. Like a bird." I grin at him and then look sideways at the seagull that's still watching us intently.

"Like a..." His eyes follow mine, and he stiffens in my arms. "Cover your eyes, pervert!" he calls out, muttering under his breath as the bird ignores him and continues bobbing.

"Why does he need to—?"

"Because"—he pulls me closer to him, his large fingers flexing against my back—"he's a nosy little fucker, and you're for my eyes only."

"Okay." I giggle, leaning into his possessive embrace where I'm more at home than ever before in my life. "Okay," I whisper again, dusting my lips against his.

"Fuck." He sighs against my mouth, screwing his eyes tightly shut as he lifts his hands to my face, holding me in place so he can kiss me in the way that sends flutters through my body and has my heart beating hard against my ribs.

I kiss him back, losing all sense of time, until I have to pull back to breathe. I pant, drawing in much-needed air.

"I love you so much." He reaches for me again, kissing the breath out of me once more. "I will worship you. I swear on my life, you'll never question my love for you. You are everything to me," he growls softly as his lips travel from my lips, across my jaw and down my neck, drawing a gasp from my lips.

"Your lighthouse?" I murmur as his lips reach my collarbone and dance their way along my skin.

"Fuck yes, Sweetheart." His hot lips continue their path over my skin. "You. Are. All. Mine."

"No." I place my hand against his chest until he draws back his lips and lifts his eyes to mine. They shine like crystals in the moonlight.

"No?"

I take his hand and place mine over it, uncurling my fingers and letting go.

His eyes drop.

Drop to the bright blue diamond shining in his palm.

Shining with possibilities.

For our future.

Together.

I take a deep breath and look into his beautiful eyes, which light up as he realizes what I've just agreed to.

To a lifetime with him.

And everything that means.

"Sweetheart?"

I lean forward, inhaling.

Tropical air after a storm.

I may be his lighthouse, but he's this—my air. We've weathered one storm together. And I know we can survive the next.

Because life isn't always a smooth flight, or even plain sailing.

But with him, every single wave, bump, riptide, whatever the hell it can be called, is worth it.

We are worth it.

Me and him.

My lips press against his, and I speak into his mouth, letting my words rush down into his body, toward his heart.

"No, Griff. It's not just me who is yours."

His arms tighten around me as he breathes me in, and his heart beats against my chest.

"Now, it's you who is mine, too."

"All. Mine."

The (Almost) End.

Chapter Forty

Maria

Extended Epilogue

"Come on, Sweetheart. There's something important I want to show you." Griffin wraps my hand tightly in his and leads me down the corridor.

"Griff... the party... they'll realize we're missing." I stop, my hand firmly inside his as I glance back toward The Songbird ballroom, and the venue for Earl and Will's joint leaving party.

He turns and arches a dark brow at me. "Five hundred people, and you think they'll miss us for twenty minutes?"

Twenty minutes? What does he want to show me that will take twenty minutes?

I smile back at my gorgeous, demanding man in his tuxedo. He smirks and pulls my arm until I follow him again.

We stop outside a door and he scans his master keycard, granting us entry.

"After you."

I step past him into the room, and the small hairs on my neck stand to attention as his warm breath grazes my neck.

"What are we doing here?" I turn as he closes the door behind us.

"Reminiscing." He smirks and then pulls me into his arms, cloaking me with the scent of tropical air after rain.

Him.

"Griffin Parker. You did not bring me into a meeting room to reminisce." I smile up at him as his blue eyes glitter at me.

"Not just any meeting room, Sweetheart."

I glance around, my smile widening. We are in the room we came in all those months ago, the night of the charity gala. The night we were almost caught in the act on the meeting table... the night he stayed in my apartment with me whilst I slept, worried I had concussion... the night he buried himself a little deeper into my heart. Even if I didn't want to admit it to myself at the time.

"Hmm, there is a romantic soul hiding underneath that brooding, control-freak of mine, then?" I turn back to him, biting my bottom lip.

He reaches up and pulls it free with his thumb, his gaze darkening as he stares at my lips, his other hand firmly gripping my ass and pulling me against his erection.

I love that he gets hard just from looking at me.

"Turn around and place your hands on the table, Sweetheart."

His voice is deep and rough, and it sends shivers racing up my spine as I do as he says and walk over to the long meeting table in the center of the room, turning and placing my hands on it.

"Now what?" I whisper, looking back over my shoulder at him.

He stalks over, unzipping his pants in one swift move as his eyes land on mine.

"Now I fuck your pretty cunt the way I wish I had the first time we were alone together in this room."

Oh, God.

He does this. Gets all dark and filthy, and commanding, and bossy... and *Griffin.*

This is so him. He loves taking control, watching me quiver at his touch, making me lose all sense of control as he commands my body in the way only he knows how.

I live for it.

I love the way his eyes roam my body like he's never seen a more captivating sight, the way his breathing catches in his throat and he lets out a low groan as his hands flow over my curves. The way he can both make love to me like we are the only two people in the world to exist in that moment, and then fuck me with passion and energy radiating from him like he will literally die if he doesn't bury himself deep inside my body at that exact second.

I live for every moment with him.

"So beautiful," he rasps.

I shiver as his breath falls over my neck, and he hitches my long red evening dress up around my waist. He lifts one of my legs, placing my knee on top of the meeting table so I'm spread wide open for him.

"And it's all mine."

He drags my already soaked panties to the side and hisses as he strokes his thumb from my clit to my entrance, and then pushes it inside, swirling it around.

"Griff," I moan.

He chuckles. "You like that, Sweetheart?"

"Yes," I murmur as tingles spread across my skin, skating up my inner thighs as my body clamps down on him.

"Would you like my cock more?"

He pulls his thumb back, the sound of him groaning deep in his throat as he sucks it into his mouth vibrating through me as my breath hitches in anticipation.

"So fucking sweet."

His hands drop to my hips and he nudges the head of his thick cock against me. "You're always so wet and ready for me, Sweetheart."

"Griff," I moan as he presses his cock inside me in one long, slow, delicious thrust.

God, this man... I will never get enough of his body inside mine.

"Fuck! You've no idea how much I love your tight cunt squeezing me like this."

He pushes me forward so my cheek is pressed up against the cool wood, and then leans over the top of me, encasing me between the solid tabletop and his hard body.

"Hold on, sweetheart. I need to fuck you hard."

I shake underneath him as he thrusts into me, his ragged breath in my ear as I whimper with each pump that hits my G-spot.

"Griff."

"Yes, Sweetheart?"

He thrusts harder, his balls hitting my skin.

I swallow down my moan as I pant beneath him. "You feel so deep like this," I whisper.

My cheek presses harder into the wood as he growls and snakes a hand between me and the wood and finds my clit.

"You're so swollen," he grits outs, sucking in a sharp breath.

I know what it does to him when he feels how turned on I get, how my body reacts so quickly to him.

It drives him wild.

He rails me against the wood, thrusting into me as his skin slapping against mine joins the sound of my wetness and fills the air around us. I shake beneath him as the muscles in my core pull everything in and clench around him.

"I'm going to come," I moan, struggling to think straight as the pressure in my core sends electricity racing across my skin.

"Yes, you are," he growls in my ear. "And I'm going to fill this pretty cunt whilst you do."

"Griff!" I cry, my muscles trembling as everything draws tight.

"Do it," he growls.

Then he pinches my clit.

A giant sob leaves me as I come apart, pinned against the wood. I squeeze my eyes shut, gasping in air as I spasm around him in waves, shuddering and shaking. Giving him everything. And more.

"Fuck," he groans long and loud.

He swells inside me as he growls into my neck, coming hard.

Fucking me. Filling me. *Owning* me.

He's right, he's always right.

I am his.

I will always be his.

"I love you," I pant as he grinds his orgasm out inside me, his cock deliciously deep, making me full and sated.

He buries his head deeper into my neck, his breath skittering over my skin in a sweet caress as all tension leaves his body and he stills against me.

He holds me to his chest and peppers gentle loving kisses over my neck and then along the skin on my shoulders.

"You better. Because I exist for you, Maria. I love you with everything I am, sweetheart."

I smile as he strokes his hands and lips over my skin.

This. My man. Everything we went through to get here.

Every tear was worth it.

I love him so much.

"You romantic."

My breath leaves my body as he pulls back and straightens my lace underwear, helping me back onto my feet. "Don't tell anyone." He smirks as I turn to face him.

I run my fingers up into his dark, inky hair as his crystal blue eyes assess me.

"Back to the party, then? Now that you've shown me what you wanted to." I smile, running a finger along his jaw. The hint of stubble creates a delicious friction against my skin, which makes my core clench.

He couldn't be any sexier. No matter how many times I look at him and feel his skin against mine, it never loses that shine... that magic.

"I love you," I whisper again, drawing my hand back and waiting for him to make a move toward the door.

He doesn't.

He stands and stares at me, looking over my face with a soft smile on his lips. "That isn't what I wanted to show you."

"It isn't?" My brow furrows as he reaches to a chair at the meeting table and pulls it back.

There's a large velvet box on top of it.

"Remember how you lost something that first night we were in this room together?"

He takes the box and opens it.

"Today you found something."

Both hands fly to my lips as I stare at the sparkling contents.

Diamond after diamond link together forming a never-ending loop.

All blue. Every single one blue like drops of the ocean... just like his eyes.

Griffin takes it and fastens it around my neck, brushing my hair away from my ears, his gaze landing on the matching blue diamond studs.

"You said it was like having my eyes on you. But, Sweetheart..." He pulls me to him and dusts his lips over mine. "I want my eyes all over you. All. The. Time. If we are ever apart, I want you to be covered in reminders of me. Reminders of what you mean to me. How much I love you. Reminders that for all eternity, you are mine. All. Mine."

I stroke the stones where they rest against my collarbone, allowing my lips to part for him, sharing his breath, *sharing everything I am with him*.

"I could never be anyone else's. You know that."

He looks between my eyes. And then he kisses me. Kisses me until I could pass out from the emotion and weighted meaning passing from his lips onto my mine.

"I love you, Sweetheart." He cups my face, pressing one final gentle kiss to them, and then takes my hand to lead me from the room.

We head down the corridor in the direction of the ballroom.

"Shh!"

Giggles erupt from The Songbird's kitchen as we pass.

"It's a free bar, and someone still has to sneak into the kitchen." Griffin scowls and strides over and through the swinging door, pushing so hard that it bangs against the wall.

"Shit!" Suze claps a hand over her mouth as Will pauses with a can of whipped cream over his mouth, a mountain of foamy white spilling from his lips.

"We..." He struggles to swallow, trying to gulp it all down.

It takes three attempts.

"We were just taking a breather from the party, Mr. Parker." His eyes widen as he waits for Griffin to respond.

Suze, Harley, Fraser, and Reed all stand watching.

Waiting.

Caught red-handed.

"You're lucky you're already leaving, Will. Now I don't have to fire you."

The kitchen falls silent as everyone looks at Griffin.

Then he smirks, a vision of devilish charm. "Fuck, the look on your faces, anyone would think you work for a tyrant."

The energy in the room shifts as Griffin laughs. Suze pushes Will in the arm, then grabs the can from him, extending it toward Griffin's face.

"No." He holds up a finger, and she rolls her eyes, then turns to Harley, who tips her head back with a giggle as she opens her mouth, letting Suze fill it with cream.

"You're wicked," I whisper in Griffin's ear, delight dancing through me as he turns and fixes me with his brilliant gaze.

"I can't have my staff thinking love has turned me soft."

"Believe me, they know there's nothing soft about you."

He smirks as I curl into his side.

"Besides, these are our friends."

We both watch as the chaos resumes in front of us—cream, strawberries, flutes of champagne being re-filled as our friends carry on their own private party, laughing and joking with one another.

Suze sprays the cream again, and it goes over Harley's pink dress, covering her cleavage with bright white speckles that catch the light like glitter. Reed grabs a napkin and passes it to Harley, his eyes lingering on her coated skin before he tears them away and clears his throat.

Griffin follows my gaze.

"Do you think—?"

"No, Sweetheart."

"I wasn't suggesting anything." I smile sweetly. "Just, you know..."

Right then, the door opens.

"Charming! This is where you young lot got to! I've been holding down the dancefloor by myself. No one else out there could hip shake if their life depended on it!"

"Earl!" Harley cries, abandoning her dress clean up and rushing over to usher Earl and his wife into the kitchen. "We're going to miss you so much! Both of you!" she adds, looking to Will, who's standing, holding hands with Fraser. "Do you have to retire? And Will"—she turns—"do you have to both move to Paris? Surely there are enough ridiculously rich people in New York to buy all the diamonds and jewelry!"

"The girl's right," Reed says, his voice laced with amusement as he comes to stand at the other side of Griffin and clasps a hand around his shoulder.

"Don't," Griffin warns. But there's a playfulness in his voice.

Each day since we got back together, he has softened. Smiled more. Laughed more. Become ever easier to love.

He's still a control freak, of course, and strives for perfection, especially in business. But he's also more open... easier to coax into having fun.

Reed grins at me, looking at my neck. "Beautiful necklace, Maria."

"Thank you." I grin back at Reed, both of us chuckling as Griffin bristles, his jaw ticking.

And fun to wind up.

"All right you two, that's enough."

"Did this one get its own private jet and personal bodyguard to deliver it to you as well?" Reed takes my hand and admires the giant blue diamond engagement ring on my finger.

My mouth drops open and I turn to Griffin. "You did not! Griff! All of New York, and you couldn't find a diamond you wanted?"

He stares straight ahead, a muscle in his jaw twitching. "Not the right one. It had to be perfect for you, Sweetheart."

"Wow," I murmur.

I look down at my ring.

I loved the stone the moment Griffin gave it to me that night on the beach. It's perfect and symbolic of how far we've come, what we've endured to get to where we are. And then when Will's boyfriend, Fraser, set it onto a platinum band for me, it made it even more breathtaking.

I haven't taken it off since.

"A little circle of trust."

That's what Griffin had said to me that night.

Trust.

I trust him with my life. I always have. Even after everything that happened, a part of me knew, deep down, that he would give his life for me if he had to.

Griffin control-freak Parker.

The beautiful, complicated man who says I'm his. But who undoubtedly is mine, too.

I lean into his side, inhaling his scent, letting it wash over me.

"Thank you," I murmur, as Reed excuses himself to go over to Earl and says something to him and his wife that has them laughing out loud.

"For what?" Griffin turns his head, his lips grazing my temple.

"For being you. Please don't ever change." I sigh as he wraps an arm around my waist.

"Anything you say. Nothing pleases me more than pleasing you."

"Pleasing me, Mr. Parker?" I smile up at him as Earl claps his hands together and gets everyone's attention.

"Always."

He smiles back as Earl pipes up, "Now, when I first began working here, there were three young boys who said I make the best hot chocolate on the entire East Coast."

"Yes!" Harley bounces up and down as Earl laughs, his eyes crinkling at the corners.

"May I?" He turns to Griffin, who smiles at him and tips his head.

"The Songbird kitchen will always be yours whenever you want it, Earl. You know that."

Earl's eyes mist over and his wife squeezes his arm with encouragement.

"All right, then," he sniffs, plastering a smile back onto his face. "Call those two brothers of yours! Tell them they're missing out," he says to Griffin. Then he turns back to the others. "Now, who's up for hot chocolate?"

Cheers and laughter erupt, ringing out in the space as my heart swells.

Griffin lowers his lips to my ear. "You want to go back to the meeting room?"

I swat him on the chest. "And miss all this? You're kidding!"

"I could make you come before the milk's even warm," he whispers, making my body hum in delight.

"I'm sure you could," I whisper back. "But you'll have to wait."

He grumbles and draws me closer to him.

"Tell Earl to make yours strong. Extra caffeine."

"Why?"

He tightens his grip around me. "Because, Sweetheart, you're not getting any sleep tonight."

Oh.

I melt into him, enough energy vibrating through my body to keep me awake for a year.

"Please yourself, Mr. Parker."

"Oh, I intend to, Sweetheart," he growls into my hair, "but first I'm going to please you. Over and over... and over again."

The (Actual) End.

Elle's Books

Pleasing Mr. Parker is book 5 in 'The Men Series', a collection of interconnected standalone stories.
They can be read in any order, however, for full enjoyment of the overlapping characters, the suggested reading order is:
Meeting Mr. Anderson – Holly and Jay
Discovering Mr. X – Rachel and Tanner
Drawn to Mr. King – Megan and Jaxon
Captured by Mr. Wild – Daisy and Blake
Pleasing Mr. Parker – Maria and Griffin
Trapped with Mr. Walker – Harley and Reed
Time with Mr. Silver – Rose and Dax
(Also available by Elle, **Forget-me-nots and Fireworks**, Shona and Trent's story, a novella length prequel to The Men Series)

Get all Elle's books here: http://author.to/ellenicoll

About the Author

Elle Nicoll is an ex long-haul flight attendant and mum of two from the UK.

After fourteen years of having her head in the clouds whilst working at 38,000ft, she is now usually found with her head between the pages of a book reading or furiously typing and making notes on another new idea for a book boyfriend who is sweet-talking her.

Elle finds it funny that she's frequently told she looks too sweet and innocent to write a steamy book, but she never wants to stop. Writing stories about people, passion, and love, what better thing is there?

Because,

Love Always Wins

xxx

To keep up to date with the latest news and releases, find Elle in the following places, and sign up for her newsletter below;

https://www.subscribepage.com/ellenicollauthorcom

Facebook Reader Group – Love Always Wins –
https://www.facebook.com/groups/686742179258218
Website – https://www.ellenicollauthor.com

a
http://author.to/ellenicoll

f
facebook.com/ellenicollauthor

O
instagram.com/ellenicollauthor

BB
bookbub.com/authors/elle-nicoll

P
pinterest.com/ellenicollauthor

d
tiktok.com/@authorellenicoll

g
goodreads.com/author/show/21415735.Elle_Nicoll

Acknowledgments

My first thank you must go to the incredible TL Swan. As with my earlier books, you gave me the courage to chase a dream. You've had a huge impact on my life, and others too. No amount of thank yous will ever be enough for the support you give so selflessly. You are an inspiration. Thank you to the wonderful author friends I have met on this journey; many fellow cygnets. I really wouldn't have gotten this far if it wasn't for such an awesome group who are always there to support one another. And a huge virtual hug to Layla, Vicki and Sadie, purely for putting up with my daily ramblings and still wanting to be my friends. Love you all.

My beta readers; Layla, Hannah, Rita, Kelly and Taye. Thank you all so much for your time, wise words, support, and late night emails.

To my editor, Zee; thank you, thank you, thank you! You are amazing! Your comments have me giggling, and make editing so much more fun. I think of you every time I spot a dangler.

Thank you to Abi at Pink Elephant Designs for making such a beautiful cover.

To my wonderful PA, Zulfa, for being so calm and knowing how to do all the techy stuff, and being just so blooming lovely.

Thank you to my family for putting up with all of my late nights and constant book talk and still remembering who I am when I emerge squinty eyed from the writing den.

Thank you to my amazing ARC readers and street team, to Jo and the team at Give Me Books, and to the bloggers, bookstagrammers, booktokkers, and everyone who has shared reviews and made beautiful photo edits. They make me emotional, they really do! I love seeing how you picture the story.

Finally, a huge thanks to you, the reader. Thank you for reading Maria and Griffin's story. I hope you enjoyed it and come back to read more about Harley and Reed in Trapped with Mr. Walker.

Please consider leaving a review on Amazon. It's one of the best ways to help other readers try out a new author. I never realised just how helpful they can be until I started on this journey.

Until the next book...

Elle x

Made in United States
Troutdale, OR
11/02/2024

24369903R00335